The Nightmare in Their Blood

The Progeny of Devils book 2

Viktor Bloodstone

FORTRESS PUBLISHING, INC.

WWW.FORTRESSPUBLISHINGINC.COM

The Nightmare in Their Blood
© 2024 Fortress Publishing, Inc.
ISBN: 978-1-959797-04-3

Edited by: Catherine Jordan

Cover by: Koa Beam

This book is available for wholesale through the publisher, Fortress Publishing, Inc.

PUBLISHED BY:
Fortress Publishing, Inc.
1200 Market Street
Unit 17 / Box 137
Lemoyne, PA 17043

WWW.FORTRESSPUBLISHINGINC.COM

CHAPTER 01

July 6th, Las Vegas

Wearing a mint green sun dress and black flats, Celina Davenport felt underdressed in her own café. *Her* café.

The Roll and Role Café crackled with warm energy. A couple blocks off the strip, it leaned into whimsy with menu items named after pun-filled variations of tabletop games. No table was empty, but it wasn't standing room only either – customer flow was at perfect equilibrium. When the smiling cashier behind the register said, "Have a great day," a seat opened for the patron who wanted to enjoy the ambiance while eating a recently pressed panini. This made Celina, part-owner and manager of this establishment, want to vomit.

Today was the grand opening. Wringing her hands together, she was excited by the number of patrons – she'd be insane not to be – but what if this was a fluke? What if there was no way to replicate today's success? "What if none of these people come back tomorrow?"

"Oh my God, woman, you need to lighten up," Victor Vegas said. Standing next to Celina was her best friend, roommate, rock, café co-owner, never-ending well of strength to drink from, and whatever lame cliché Celina could think of to describe the one woman who could pull her from an existential spiral.

"Breathe," Victor continued. "Since you can't see tomorrow, you might as well close your eyes, take a few breaths, and then take a new look at today."

Celina closed her eyes and took a deep breath. One more. Two more. Eyes opened.

Smirking, Victor took her hand and squeezed. "Better?"

"Better."

"Good. Now, please take a moment to bask in your glory." Victor spread out her arms like a liege displaying the kingdom over which she ruled, her smile wicked and maniacal. The three-piece suit – black with a stand-of-hair thin red pinstripe – made her look even more like a power monger.

Although the café was really Celina's baby, she couldn't have done any of it without Victor. Though, if the question ever came up to anyone, she'd shovel the accomplishment onto Celina. It took only two months to go from concept to open doors. Victor did that. Sure, Celina made a lot of the decisions and crunched the numbers as far as inventory and pricing, but it was Victor who gave her the options to choose from and Victor who haggled with vendors. She found this storefront and negotiated the lease, then found the contractors and got them to make the interior match Celina's specs in mere weeks. Celina knew that Victor motivated them with threats and fear, but it was impressive, nonetheless. Now, she and her business partner stood in the middle of The Roll and Role Gaming Café.

Seating was to the left, the counter at the front, and shelves of tabletop games for purchase along the back wall. To the right was the rental space with plenty of tables and comfortable chairs for customers to rent and play the same games available along the back wall. Everyone was smiling, except for Celina – too nervous – and… Orion?

Orion Fogelberg was usually upbeat, never letting the weirdness of his life get him down. Poor kid. Only eighteen and he needed to flee from his home in Maryland and change his identity to John O. Miller. A few months ago, his adoptive parents confessed that when he was an infant, they were assigned to observe him by a man so powerful they had refused to speak his name. And this was in the midst of being hunted by an assassin named Calista Lindquist. Had these pressures finally caught up with him?

"Orion looks glum," Celina said.

Victor frowned. "Hormones. You remember what it was like to be twelve. Nothing but mood swings and angsty ennui."

Celina swatted Victor's arm. "He's eighteen. I'm not discounting hormones… but he's always been chipper."

"Well, if he doesn't start smiling for the customers, I'll give him something to be moody about."

"Victor! Be nice. He's been through a lot lately. He graduated from high school a couple of weeks ago via the internet and it's not even his name on the diploma. Graduating is supposed to be a big deal, and even though he didn't like high school, he had to do it with no family, no friends. Just two older women."

"Older? Hey, we're younger than his adoptive parents and you're the one pushing thirty, not me."

"You're only a year younger than I am, and I'm serious. I think we should talk to him tonight."

"Fine. I'll agree to talk to him tonight if that means you'll allow yourself, like, a minute to enjoy your accomplishments."

"I'm enjoying them, I swear, but I want all my friends to enjoy them, too. Including Orion. And, if I'm being honest, I'm missing my New York friends."

Victor said, "Well, you're in luck," with her naturally mischievous smile, one that teetered between pure evil and lighthearted fun. Celina couldn't always tell which side of the line she'd find herself on, and grabbed the sides of her dress as if a sudden gust of wind threatened to embarrass her. Victor nodded toward the door, and said, "Look who's here."

Anson and Branson, owners of the Roll and Role Gaming Café in New York City where Celina used to work. The brothers stood at the café's entrance, beaming with pride.

Celina stifled a squeal but couldn't stop herself from loping halfway across the restaurant to give them each a bone crushing hug. "It's so good to see you two! I had no idea you'd be here!"

"We wouldn't have missed this for the world, Cel," Anson said.

"Oh, Lina, this place looks great!" Branson added. "Maybe even nicer than ours."

Anson frowned and cleared his throat. Celina knew that meant he was upset that his brother had been both blunt and correct. "Well, I am very happy to see a great turnout for our first franchise."

"Well, I'm happy that our Lina is living her best life."

And Celina was happy that they were happy with her. Three months ago, she had gone through many life-changing events and knew that she needed to expand from the tiny world that she created for herself, yet was frightened about how to do so. Victor suggested that she bring some comfort of her old world into her new one by contacting Anson and Branson about opening a franchise in Las Vegas. They said, "Yes," followed by nonstop words of encouragement and support, every day. Still, she sought their approval. "I'm definitely trying. It's a challenge, but I'm trying. I'm surprised to see you!"

"Well, you're succeeding, sweety," Branson said. "Your firecracker of a partner contacted us and told us when and where to show up."

"She paid for everything, too," Anson said.

Branson punched his brother's shoulder and mumbled, "You're so rude."

"That wasn't rude," Anson said. "I was just noting her generosity."

"Is this going to turn into another argument for attention?"

"I so fucking hate you."

"But I'm still your favorite brother."

"I'll buy a better brother off the internet."

"Fine! Now, if you're done making a spectacle of yourself, let's go grab a Sheriff of Nottingham and Swiss panini and a gingerbread meeple cookie, sit at that table over there, and bask in the glory of Celina."

Branson winked at Celina, and as they made their way to the counter, Anson muttered, "The whole Roll and Role Gaming Café was my idea."

"Of course it was," Branson said. "And Mom loves you more. Now, stop being a sour-patch kid."

Memories of being with the brothers flooded Celina's thoughts, both inside the New York café and outside in social settings. Anson was quick to share his thoughts, no matter how negative or direct, but he always valued his friends above anything else. Branson valued life and experience but did his best to make sure everyone around him was having a good time. Nothing made her giggle more than when they bickered.

"Those two seem like a handful," Victor said.

"They are. But they're great."

"Yeah, doesn't change the fact that I'm super happy that I'm an only child."

Celina crossed her arms over her chest and frowned. "Not any more you're not. We're honorary sisters now, especially after all we've been through. Living through situations that bring people perilously close to death has a habit of forming indelible bonds." And there was nothing more deadly than being hunted by Calista Lindquist.

"Yeah, yeah, yeah. And my mom loves you more."

"Oh, she so does not! She and your father dote on you, you spoiled brat."

"Okay, it's true that they worship the ground I walk on."

"Don't forget that your mom's birthday is coming up."

"How do you know that?"

"Because I'm her favorite."

Victor ground the heels of her hands into her eyes and mumbled, "I so fucking hate you."

"But I'm still your favorite sister."

"I'm going to see if Anson will go halvsies on purchasing new siblings. Maybe we can get a bulk discount."

"No, you won't, because you love me and help me through my insecurities."

Victor sighed. Strength was something Celina admired in other people, because it was an elusive quality she rarely saw in herself. The thing about Victor's strength was she was so willing to share it. She stepped forward and took both of Celina's hands into hers. "Please, please, please listen to me, you amazing goofball, when I say you have nothing to be insecure about. You are sweet and lovable, which are qualities I'd love to learn from you if I didn't enjoy being so acerbic all the time. More importantly, you are intelligent and capable."

Celina closed her eyes and inhaled Victor's strength as if it were perfume, as if this was all she had to do to imbue her essence. Victor wasn't inaccurate about being acerbic, yet she had unending patience and provided a calming effect for Celina. Doubts would always skulk around the dark recesses of Celina's mind, but she knew in her heart that she had made the right choice to trade away her old, passive life in New York for a new life in Vegas where she was in control.

Victor muttered, "Oh, shit."

Celina's heart sped up. She opened her eyes and scanned the café, stopping on the door. Her heart fluttered with an ambiguous feeling between excitement and fear. In walked someone she hadn't seen in three months and thought she'd never see again.

Robert Harrington.

CHAPTER 02

July 6th, Las Vegas

The mural on the ten-foot section of the wall in the Roll and Role café was Orion Fogelberg's favorite thing in the world right now.

Orion hung back and admired the work – the painting was damn good, if he thought so himself. Although he had small explosions of pride for finishing such an undertaking – the planning, timing, outlining – he couldn't help hyper-analyzing the finished product, as most artists do. Color choices. Brush strokes. Lines. In the center of exposed space – a field of green grass on the bottom and light blue sky inhabited by two white clouds – stood a single turret castle and a big-belly, tiny-winged dragon with round teeth and sausage-like claws hovering above it. The exaggerated frown let the viewer know that despite ridiculous proportions, it was indeed evil. A dozen meeples defended the castle. Since meeples were game pieces that represented a person in both concept and approximate shape in tabletop gaming, there were no better characters to fend off a dragon. He gave his work a nod, proud of himself for this wall.

"Excuse me? Johnny? Could I have a refill on my water? And another box of pocky sticks for the table?"

Orion blinked out of his reverie, then looked down at the nametag on his chest. Johnny O. was printed in bold, the moniker suddenly bigger than the mural.

Three months ago, his name was Orion Fogelberg. After Aika – his lifelong, live-in nanny – tried to kill him, he learned that his parents only adopted him as part of a mission for some unnamed man who knew that Orion had some kind of dream demon residing in his head. Now his name was John O. Miller. That was the name on the social security card locked in a safe in his apartment. That was the name on his high school diploma he earned from an online school. That was the name on his driver's license, despite Victor betting – and losing – a hundred dollars to Celina that he'd fail the test. Three months ago, Orion Fogelberg died in a car crash, according to all official reports.

Orion forced a smile to the young man sitting at a table with three other people playing a card game. "Sure. Water refill and more pocky sticks. No problem."

On his way to the counter, he glanced at his mural, but it didn't make him smile this time. John O. Miller was the signed name on the mural, not Orion Fogelberg.

When Celina had first asked him to paint the mural for their grand opening, he declined, too unsure of his abilities. It wasn't like the mural was ever going to come down! Then Victor stepped in and said, "C'mon, kid, I believe in you." He was self-aware enough to know that at his young age, he didn't always hear unspoken words in conversations or read between the lines. He believed he had Asperger's, but his adoptive parents had him tested. Since he didn't fall on the spectrum, they had assured him he only suffered from lack of experiences.

He first thought Victor's six-word peptalk was a load of crap. But something about the way she said it made him feel like she was telling the truth. She was a powerful businesswoman, a partner in a venture capital firm. Heck, she was the most powerful, and sometimes the most terrifying, human being he knew!

Melancholy had come along and crapped on his good feelings as he – "Johnny" – delivered water and pocky to the table.

Then he saw someone who made him break out in an honest, heartfelt smile – Robert.

They used Whatsapp to keep in touch, despite the events from three months ago. Robert was the coolest person ever – smart, well-spoken, ran an art gallery. A mentor of sorts, encouraging Orion whenever he felt down, giving him in-depth critiques on a few pieces of his works. Every once in a while, Robert asked about Celina and Victor, and if they had contacted anyone else on the hit-list. But Robert never mentioned visiting Orion in person. He hurried to the front door and said, "Oh man, what a surprise!"

"Orion! It's great to see you." He and Robert hugged, patting each other hard on the back. It was nice, comforting and paternal enough to make Orion miss his parents.

Victor and Celina must have seen Robert enter the café as well, because the two women made their way toward him through the throng of customers.

"The mural looks amazing," Robert said.

"Thanks," Orion said. "Did you come all this way just to see it?"

"That, and a couple other reasons."

Robert looked over at Victor sauntering toward him, Celina bashfully following. He hugged the women amid a flurry of happy greetings, though Celina and Robert did a weird dance, their heads almost colliding on several occasions. One of the many reasons Orion loved Celina – she was probably the only person more awkward than him. Cheeks pink, Celina seemed relieved when Orion said, "He's here for the grand opening."

"I couldn't miss it," Robert said, making Celina's cheeks flare.

Celina tucked a lock of hair behind her ear. "Thank you."

"I'm impressed. This location looks better than the one in New York."

"Hey! I heard that," Anson said, pouting as he and Branson passed by.

Grabbing Anson by the arm and guiding him away from the conversation, Branson said, "He just meant that it looks newer. But he's right. This location is way better than ours."

"Heeeeey!" Anson whined again.

"Shush and have a cup of tea." Branson handed him a light purple cup containing *St. Chai's Place*, one of the flavors of the Tea-opoly line, and they continued their tour deeper into the café.

"The owners of the Roll and Role in New York, I assume?" Robert's smile brought out the finer points of his chiseled face, handsome enough to make plenty of women swoon. Orion so wanted to be like Robert when he grew up.

Celina seemed too hypnotized to speak, so Victor answered. "Yep. They own the name. Celina is franchising from them."

Robert leaned in like a coconspirator ready to drop secrets. "I meant what I said, Celina. You did a great job, especially in such a short time."

"Thank you." Her blush seemed to be pulsing. "But it was mostly thanks to Victor acting as project manager."

"Let me guess, the contractors moved at twice the speed for half the price because of her pure intensity."

"Yes," Celina and Orion said at the same time.

"I know how to motivate," Victor said.

"Through surliness," Celina replied.

"And with fear and threats," Orion added.

Victor flicked her fingers at them as if shooing away a fly. "You say potato, I say vodka. So, Robert…" She squinted slightly, and the curl of her upper lip was both a snarl and a smile. Orion had seen this look before and referred to it in the privacy of his own mind as the "barracuda face." She was ready to call bullshit. Orion so wanted to be like Victor. "You kind of implied that there was at least one more reason for your visit than the grand opening."

"Nothing escapes your intuition."

"It's like a spider's web."

Robert winced and Celina looked away. Orion's insides went squishy.

"Too soon for spider jokes?" Victor asked.

Considering what had happened in L.A. was only three months ago… They nodded collectively.

Robert cleared his throat and reached into his pocket for his cellphone. With a few taps and swipes of his thumb, he pulled up a picture. Calista Lindquist's hitlist – twenty people, including the four of them. He zoomed in on the image and pointed to the person in the middle of the screen. Jacob McGovern, according to the caption under his face. "Any of you heard of this man?"

Orion appreciated Robert including him in these conversations even though he couldn't add anything more than a head shake.

"Nope," Victor said.

"Me neither," said Celina.

Since neither of them knew him, Orion didn't feel quite as useless.

Victor asked, "Have you met him?"

"No, but apparently he's a Philly based philanthropist."

"Philly, where you live," Celina said. "Have you reached out to him yet?"

"No. Only minimal research so far. He owns a few companies that focus more on doing good than on the bottom line. One company is called ReSole La Soul. They developed a technique that recycles used tires to make rubber shoes. They donate two pairs for every pair purchased. What I found more interesting is that ReSole La Soul is based in Las Vegas. I figured since I was coming here to visit the café, we'd get the band back together and do a little more recon."

Celina worked her bottom lip and looked at Victor for guidance.

Victor squinted a little more, but then her expression softened, warm and inviting. "Yeah. Yeah, that's a good plan. But tell me… How'd you find out about him?"

She was dubious. Pride tickled Orion's heart – he was getting better at reading faces and non-verbal cues!

"He was on the news a couple times and he looked familiar, so I checked the list and sure enough…" Robert tapped the face on his phone. "There he is."

Victor's phone buzzed. She frowned, then smiled at the text she received. "Maybe tomorrow? Gives everyone a chance to research this Jacob guy and his ReSole La Soul.

"Everything okay?" Celina asked.

Victor slipped her phone back into her pocket. "Yep. Just an investor who needs special attention. Robert? Are you able to stay in town for a day or two?"

"I assume 'adventure' whenever you're involved, so I planned ahead and scheduled a few days away from the gallery."

"The sky's the limit when I'm involved. But enjoy the café and then enjoy my town. It is named after me, so you should have a blast." She swiped a cloth napkin off a nearby table and snapped Orion in the butt. "Orion, get back to work." She threw the towel to her roommate. "Celina, I'll see you tonight. Or tomorrow morning. The four of us can meet up for lunch tomorrow and share what we learned. Okay? Okay."

Victor made a beeline to the door and Robert chuckled. "God certainly broke the mold with her, didn't He?"

A quick head shake as if waking up from a dream, and then Celina turned her smile to Robert. "Sometimes I'm not entirely sure He was the one who made her. But Victor's right about one thing. You're welcome to enjoy your time here. The café, not the city. Of course you're welcome to enjoy the city, you don't need my permission for that. And it's not permission, it's an invitation. An invitation to the café. Not the city. Not that —"

"Dude." Orion had to interrupt. Celina's face was getting redder the longer she tripped over her words. He'd watched this scenario a few times in the high school hallways, when one classmate liked another and the conversation didn't go according to plan. *Wait…? Does Celina like Robert?* That didn't matter at the moment, but Orion felt so much pity that he needed to intervene. "I think there are customers looking at the dice games."

Folding her hands together, Celina took a step back and said, "Thank you, Orion. I better go see if they need help. Robert, it means a lot to me that you visited. I'll see you tomorrow."

Robert waved and chuckled, then turned to Orion. "I'm going to admire the mural, grab a coffee, and then head out. Tomorrow morning, I want to check out the local art scene. Care to join me?"

Pleasantly surprised, Orion said, "Yeah! I don't work tomorrow, so yeah. Text me the details."

"I will. It's great seeing you."

"You, too."

Orion's enthusiasm had been raised a level, thanks to Robert.

An hour after Robert was long gone and Celina had gone back to flitting around the store to check on customers and help her employees when necessary, Orion's phone buzzed. Sneaking away to a far corner of the cafe, he saw an email. Since very few people had this address, he clicked on it expecting something from Robert with details about tomorrow. To his surprise, he didn't recognize the sender's address and the subject line was blank. Then he gasped and almost dropped his phone when the entirety of the email read:

"I know who your birth parents are."

CHAPTER 03

July 6th, Chicago

Club B-Sides was a nice enough venue for music and drinks. Tucked between a salon (closed at 6:00) and a pizza shop (always open well past when the area bars closed), the club had a small marquee that doubled as an awning jutting out from the building. On the front in blue, a few letters a different shade than the others, read: 07/06 Dog Food Lawyers, 07/09 Genocide and the Doomsdays. The latter was Blaze Stanford's favorite band.

Across the street, he lit a cigarette and debated about heading inside. *Naaah*, he thought. *Better to be fashionably late.* Too much sunlight behind the buildings, and the neon signs of the store fronts hadn't started to glow yet. Blaze pulled out his cell phone and sent a text to Jerry: Change your mind yet Chicago's fun

Less than a minute later, his phone pinged. No and if its so fun why you texting me

Blaze chuckled to himself. Sissy

Melissandra aint dead

Your being paranoid

Youre not being paranoid enough Go make some new friends

Blaze laughed. Back in Los Angeles, he had a small network of "friends." Of course, in that city, they weren't the kind he'd trust with his life, mostly just acquaintances who would need a *hefty* paycheck to screw him over. Jerry was more of a real friend, but after what had gone down three months ago, he moved to an undisclosed location. With impressive computer skills, he made his living tapping away at a keyboard while most of his associates were virtual. Blaze, on the other hand, was a people person who made his living with favors. To exchange one favor for another, he needed "friends." He'd only been in Chicago for two months, hardly enough time to make "friends," but he was getting there.

One "friend" that he made was his landlord. A dirtbag made up of black body hair, greasy head hair, and stubbly facial hair, he was never without a cigar in his mouth and wore nothing but tank tops since he was too cheap to install air conditioning in the unit he lived in. But he lived in the building he managed; always around when rent was due, but never home when something needed to be fixed. Blaze prepaid five months' worth of rent in cash but learned that the landlord worked with the barter system. A single mother of two on the third floor lived there rent-free, but she put a smile on the dirtbag's face a couple times a week. Blaze wasn't about to do that. However, he had another favor in mind.

Two thugs hung out on the block. They were locals and mostly sold a drug called "rec," but lately they'd been bothering people on the sidewalks. They pushed the landlord around and harassed a few of the tenants. Calling the cops wasn't an option. A police presence too close to the building would make more than a few tenants uneasy, and if the thugs had a spiteful boss, then the situation could worsen should they find out who made the call. So, Blaze worked out a deal – four months free rent if he could get the thugs off the block permanently. Of course, the dirtbag landlord implied that Blaze should put the miscreants in body bags. That wasn't Blaze's style. Instead, he told the drug dealers that someone in Club B-Sides had been selling rec for cheap, taking away their business, and talking shit about them.

As Blaze lit another cigarette while watching Club B-Sides, a voice from behind him asked, "Got one to spare?"

A young woman in painted-on shimmering red pants and a tiny pink tube top barely containing her chest. The fluffy fur half jacket looked like a stole with sleeves. It, too, was red. With red hair straight and long enough to touch her shoulders, it was the muted shade found in a rainbow but with a metallic sheen. Blaze assumed it was a wig. He also assumed she was a hooker, since one might assume he was a john standing at the corner of an alleyway.

"Yep," Blaze said.

She accepted one from his pack of Marlboros, and he lit it for her. With her cherubic face and baby doll features, she looked far too young to be slipping a cigarette between her rosebud lips let alone skulking around alleyways in four-inch heels. "Thanks."

"Yep."

After a deep pull, a dragon's plume shot from her nostrils. "I'm Scarlett."

Blaze smiled. He needed something to do for about an hour, and Scarlett would fit into that slot perfectly. "I'm Blaze."

"Your name sounds fake."

"So does yours."

"It's not." Scarlett might have been able to pass for a teenager, if not for her eyes. Dark. Sunken pits-of-the-Abyss dark. Within that darkness was knowledge, experience, and an understanding of how the world worked. And… something else about her. A feeling. A small, tiny itch of a feeling that Blaze got when he was around… others similar to himself.

Blaze took a drag, long enough to debate what to say next. As with most conversations he had with himself, it ended with, *Fuck it.* "Neither is mine."

Another billowing stream of smoke from her button nose. She squinted, examining him. Judging him. Arguing with herself. Blaze knew she had that same small itch, that feeling that told her he was different than most people. Did she know what it meant? If she did, then she ignored it or moved past it, because she said, "You want some company?"

"How much for an hour?"

"A hundred. And you pay for the shitty hotel."

Blaze grabbed a wad of bills from his pocket and peeled off seven Jacksons. "Follow me."

Blaze led the way to a diner and even held the door open for her. Her face contorted in confusion, then she paused at the threshold and said, "If you wanna do some kinky shit in public, it'll cost more."

"I'm sure it would, but that's not what's happening."

"Then what is?"

"Dinner."

Scarlett crossed her arms over her chest and glared. There was nothing childish in those eyes. Blaze doubted that she ever was a child. She'd probably been a suspicious adult from birth. She needed no words for him to understand that she was all, "Oh hell no." So he followed up with, "Hey, I paid you for an hour and even gave you a tip, so in you go."

"I got a knife in my purse," she said as she finally went inside.

"I'm sure you do."

They sat, they ordered. They didn't speak until their food arrived, her stare too icy for Blaze to start any kind of conversation. He opted for breakfast platter number seven. Nothing like a large stack of pancakes and a heaping side of bacon for dinner. Scarlett ordered the same thing. Halfway through her pancakes, she asked, "What's your deal?"

"Nothing. What's yours?"

"I carry a knife in my purse. That's my deal. I use it on weirdos who try to take advantage of me."

Blaze offered a soft smile, showing he meant no harm and that she could trust him. "Not trying to take advantage of anyone. Just trying to do something kind because there are too few kind people in this world. If you feel uncomfortable at any time, you can leave. I know what you do can be thankless."

The tension eased in her shoulders and her scowl softened. It was obvious that she still didn't believe him, but she relaxed enough to focus on her meal instead of eyeing him the entire time. "Okay, Mister Kind, what do you want?"

"Nothing."

"Nothing right now. Maybe something later."

"Maybe you're right."

"I know you're new to the area. I also know you've been chatting up the locals. Tipping well at the mom-n-pop shops, helping the homeless, *not* having sex with girls like me."

"Just trying to be a part of my new community."

"Just trying to learn the inner workings of your new community to exploit the people living in it. What do you want?"

With a strip of bacon in his mouth, he leaned forward on his elbows. What he wanted to know was why he felt an itch with her, the same itch he had felt around other people he had met a few months ago. "A story. Tell me the story of how Scarlett ended up walking the streets of Chicago."

"I made bad choices, and sometimes bad choices were made for me. End of story."

"And you can't turn to your parents?"

"Fuck them."

"Meaning you don't know them?"

"Meaning I know enough about them to make me not want to know them. End. Of. Story."

Blaze held up his hands in surrender and leaned back in the booth. "Okay. Okay. Didn't mean to upset you. So... Where can I get some rec?"

Scarlett paused mid chew. "You don't use. Why are you looking for it?"

"I have interested parties and I'm helping them out."

"Sonny and Teabag. They hang around a block from here."

"I know who they are. Just in case they're not around, who else is there?"

Pointing her fork at him, she frowned. "I don't know what you plan on doing to them, but don't. They, and everyone involved with rec, are dangerous."

"Who is 'everyone?'"

"No one, that's who. End of story." Scarlett wiped her mouth and tossed the napkin on her plate. "And unless you want to have sex, this is the end of our date, or whatever the fuck you want to call it."

"No sex, Scarlett. And not a date. I only wanted to give you a break."

"Uh-huh," she grunted as she stood up. "I'm not stupid. I'm picking up a lot of subtext here. See you around, Blaze. But remember what I said about people involved with rec."

"I'll never forget."

Blaze took his time with the rest of his meal, paid with a generous tip, and left.

Back to standing outside Club B-Sides, wondering if he should head in for a couple preshow drinks... until he saw The Doomsdays' bassist leave the establishment. Curious, Blaze followed.

Over six feet tall, well-muscled, and long, black hair flowing as he walked, the bassist – named Venom, according to the band's social media pages – was easy to track. Hands in his pockets, Blaze crossed the street. He gazed around while keeping pace a half block behind Venom, even with a seemingly relaxed swagger in his step. Down the block. Over two blocks. Up three. Then Venom cut down an alley.

Blaze hastened his step and turned down the alleyway as well. It was surprisingly dark, and he couldn't see where he was going. Or what grabbed his ankle and pulled him deeper into the alley. He fell on his right side, his hip and elbow screaming, but by the time whatever was dragging him let go, his eyes had adjusted to the darkness.

Standing in front of him was a human-sized, black spider.

CHAPTER 04

July 6th, Chicago

Club B-Sides bustled with a good crowd. Genocide Stone smiled as she meandered among the people flowing between the bar to the stage, a few hanging out in the darker corners, some sitting at the high-top tables. Vinnie, her bouncer and doorman, had told her they numbered sixty so far, with a steady set of stragglers expected to arrive. Not bad. About twenty regulars from what she saw, so tonight's band – a punk trio – had brought in the rest. Gen was pleased. As owner of the club, she was allowed two hundred, per the fire marshal.

As singer and leader of the band, Genocide and the Doomsdays, she was liking the drummer of the band about to take the stage in an hour. He had been the guest drummer for her band at a few shows in this and surrounding venues. For the moment, Genocide and the Doomsdays didn't have a permanent drummer. Three months ago, her former drummer died from a drug overdose. Actually, it was a combination of two drugs, latro and rec, and the reaction was so intense that his skin split open, his organs melted, and his muscle fell away from his skeleton. After that incident a billion rumors swirled and grew in outlandishness until Genocide and the Doomsdays got the reputation for losing more drummers than Spinal Tap. Now no drummer wanted to join the band, instead satisfied with the phrase "guest drummer."

It might take a while for the exploding drummer story to fade away, so Gen tried to emphasize that it was caused by latro and rec. A cautionary tale to highlight the dangers of the drugs. Before she became owner of Club B-Sides, she had spent a considerable amount of time and effort to rid the streets of latro. The drug had taken too many people close to her. It had recently resurfaced, but her removal of it was swift, and almost as deadly. Rec was still making its rounds, and she wouldn't stand for it. Especially when it made its way into her club.

Leaning against the bar were two young men, their fake licenses stating that they were twenty-five. Gen allowed a fake license through the doors as long as the kid was as subtle as tan on beige. As soon as they caused trouble, then out they'd go. These guys here now? As subtle as a brick through a window, and one of Gen's bartenders texted her that they were trying to buy rec. Nope, not happening in her club, and it was time to tell them that.

Since she wasn't performing tonight, she kept her look mellow – black spandex, midriff baring white tee shirt, black booties covered in spikes – enough to turn heads should she add a little sway to her hips when she walked. And it was hard not to notice her mess of platinum hair, random streaks of blood-red throughout. Ten feet away and she caught the attention of the two numb-nuts asking for rec.

Their impressive scowls softened, and their postures improved by the time she approached. She smirked. "Hey."

One taller than her, the other her height, their corded muscles let the world know they had access to weights and enough time on their hands to use them. The shorter one had a scar running the length of his left eyebrow. "Hey," he replied, his lust deeper than his scar.

"Heard you're looking to party." Gen took the half-finished beer from his hand and emptied the glass in a few gulps. It was stupid thing to do, but for some reason, men loved that move. Idiots.

"Depends," the taller one said, posture stiffening.

The shorter one elbowed his friend. "I'm Sonny and that's Teabag. Don't mind him. He's just grumpy."

"Yeah?" Gen moseyed up close enough for her words to warm his neck. "Why's that?"

"Can't quite find what we're looking for."

Gen kept walking, heading toward a dark corner of the club, her maintained eye contact dragging them along. "And what's that?"

"Heard there was someone in the club who's selling rec."

Gen winked and gave a half shrug as she continued walking, them following. She felt stupid, but it was the only way to lure them into her trap. Teabag sauntered behind Sonny, hands in his pocket and a dubious look on his face. Gen tapped a quick text. After she hit "send," and by the time she reached the back corner, the lights dimmed to their lowest setting.

Crossing her arms over her chest, she leaned back against where the walls met. "So... Who told you that someone was selling rec?"

Sonny opened his mouth, but Teabag grabbed his shoulder and said, "Weird question to ask."

"I want to know who to thank for bringing you guys in."

Sonny pushed away Teabag's hand and said, "Don't know his name, but he wears a gold snakeskin jacket."

Gen huffed, then frowned. Blaze. She thought she had seen him hanging around the club, but now she was certain he was in Chicago. But why would he be here? *I'll worry about that later.* She had these idiots to deal with now.

Standing in enough darkness to play tricks on a person's eyes, Gen said, "Okay, morons, there's no one here selling rec."

Sonny reeled back as if she had spit on him while Teabag clenched his fists and took an aggressive step forward. "Look, bitch."

Perfect. They were close enough to see her discreet transformation. Eyes first. She blinked them to their more natural state – black orbs like shiny marbles. That was all it took to make Teabag stop in his tracks.

Gen bared her teeth, easily mistaken for a smile, and a set of black mandibles slowly extended from her upper gums. "Funny thing about rec, it makes you hallucinate. Makes you see some crazy shit."

Despite their faces snapping back to default scowls, their eyes remained wide, worried. There was a tremor in Sonny's hand when he smacked Teabag's chest as a sign to back away. Gen's growing mandibles made it more difficult to talk, but she continued. "I'm the owner of this establishment and rec is not welcome. So, get your dumbasses out of here. If I ever see you here again, I assure you I will be the last thing *you* see."

They heeded her threat, turning and racing through the club to the exit. Gen retracted her fangs and blinked her eyes to human. She texted Lucas and Venom to meet her in the office, and gave a thumbs-up to the bartender to brighten the lights in the corner.

Her office was in a nearly dilapidated back room of the club far enough away from the main area's regular noise. It also served perfectly as a hospice for ignored paperwork. A stack of papers sat in the center of her cheap-ass metal desk, and that simply wouldn't do. The equally cheap-ass metal file cabinet had three drawers. The top two were full so she opened the bottom drawer, shoved the mystery stack inside, and shut the drawer. Trudging across the threadbare carpet to the rickety chair behind her desk, she wondered if she'd have to buy a new cabinet when she could no longer close this final drawer. She propped her feet up on the desk just as Lucas opened the door.

"You know, I put those papers there because they looked important," he said, shutting the door behind him. With spiked hair a shade of bright blue and metal studs festooning his black leather pants, no one would mistake Genocide and the Doomsdays' guitarist for a business advisor, but Gen trusted no one else with the position. Plus, he rarely gave pushback when she said things like, "I'll look at them later."

"Gen, I know you love Club B-Sides more than your other business, but—"

"I know, I know." Okay, so this was one of those times when he was going to pushback. Sneering, she waved her hand as if trying to erase his words from the air. "I have great managers in place for the other businesses and they'd contact me with anything too major. Plus, we have potentially more important things to deal with."

Lucas' face had all the angles of a handsome statue, so every muscle in his jaw rippled as he chewed his words. After a dramatic sigh, he dropped the topic and asked, "What's up?"

"Remember my misadventures a few months ago?"

"When you ran off to Los Angeles with a guy you never met before to kill a crime-lord named Melissandra as well as a crazy woman who was hunting you and a handful of other interesting characters? Sounds vaguely familiar."

"A bit reductive and more than a little bitchy, but yes. The guy that I shared a van with from here to there? I think he's in Chicago."

Lucas rolled his eyes. "Wonderful. What's his name?"

"Blaze."

"Blaze?"

"Blaze."

The door flung open, and Gen dropped her feet to the floor, ready to jump or duck. Venom stormed in, pushing a blond man in a gold snakeskin jacket in front of him.

"Blaze?" Gen said.

"Holy shit," Lucas whispered. "This dude is like Beetlejuice or Candyman. Say his name a bunch of times and he appears."

Ven shoved Blaze to the center of the office and shut the door behind him. "Found this following me. Says he knows you and he knows our secret."

"Secret?" Lucas asked.

Blaze cracked his neck and adjusted his jacket. "The secret that you three are giant fucking spiders."

Lucas pointed to Blaze, but looked at Gen. "This is the guy?"

"This is the guy," she replied, eying Blaze. He was thin, but nowhere near the realm of skinny, with blond hair upswept into a fauxhawk. Black pants fit him nicely while his Hawaiian shirt offended horrifically – bright green pineapples on a red background, the top three buttons undone to show off a few gold chains, a three-inch shark tooth, and a black rosary. Few people noticed any of that other than his gold, snakeskin jacket.

He approached Lucas with a smile of implied brotherhood. The two circled each other, eyeing each other up and down. Gen wondered if a fight would break out in her office. She couldn't have been more wrong.

Pointing to Lucas' bright blue hair, Blaze said, "That is amazing, my friend, absolutely amazing. Perfect color. I was thinking of going green for myself one of these days."

"May I suggest more of a purple due to your skin tone but keep the style. It works for you. I have to confess, I'm digging the jacket."

"Thanks. You have one as well?"

28

"Naah. I'd feel funny about wearing a snakeskin jacket since I'm... you know... a giant fucking spider. I gotta ask – is there a species of golden snake I'm unaware of?"

"No, sir. Just a fancy dye job."

"And the boots?"

Everyone looked at Blaze's boots. Dark brown and tan. "All natural. Python. And yours?"

As blue as his hair. "Ostrich."

Smiling like a kid who just got a puppy for Christmas, Blaze looked at Gen and said, "You never told me your bandmates were awesome."

Gen buried her face in her hands. "This can't be happening. You two cannot like each other. I fucking forbid it."

Lucas laughed. "Oh, come on, Boss. He's all right. Hell, if he can play drums, I say he's in the band. Do you know if he can play drums?" Turning back to Blaze, he asked, "Can you play drums?"

Gen moaned. "He's not in the band."

"He can't be in the band," Venom said with a growl. "He's not one of us."

Blaze laughed and held out his hands as if showing he was unarmed. "Sorry, Lucas, but the only musical instrument I can play is the stereo."

Lucas patted Blaze's back. "No worries, my friend. No worries. Can't blame a guy for trying."

"Trying to do what?" Gen asked, slapping her hands on the desk. "Give me an aneurysm? 'Cause you might be succeeding."

Blaze sauntered over and leaned against the desk, half-sitting on it. "It's good to see you, Gen."

"Oh, he's ballsy," Lucas said. "Very bold move to try..." Lucas finished his comment by sliding the index finger of his one hand in and out of the fist of his other hand.

Ven clenched his jaw and grit his teeth. "He better not be."

"Oh my God! Will you two leave my office?" Gen yelled.

"No. I don't like him," Ven said.

Blaze extended his arms and smiled like a used car salesman. "C'mon, man, what's not to like?"

Ven shifted his weight from one leg to the other and frowned. "There's something... *different*... about you."

Lucas leaned against the far wall and squinted. "Yeah, I get that feeling, too. Like an itch inside my brain. Reminds me of when...?"

"We met those two women a few months ago," Ven finished his thought. "What were their names?"

"Victor and Celina," Gen said.

"Yeah. Yeah, that's right," Lucas said. "Something special about them gave me that feeling. Something special about Blaze, too."

Seeing Blaze had made the distance between today and three months ago disappear. Top drawer held a pack of cigarettes, and she reached inside – she needed one right now.

"Mind if I borrow one?" Blaze asked. "I'll give it right back."

Gen grabbed two from the pack and slid them between her lips. After a light and a quick puff, she handed one to Blaze. Eyes closed, he took a long draw, the tip flaring orange. Smoke curling from his mouth as he spoke, he addressed Lucas and Ven. "You're right. There's something special about me. Celina and Victor, too. Not entirely sure what. The current theory is that the 'specialness' has something to do with at least one of our parents. Celina's father was a crazed murder psycho." Blaze took another drag, then addressed Gen. "Orion's dad is apparently a dream stalker or something. Victor didn't know anything about her birth parents."

"How about yours?" Lucas asked.

Blaze shrugged. "My mom was a saint, but I don't know shit about my father."

"Is that why you're here?" Gen asked.

"Nah. Just got bored with L.A., so I wanted a change of scenery." Then he smiled and something within Gen's chest melted. She hated that smile, because... she liked it. He referred to himself as a person who dealt in favors, which screamed, "Con artist," to her. Yet, she spent an entire van ride alone with him from Chicago to Los Angeles, and never once did she feel uncomfortable. Quite the opposite. A few occasions, she'd let her guard down. Sure, he tossed out a couple flirtations, but he accepted Gen's rebuffs and moved on.

"I'm assuming you're to thank for sending the two douchebags looking for rec into my club?" Gen asked.

Blaze's smile shifted ever so slightly, but it made Gen feel a connection, a coconspirator of a secret mission. "I knew you were looking for someone who sold rec. Those two ass-hats have been sellin' that shit around my new neighborhood."

"They sell it?" Gen asked.

"Yep. They're also fuckin' with the locals, so I'm more than happy to follow them around for a bit."

This was the lead Gen was looking for in her crusade to find rec's producer. Lucas was overjoyed by the news, and even Ven smiled. Well, his stone face cracked into a shape that could be mistaken for a smile. She was still suspicious about Blaze's reasons for moving five states away from his last home, but... "Thank you for the information."

Lucas laughed and approached Blaze. Arm around his shoulders he escorted him out of the office. "Nicely done, my friend! Especially since finding a rec dealer is something Ven hadn't been able to do. Let's hit the bar and I'll buy you a couple rounds. I seriously would love to know the story behind the jacket."

"No!" Gen shouted as they exited. "No story sharing! No becoming friends! I forbid it! Fuck."

Ven followed them, but turned back before leaving the office and said, "He's not one of us."

Gen growled and waved her hand to dismiss him. "I know! I know!"

Alone in her office, Ven's words dropped the boulder of responsibility – being the queen of the black widow cluster – squarely on her shoulders. The file cabinet full of ignored paperwork added the weight of half a dozen businesses that she owned. All she wanted to do was sing in a punk band.

Slouching in her chair, she lit another cigarette and sighed.

CHAPTER 05

July 7th, Las Vegas

Victor Vegas woke up in a bed, the sun warming her face. Her bed. And she wasn't alone.

Fitted silk sheet half removed and top sheet twisted around her left leg, all very *déjà vu* as she rolled onto her side and propped her head on her hand, contemplating the blonde woman's naked back. Victor remembered what she had said the last time they had woken up together. Even though she knew the answer, she asked, "Is this my room or yours?"

"Yours," Jaime Ashton answered, voice as raspy as a nailfile against stone. "Are you going to be an asshole and kick me out like last time?"

"Depends. Are you going to be a bitch like last time?"

Muscles tensed along Jaime's gym-toned form. She rolled over with a scowl on her face, but her features softened at Victor's smirk. She propped her head on her hand, face to face with Victor. "You're a dick."

"Can't argue with that."

Last night's mascara-streaks running down Jaime's cheeks looked like shadows of tears. Victor didn't like the implied sadness, so she gently placed her hand on Jaime's cheek and thumbed away the makeup. "At least you're starting to get my sense of humor."

The false tears were gone, but the sadness remained. "No, I'm really not."

Victor kept her hand on Jaime's cheek. For the briefest of moments, there seemed to be a flicker behind her crystal blue eyes that indicated she wanted to stay. But then Jaime abruptly sat up and slipped off the bed. She slid back into the little black dress she had quickly slid out of last night.

Victor had met Jaime and her brother, Jackson, a few months ago at Victor's investment firm, Bouch & Becker. The Ashton's were looking for extra capital and leadership to take their company, Sugar Fix, Incorporated, to the next level. Victor had pressured them into handing over fifty-one percent of the company to collect the funds and experience from Bouch & Becker, which didn't make either sibling happy. And that was after she had sex with them the night before the deal, without disclosing who she was. "Are you going to tell your brother about us?"

Pulling her hair back into a ponytail, Jaime offered a sadistic chuckle. "There is no *us*."

After the paperwork had been signed, their communications had been brief, professional, and mostly electronic. So, Victor was caught off guard when Jaime texted her yesterday to meet her at a nearby bar. One drink later, they were in Victor's bed. The sex came from frustration and loneliness, not that Victor was complaining. More than once through the night and early morning, Jaime put her hand over Victor's mouth and said, "No talking." Victor was just thankful that Jaime hadn't tried to choke her. Or shoot her. Or stab her with an ice pick. A quick glance at Jaime's clutch confirmed that it wasn't big enough to fit a gun or an ice pick.

"You know what I mean," Victor said.

"My brother and I don't share our sex lives with each other."

"But you two—"

"Stop. It's not what you think. It's not what most people think."

"Then what is it?" Victor asked.

"Were you born rich?"

"Honey, I was born—"

"Please don't be a dick. Were you born rich?"

Victor had an idea of where Jaime was going with this. Awkward pillow talk was probably a better form of therapy for Jaime than any of the shrinks she undoubtedly saw, so Victor cleared her throat and ditched the smarm. "No, I was not."

"Jackson and I were. Old, disgusting money, to the point of aristocracy. Our parents looked down upon everyone who wasn't in the three-comma club. From birth, they taught us that we were above *everyone*. Through our parents' eyes, people were either tools or cattle to buy or rent. Things to use. You can't fall in love with tools or cattle, can you? So, Victor, who do you love when there's no one worthy?"

"That… sounds lonely."

A soft smile touched Jaime's lips. There probably weren't many people who'd sympathize. "It is. Jackson's not a bad person. He can be a nasty son of a bitch, but he doesn't look at people like our parents do. Neither do I. A couple years ago, we snuck a couple million into our own accounts and made a break from them. We wanted to show them that we could be successful. Unfortunately, our college degrees are just for show, paper Mommy and Daddy purchased for us. Neither Jackson nor I attended enough classes to learn anything."

"Hence the need for our help."

"Yes. We have a little bit of money and determination, but no experience or knowhow."

"I got all four, so you're in good hands. First thing next Monday, we're signing the paperwork for your new space and then the sky's the limit."

Jaime frowned in confusion. "What paperwork? The owner sold to someone else yesterday, a last minute, secret backroom kind of deal. That's why I was at such a low point that I decided to sleep with you again."

Victor sat up in bed. "Wait, what? The place was sold?"

Whatever modicum of warmth Jaime had displayed by opening up to Victor was gone. A smirk like frozen mud cracked across her face. "You didn't hear? Hmmm. I'm beginning to wonder if I'm truly in good hands or not."

As Jaime marched out of the bedroom, Victor gave chase, right after throwing on a pair of sweatpants and a tee shirt.

Victor had a four-bedroom penthouse apartment, the massive space between one pair of bedrooms and the other served as living room and dining room, the kitchen separated by a half wall. Her roommate, Celina Davenport, was standing in the kitchen divvying up a breakfast of eggs, bacon, and hashbrowns onto two plates, the stove vent still humming. In plain blue pajamas with fluffy bear-claw slippers, she looked too soft to be in the kitchen's hard, sharp lines of silver, black, and white. With big, brown eyes, she watched in silence as Jaime headed for the door to the outside world.

Jaime paused and regarded Celina. To Victor, she said with a chill in her voice, "I fucked you and she's making you breakfast. Nice little concubine you have. Bye, Victor."

"Until next time."

"God, I hope not."

The door clicked shut softly.

Victor ran back to her room for her cellphone, then walked to the dining room and sat at the table, tapping the phone's screen. Placing one of the full plates in front of Victor, Celina sat beside her.

Nibbling on a piece of bacon, Celina said, "Another satisfied customer, I see."

"Ha ha," Victor grumbled. "You know, you shouldn't wear those slippers. The Sasquatch jokes write themselves."

Celina stuck out her tongue as Victor brought the phone to her ear. Two rings and a cheerful young man answered, "Good morning, Bouch & Becker. How may I direct your call?"

"This is Victor."

"Good morning, Ms… Ummm…? Mister…? Ummm…?"

"Victor is fine, don't hurt yourself. What kind of access do you have?"

"Access…? To…?"

"Files. Records. The portfolio. Anything with dollars signs."

"No access."

"Okay, that's changing right now. Congratulations, you just got a promotion. I'm claiming you as my personal assistant. First thing… Wait… What's your name?"

"Bailey."

"You don't even know his name?" Celina whispered.

"I do now!" Victor snarled at Celina. Much less snarly to Bailey, she said, "Okay, first thing – go to HR and tell them about the promotion and that your salary has been doubled. Second, go to Marshall—"

"Marshall? You mean Mr. Becker?"

"—and… Yes, the fat, old man who has half the name on the big sign outside the office. Go to him and let him know that you're now my new assistant and that I, Victor fucking Vegas, your new boss, needs to know who the fuck bought the building *we* were getting ready to buy for Sugar Fix, Inc. You may alter your level of profanity depending on your comfort level for swearing at fat, old men. You got all that?"

"Umm... Yeah?"

"Good. Text me the name as soon as Marshall gives it to you. Bye."

She slammed her phone on the table and dropped her head into her hands, digging her heels into her eyes until stars burst through the blackness.

"So..." Celina started, voice soft. "Things aren't going well?"

Victor looked up, her curtain of hair – shoulder length and black, except for two streaks of blood red running from her forehead all the way to her ends, "devil horns" as she referred to them – remained in front of her face. "What gave it away?"

"What's wrong?"

Victor grabbed her fork and shoveled food from her plate into her mouth. Delicious, but she was too angry to savor it. After a few gulps, she grunted, "Fuckery. Lots and lots of fuckery that I am not yet a part of. What's wrong with you?"

"Me?" Celina's reply was very close to a squeak.

"Yeah, you. Sister Squirrel, you're nuttier than usual. You barely touched your breakfast."

Celina wrapped her arms around her waist and slouched. "I'm nervous."

"Nervous? Why?"

"About yesterday's grand opening."

"You mean the perfectly executed grand opening? Anything specific?"

Celina looked away and shrugged. "I don't know. Everything. That no one will show today? That it sucked? That I'm wasting our time and money? That I'm going to fail?"

"Seriously? We've been open for a month. I've never seen such a successful soft open. Each day we're getting more customers to the point of making yesterday's 'grand opening' purely a formality."

"I know. Maybe... Maybe it's because... Robert is in town."

Victor cleaned her plate with one final scoop and then grabbed Celina's plate. While working on her second breakfast, she said, "Yeah? Anything specific about that?"

Celina folded her hands together and rested them on the table. "I haven't actually thought about him since the last time we saw him. He's... Well... He's..."

"Fuckin' hot? Intelligent? Kind?"

Celina's cheeks turned red so quickly that Victor expected an explosion to accompany the blush. "Obviously, he's all those things. But also...?"

"Mysterious? Standoffish? Cagey? Suspicious?"

"Yes. All those things as well. And I feel guilty for not researching any of the other names on the hitlist. Over the past few months, whenever I pulled it up and looked at it, I can't help but think about how scared I was in Los Angeles. Seeing Robert makes me feel both guilty and scared."

"Those are valid emotions. Do you wanna call off work today?"

"No. I'm either going to worry about the list or the café. I can at least work on the café."

Victor's phone buzzed. A text from Bailey. "Wow, that was fast. Guy's got potential." `Munition Investing. Mr. Marshall had some choice words for you that I'd rather not repeat to my new boss on my first day.`

"Munition Investing? Sounds like they're aggressively overcompensating for tiny penises. Well, I now have a new mortal enemy to investigate."

They stood from the table and Celina went to hug Victor but stopped herself. At six feet tall, Celina was looming, even though Victor was only a couple inches shorter. Strong, striking facial features could take Celina from pretty to pretty terrifying in half a second. She stood with her arms spread wide and frowning, and Victor had no idea where she was on the emotional scale. Celina dropped her arms by her side and softened her features. "Naah, no hug. I don't want you getting any hooker smell on me."

Victor crunched her eyes shut and pinched the bridge of her nose. "She wasn't a hooker. I don't need hookers. She's the president of... She needed someone last night. She's not a...." Victor stopped talking when she heard giggling. She opened her eyes to see her roommate's gleefully impish face.

"Thanks," Celina said as she skipped to her bedroom. "That cheered me up."

"You're a psycho!" Victor yelled at the closed door.

Victor snatched her phone from the table and headed back to her bedroom, wondering how bad she truly smelled. Looking at the text again, all she saw were the words, "Munition Investing." Who were they? Why'd they buy the building in the dead of night? She knew this was business, but… something about buying the building from under her felt personal. She had research to do.

CHAPTER 06

July 7th, Las Vegas

Orion Fogelberg had been afraid of the dark since he was about four or five, right when most kids grew a sense of trepidation about the unknown and what they couldn't see. His biggest anxiety had been the monster under his bed. His adoptive parents gave him words of encouragement and tried their best to prove that monsters didn't exist. When their efforts failed, they were supportive enough to put glow-in-the-dark stars on the walls and ceiling. Like many people with that fear, he got over it as he got older. How did he work through it? By believing his parents? By deducing that a monster the size he envisioned couldn't fit under the bed? No. By boredom.

Most nights he'd stare at the stars, letting his mind drift while concocting his own stories and myths. The next day, he'd grab crayons, pencils, markers, whatever he could find, and give shape to the fantasies that helped him find slumber. One night, he couldn't sleep. Back then he didn't know why, but now he was certain he had drunk too much soda. Staring at the constellation of Orion the Hunter to lull himself to sleep wasn't doing the trick, not with a gallon of caffeine coursing through his blood vessels. He decided to play with his action figures. But he had shoved them under the bed earlier that day.

He grabbed his iPad – his parents had set the timer so he couldn't access the internet or any apps, but he didn't need apps for it to provide light – and turned it on. Step one was a quick head peek over the side. Step two, a longer peek. Step three had him on the ground and under the bed fetching his action figures. And that was how he conquered his fear of monsters under the bed.

Now that Orion was eighteen, despite being an adult, boredom still helped him face his fears. Instead of worrying about the darkness under his bed, he wandered around the darkness of his own mind, his dreamscape.

Three months ago, his life got turned upside down. He had always known that he was adopted – he never considered himself overly intelligent, but he caught on at a young age that two blond people usually didn't have children with East Asian features. They had been forthcoming about the adoption, but not the motivation – they were *hired* to be his parents. Hired to keep tabs on him, and observe him, because within him was a nightmare monster named Bigby who could kill people in their dreams. And Orion had unwittingly unleashed Bigby.

Orion had witnessed Bigby slaughter his best friend, Brennan, in a dream. Bigby had also killed Orion's high school nemesis, Lance, in a different dream.

The dreamscape. That was what Aika, his nanny – a ninja who tried to kill him despite helping raise him – had called the black void within his sleeping head. Aika had fought Bigby with the help from an unseen, mysterious woman, and captured the monster. Orion swore he'd never come back to the scene of the fight, but lately he'd been thinking of this place. He needed to return.

As with beating his fear of the dark, he came back to the dreamscape in steps. The first visit back had been brief, just long enough to witness the sprawling black void, and then wake up. Two nights later, his next trip was only long enough to move around the space. During this trip, he noticed broken glass on the ground.

Orion picked up a triangular piece about a foot long, careful not to cut himself since he didn't know all the dreamscape's rules. Actually, he didn't know *any* of the rules. Only what he found on the internet, and he doubted that many, if any, of them, were accurate. Since Aika had tried to kill him here he felt confident about the rule stating that if he died here, then he'd die in the real world as well. What about getting cut with dream glass? Would it hurt? Would he bleed in the real world? Would he still have a cut the next time he returned to the dreamscape? A dream scar?

A flicker of pink light skittered across the surface of the glass in Orion's hand. An image started to form, a picture of him when he was seven, with a skinned knee. Aika was applying a band aid. The image grew clearer and then transformed from a picture to a movie where he had fallen on the sidewalk outside his house and Aika came to his rescue and patched him up. The minute long scene repeated. Other shards of glass on the ground had come to life, each playing a different scene with Aika. She cheered him up when he was sad, she made him feel better about himself and how he fit into the world. Her smile gave him strength. And her cooking was unparalleled. A scene of her making pancakes laid by his feet, and his gut twisted, knowing he'd never have them again. None of the scenes could ever happen again. The joy. The kindness. The love from when he was younger, when he thought Aika might have been his birth mother. Tear droplets splashed the glass and rolled along until they dripped off the edge. *Well, I now know I can cry in the dreamscape.*

Orion wiped his nose with the back of his hand. Over the years, he deduced that Aika hadn't given birth to him. But when she tried to kill him... that sealed the deal. No mother would do that to her child. But then, who was his birth mother? And his father?

Conner and Madison, his adoptive parents, eventually told Orion that his birth father could go into people's dreams and manipulate them in order to commit murder. What about his mother, though? And who was Bigby, the monster that killed Brennan and Lance in their dreams? When Aika brought Orion to his dreamscape, Bigby was there as well and wanted to kill Aika. Then a woman called out, a woman who Aika knew. A woman who captured and trapped Bigby. Was she his mother?

Orion concentrated on the woman's voice. He tried to recall the exact sound, the pitch, the timbre. She spoke English, but had an accent, Japanese he presumed. The woman had access to his dreamscape, but this was *his* dreamscape so he should have control over it. After all, he just made all the glass shards come to life with memories of Aika. He had to have some memory of his mother, some primal connection from being sustained by her for nine months. He glanced at the glass on the ground. They all played happy memories of Aika.

He'd never seen his birth mother, so he couldn't conjure memories of her. Nor would he. According to Conner and Madison, she was dead. But they had lied to him his entire life, so maybe they were lying to him about his mother. The only way to find out was to contact them. No... They told him that his life was in danger by the man who had hired them to adopt him.

Trying to contact them would be catastrophic. He was now relegated to searching his dreamscape, but it was no use trying to find his mother here.

However, he learned how to play memories like movies, so that was pretty cool.

He wandered around the dream-area, watching all kinds of happy times play out before him, careful not to step on any of the pieces. He didn't want to break them. What if he did? The piece in his hands still showed him his skinned knee. What if he broke it into two pieces? Would the same scene play on each piece? Or would this scene play on one piece and a different scene play on the other? Would it be another random scene, or one he could pick?

Orion gasped as a thought struck him – what if he could change the channel? Standing in his own dreamscape, one hundred percent *aware* that he was dreaming, he had to be able to exact some level of control.

Watching the scene of Aika patching him up, he focused on something different. A moment with Aika. Something meaningful. He wanted to see one of those memories. Any year. Any grade.

Concentrate.

The scene started to change. It morphed to where he was standing at the front door wearing his Star Wars backpack, and Aika had crouched down, beaming. He was doing it! He was altering his dream; he was changing the channel! His first day of first grade. On the first day of school every year, Aika would say, *"Senri no michi mo ippo kara."* She said it meant, "A journey of a thousand miles begins with a single step." He had heard that sentiment from a dozen other sources in his life, but it meant something more to him when it came from her. It gave him power and purpose and strength. But the image wavered, flickered. Then the scene started to fade, and another image was forming. A face? Yes, a face. The skin was twisted and folded, gnarled like tree bark. Angry black eyes held nothing but hatred. Split and cracked lips sneered, exposing razor blades instead of teeth.

Bigby.

Was this Orion's father? As much as he didn't want it to be true, he had been told his father did what Bigby could do. Orion wasn't sure if he believed in God or not, but he prayed that Bigby wasn't his father. Though, that might explain why his mother was dead.

Bigby shifted in the scene playing on the glass, turning as if trying to get a better look at Orion. Bigby reeled back, then lunged forward, snapping his teeth. Orion jerked away and Bigby laughed, a noiseless chuckle through his sharp teeth and smiling mouth.

"Fuck you!" Orion screamed.

Angered, Bigby reached for Orion, but his hands bounced back as his fingers slammed into the glass. Bigby shook out one of his hands and then reached again, this time slower. At first, his fingertips pressed flat against the glass, then the tips suddenly rounded. His fingers were through! Orion thought he was imagining it, but Bigby's bony hand kept coming through, kept reaching for him. He held the glass as far away as he could, but the hand didn't stop reaching. Inches from his face, Orion screamed and slammed the glass to the floor, shattering it into pebble sized pieces. The scenes along the floor all disappeared, winking out of existence, leaving Orion alone in his dark and empty void. *Wake up!*

Sitting straight up in bed, Orion was drenched. At first he laughed, excited that he found some form of control in his dreamscape, then cried from losing it, his tears getting lost within the sweat pouring from him. Every time he awoke after being in the dreamscape, sweat flowed over him like he got caught in a rainstorm. He shook his head to snap himself out of his funk and hopped out of bed.

The thought of breakfast turned his stomach and he felt too weak in the knees for a shower. He needed a few minutes to calm down, so he flopped in his desk chair and turned on his computer. Might as well use his time wisely and continue researching the topic of lucid dreaming. But he had a message in his inbox: "The last email wasn't bullshit. I know who your parents are. You need to come to Philly."

CHAPTER 07

July 7th, Las Vegas

Victor straightened her tie, the last necessary adjustment. Mirrors for her bedroom closet doors reflected her image, and she liked what she saw. Hair slicked back, her two red streaks vibrant and eye catching. She opted to go three-piece Armani, solid black with a black shirt. The tie a bold red, but not ostentatious. Flashy excess with expensive suits and shoes and watches showed what was to come should potential clients allow her to invest in their businesses. Meeting potential adversaries was different – she wanted to show she meant business.

Bailey was a miracle worker. He had sent her information about Munition Investing mere minutes after being promoted. To Victor's surprise, Munition Investing was a small firm somewhere in the southwest. Where it was located didn't matter to Victor. Who ran it did – a woman named Corette Remington.

Sure, she fell into the same trap most people did with a word as aggressive as "Munition" in the company name, that the owner would be a man. Her sisterhood half wanted to congratulate Corette, but her competitive half wanted to strangle the bitch for stealing her shtick. Thanks to Bailey – actually it was thanks to Victor for brilliantly promoting such an industrious young man to the position of her assistant – he discovered that Corette was in town due to Munition's last second purchase of the building. Also, thanks to Bailey, he set up a meeting between Victor and Corette for this morning. Though, during Victor's last conversation with him, he made her promise not to bring brass knuckles. She acquiesced to his request, but she was still going to bring intimidation. Time to check on Celina.

In the living room, Celina paced while looking down at her chest, desperately fumbling with the tie around her neck. "I can't tie this stupid thing. I think it's broken."

Victor chuckled as her fingers worked their magic. "First of all, you should be in front of a mirror. Second of all, it takes two to three decades to learn how to tie a Windsor knot, so no worries, okay? And before you ask, yes, I was tying ties in elementary school."

"No, you weren't. I know for a fact that you were a perfectly normal little girl."

Victor sneered as she put on the finishing touches. "You shouldn't be mean to someone messing with a silk garrote around your neck. Okay, done. Let's take a look."

Victor backed up and admired her handywork. Celina looked stunning, even though she fidgeted and pulled at the bottom of her suit jacket. She complained whenever Victor took her clothes shopping, but not so much this last time. Maybe because after Victor picked out the light gray two-piece Armani, white shirt, and radioactive yellow tie, she allowed Celina to pick the shoes – gray with a faint snakeskin pattern. "You are one impressive human being."

"Thanks… I think?"

"You suck at taking compliments."

"Maybe you just suck at giving them."

"Make sure you bring that sharp edge to the meeting. And thank you for doing this. I know you'd rather be at the café."

Another tug of the suit jacket. "Is there a script I need to follow?"

"Nope. You probably won't even need to talk. I need you to look intimidating."

Celina frowned. "How's this?"

"Like a teddy bear with constipation."

"Dick."

"I'm just trying to make you look meaner. Throw a snarl in there."

Celina pursed her lips, but that only added to their fullness. She squinted, and then growled. Victor waved her hands. "Okay, stop, stop. I don't think it's going to happen."

"Why are you always trying to change me?"

"Change you? I don't want to change you. In your tree trunk body, you are nothing but sweetness. You're the living, breathing tree of kindness."

"I'm having unkind thoughts about you right now."

Victor huffed and then placed her hands on Celina's cheeks. Looking deep into her eyes, she said, "I don't want to change you. I just need you to play pretend for an hour or so. I'm asking for your help because I trust you and believe in you. I need you in my life, as you are, because you're awesome and you keep me grounded."

"I do?"

"Yes. Without you, I'd be all fire and brimstone and I'd want to burn Corette Remington and Munition Investing to the ground. Instead, I asked myself, 'What would Celina do? Oh, she'd bake Corette a pie and kill her with kindness.'"

Celina huffed. "I think that's an over-simplification as to who I am. And I don't know how to bake."

"I was being metaphorical."

"You're being an ass. You're nervous about the meeting and instead of dealing with uncomfortable feelings, you decide to bury them and be an ass to the people who love you."

Victor sneered, showing Celina how to do an effective one. "Ugh! Feelings? Gross."

"You should try them sometime. They're good for you."

"That's what a drug pusher would say."

As if they had a life of their own, Celina's fingers prodded her tie's knot. "So… this metaphorical pie of kindness you have me baking. What flavor would it be?"

"Anchovy, calf liver, and nutmeg, obviously."

Celina grimaced and reeled back. "Eww!"

"There!" Victor said. "Keep your face just like that."

Freezing her entire body, Celina whispered, "Like this?"

"Yes. Now deepen your frown. And widen your eyes. And clench your teeth. And…" In nature there was a fine line between exquisite beauty and terrifying ferocity, the way a jungle cat is the symbol of graceful perfection one moment and a roaring creature of pure death the next. Celina was that line. And Victor just made her cross it. The left corner of Celina's lip pulled up to expose a few teeth and the ripple in her jaw muscles showed a beast ready to devour. The sharp furrow in her brows could cut diamonds, and the lines partially framed her eyes. It had been discovered that Celina's birth father was a monster named Zebadiah Seeley, a depraved soul who had kidnapped, raped, and murdered young women until he was eventually arrested and jailed. Victor never reconciled how such a sweet woman could come from such a horrible man. Now, she saw it, easily envisioning the expression on Celina's face being the last thing that those poor victims saw. "And... You know what? Don't worry about it. I'll just let your impressiveness speak for itself."

Celina nodded and tugged one last time at the bottom of her suit jacket. "That's more like it. So, where are we going?"

*

The conference room was small with lame two-colored paintings adorning dull gray walls. Victor had hoped for more but expected as much from a complimentary hotel conference room. Corette was just visiting Las Vegas, and Victor would be damned before suggesting that they meet anywhere near her office in Bouch & Becker, so the hotel conference room it was.

"These chairs suck," Victor mumbled as she tried to get comfortable in the non-luxury foam pieces wrapped in an indeterminate material that could be found in any office supply store.

"You're just spoiled," Celina whispered, sitting straight with her hands on the table, fingers folded together.

"You just don't know any better." Victor whispered as well, the smallness of the room ready to pass along any secrets spoken. Wheeling the chair closer to the table, she shifted in her seat one last time, leaning on the right arm rest in a pose of relaxed aggression. The conference table was barely big enough to fit the six chairs around it, and there was no way Victor wasn't sitting at the head of the table – her intimidating face would be the first thing anyone saw when they entered. However, when Corette Remington entered, Victor doubted that any intimidation tactic she'd come up with would work.

Corette was a wisp of a woman with straight, shoulder length dishwater blonde hair and wirerimmed glasses. She wore a shin-length beige business skirt and matching jacket. At first Victor wondered if Munition Investing sent their accountant instead, but there was something in her eyes... Even from this distance Victor could see the machinations of an unstoppable machine chugging away in this woman's mind. The eyes were the windows to the soul and Corette had no curtains hiding the intelligence within.

Victor thought about standing up, which would be Celina's cue to stand as well, to give her a psychological edge by using physicality, since Corette wasn't even five and a half feet tall. She decided against it. Despite the intensity behind her green eyes, Corette had the sleepy-eyed look of boredom while her lips were drawn tight into disappointment. No, being significantly taller than her opponent would be no help at all. Plus, Corette sat down too quickly in the chair at the other end of the table.

"Victor Vegas?"

Victor appreciated that she didn't call her Victoria Vargas, though it would have been a successful tactic to get deeper under her skin. *Wait... Why do I feel itchy on the inside? Like I did when I first met...* Victor glanced to Celina. She must have felt it, too, because she stared at Corette and shifted as if her chair had suddenly turned to stone. This strange sensation unnerved them when first meeting Genocide, Orion, and Blaze.

Sitting up straighter and pushing aside the strange feeling, Victor answered with, "Corette Remington."

Corette assumed the same stiff-backed, fingers-folded position as Celina, and cocked her head to look at the taller woman. "My assistant said that your assistant was a man. Bailey, I believe?"

Celina's eyes widened. Victor cleared her throat and said, "This is my numbers guy, Monique Deveraux, a world renown financial analyst from France."

"Hmm," Corette hummed, probably assessing the validity of Victor's statement. "I've never heard of her. Must be exclusive."

"I am very exclusive," Celina added, using a fake accent. Her attempt was French, but it sounded like Russian. Next time she employed Celina, she'd say, "She's from Moscow," to avoid confusion.

Before Corette could openly call bullshit, Victor asked, "How about Calista Lindquist? Ever heard of her?"

No reaction. No frown or smile or minute twitch. Nothing. "I have not. Another world famous and exclusive 'financial analyst,' I assume?"

No. An assassin who had tried to kill Victor and her friends. Victor's fingers actually itched with the desire to pull out her phone and check the hitlist she had stolen from Calista – the same list that was the impetus for Victor meeting her merry band of misfits – to see if Corette was on it, but stopped herself. The meeting hadn't even started, and she already felt like she was at a disadvantage, so checking her phone would make her look needy or distracted. Time to get back on track.

Victor leaned forward, ready to grab the last piece of pumpkin pie at Thanksgiving dinner. "Nah. Just name dropping to see if you knew any of the cool kids."

"Sorry to undoubtedly disappoint. Do you know the name Sylvester Kromesky?"

Yes. The man who owned the building that should have been sold to Sugar Fix, Inc. "Oh, I most certainly do. I'm guessing you know him better than I do to get him to make such a dirtbag move, like sell it to you after he had a deal with me." Victor added an eyebrow wiggle and a wink.

"Interesting. I heard rumors that you tended to be crass. Shame that they're true. But, no. Not that it's any of your business, but I didn't need to sink to such depths. Sylvester Kromesky did that all on his own."

"He still needed a motivation, and I think you gave it to him."

"Alas, I did no such thing. He caught wind that my newest investment partner was looking to expand his production. Since it's the rare mix of having a profitable future while helping others in need, Kromesky wanted to sell the building to ReSole La Soul, instead of to you."

Oh, Victor didn't like this at all. A hunch twisted behind her chest, demanding to be released. She had no other choice than to let it go. "ReSole La Soul. You're partnering with Jacob McGovern."

Corette's facial expression didn't change one iota, but her voice dripped with smugness. "Oh, you finally said a name I've heard of."

Celina gasped and looked at Victor.

There was a fine line between coincidence and fuckery, and Corette just crossed it. Victor didn't have the best poker face and her anger started to display itself. "I don't know what you and Jacob are planning, but I assure you I have access to nasty lawyers. I'm going to hand them the contracts Kromesky signed, give their nuts a good twist, and then sick them on you, Jacob, and Kromesky."

"No, you won't."

Victor sat back, feeling lightheaded. Something about Corette's voice had changed, and Victor heard it with her whole body, not just her ears. A quick headshake and she straightened up again. "Oh, you better believe I will."

"How would those optics look?" Every word shoved a pound of cotton into Victor's head. And Corette didn't stop. "Local venture capitalist throws tantrum and sues company focused on helping both the environment and the impoverished."

The room started to spin, and Victor felt drunk. She needed to sit down... Wait, she was already sitting. She needed to lay down. No. She needed to stand up.

"Victor?" Celina asked, but she was so far away and underwater. No. No, she was close enough to put her hand on Victor's forearm.

Corette continued, the weird effects of her voice unyielding. "Is that what you want headlines to say? Is that the kind of exposure you want for Sugar Fix, Inc.? For Bouch & Becker?"

Fight or flight time and Victor was too woozy to throw a punch. Using the table for balance, she stood and whispered to Celina, "C'mon. We're leaving."

Nodding, Celina followed Victor to the door. On her way out, Victor snarled at Corette and said, "Keep the fucking building."

Out of the room, the unusual feelings wore off, and they were completely gone by the time Victor stepped outside. She stormed across the parking lot so quickly that Celina struggled to keep up. "Victor? Victor? What happened in there?"

Victor jammed her hand into her jacket and pulled out her cell phone. Her pace didn't slow as she thumbed through various screens. "Did you feel it?"

"Umm...? Do you mean the weird feeling we got when we first met each other and the others?"

"Yes. That's because—" Victor stopped in her tracks and squinted. "Shit! She's not on the list."

Celina pulled out her phone and joined the search. "You're right. But... I felt it, too. She *has* to be like us. What's going on, Victor?"

Victor put her phone away and glared at the hotel as if it were the only thing keeping the answers from her. "I don't know, but I'm sure as hell going to find out."

CHAPTER 08

July 7th, Chicago

The air was weird. Blaze didn't know what to make of it. It must be this "humidity" thing he had heard about. Los Angeles didn't have it. Well, not much of it because the ocean had the decency to keep it to itself. Lake Michigan? All too happy to share its moisture, even on a mild afternoon. Not smoggy like L.A., but the air quality still sucked, just in a different, strange way.

Blaze leaned the back of his head against the brick building and savored the coolness of it. Hands in his jeans' pockets, the center of his back against the corner of the building, he slowly rocked from side to side. The building was only two stories but ran the length of the alley to a half-ass side street, riddled with pock marks and divots. Across the alley, in front of a chain link fence overgrown with weeds and surrounding a scrap metal recycling center, Gen puffed away at her cigarette, glaring to her left then to her right. Blaze smiled at her.

"Don't smile at me," Gen said, not even bothering to look at Blaze.

"Yeah? Why is that?"

"Your smile makes people feel… strange. Makes *me* feel strange." She then turned to address him eye to eye. "And I know you know that."

Blaze downshifted his smirk to one evoked when caught raiding the cookie jar. "Not sure I understand or agree, but I'll respect your wishes. No smiling."

Gen grunted, columns of smoke blasting from her nostrils, and went back to leering down the sidewalk. Another grunt and she then scoped out the alleyway.

"So," Blaze said. "What kinds of movies do you like?"

"No."

"No, you don't like movies?"

"I do, but we're not going to do this."

"Do what?"

"Don't play fucking dumb. You want in my pants and you're now resorting to the tactics of a twelve-year-old on his first date."

"Just trying to get to know you."

Gen snapped her head around, the fire in her eyes burning all the way to his spine. "Well don't. You know too much about me already."

"The only thing I really know about you is that you're lonely."

The cigarette tip bloomed orange while Gen telegraphed her ire through squinted eyes. Once the embers hit the filter, she dropped the butt to the ground and crushed it so hard that the ligaments of her neck flared. Smoke curled from her open-mouth snarl, the portent of a dragon ready to rush forth from its cave. Blaze readied himself to get fried. To his surprise, she blew the smoke away and said, "I have my band, my cluster, my club, my businesses, and my fans. Being alone is one thing I don't have to worry about."

Blaze tilted his head downward, rounding his eyebrows to express empathy. "I said lonely. I saw how you keep your paperwork for your businesses. Your fans adore you, but that's because they look to you to bring something out within them. I know Ven hates me, but not because of my personality – we all know it's sparkling as fuck – but because I'm not one of your kind. You're the queen of a whole species, and with that comes a level of pressure very few people can comprehend. Everyone you mentioned looks to you as a form of leader. I'm the only person who doesn't, so I'm just trying to offer you an opportunity to be yourself, to be something other than someone's boss or idol."

Heel tapping in rhythmic agitation, Gen set her jaw and looked to the heavens. A quick swipe of her hand over her cheek which Blaze assumed was to wipe away a tear or two. But before he could say anything else, a voice from the other end of the alley interrupted the moment.

"Hey! You!"

Gen quickly stepped out of the alley to avoid being seen.

Blaze walked into the alley and greeted Sonny and Teabag, shrugging his shoulders to feign innocence. "Me? Me what?"

53

Of the two, Sonny had been the more personable one, willing to try fast talking before resorting to threats. Now, the crags from his scowl were just as jagged as Teabag's. Eyes afire, he pointed at Blaze, a foreshadowing of the knife he undoubtedly had in his pocket. "You set us up."

"Set you up? For what? What are you talking about?"

Teabag's hot glare burned directly into Blaze's eyes. Jaw-jutting, he growled through clenched teeth. "There was no one selling rec in that club you told us to go to."

Blaze still stuck with the ignorance act. "No? Well, I did say it was just a rumor and that's the thing about rumors, right? They ain't always true."

"Nah, nah, nah." Sonny shook his head for emphasis. "This felt like a set up."

"What's the big deal? Now you've got it confirmed, and you and your boss should be happy no rec is being sold where you sell."

"Our boss ain't happy that we got set up."

"Yeah? Who's your boss? I'd be happy to talk to him and smooth things over."

Sonny and Teabag leaned in closer, rancid breaths assaulting Blaze. Teabag snarled, exposing gold-plated canines. "You a cop?"

Blaze laughed. "I've been accused of a lot during my lifetime, but never a cop."

Sonny looked upward at Blaze. "You sure act like one, asking who our boss is."

Hands back in his pockets, Blaze shrugged and backed away toward the corner of the chain-link fence where Gen remained hidden in the shadows. "Just thought I was giving you a heads up but if you two aren't interested, then there's nothing I can do."

Sonny and Teabag advanced as Blaze retreated. Teabag grabbed two fistfuls of Blaze's shirt. Immediately, Gen lunged, grabbing Teabag's arm. Faster than anyone expected, Sonny wedged himself between his friend and the other two, separating everyone. "Back off!"

Teabag reached behind his back, presumably for a knife, but hesitated when he got a better look at Gen. Sonny squared up to Blaze and Gen, but Teabag stopped him with a yank to his sleeve. "It's that bitch from the club."

"It is," Gen said. "And we're not cops. Just interested in who your boss is. A name is good enough."

Sonny and Teabag stepped back, frowning as if angry over no longer being the scariest ones in the alley. With one last snarl from Teabag, they turned and sprinted away.

"Well, shit," Blaze mumbled as he and Gen gave chase.

When Sonny and Teabag reached the end of the alley, they turned right.

Blaze asked, "Any idea what's to the right?"

"A small street that shoots off to the main road, or else they're running around the building toward another alley on the other side."

"Should we split—?" Teabag ran back into the alley, looking over his shoulder. Blaze reached out and grabbed Gen's hand. She began to pull, but he tightened his grip just enough for them to clothesline Teabag.

Head stopped, Teabag's feet kept going, and then his back hit the ground with a grimacing slap and a thud. Groaning, he scrunched his face and grabbed the back of his head.

Still holding Gen's hand over Teabag's writhing form, Blaze offered her a slight bow. "Care to dance?"

Gen yanked her hand from Blaze's. "I don't dance, freak."

"You don't like to dance?"

"I don't dance."

"Everyone dances, even if it's in the privacy of their own home."

"I don't!" Gen stomped her foot to add emphasis – right on Teabag's chest. Blaze heard the crack of ribs, and Teabag's eyes snapped open wide, accompanied by a soul-rattling wheeze. He grasped at his chest. Pinned under Gen's foot, he tried to roll over, but couldn't.

"Wow," Blaze said. "I figured you were a little stronger than a regular human, but how strong are you?"

"Strong enough to end this conversation."

Blaze smiled, his hands out in surrender. "Sorry. It wasn't my intention to make you incapacitate one of the people we wanted to interrogate."

Glaring, Gen lifted her foot from Teabag's chest. "He's fine." She looked down at him and asked, "You're fine, right?"

Still grasping his chest, Teabag's breathing sounded like two bricks scraping together.

"Shit," Gen mumbled.

Blaze opened his mouth to respond with something akin to, *I told you so,* but a distant woman's voice suddenly called out...

"Ow! Fuck! You fucking asshole!"

Gen and Blaze broke into a run again, following the voice around the building. To the left, a side street connected to a main street. Ahead, a man was running away and when he reached the main street, disappeared from view. Another alleyway sprouted on the other side of a building. Instead of pursuing the mystery man, Gen and Blaze opted for the other alleyway toward the profanity.

"Fucking fuck!" Sitting on the ground, a woman clutched her right shin while staring at her shimmering wound of a badly skinned knee. "Mother fucker."

Blaze crouched down. "You okay? What did that guy— Scarlett?"

Not vamped up to walk the streets – a simple blue skirt and white concert tee shirt – she still had the baby doll face and deep frown of an irate cherub despite wearing no makeup. "Ugh. You again? Seriously?"

"Friend of yours?" Gen asked, glaring down with arms crossed over her chest, a deity too proud to mingle with mortals.

Offering her a hand, Blaze helped Scarlett to her feet. When he noticed an abrasion on her elbow, she yanked her arm away. She rankled when he said, "Yep. Her name's Scarlett. Scarlett, this is Gen."

Sneering as if Gen were the source of her injuries, Scarlett said, "I'm sure I should be charmed."

Gen rolled her eyes. "I don't care if—"

Both women suddenly went rigid, two predators ready to fight if one or the other gave any reason. They must have felt the same bizarre itch Blaze had felt when first meeting each of them. Something special, something familiar, but possibly adversarial.

Stepping between them, Blaze focused on Scarlett. "What happened?"

Eyeing Gen, Scarlett said, "I was coming down the street, aiming for the alley." Relaxing a bit, she looked to Blaze. "I saw a dude run out of this alley, loop around the building, and run down that other alley. I didn't think much of it, didn't care, but when I turned in, I saw some shithead messing with some short kid. I musta surprised him, 'cause he ran at me. At first, I thought he was gonna try somethin', but he pushed me down like a fucking shithead and ran."

"Short kid?" Gen asked.

"Sonny?" Blaze turned his attention to the deeper recess of the alley. A few trashcans and a dumpster. The buildings were small, two stories, so no fire escapes. Movement caught his eye – a pair of twitching feet sticking out from behind a dumpster.

Blaze raced to the person on the ground, knowing it'd be Sonny, and Gen followed. Sure enough, the young man lay on his back, convulsing with his hand pressed against his neck. Skin nuclear red and dripping sweat, getting redder and tighter by the second. "What the hell?"

"Shit!" Gen spat. "He's OD'ing."

Blaze reached out, but stopped, unsure if moving him would help or hurt. "What do we do?"

Sounding rueful, Gen whispered, "There's nothing we can do."

"There has to be something—"

With the bubbling sound of screaming underwater, Sonny hocked up a glob of blood.

Blaze questioned his sanity as every part of Sonny continued to swell, the skin of his ankles folding over the tops of his shoes like fleshy muffins. Then his skin split. A tear formed along his left arm letting loose a gush of syrupy red followed by an orange ooze. A fissure tore its way along his right cheek, the skin sloughing away, taking the muscle and fat with it, exposing a slime-covered jawbone. Sounds of intestinal distress rumbled underneath his shirt. The gurgling intensified and culminated in the popping of a gore-filled balloon. The muscles and sinew gave out and continued to twist, briefly held in place by Sonny's clothes. There was a hollow snap as his pelvis distorted in inhuman ways, followed by the castanet sound of each vertebra and rib snapping apart, muffled in the growing lake of viscous liquid scattered with wrinkling organs. The skull slipped free from his split face, a loose melon rolling from a grocery bag in a half circle, inscribing an arc of pinkish slime and the yellow of fatty residue.

With his own guts feeling like jelly, Blaze didn't realize he was holding his breath until he gasped.

Scarlett said from behind him, "What the fuck happened?"

Gen said, "That is what happens when someone ODs while mixing latro and rec."

Scarlett asked with a tremble in her voice, "Who was he?"

"A dealer," Blaze answered, stumbling backward, lest Sonny's disfigured remains run onto his shoes. "He dealt rec. Gen and I were shaking him and his partner down, trying to get to their boss."

Gen shot Blaze a look of scorn, clearly unhappy that he freely shared that information. He didn't care – he was too upset from watching a human being go through whatever the hell just happened, too disgusted to think strategically.

"I guess he took too much of his product?" Scarlett said.

"Maybe not. Wait… Scarlett, you said you saw a guy messing with him?"

"Yeah, the shit stain that knocked me over."

Blaze looked at Gen. "You think that guy did this? Shot him up with that junk?"

"Maybe," Gen said with her usual cold and emotionless shrug.

"All right. As much as I hate to leave this kid here, let's get Teabag to a hospital and let him know what kind of danger he's in."

"Teabag?" Scarlett asked.

"The other kid you saw run out of the alley. Gen and I… incapacitated him on the other side of the building."

Blaze hurried along the building and then back down the other alley. He stopped in his tracks so abruptly that the women stumbled into him. He wanted to tell them not to look, to turn around, but his tongue went dry and stomach acid tickled the back of his throat.

Teabag must have torn off his shirt, because skeletal fingers held a strip of material soaked in red. His exposed ribs glistened in ooze, his beating heart resting in a gelatinous pool of crimson. Lower half of his face missing, Teabag looked at Blaze, the skin on the top half of his face swelling, pushing his eyeballs out of their sockets. With a sloppy slosh, they popped from his head, and dangled over his face.

"Fuck this!" Scarlett cried. Both hands over her mouth, she turned and ran.

Blaze's world turned sideways and his vision blurred. He spun away from the pulpy mess on the sidewalk, hoping to see which direction Scarlett ran. Too wavy, hazy, warped from angry tears, he only saw blurry colors. A step, a stumble, he crouched down and willed himself not to fall over, but readied himself for impact just in case he did.

"C'mon," Gen said as she grabbed his arm and yanked him to his feet. "Someone's gonna stumble on one of these two soon enough and we can't be here when they do. I didn't see any security cameras, so we should be fine."

"Fine" wasn't a word Blaze would use to describe this situation or his place in it. He wasn't going to be fine for a while, but he got moving, one unsteady foot in front of the other. By the time they staggered out of the alley to the main street, he could walk on his own.

A block later, after he'd caught his breath, Gen asked, "You gonna make it?"

"Yeah. I'm better."

"Good." She wheeled around on him and stopped him in his tracks. "Something's up with Scarlett."

Hands on his hips, Blaze took a moment to grab a few more deep breaths. The sidewalks had a couple people walking them, and a car zipped by now and again. Nothing suspicious, no reason not to speak freely. "I sensed it too. Is she a spider like you?"

"I can only recognize my kind, but she's… unique. I got the same weird feeling that I got when I first met you. What do you know about her?"

"Nothing."

"No? Or are you protecting her? She's one of your friendly neighborhood hookers, right?"

Blaze mashed his lips, an unusual expression for him, and judging by how Gen took a step back, it wasn't a natural one. At least she no longer looked pissed when he followed up with, "I met her once. That's it. I don't know anything about her other than name and occupation. How about you explain what the fuck we witnessed and why it's not freaking you out."

Gen crossed her arms over her chest and looked away. "Like I said in the alley, it's a combination of latro and rec. As you know, latro is made from black widow venom. Rec is made from the venom of another spider species. Ven, Lucas, and I have been trying to figure out who's making the drugs."

"Your band playing tonight?"

"No. Why?"

"I'm going home to freshen up and ask questions around the neighborhood. Let's meet at that diner by Club B-Sides."

"Blaze—"

"It ain't like that, Gen. Scarlett is… different. Like us. Like the others in Vegas. Let's take a beat and exchange information, okay?"

"Fine. Food." As Gen walked away, she said, "But no dancing."

Blaze smiled.

CHAPTER 09

July 7th, Las Vegas

Phone pressed to her ear, Victor glanced at the hotel bar from where she sat in the lounge. Still not open. Of course, it wasn't even noon yet, so it didn't surprise her. "I'm fine."

"Are you sure? It's only been an hour since we met with Corette," Celina said.

Victor smiled. "It's sweet that you called to check up on me. Something had come over me, but I'm better now."

"Yeah," Celina said softly. "I felt the weirdness, too. I wanted to make sure you weren't doing anything crazy. Or destructive… to your soul or your liver."

Crazy or destructive like coming back to the scene where Corette's voice fucked with my head? Naah. It'd only be crazy or destructive if I called my assistant and asked him to bring a care package to Corette.

As soon as she finished the thought, Bailey entered the hotel carrying a sturdy paper bag with "Bouch & Becker" on the side. Inside the bag were soaps, coffees, chocolates, bourbon, and other items from companies Victor invested in, including single servings of cherry cheesecakes from Sugar Fix, Inc. "I, my soul, and my liver appreciate your concern, but we're all good. I have to get back to work, and you have to go be an awesome café owner."

"Well, I appreciate you."

"I appreciate you, too. Bye."

At the front desk, Bailey informed them he had a delivery for Corette Remington, and politely yet firmly stated that it needed to be hand delivered. Victor knew this because she had given him a script. She assumed he redacted the profanity. But her plan worked.

Mere minutes after the desk clerk dialed Corette's room, the elevator doors opened. An attractive man in a shimmering dark blue Brunello Cucinelli two-piece suit exited. On his way to the front desk, he tugged at his shirt cuffs to bring attention to the diamond cufflinks. He was handsome enough that he didn't need to draw attention to his expensive addons, but Victor had made that same move a few times herself, so no judgement. With an exchange that lasted with only a few words, Bailey offered him the gift. Corette's assistant looked in the bag, accepted it, and went back the way he came.

As Bailey left the building, he texted her that the delivery had been made.

Perfect. Now all she had to do was wait.

Forty-five minutes later, her assumption paid off – Corette's assistant exited the elevator one more time and strode across the lobby to the exit. Victor gleefully followed.

A coffee shop, a trendy one that Victor had never heard of. It was modestly busy, and she didn't have to skulk too long by the entrance as Assistant ordered two large coffees. A coffee in each hand, he got halfway to the door and Victor pounced.

A little extra roll in her hip, she sauntered by and took the cup from his right hand. Taking a seat at the closest booth, she drank from his cup and eye-banged him so hard she was afraid she might have made him pregnant.

He smiled, and – *oh, shit, those are nice dimples* – took a seat across from her. "You took my coffee."

"You got one right there."

"It's my boss'."

"So, he'll fire you if you drink his coffee?"

"She. And no. She likes it black with no flavor shots, no cream, no sugar. It's disgusting, like filtering water through dirt and then drinking it from a used ashtray."

Victor chuckled and took the second cup from him while gliding her fingers over his hand. One gulp and she needed to fight with her tongue to keep it from mutinying and running away. "Oh, it's every bit of delicious as you described."

"Glad I didn't oversell it. I'm Gavin."

"Victor."

"Well, Victor, I can't help noticing that you're very aggressive, seeing as you have stolen *both* of my coffees," said the dimples.

"It's lunch, I'm bored, and I got about an hour to spare. I'm willing to invest a few minutes to see if you'd be someone I'd like to be with for that hour. If you're truly heartbroken about the coffees, I'll buy you two more and be on my way."

Gavin pulled out his phone to send a text, undoubtedly to Corette letting her know he decided to take a lunch break. "So, what do you like?"

"What all women like. Money. Power."

Gavin sat straight and tugged at the shirt cuffs. "Lucky for you, I have both."

"Really? I'm not buying it. You mentioned that you have a boss. Not many people with money and power have bosses."

"My boss is a venture capitalist. She's very good at what she does, and I get a generous cut of her deals."

Victor smirked and nodded, approving yet dubious. "Yeah? What's your latest deal?"

"Can't talk about that."

"Then it's obvious to me that you're bullshitting."

Gavin looked away, his eyes focused and calculating, weighing the pros and cons of sharing. Looking back in time to see Victor bite her bottom lip, he asked, "Ever hear of Jacob McGovern?"

"The philanthropist from Philly?" she asked.

"Yes, him."

"Oh, damn. Does that mean he's in town? Where's someone like Jacob McGovern staying?"

Gavin's smile left and took his dimples with it. "Why do you want to know? Are you a stalker?"

"Yeah, stalkers wear suits that cost four figures."

"Maybe you tracked him from Philly. Like a private investigator or reporter."

"Do I look like a skank or an angry sociopath?"

"No."

"Then that should tell you I'm not from Philly. Look, you're the one bragging about being a venture capitalist working with a premier philanthropist but giving no details. Lack of details is one of the signs of a bullshit artist, and I don't have time for that." Victor sat back and turned in her seat to imply she was leaving.

"Ever hear of Oasis Life?" There was a gruffness to his voice. Not panic, rather frustration for needing to play a trump card sooner than he wanted. Victor liked it.

"The Air BnB for the ultra-rich?"

"Since my boss is a major investor in the company, I think it's better described as an opportunity to view exotic locations through the lens of luxury."

"I wouldn't consider Vegas exotic."

"Lake Las Vegas may not be exotic, but there is plenty of luxury there."

Satisfied with the amount of information she had received, Victor stood and dropped a twenty on the table. Gavin stood as well and stepped close enough for Victor to feel the heat radiating from his body. He put his hand on her arm. Victor's first thought was to deliver an upper cut, but he hadn't grabbed her and the look in his eye wasn't of anger, rather of curiosity. Plus, he smelled vaguely like cinnamon, and said, "I thought I'd be someone you'd like."

"Give me one reason why I'd like you?"

He summoned his dimples again, which was reason enough for Victor to like him for the next hour or so, but he leaned in and whispered in her ear, "I reciprocate."

*

Victor walked into the Roll and Role Gaming Café with a bounce in her step and whistling a jaunty tune, one she wasn't sure if she had heard before or if she was just making it up. She briefly wondered if Gavin would get in trouble with Corette for the two-hour lunch break and for returning to work without coffee. *Meh, doesn't matter. Just like the muscle he pulled in his back, whatever scorn Corette dumps on him would be worth it.* She smiled at the memory.

Celina rushed over, her eyebrows knitting with worry. "Are you okay?"

Speaking of coffee... Victor sauntered to the counter and ordered a large Hawaiian blend. While the barista filled the cup, Victor answered, "Yes. Better than okay, actually."

Celina frowned and cocked her head. "Yeah? Then why'd you show up for no reason and... Wait. That isn't the suit you were wearing this morning. Did you go home and change?"

Coffee in hand, Victor led Celina to a table for two at the back of the café. Business was good, so most of the tables were occupied, but this was the farthest away from everyone else. Victor knew how Celina was going to react, and wanted to get her as far away as possible from the rest of humanity. Once they both sat, Victor said, "I went home to shower and change."

Celina tilted her head the other way. "A shower? Why would you need...?" Her words faded as realization grew. Eyes wide and lips tight, she all but shouted, "Oh my God! You had—" In the rare moment of situational awareness, Celina stopped herself. A glance over each shoulder, she leaned forward and overcompensated with a barely audible whisper, "You had sex."

Celina's raw reactions made Victor laugh. Leaning forward as she whisper-shouted, "Yes. And he was pretty good, too."

Celina looked away. Victor could almost smell smoke from the gears grinding within her roommate's head. Turning back, Celina said, "You are a piece of work. Jaime yesterday and now today... Was it Jackson?"

Victor rolled her eyes and took a swig of coffee. "You know there are more people in Vegas than Jaime and her brother, right?"

"And you're trying to sleep with them all?"

"Ha ha, you prude."

Crossing her arms, Celina struck her ridged defiant pose. "I am not. I'm just more traditional. And I spent all my time in this city getting the café ready to open, so I've had no time to meet any men."

As much as Victor loved teasing her roommate, Celina's words stung. Just because she wasn't as aggressive in pursuing a social life didn't mean she didn't want one. She was a stranger in a strange city. Victor's city. "You're absolutely right and I'm gonna help you fix that. A few proper girls-nights so you can learn the lay of the land."

No longer pouty, Celina said, "Okay. I'd like that. So... your afternoon delight... Anyone I might know?"

"No, but that reminds me..." Victor pulled out her phone, her thumbs dancing over the screen. "I'm texting Robert and Orion to meet us here. I have information about Jacob McGovern."

"How did my question remind you to do that?"

Wickedness radiated from Victor's smile, a furnace blasting heat. "Because my 'afternoon delight' was with Corette's assistant. He told me Jacob is in town and the neighborhood he's staying in."

Skin paling, Celina's face went slack. "Victor! I can't believe you did that."

"Ummm...? Can't believe what? That I got laid? We've established that I like to and that I'm really good at it."

"No. That you used your body to get information from a guy like you were some kind of... like you were a... like a..."

"Hooker? Are you implying that I'm a hooker?"

"No! Maybe. I don't know. I just never thought you'd stoop to using yourself like that."

"You do know I'm an adult, right?"

"Yes, of course! But we've both said on more than one occasion that we're sisters and this is upsetting. You're smarter than that. More capable. How would you feel if I had sex with a stranger in exchange for something of value."

Other than her adoptive parents, Victor never had anyone care about her. All through her life, her friends were mere acquaintances, outfits from which to choose depending on situation and mood. Letting her emotional guard down enough to let someone care about her, like Celina who was a staunch defender of her virtue, tugged at Victor's admiration for her friend.

Reaching across the table, Victor took Celina's hand with a firm grasp to punctuate the earnestness of her words. "You're right. I'd be pissed if you did something like that. You're also right about me being smart and capable, which is why I fucked Gavin's brains out *after* I got the information."

"Really?"

"Really. I got the information within mere minutes of meeting him. Then he caught the Victor-fever and there's only one cure for that."

Crinkling her nose, Celina curled her lip. "I think that sounded better in your head."

"Yeah, probably."

"So, what did you find out?"

"Spoilers, dude! I'm not gonna ruin the surprise."

Celina stood. "You just don't want to repeat yourself. I'll grab a round of coffee. You go find a table for four."

"You got it, captain." Victor saluted. And then smiled again.

CHAPTER 10

July 7th, Las Vegas

Away from the casinos, Las Vegas looked like any other small city. Well, considering Orion's limited scope of the world, it seemed like any other small city. Random buildings lined up on either side of two-lane streets, with traffic lights or stop signs at the intersections. A three-bay mechanic shop on the corner, a squat square of bricks with a "for lease" sign across the street next to an insurance company.

Orion sat at a metal table built for two outside a café with a fancy name, something French he assumed. It was only a block away from Tools of the Id, an upscale, yet hipster, art gallery. The third and final gallery he and Robert had visited for the day, and Orion's appetite took over. He needed a late lunch. Of course, it had only been two hours after lunch, which was two hours after brunch, which was an hour after breakfast.

About three-quarters through his prosciutto, wild mushroom, smoked gouda flatbread – the closest thing this place had to a pepperoni pizza – Orion checked his email while Robert used the restroom. His brows pinched at the offering.

After this morning's email had demanded he go to Philadelphia, he had replied, "Lemme guess, you're a Saudi prince looking to move millions because you're being hunted. Sorry, I'm not buying what you're selling."

Feeling smug by replying the way Victor would have, he tried to put it out of his mind and enjoy the day with Robert. After the first gallery, a follow up email shook him: "Your name is Orion Fogelberg, your adoptive parents are Conner and Madison. Recently, you've been entering people's dreams."

He had replied with, "How do you know? Are you spying on me?"

At the second gallery, Orion had been quiet, allowing Robert to do most of the talking, pointing out contemporary styles and techniques of the gallery's offerings. Afterwards, during lunch, Orion received: "Not spying on you. I know about you because I know about your real parents."

Before going into Tools of the Id, Orion quickly typed, "Who are they? What are their names? Who are you? Why do you want me to go to Philly?"

Having shoved another piece of flatbread into his face, Orion pondered the response: "One answer will lead to more questions. It'd be easier to show you. I know how it sounds and you're right to be suspicious. I knew your nanny. You need to come to Philly."

"Show me?" Orion whispered to himself. "Show me what?"

Robert exited the café and Orion flipped over his phone, displaying the artwork on his phone case, an image of Pikachu riding Godzilla like a horse. Grabbing the remaining half of his panini, Robert said, "Thanks for accompanying me to the galleries today."

Orion chuckled. "I should be thanking you for sharing your insight about running a gallery and the current trends." Robert had mentioned that it was good to research what other galleries in vastly different parts of the United States had to offer. That gave Orion and idea… "Do you think I could be in your gallery? I mean, someday?"

Robert smiled softly, the same kind of smile Conner or Madison would have given if he had asked about becoming an astronaut. "As long as you remain diligent to the craft. Experiment, explore, and learn, learn, learn. Discover your own eye. Then absolutely someday."

"How about I go to Philly with you when you leave."

The smile faded. "I certainly can't stop you from going wherever you'd like, but when I get back, I don't know how much time I could devote to mentoring you."

"I can hang out around town and do whatever until you're free."

"If you don't mind waiting, we could schedule some time in a couple of weeks."

Not soon enough. Orion needed to go now and without a good excuse, Victor and Celina would ask questions about why he'd want to go to Philly. "Hookers and booze," was the best he could come up with, but no one would buy it. Victor would respect it, but not believe it. Visiting Robert's gallery was way more believable. He shrugged and said, "S'alright. I have no problem just hanging out."

Robert finished his sandwich and wiped his fingers on the napkin while regarding Orion. Finally, he said, "You have the same look in your eye you had a couple of months ago when we were in Los Angeles, when you wanted to follow the others to the warehouse. Any reason for the tenacity?"

Shit, he saw through my ruse. Orion shoved the last piece of flat bread in his mouth and wiped his hands. Shaking his head, he said, "No, nothing. Just really excited to get started on my art career. Kinda nerding out that I'm friends with an art gallery owner."

Whatever Robert believed, his smile wasn't betraying him. "I appreciate the exuberance, but maybe you should focus a little more on goal setting first."

Orion nodded. Even though his plan had failed, Robert hadn't pressed him. "Yeah. Yep, yep, I totally will."

Before Orion could think of a way to change the subject, both of their cellphones buzzed with a message from Victor to meet at Roll and Role.

Robert stood up, and mumbled, "This ought to be interesting."

They took a ride share to the café in silence, Orion not knowing what to say, as well as seething with guilt for patronizing a competitor café. *I'm not an indentured servant to the place, and I'm allowed to meet my café needs elsewhere.* But when he walked into Roll and Role, he avoided eye contact with Celina and Victor and went directly to the front counter to order a panini. No drink; there were three coffees and a can of Red Bull at the table in the back where he joined Robert, Victor, and Celina.

"Should we assume you found some information?" Robert asked.

"Jacob McGovern is in town," Victor answered. "He's staying someplace around Lake Las Vegas."

"How did you find this out?"

"She had sex with Corette's assistant – well, she met him got the information out of him and then had sex with him," Celina blurted in one word-cramming breath.

Victor dropped her forehead to the table with a thunk hard enough to make the contents jump. "Why? For the love of all that is holy, why?"

"You would have eventually told everyone anyway, and then probably doled out high-fives."

"I never knew it was possible to simultaneously hate someone and love someone as much as you," Victor muttered, forehead still on the table.

"You need to play more video games," Orion said. "That weird love-hate feeling is nonstop."

"I'm not taking life advice from someone half my age."

Orion crossed his arms and slouched. "I'm only ten years younger than you."

"Close enough."

Robert chuckled. "Is Corette's assistant going to try to kill us like your last dalliance who Celina told everyone about?"

Victor lifted her head and glared at Celina through a cascade of hair.

Celina shrugged her shoulders, pointed at Robert, and mouthed the words, "He said it, not me."

Sitting up, Victor tamed her hair and sighed. "No, he's nothing like Calista."

The mere mention of Calista's name sent a jolt of electricity to Orion's bladder. He had been doing so well dealing with the Calista Lindquist trauma by ignoring it. "Children of Monsters," Calista had called them, her gun pointed at Orion. And that was after being caught in a massive web spun by human-sized black widows. That memory wrung his spine like a dish towel. "Maybe he's a giant-ass spider."

A chill rippled over the table. Victor softened her tone and said, "Jesus, kid. Sorry for teasing you about your age. Next free night, I'll game with you."

Robert cleared his throat, an instant reset of the group's mood. "You mentioned that Jacob McGovern is in town. What are you proposing?"

"That we figure out where he's staying. Then I'll visit him to see why he's on the list." Celina opened her mouth, but before she could speak, Victor huffed. "For the love of God, Celina, I promise I won't sleep with him."

Celina frowned and said, "I don't care about that. I was wondering why it should only be you and not all four of us."

"It just makes more sense. He's a businessman, I'm a businesswoman. I need to talk to him about a piece of property that he's buying, so the hitlist will be a natural segway."

Eyebrows raised, Celina leaned forward. "The hitlist of us that Calista had compiled? That's a natural segway? What are you going to say?" Celina dropped her voice. "'Hey, I want that building back, and oh yeah, why are you on the kill-list of a hot blonde?'"

"Your less than flattering impression of me is downright disturbing."

"Sounds surprisingly accurate," Robert said, raising his coffee cup to Celina, pantomiming a toast.

"You're not helping," Victor mumbled. "But I'd like to think I'm a little more clever than that, since, oh I don't know, I'm a partner in a venture capital firm that has secured millions of dollars in investment deals."

Orion took a massive bite from his panini and wiped his mouth with the back of his hand. After a few chews, he said, "If it weren't for you three visiting me as a group, I'd probably be dead right now."

"He has a point," Robert said.

Victor rolled her eyes and sighed. "Okay, fine. You maniacs can join me. But I do all the talking."

"Fair enough. Did Corette's assistant tell you anything else about Jacob McGovern?"

"No. He went on and on about her next big investment, a personal rental app called Oasis Life. Of course, that now makes me think I have to vet Bailey to make sure he's not telling his bedroom partners about the deals I have lined up."

"Okay, so we know where he's staying. Should we go now?" Orion asked.

Victor chuckled. "You got enthusiasm for days, kid, but Lake Las Vegas is too big to go knocking on every door until we find him."

Orion turned his phone for everyone to see. "I thought it'd make sense that if Corette was investing in Oasis Life, she'd have Jacob stay at one of the properties listed. There's only one Lake Las Vegas property listed on Oasis Life. Unless you think he's staying someplace else?"

Victor smiled at Orion. "Nicely done, kid. I knew there was a reason to keep you around."

A warmth bloomed behind Orion's cheeks. He thought his guess at Jacob's whereabouts was pretty obvious, but he liked the compliment implying that he was clever. Now, to be clever enough to get to Philadelphia without anyone getting suspicious.

CHAPTER 11

July 7th, Las Vegas

Celina hugged herself in the passenger seat as Victor drove the Rolls-Royce Phantom. Orion and Robert rode in the backseat. Though it was hot as hell outside, a chill ran through her.

She would never get used to Las Vegas, or to be more specific, she'd never be comfortable living in a desert. Sure, she and Victor shared an upscale apartment in the city, but she came from New York – *The* City. Yes, The Strip rivaled NYC in glitz, glam, and cascades of lights, but that was a fraction of what Vegas had to offer. Lake Las Vegas was outside of town, but it was across the desert. Flat, sprawling, sand desert.

Whenever Celina left *The* City, it was rarely any farther than the closest suburb, replete with verdant landscapes. The tan of the wilderness here in Vegas was borderline oppressive. Even when they drove down a street lined with mini-mansions and palm trees and chromatic wildflowers, Celina couldn't escape the sprawl of taupe-colored desert dirt. She sighed. Her existential crisis wasn't the desert's fault; it was the hitlist's.

The last person they had searched for on the list was her half-brother, whom they found dead in Los Angeles three months ago. Before that was Orion, and they walked in on his adoptive parents fighting with his nanny because she was trying to kill him. Were they headed into a similar scenario? Would they have to fight for their lives again? This situation was reminiscent to when they found Orion – driving into an affluent neighborhood with plans of first contact being a knock on the door. However, Orion came from an upper-middle class family. These houses were upper-upper-upper class.

Victor guided the car up the driveway and into the parking court of the U-shaped hacienda-style home. The arms of the main house looked like smaller houses attached to a bigger one, a different roof for each section. Evenly spaced palm trees invited guests to the property while five arches invited them into the portico.

"Wow, this place is huuuuuuge," Orion whispered.

Despite how emphatically he said it, "huge" was an understatement. Bubbles percolated in Celina's belly, adding to the disquieting flutter behind her chest. She almost jumped through the roof when her cell phone went off.

"Drama queen," Victor said.

Celina checked her phone ID: Blaze Stanford, wanting to video chat. So surprised by his unexpected call, she forgot she was sitting in a car outside a stranger's house and answered. His face popped up on the screen. He looked exactly like the last time she had seen him – upswept blond hair, dull gold snakeskin jacket over top of a red base Hawaiian shirt, unbuttoned enough to expose a few gold chains, a shark tooth necklace, and a rosary. And that smile. That damn smile. "Hello?"

"Hey, Celina, how's it goin'?" he said. His smile shifted in such a way that Celina formed one of her own, accompanied by a warmth in her cheeks. "Your hair's a bit longer, I see."

"Thanks," she replied, tucking a lock behind her ear.

The warmth within her cheeks exploded into a raging inferno of embarrassment – he had simply stated a fact, not given her a compliment.

"Is that Blaze?" Victor asked. "It sounds like Blaze!"

Celina angled her phone to capture both her and Victor in the frame. A look of worry skittered across Blaze's face, yet he maintained his radiant smile. "Hey, Victor! How've you been?"

"You owe me a car! You stole my rental."

Blaze shrugged. "Technically, I owe either the car rental place or their insurance company a new car, depending how the policy was written. When you find out, let me know. I'll get everything squared away."

Jaw muscles flexed, Victor's eyes widened as if the rage bubbling up within her was ready to blow through her sockets.

Orion leaned forward from the back seat. "Hey, Blaze! Wassup?"

Celina turned in her seat and angled the phone to capture Orion and herself, hiding Victor's erubescent face. Blaze's smile shifted again, softer, as if cooing over a puppy. "Hey, Kid! You keeping Victor and Celina out of trouble?" He then squinted and held the phone closer to his face. "Is that Robert with you guys?"

Not leaning any closer to Celina's phone, Robert tersely said, "It is."

"So, the gang's all together. What's going on?"

"We're checking out another person on the list," Orion said.

Victor scowled at Orion, though the younger man missed it, too focused on Blaze. Before Orion had a chance to overshare more information, Victor said, "Why are you calling, Blaze?"

"Coincidentally enough, it's about the hitlist. Celina, could you text it to me?"

"Sure!" Celina replied, voice squeakier than she liked.

Victor aimed her scowl at Celina, but she didn't mind the look of chastisement. Information was currency, and a person she considered a friend needed a loan. Clearly, Victor didn't want to dole out anything to Blaze.

Tone still clipped, Victor asked, "What do you need the list for?"

Blaze's smile froze on the screen while he obviously contemplated what to say. Celina thought that since she had offered information, he would also be willing to share. She was right. "I recently met someone who... I get a weird feeling around."

Celina understood and tapped away at her phone. "Okay, I just sent the list."

Victor disapproved, judging from the depth of her frown.

After a few seconds of silence while Blaze studied the list, he grunted. "Huh. She's not on the list."

"You ran into another special someone in L.A.?" Victor asked.

"I'm not in Los Angeles."

"Where are you?" Orion asked.

"Chicago."

"Hooking up with Gen?" Victor asked.

"Jealous?" Blaze winked at the screen, and Celina knew that was meant for her, a signal passed from one coconspirator to another. She and Orion chuckled.

"Careful not to get webbing on your dick," Victor said.

"Victor!" Celina snipped.

"Dude!" Orion added.

Robert remained silent.

Victor waved her hand to shoo away the aspersions. She then crossed her arms over her chest and slumped in the driver seat. As a form of apology, she mumbled, "Whatever."

Blaze laughed. "Nonstop surprises with her, right? Anyway, thank you for the list, Celina. Take care, Orion!"

The screen went black.

"Oooooh, I can't fucking stand him," Victor said.

"I like him," Orion said.

"Me, too," Celina added. "I think there's a sweet side to him."

"Too smiley." Victor grumbled. "Smiley people are hiding something."

"A bright photograph is born from a dark negative," Robert said, obviously siding with Victor.

"What's he doing in Chicago with Gen? Last we saw her, she didn't seem like she wanted anything to do with Blaze. Or *any* of us."

Celina frowned and said, "Now, *her* I don't like."

"Me neither which is why I feel like there are shenanigans afoot," Victor said.

"She seems... capable," Robert said. "I can't imagine her falling for any of Blaze's cons."

"I like her, too," Orion added.

"You just like her because you think she's hot," Victor said.

"You think she's hot, too. And I actually like her music."

"See? That's what it means to be an adult – I can think she's hot and not like her."

"I am an adult," Orion muttered as he got out of the car.

"Nothing I can add will make this situation better or worse," Robert said, joining Orion in the driveway.

After the back doors closed, Celina frowned and asked, "Why do you have to be so cynical? Blaze and Gen faced the same dangers we did with Calista hunting us. In fact, Gen saved our lives. I may not like her, but I can at least be thankful for that without being nasty. Yes, Blaze stole your rental, but he works in favors, so I'm sure he needed it. If you'd be nicer to him, then maybe he'd consider owing you a favor."

Victor opened the door, but before stepping out onto the driveway, she asked, "Did you give him your number?"

"No."

"Then how'd he call you?"

Celina was left alone in the car with that question hanging in the air.

CHAPTER 12

July 7th, Chicago

A diner. The one close to Club B-Sides. Not even two blocks away and Gen had never been to it before now. She might never have stepped foot in here if not for Blaze's overly romantic view of diners. Hell, up until a few minutes before the meeting time, she thought about not coming, especially after Lucas had teased her for half an hour about this being a date. But Gen needed to learn more about Scarlett, and Blaze happened to know her, so in the diner she sat.

In a booth, Blaze looked up from the eight-page menu and wielded his smile like a sword. "Hey, glad you showed up."

A menu laid on her side of the table. Gen pushed it aside. "So, what do you know about Scarlett?"

Blaze chuckled at a secret joke he had told himself earlier. "I know you're busy and I know you want to find out who's supplying the rec, but you're allowed to take a break."

"Don't worry about how many breaks I take."

Blaze shifted his smile; his whole expression reached inside her, and offered to take away the parts that made her feel bad about herself.

"I do worry," he said. "When I see you, I see Atlas – always struggling to keep the weight of the world on your shoulders. A lot of people depend on you and you're not giving yourself time to rest. What happens to those people when the world comes crashing down on you? I'm not saying you should shirk your duties and goof off with me for the rest of the day. All I'm suggesting is that you take a few minutes to grab a meal and breathe."

God damn it, I hate that he's right.

Gen unclenched her jaw and relief bloomed from her ears to her chin. Even though she knew what she wanted to eat, she grabbed the menu and flipped through it in silence. The menu's pictures no longer portrayed food – instead, she saw faces of her employees, and the accompanying descriptions looked frightfully like invoices and receipts she had stacked in piles upon piles on her desk.

When the waitress came by, Gen handed her the menu and said, "Double cheeseburger, rare."

Gen didn't know what Blaze ordered, too busy glaring at him. As soon as the waitress left, she asked, "Why are you here?"

Blaze shrugged. "To unpack what happened this morning and—"

"No, I mean, why are you in Chicago?"

A second shrug. "Nothing left for me in L.A. except bad memories, so I thought I'd give Chicago a try."

"It's not gonna happen, Blaze. I'm not looking for a relationship."

"Neither am I. Look, what happened in L.A. kinda shook me up a bit. When I was a kid or teen… or *ever*… I never thought about the dirtbag who knocked up my mom, until three months ago. Celina and Orion are right. There is some kind of connection among us, and it seems to be stemming from our parents. I've been thinking about their suggestion to stick together."

"Then go hang out with them."

"I can't right now. Victor would literally murder me."

"Why?"

"I stole her rental car, then gave it to a pimp as payment to release a girl from hooking."

Gen laughed. An alien noise to her own ears, a sound almost forgotten. It… felt good. "You stole Victor's car?"

A hint of pink colored his cheeks. "I did."

"Oh, God, please tell me the look on her face. Describe it in great detail."

Blaze laughed and shook his head. "From what I saw, it was priceless, but I was too busy driving like a bat out of Hell to get a really good look."

Before her smile faded away into nothingness, Gen asked, "You get that feeling with Scarlett, too, don't you?"

"That weird sense of familiarity the first couple times we meet people on the hitlist?"

"Yeah, that."

Blaze nodded.

Gen reached into her jacket for her smokes as well as a pen with a hair-thin tip. After tapping two cigarettes from the pack, she wrote on one of them, "You forsake me more than Love; want me more than Death." Blaze watched her without saying a word, even when she lit them both and handed him the one without any writing on it. "We both got that feeling with Scarlett. Is she on the list?"

Blaze pulled the list up on his phone and slid it to Gen. "Nope."

"Doesn't mean she's not special or somehow involved in this."

Their meals came. Two eggs with jiggly yolks and a slab of ham that went beyond the confines of the plate for Blaze. Gen's burger was as greasy as a tanker spill, just as she had hoped.

"True," Blaze said. "Melissandra wasn't on the list either. Neither are Venom or Lucas. Anyone on that list from your cluster?"

Gen looked at the list one more time. "No. But Scarlett—"

"Could be involved? I doubt it. She's just a kid, probably Orion's age."

"Orion's on the list."

Blaze chuckled and shook his head. "Good point. All right, I'll find Scarlett."

Gen wanted to threaten him or give him an order or both, but what he had said earlier resonated with her – he was the only person in her life that didn't answer to her in some way. She wasn't responsible for him. God, she hated to admit it, but it was liberating. "Okay."

They ate in silence until Blaze crossed the halfway point with his meal. "So, your crusade against drugs... Seems like it runs deeper within you than just being a good Samaritan in the neighborhood watch."

Gen chewed the last of her burger slowly, debating what to share. She only shared herself with her friends, but they were all gone. "Growing up in the system sucked."

"I can't imagine, but I've heard stories."

"They're true. And there are stories worse than what you've heard. Abuse. Gang activity. Drug use. Preteen felons. Friends in the system are few and far between. The ones I did have... Well, I don't have them anymore."

"Sorry to hear that. What were their names?"

Blaze was a con man, and he used words, facial expressions, and his smile as lock picks to break into the most valuable vault – a person's soul. But his sincerity seemed pure. Was he that good at deception? Was Gen so desperate to unburden herself that she was willing to believe the lie? Perhaps she was. "Sophie and Alexis," Gen said. "Sophie often mistook attention for affection. She never learned that just because a boy seemed nice, it didn't mean she wouldn't end up with a black eye. She always made excuses, and needed a needle to believe them. One day she needed too much belief. The three of us met in a state-run home. Alexis hated it but stayed for Sophie. When Sophie left us, Alexis found other places to stay, mainly houses of gang members. One day, the gang hit a pharmacy. They had no fucking idea what they took, so that night they played mix-n-match. That game has no winners."

"And you?"

Gen didn't realize that she had been talking to Blaze's ham until he cut off a long piece and offered it to her. She grunted as a form of thanks and plucked it from the fork. Chewing, she continued. "Never did any of it. Never tried it. Alexis always said I never needed to because I was the strong one. That was why she started leaving me behind at the home when she hung out with the gang, because I was strong enough to handle being there." She paused while she finished the ham, debating about telling him the whole truth. *Fuck it.* "She was wrong, though. It wasn't strength that kept me from trying drugs. It was fear. I was too afraid to say yes. When word spread that I said no, then assumptions were made. No one messed with the girl tough enough to turn down drugs."

"So, drugs took your friends and you decided to rid the world of them?"

"Not exactly. It wasn't until a few years ago that my crusade began. The drug, latro, hit the streets. It's made from black widow venom."

Blaze took another bite of his ham. Gen was getting ready to go into more detail, explain the ramifications, the people she lost. She didn't need to; he nodded with understanding. "And rec?"

"Venom from an unknown species of spider."

"That means that this unknown species is close by, in your territory."

Gen nodded. "And how Sonny and Teabag overdosed? That's the result of mixing the two drugs."

"So that means latro is still being made."

"Yes."

Blaze finished his dinner. He tossed the wad of cheap napkins on the plate after wiping his fingers. "Okay, then. I understand a little better. Now what?"

That question had a hundred different interpretations, everything from, "What's the bigger picture?" to, "My bed or yours?" But Gen knew with certainty what he wanted, the message was written on his face, in his eyes, with his eyes – he wanted more conversation, wanted to get to know her. God help her, she desperately wanted to stay. "Now, I'm gonna go."

"Okay. I got dinner."

Favors were currency and he was a loan shark. She didn't like owing him, but she needed to leave before she changed her mind and vomited up more details of her life story. Hating that she felt like an awkward teenager, she said, "Thanks. Bye."

"Bye, Gen."

Out the door, down the couple blocks, and into Club B-Sides, her sanctuary.

"Hey, Boss," the swollen-muscled bouncer said as Gen entered.

"Hey, Vinnie." No band tonight and it was barely after quitting time for the local stores and offices, so the crowd was light. A dozen people or so. Two bartenders. She waved to the closest one, Chet, a lanky goth kid in a black leather vest and black pants. He flashed heavy metal horns as she breezed by.

In her backroom office, Ven and Lucas were waiting in their usual spots: Lucas leaning against the flimsy metal file cabinet, Ven standing like a terracotta soldier in the middle of the room. Neither of them sat in her chair. They knew better.

"Damn it, guys, don't you have any place better to be?"

"No," Ven grumbled.

"How was your date?" Lucas asked.

"Not a date," Gen said as she flopped down in her chair and propped her feet on her desk. "It was nice to get the fuck away from you two for a minute."

"There are better ways to do that than spending time with a con man," Ven said.

"I wanted intel on that hooker who witnessed Sonny and Teabag ODing. Blaze knew her, so now he's gonna find her and see what she knows."

"I don't trust him. You shouldn't have met with him."

Lucas sighed. "Okay, you pitbull, we get it. You're so fucking annoying."

Ven took a threatening step toward Lucas. "It doesn't matter how annoying I am, this is a black widow problem and as queen she shouldn't be seeking help from the likes of a con man."

Lucas remained unflinching. "As queen, she can seek help from anyone she fucking wants to, especially if it helps with a black widow problem."

"Uhhh, hey, excuse me?" came from the door. Chet, holding his right hand to the side of his neck.

"Come in," Gen said. "Ignore these two. What's up?"

"So, this guy came to the bar. A real weird guy with a face that didn't seem like it fit his head right, like he was wearing a mask and trying to act like he wasn't wearing a mask, you know? Well, he mumbled something and when I leaned closer to hear him better, he pinched my neck." Chet moved his hand to expose a mound of swollen skin, two tiny red marks on the peak.

"Fuck!" Lucas yelled, snapping to attention.

Ven hurried behind Chet and slammed the door shut.

Gen jumped out of her chair. "Chet, that guy injected you with either latro or rec or both, so you need to tell us how you're feeling right now."

The redness flowed over his skin like spilled wine, leaving raised, puffy skin in its wake. "Stiff. Warm. No... hot. Tight, like my skin doesn't fit no more."

Right arm now twice the size of his left, veins surfaced along his shoulder and wriggled like discontent worms. By the time his right eye swelled shut, his pants strained against his bulging legs.

"Gen, we need to do something," Lucas said.

"It's too late for him," Ven added.

"Too late?" Chet squeaked. "What do you...? What...? Do...?" Chet's swelling neck crushed his throat, his voice reduced to gurgling vowels.

"Fuck!" Gen yelled, as Chet's body continued to swell.

"Gen!" Lucas yelled. "We can't have another mess. Not after the last time."

Three months ago, they lost their drummer the same way, in the exact same spot. Lucas was right – they couldn't have the police involved again, not so soon.

A line of skin split open from Chet's right temple to his shoulder, enflamed muscle separating from the bone as a foamy orange mass oozed over his chest and arm. Before it could slop to the floor, Gen's arms and legs each split into two spindly black appendages, her head merged with her chest to form a cephalothorax while the rest of her torso ballooned into an abdomen, a red hourglass on the back of her black exoskeleton. She wasted no time spinning a web around Chet's ripping body.

Shredding their clothes, Ven and Lucas morphed into their black widow forms as well – Lucas's body brown, Ven's black, but neither bore the red hourglass reserved for the female of the species. The three of them spun webbing over Chet, trying to contain the sloughing skin and liquified organs. More webbing. Faster. With a thump, Chet – cocooned in spider webbing – toppled to the floor, a few crimson patches blooming.

Panting, Gen's black body shrank while her eight limbs folded into four. Ven and Lucas followed her lead, a sheen of sweat shimmering on their naked, human bodies.

"Blaze did this!" Ven yelled.

"No, he didn't," Gen replied, staring at a few tiny splashes of red on the carpet.

"He said a man did this to him, that a man—"

"It wasn't him!" Gen snapped, her chelicerae flaring from her cheeks.

Ven stepped back and averted his gaze to the floor.

After a few breaths, Gen continued. "It wasn't him, but... I'm going to follow him."

She hated to do that. It hollowed her gut, but it was the right thing to do. Looking down at the mass of webbing that contained an innocent victim, she wasn't sure what was right anymore.

CHAPTER 13

July 7th, Las Vegas

Orion got out of the car and slammed the door shut. Why did Victor have to be such a bitch sometimes? *No, wait. She'd rather be called a bastard. Screw that! Bitch or bastard didn't matter. She was being both!*

Robert got out of the car next and stood beside Orion. Robert was cool. So was Celina. And, of course, Victor was cool, too, when she wasn't being surly. At the moment, Orion hated to admit that he admired her – her toughness, her smarts, success, generosity. Why was she so nasty to Blaze? Okay, he stole her rental car, but in the brief time that Orion had known him, he didn't seem like the kind of person who stole for no reason. That also wasn't a reason to hate on Genocide either. What was Victor's beef with her? Her music was great! Yet, he still couldn't help but admire Victor.

Orion admired all of them. In a similar situation, they had burst into his house to help fight off Aika. They were complete strangers who had put their lives on the line to save him and his adoptive parents. Orion would forgive Victor, and so would the others. In fact, he'd forgiven her already as she led the way to the front door.

Palm trees were symmetrically planted along the perimeter of the parking court. Someone had recently swept the court meticulously clean from tree droppings. Pristine cream-colored stucco walls and red brick looked brand new. The tan tiles on the floor of the covered porch were without scuff marks. Orion tried not to look like a noob tourist as he admired everything.

Victor pressed the doorbell and a standard, unremarkable bong snapped Orion out of his hypnotic gaze – he'd been staring at the swirling shapes carved into the double door of dark wood. Side note – should he ever find himself owning a hacienda, he'd make sure to have a much more interesting doorbell.

As the final echoes of the bong faded away, a cry for help sounded.

"Hear that?" Orion asked.

"What?" Victor replied.

Orion held his hands up for quiet. After a few thumps of his heartbeat, a man's voice yelled, "Help!"

"God damn it," Victor snapped as she tried the door handle. It clicked open with ease.

She charged forth, shouldering between the heavy doors. Robert pushed the right-sided double door farther open and ran in. Orion tried to hurry in behind Robert, but Celina held him back. "Stay behind me."

Orion struggled to see around her. A wide hallway tiled in earthen colors led right and left. The continued cry for help and clanging of kitchen items sounded like it came from the right. "Get away you crazy bitch!" a man yelled.

"Fuck! Is it *her*?" Victor yelled as she rounded the counter.

Who? Orion wondered. He bolted from behind Celina as the four of them rushed into a spacious living room. Victor released breath-infused profanity just as Robert and Celina stumbled up beside her.

A long counter separated the kitchen from the living room. The man yelling, "Stay away from me," couldn't be seen, presumably on the floor behind the counter. Standing in the kitchen was a long-haired blonde wearing a black bodysuit and boots, guns strapped to her thighs. At first glance, Orion thought it was the woman who had tried to kill him in Los Angeles.

Calista Lindquist.

The attacker darted from the kitchen, disappearing behind a wall between the living room and another area of the house.

Victor and Robert snapped into action and took off after her.

Orion and Celina hurried around the counter. On the floor and gripping his left arm was a wide-eyed, shaking man. "Jacob McGovern?" Celina asked.

Breath quivering, he pushed himself against a set of cabinets. "Who are you? What do you want?"

Celina held out her hands to show that she was harmless. "We're friends. We're not here to hurt you. We're here to help."

Jacob shook his head. "How... How did you know I was being attacked?"

Mimicking Celina's actions and as if speaking to a spooked horse, Orion said, "We didn't. We are all on a list of special people. The four of us and you. When we found out that you were in the area, we drove here to talk to you."

"A list? What list? What are you talking about?"

Victor and Robert came clamoring back into the kitchen, both breathless.

"It's a hitlist," Orion said, pointing in the direction of the attacker's escape. "Written by the woman who attacked you."

"It might not be her, kid," Victor said.

"She ran outside and then disappeared," Robert said. "We didn't get a good look at her."

"And she died three months ago," Victor added.

Jacob eyed the two newcomers, blood from his arm dripping between his fingers. "Who? Who are you talking about?"

"A killer named Calista Lindquist," Orion said.

Victor tightened her lips, then asked Jacob, "What did the woman who attacked you look like?"

Jacob blinked quickly and shook his head. "Umm… Blonde."

"Yeah, besides that. We saw the back of her. Gimme details we didn't see."

"She had a few faint scars on her face. Her top was unzipped, and she had a tattoo on her chest… A name. Linda, I think."

"Fuck." Hand on her hips, Victor looked to the ceiling and walked into the living room.

Celina stepped forward. "We're sorry that you got attacked, but it could have been worse. Let's help with the cut."

Jacob squinted, a dubious look, but got to his knees, and then stood. He removed his bloodied hand to examine the wound. He grabbed a nearby kitchen towel and pressed it against his arm. "Doesn't look all that bad."

"Do you want to go to a hospital?" Celina asked.

"No. But if someone could run to the bathroom and see if there's any kind of first aid kit. It's down the hall, first door on the right."

"I'll get it," Robert said.

Celina made introductions. By the time Robert returned, Jacob was washing his wound at the kitchen sink. Robert helped apply antiseptic and ointment, then wrapped his arm.

"Thank you," Jacob said. "She got me good, but I don't think I need stitches. And I think I need a better explanation about what the hell is happening. Who is this Calista person? Why did she attack me? Who are you four?"

Flopping down on the couch, Victor scrubbed her fingers through her hair as she growled. After a few seconds, she said, "Grab yourself a drink and get comfy, Jake, because it's a doozey. In fact, grab me a drink, too, strongest thing you got."

Jacob squinted at Victor, then moved to the refrigerator. "It's Jacob, please. Anyone else want anything?"

Robert and Celina declined his offer. Feeling immature as the words left his mouth, Orion asked, "Red Bull? Or anything like it?"

Jacob found a can in the fridge. He then opened the freezer and grabbed a bottle of vodka with a name Orion couldn't pronounce. Robert and Celina settled into seats in the living room while Orion stayed in the kitchen, satisfied to lean against the counter.

Celina explained everything regarding the hitlist and Calista Lindquist. She shared that her own birth father was a psycho-murder-rapist of mythic proportions, but withheld the fact that they confronted an organized crime boss named Melissandra who could turn into a human-sized black widow. And she kept mum about Bigby, the nightmare monster living in Orion's head, the fiend that was capable of killing people within their own dreams. She concluded by stating Gen had killed Calista, though she left it vague, never mentioning that Gen was also a black widow creature. Though Celina had such an easy way about her that she could tell Jacob the truth and make it seem right as rain, it was better to ease Jacob into this strange world of monsters.

Staring at something a million miles away, Jacob took a swig of vodka straight from the bottle. Running his thumb over his bottom lip, he said, "That... That sounds crazy."

"I understand," Celina said. "We all do. That's why we're here. We saw you were in town and wanted to meet you, see if you knew anything about your parents, or if there was anything... I don't know... unusual? Anything unusual about your life?"

Jacob shook his head and set the bottle on the coffee table. "My parents died when I was seven and I was raised by my Aunt Shirley. The only thing truly unusual about my life is happening right now. You four. Calista."

"We still don't know that it's Calista," Victor mumbled.

Tone as somber as talking in a church, Robert said, "The way he described the attacker certainly sounds like her."

"Actually," Victor started as she leaned forward, elbows on her knees. "Can you tell us exactly what happened here, Jacob?"

"Not much to tell. I went to the kitchen to grab a bite to eat. I saw something from the corner of my eye and when I turned, Calista... or whoever she was... slashed at me with a knife. I tried to fight her off, and then the doorbell rang. Now you're all caught up."

"See? I can't believe it's Calista, because she would have used a gun, not a knife."

"What weapon did she use when she first attacked you?" Orion asked Victor. He didn't intend to say anything, but the caffeine was kicking in, and he thought about disavowing responsibility for his mouth.

After a quick glare in his direction, Victor answered, "With a knife, but it was a different situation.

"Different how?"

Now focusing her glare on Celina, Victor said, "I was doing reconnaissance and that's how I discovered her list."

It was Jacob's turn to lean forward. "The list. It's been mentioned a few times. Does anyone have it?"

Celina tapped away at her phone, and handed it to Jacob. His eyebrows knitted, scrutinizing it as if it were a treasure map. Suddenly his head shot forward, eyes wide. "Oh, wow. Wow, wow, wow. I actually know someone on the list. Knew. I knew someone on the list."

Furtive glances were tossed about the room, a couple Orion's way.

Celina asked, "Who?"

"Preston Albright. I met him when we were children. I was at a playground for a play date, although I think it was a date for our dads."

Orion pulled out his phone and studied the list. He assumed that Preston was thirty-something, though his gaunt face and sunken eyes made him look like forty was having its way with him. He then swiped to his search bar and tapped away.

"I think it's pretty obvious what we have to do next," Celina said.

"Are we really doing this again?" Victor asked.

"Jacob was attacked. Regardless of whether or not it's Calista, we need to follow up."

Victor turned to Jacob and said, "You're a smarmy businessman. I'm sure plenty of people want to kill you."

Athletic build with perfectly styled hair, he had a face that belonged on a yacht while live streaming for tens of millions of followers. Orion felt Victor's assessment was accurate.

"I may be a businessman," Jacob said, "But in the limited time that I've known you, you seem to be way smarmier than me."

"Well..." Celina said. "I suggest that we find Preston Albright and visit him, like we did with you. If he's in trouble, we can help. Even if he's not, maybe he can help us figure out what we all have in common."

Jacob sat back in his armchair, glanced at Orion, and then stared out the window. Orion had no idea what that look meant, so he went back to researching on his phone.

"I don't think so," Jacob said. "I don't want any more to do with any of this. My business in Las Vegas is done and I'm going back to Philadelphia. If you feel the need to hunt Preston down, then I'm certainly not going to stop you, but—"

"He lives in Philly!" Orion blurted, heart racing, wanting to crash free from his rib cage. He tried to hide his excitement, but from the sound of his voice, he knew he was failing. "Preston Albright lives in Philadelphia."

Victor pinched the bridge of her nose and slouched back into the couch. "Jesus, I guess we're going to Philly."

Jacob flinched, a stunned look now on his face.

Orion wanted to jump around and punch the air, electricity racing from joint to joint, but he contained himself. Finally, he'd found a way to get to Philly without raising anyone's guard. He had to meet with the mysterious person sending those emails.

"I was going to leave tomorrow," Jacob said, standing. "But I don't want to stay here any longer than necessary should *whomever* change her mind and come back, so I'm leaving tonight. But... I'll free up time to meet tomorrow morning."

Orion couldn't tell if anyone liked the idea or not, faces slack from fading adrenaline, but everyone stood. Time to leave, so Orion joined them.

Celina smiled and said, "Tomorrow it is. We can catch an early flight and meet you."

As Orion walked past, Jacob snatched his phone. "Here's my contact information. Let me know when you arrive."

"We will," Celina said.

"Wait...," Victor said. "One of the reason's I came to see you was to talk about the building you stole from—"

Arm around her waist, Celina escorted Victor out the door. "Not now. You'll have plenty of time later."

A wave of confusion swept across Jacob's face, but it disappeared when he looked into Orion's eyes as he returned the phone. There was knowledge there, like when he played a card game with a partner and they both knew they'd win the game. Orion opened his mouth to ask what Jacob was thinking, but Jacob closed the door.

CHAPTER 14

July 8th, Chicago

Blaze loved Los Angeles but there were a billion differences between that city and Chicago. Much like L.A., Chicago sprawled across the landscape, collecting and stitching together differing neighborhoods. Away from the watchful eye of Willis Tower, nowhere near Grant Park, and no tourist traps like The Bean, he leaned against a graffiti covered wall and viewed a three-story block of bricks that had once been an apartment building. It stood apart from the rows of single-family houses nestled together, each barely large enough for half a family, but all separated by chain-link fences. The sidewalks, cracked and uneven, led past the train tracks to pawnshops, convenience stores, and coin operated laundromats. He'd been in Chicago long enough for the trains to become ambient noise as they rattled past.

"Jesus, dude, are you standing right in the middle of the train yard?" Jerry asked.

With his phone to his ear, Blaze chuckled. "It ain't that loud, Jerry."

"Well, I don't have to worry about trains where I'm at."

"Yeah? Where's that?"

Silence.

"C'mon, give me a hint," Blaze said, egging on the closest person he had to a friend. "Are you still in the U.S.? North America? Planet Earth?"

"Oh, you're such a funny guy," Jerry moaned.

"Don't you trust me?"

"You? Meh. The eighteen agencies with three letter initials listening in? No."

"Hey, you've been smart enough to get the information I've needed, so I know you're smart enough to avoid the alphabet trios."

"Yeah, yeah, yeah. You're as subtle as a brick through a window, Blaze. I got the info you're looking for. Sending it to you now."

Blaze paused from the conversation long enough to check his inbox. A few PDFs of documents probably long forgotten. In one of them, though, was info on the owner of the apartment building that should have been condemned long ago. "Thanks, Jerry. And thanks for getting Celina's number for me."

"Those two tidbits were nothin'. The info I got on your girlfriend? That I had to dig deep for."

"Heh. You'll have to come to Chicago to collect."

"Screw you, pal. I'm wondering how you're gonna pay me back."

Jerry wasn't lying. As soon as Blaze had set up residency in Chicago, he tried to learn everything he could about Genocide Stone. Not much – every avenue he turned down, he was met with a brick wall. He wasn't sure if he was collecting a favor from Jerry or going into debt, but Jerry found interesting information about a "Jennifer Faustino." Not only did she own Club B-Sides, but quite a few other businesses as well, all sold to her for one dollar. Blaze wanted to know more about the seller, and he was confident that Jerry already had the intel. But now didn't seem like a good time to ask for it, especially since he just got the name of who owned the three-story shithole he was looking at. "All right, all right. I was bein' a dick. I owe you."

"Fuck right you do."

Hanging outside the building finally paid off – Scarlett exited. Tracking where she lived was easier than expected and he hadn't needed any help from Jerry. A few questions around town had led Blaze here.

"I know you'll figure out a way for me to pay you back. But I gotta go."

Blaze waited for her to walk ahead a couple blocks before he started following. Hands in his pockets, he tried to keep his footsteps natural, but quiet. The sun had about an hour left in the sky, so if she turned around he'd have nowhere to hide. He wanted to talk to her, but he didn't want her to think he was stalking her. When the shadows of the underpass absorbed her, his hopes of being inconspicuous disappeared.

Chunky cement columns held the train tracks about thirty feet above ground and provided plenty of canvas space for spray paint artists. They also became walls for the homeless, a half dozen tents and tarps spread among the columns. Suspicious eyes watched Blaze, at least one pair he recently paid to help him track down Scarlett.

Once she reached the other end of the underpass, she turned left. Blaze hastened his pace, but when he exited the underpass, she was nowhere to be found. He chuckled and leaned against the closest column, lit a cigarette, and waited. Not even a few puffs later the tip of a cold switchblade was against his neck.

"Why are you following me?" Scarlett asked, the hold on her blade unwavering.

The eyes of the devil in the face of a baby doll. Blaze snickered to himself and wondered if those lyrics would be good enough for Gen. "You owe me a cigarette, so I figured I'd collect."

"Real funny, guy with a knife at your throat."

"I've been in worse situations. Yesterday's a perfect example."

The hard edges of Scarlett's frown softened as she took a step back and looked away. She tightened the grip on her knife. "Yeah, I'll say. What the fuck was that mess about?"

"Apparently that's what happens when you OD from mixing latro with rec."

"I've never seen anything like that before."

"Me neither. That's why me and my friend are trying to find who's making rec and latro."

Scarlett took another step back, her calculating eyes dark and stern. Finally, she retracted the blade and slipped the knife into a pocket of her half jacket. "I told you to stop asking questions about rec."

Blaze read the story on her face. The loneliness. The pain. The struggle. He wanted to help her and he needed her help. There was only one way to achieve both. "I felt it, too."

Squinting as if confused, Scarlett asked, "Felt what?"

"Something weird when we first met, like an itch inside my head."

With a motion as natural as waving to a friend, Scarlett pulled her knife again. "Are you this creepy with everyone, or is it just me?"

Blaze shook his head and smiled, a friendly one, welcoming. "What I meant to say is that when we first met, I saw the way you reacted, some flicker of recognition behind your eyes. I had that same feeling, like from a dream or *déjà vu*. I have a group of... friends... that I feel the same way with. We're different, Gen is different. And we need your help finding out who is making the rec. Who knows? Maybe you could use our help, or maybe you'd like to have a couple friends who are like you."

"I have no idea what you're talking about," she said, still pointing her knife at Blaze. "So how about you fuck off and stay away from me."

She was lying, Blaze knew it. He opened his mouth to let her know she was safe with him, but... was he safe with her? Different sometimes meant dangerous. He simply closed his mouth and let her walk away.

CHAPTER 15

July 8th, Abington, PA

Sitting in an SUV, watching Preston Albright's house, Celina couldn't help thinking that this cliché neighborhood could be found near any city in any state in the country. A microcosm of single-family houses, ranging from "almost nice" to "not so nice." One side of the street had no sidewalk, the sidewalk on the other side was barely there, grass filling in large missing patches. Even though the sun was shining, a filter in the sky added a grayness to everything.

Celina grew up in a similar neighborhood, the only difference being the level of upkeep. She also knew that in these kinds of neighborhoods there would be plenty of people watching her and her friends. From the corner of her eye, she thought she saw the blinds flitter in the window of a nearby house, but when she looked again, no curious eyes stared at them through the slats. But she felt them. *Darn Victor for making me paranoid!*

The flight from Vegas to Philadelphia earlier this morning had been quiet after the kerfuffle between Victor and Orion on the plane. As they were getting comfortable in their first-class seats, Victor had asked him, "So, what happened to your airplane allergy?"

"Ummm…? Dramamine?"

"Yeah? Let me see the bottle."

"It's in my bag."

"The one in the overhead compartment? Why don't you grab it and show the class."

Orion frowned, an expression Celina had never seen on him before. "Okay, *Mom*, I don't have motion sickness."

Celina didn't like to see Orion squirm, especially from under the weight of Victor's antagonistic words. "Victor, that's enough. This isn't necessary."

"It is. It's very necessary. Don't you remember why we had a super fun road trip from his home in Maryland to Los Angeles? I sure do, four of us in a car for 3,000 miles. I wanted him to admit that his motion sickness story was bullshit."

"Why does it matter?" Orion snapped.

"It's about trust, kid. Someone's lying to us. Calista is either still alive or very much dead. If she's alive, then that means Genocide lied about killing her, and who knows about Blaze? If she's dead, then Jacob is lying to us."

Orion's frown deepened. "Why would Jacob lie to us?"

"I haven't figured that out yet."

"Well, I don't think he's lying. If he is, there must be a reason."

"The reason is he's suspicious," Victor said.

"You're suspicious," Orion grumbled under his breath as he wriggled in his plush seat one last time before closing his eyes and putting in his earbuds.

When they landed in Philadelphia, Victor rented a Chevy Traverse. "The way our luck has been going with knocking on strangers' doors, we'll need the extra room to take this Preston guy to the hospital."

Hands wringing together for the entire drive from the airport to Preston's house, Celina obsessed over Victor alluding to bad luck. Now, sitting in the passenger seat of the Traverse while parked in an unfamiliar neighborhood, hungry eyes glowed in the shadows and denizens whispered that she didn't belong here. "I feel so exposed."

In the driver's seat, Victor tightened her grip on the steering wheel. "I know. Me, too. I say we give Jacob five more minutes, then we go in."

Sitting behind Celina, Orion huffed. She felt his warm exhale on her neck. "We should wait for him no matter how long it takes. He's the one who knows Preston."

"There's a good chance he's not going to meet us here," Victor said. "Think about it – we showed up at his rental house right when he got attacked by some blonde woman. We scared her away then barfed all kinds of crazy information all over him and told him we're going to fly across country to knock on this Preston guy's door. What sane person would actually agree to meet us here?"

"Someone who got attacked by the same person who attacked us. He went through the same thing we did."

Victor glared into the rearview mirror and Celina wondered what kind of debate raged behind those eyes. Victor had a soft spot for Orion, as did Celina, but she also had a short fuse. Luckily, the topic became moot when Robert looked out the back window and said, "Jacob just pulled up and parked behind us."

"Told you he'd be here," Orion said. He opened the passenger door and hopped to the back row of seats, making room for Jacob to sit beside Robert.

"Well, this doesn't look suspicious at all," Jacob said, shutting the door behind him.

"We wanted to wait for you," Orion said.

Jacob locked eyes with Orion, and Celina didn't like it. The look. The vibe. The weighing and measuring. The way he smiled like the fox talking to Pinocchio. He'd have bowed if the environment allowed it. Jacob said, "Thank you. I appreciate that."

Orion nodded back. "You're welcome. Okay, let's go meet Preston."

"Not so fast, kid," Victor said. "I don't think it's a good idea for all five of us to swarm his place. I'm sure people in a few of these houses either have their cell phones out and ready to record, or they're ready to call the cops if we fart in the wrong direction. So we don't freak Preston out, I think it should only be two people, and it's obvious that Jacob needs to be one of them."

"Okay," Orion said. "I'll go with him."

Shoulders slumped, Victor turned to Celina with eyes that wordlessly pleaded for assistance.

Clearing her throat, Celina said, "Your enthusiasm is admirable, Orion, but I think it should be someone who has a little more experience with unknown variables, so you and I should stay in the car."

"And Victor thinks faster on her feet than I do, so I'll stay as well," Robert added.

Orion glanced back and forth between Robert and Celina, then slouched in the seat. "Yeah, makes sense, I guess."

Victor pulled out her cell phone, put in an earpiece, and dialed Celina. "Answer, and put your phone on speaker. That way you three can at least hear my side of the conversation."

Jacob and Victor left the Traverse, and Orion returned to the center seat.

The crunch of footsteps and the soft muffles from outside intermingled with Victor's breathing came through Celina's phone. The faint knock on the door. Celina increased the volume to maximum and held her breath, concentrating on Jacob's far away voice as he called through the closed door. "Hi, Preston? Preston Albright? My name is Jacob McGovern. We, uhh… We knew each other back when we were kids." Another knock on the door. "I know this is weird, but your name came up recently and got me thinking and I saw that you and I still live fairly close together."

Silence, other than Celina's pulse thumping between her ears.

One more knock.

After a few more slamming heartbeats, Victor said, "Hey, the door's unlocked."

"Hello? Preston? This is Jacob McGovern. Your door is unlocked. Is it okay if I come in?"

No. No no no no no.

"Fuck it," Victor said.

"Wait. We can't just…" Jacob's words faded away as Victor entered.

"Fucking fuck!" Victor yelled.

Orion launched out of the car, racing to the house. Robert and Celina followed.

The front door opened into a living room with sparse, faded furniture. Preston laid on the blood-saturated couch, his red-stained lifeless hands limp on his lap beside a gaping wound in his gut. Dark blood soaked the bottom half of his plain white tee shirt and top half of his jeans. Celina didn't like how fresh it looked, wet with a red shimmer. "Is this… Did this happen recently?"

"It had to have, right?" Orion said.

He was doing much better than the last time they discovered a dead body, which saddened Celina. No one should get used to seeing dead bodies, especially someone so young. He stood close to Robert, a totem of bravery and security, and his skin had a hint of sallowness, but he wasn't puking this time.

"I mean, we saw Calista attack Jacob," Orion said.

"Whoa, whoa, whoa," Victor said, waving her hands. "You packed a lot of supposition in a tiny little suitcase. You're assuming Calista is involved, but I keep reminding you that the last we saw her, she was dead. We also don't know how many people are involved. If this is the work of one person, then think of the logistics involved. He or she would have had to leave Jacob's place almost immediately after we scared them off."

And I don't trust Jacob. Celina knew those words would have been the next out of Victor's mouth if Jacob hadn't been standing right here. Celina wasn't sure what she thought about Jacob yet, either.

Skin pale, Jacob struggled to focus on Victor, but his wide eyes kept drifting back to Preston. With a bit of a quiver in his voice, he said, "Okay, you mentioned before that your friend, Gen, had killed Calista." He turned away from Preston and put his hands on his knees, leaning over the coffee table. Deep inhale, slow exhale. "I'm sorry. I just... I'm confused."

"It's okay," Orion said.

After a few deep breaths, Jacob stood straight. "You've had to deal with something like this before?"

Orion nodded and gestured to everyone else. "Yeah. We all did, but we helped each other through it."

Jacob shook his head and worked his bottom lip. "Wow. That's... Just wow. Okay, this is real. This is real. Okay. As I was starting to say... How do we know Calista is dead?"

"Gen—"

"Stabbed her," Victor interrupted. "Stabbed the hell out of her. And then a burning warehouse collapsed on her."

"Did anyone verify it, though? Find her dead body? Check her breathing? Take her pulse?"

"Did you miss that a burning building fell on her? If we tried to do any of that, then the aforementioned burning building would have fallen on us."

"I'm merely suggesting," Jacob said, "that if she is some kind of professional assassin, then it's safe to assume she'd be hard to kill. Unless there was verification of a dead body, then there's a possibility – no matter how slim – that she might have found a way to live through all that."

Celina wanted to share her thoughts, but they were as messy as the coffee table. The half-eaten food from two pizza boxes, a few Chinese takeout containers, a bunch of empty beer bottles. She caught a glint of brightness, the shimmer of gold. A hair. A long, blonde hair on the coffee table. Pinched between her thumb and index finger, she held it up for everyone to see.

"That could be from anyone," Victor said. She frowned at the table, her words as limp as the noodles in the opened box of Chinese takeout.

"I hate to speak ill of the dead," Robert said, "but he doesn't seem like the kind of person who entertains too often. We should take a moment to search the house."

"Is that a good idea?" Jacob asked. Making and releasing fists, he glanced around. "Shouldn't we call the police? Especially since half the neighborhood probably watched us walk in here. So, we shouldn't touch anything, right? Tampering with evidence?"

Victor walked over to the coffee table and reached for the pizza box. No, not the box itself, something under it. A business card. "Corette Remington. Munitions Investing. What the fuck is he doing with one of her business cards?"

"Didn't you hear me about tampering with evidence?" Jacob asked.

"What the cops don't know won't hurt us," Victor said, taking a step closer to Jacob. "Why was it sitting right there?"

Color returning to Jacob's cheeks, he frowned and took a step back. "How would I know?"

"Oh, gosh, gee willikers, maybe it's because you and Corette screwed me in the not fun way in Vegas."

"Not me. Corette."

"Right. Sure. And how did you two meet?"

"She caught wind that I was expanding Resole La Soul and told me about an investment opportunity. *She* contacted me."

Victor squinted and growled. After a minute she broke eye contact and said to the room, "We have to go to Chicago."

"What?" everyone asked at once.

Victor slid the card into her back pocket. She ran both hands through her hair, her eyes darting back and forth – a sign that she was scheming. Celina was usually in tune with Victor's crazy ideas but had no idea where Victor was going with this, other than to Chicago.

"We have to involve Gen and Blaze," Victor said. "Fuckery is afoot and Corette is part of it. If we visit Gen in her club, then she has to listen to us. Plus, we can confirm with Gen that she… stabbed… Calista."

"Are you serious?" Jacob asked. "I can't just drop everything and go to Chicago."

"Why not? You dropped everything to come here?"

"Yeah, because I live about forty minutes away. I…" He paused and looked back to Preston. "Look, I've never been attacked before. I've never seen a dead body before either. I'm low-level *freaking out*. But I can't go to Chicago with you. I'll stay here. *I* will contact the police and stay here. I'll tell them some story about being childhood friends with Preston and learning he lived nearby, so I stopped in. It's all but the truth. Contact me later and keep me posted about what you find out."

"Speaking of being close to home," Robert started. "I don't think I can miss more time away from the gallery. I'll stay vigilant and keep you informed if I see anything unusual."

"No problem," Victor said. "No one's forcing anyone to do anything. How about you, kid? You're coming with us, right?"

"I think I'd like to stay in Philly," Orion said.

Celina would have wagered her life's belongings that Orion would have chosen to go with her and Victor. "Really?"

"Yeah. I'm starting to build a life for myself, starting to focus on being an artist. Robert and I talked about it a couple days ago."

All eyes turned to Robert. Celina almost chuckled – he looked like he got caught with his pants down. "Well… Yes, Orion, we did discuss it, but if you recall, I mentioned that I'd be a bit too busy these next few days to spend any time with you."

Orion shrugged. "I'll hang around the city and visit other galleries."

"As long as you're okay with that."

"Yeah. Totally."

Orion was right, though, about establishing a self-sufficient, new life for himself. Celina yearned to go back to Vegas, to her new café, but she'd be hiding her head in the ground and abandoning Victor. She often argued with Victor about Orion being an adult, and now she was the one looking at him as if he were a child. "Are you sure?"

Hands in his pockets, he nodded. "Yeah. It'll be fun. And if this *really* is Calista, and she comes looking for me? She'll find Orion Fogelberg's obituary. She's not looking for John O. Miller."

Celina didn't like the idea of him going off by himself, but they had to allow him his freedom of choice, and his independence. He had seemed sad these past few weeks. Life with a fake name had to be trying, so she bit her tongue and let her roommate do the talking.

Victor put a supportive hand on his shoulder. "Okay, kid. Just remember, Celina is going to text you twenty times a day."

Orion nodded.

Victor then addressed everyone. "Let's figure out a plan."

Within five minutes, everyone knew their part to play over the next day or two. They verified contact info and instructions, agreeing to share whatever they learned as soon as possible. Jacob stayed behind, all set with his cover story.

Leaving the house, Celina stole one last glance over her shoulder into the living room. Arms crossed and lips pulled tight like drinking a tea too bitter for his taste, Jacob hovered over Preston, staring down at him. Any unease he had displayed earlier was gone, replaced with disappointment. Celina shuddered as she closed the door behind her.

CHAPTER 16

July 8th, Chicago

Cloaked by the shadows, a hint of alarm scurried through Gen as she spied Blaze conversing with Scarlett. The young hooker held a switchblade to his throat. However, when he smiled, Gen squashed her concern like a bug. He wasn't afraid of Scarlett hurting him. Clearly, he was handling the situation just fine. He was up to something, but what? Everyone had an angle, an agenda, a motivation. What was his?

According to everyone Gen had talked to regarding Blaze, he was a saint. She called bullshit. Blaze monetized information and he used people as a conduit to get it. Gen wasn't without her resources; she had lived in this city her entire life. She knew people, too. Fans. Neighbors. Store owners. Hookers. But when she asked them if they knew "Blaze, a dirtbag in a gold snakeskin jacket," she got confused looks and had to listen to them extol his virtues. Either they didn't know he dealt in favors or whatever he gave them was worth what he collected. Eventually, she found where he lived and followed him. To Scarlett.

Gen didn't like her, especially after "the feeling" when they had first met. Too coincidental that Scarlett was in the alleyway the same time Sonny and Teabag ingested a lethal dose of the latro-rec mix. Yes, Blaze was trying to get information from Scarlett, but after Chet's OD yesterday, Blaze wasn't moving fast enough. Time to take matters into her own hands.

Blaze and Scarlett concluded their conversation and went in opposite directions, neither of them toward the apartment building. As she often did with every aspect of her life, Gen put her hands in the pockets of her leather half-jacket and acted casual, like she belonged, like she was moseying toward her destination.

The outer door of the apartment building opened with ease and Gen paused once she stepped inside. The nasty place was uninhabitable.

To the left was a roughed afterimage of where a set of stairs had been. A massive rectangular gouge was in the wall, presumably where the resident mailboxes once were. Without the staircase, Gen could see directly down the hallway to the back door of the building. Four apartments lined the right side, two on the left, doors missing with most of the walls bludgeoned down to the studs.

Gen walked into the first apartment on her right. No furniture, no appliances, no features. Cautiously, she crept through the apartment's skeleton as if it could come to life at any moment, stepping over the occasional metal guts and the flaked skin of drywall on the floor, ducking the electrical nerves. She walked through all four apartments, the entire length of the building, and then back into the hallway by the back door. She looked up into the gaping hole in the ceiling to the second floor where a set of stairs should have been, their memory a dirty shadow on the wall.

Kicking aside a chunk of rubble, Gen slowly spun, reexamining the first floor, wondering where Scarlett lived. The second floor? But how would she get there? There should be two sets of stairs, and neither of them...

Realization slapped her so hard that her cheek actually stung.

Spiders wouldn't need stairs to get to the second floor.

Gen opened the back door to a small parking lot, weeds growing tall and wild through the multitude of cracks. One abandoned car, no glass or tires, layers upon layers of graffiti. She thought about getting Venom and Lucas, or a few members of her cluster and bring them back to... what? A den with an unknown number of enemies. Hell, she didn't even know what kind of enemy. And it'd be dark soon; spiders had terrible night vision. Gen sighed and closed the door.

Clothes off and tossed in a pile by the back door, Gen stood under the hole to the second floor and looked up. Fuck it. In spider form, she scurried up the wall, but only extended the tip of her right front leg through to the second floor, allowing the finest of fine hairs to do their job. The odors of other spiders were abundant as were the smells of rec. Not only had Gen stumbled on where the enemy lived, but a drug lab for rec as well. Everything within her told her to retreat and return with a few gallons of gas and a match, but that'd be treating a symptom, not finding a cure. She needed more information.

One leg at a time, she pulled herself halfway through the opening, just enough to get a better idea of what she was dealing with. Similar floor plan as below, two apartments on one side of the hallway, four on the other. No stairs to the third floor. And no doors into any of the rooms either. But webbing everywhere.

Unsure which spider species she was dealing with, the mounds of webbing scattered about the walls and floor told her that they used it more for shelter than as a means for capturing prey. Careful to avoid the silky strands connecting one mound to the next, Gen crept up the wall and along the ceiling, toward the first doorway. Unlike the first floor, she didn't enter, content to peer inside. And unlike the first floor, the interior of the apartment had walls. Furniture as well, but due to the amount of web mounds throughout the place, she doubted anyone wiled the time away by sitting on the couch and watching television.

Gen continued to scuttle along the ceiling, crossing the hallway to look into the next apartment, then back again. Two more apartments and she still couldn't determine which species she was dealing with. Ven had taken a picture a couple months ago. It was blurry and of two hind legs – long, brown, thin. Webbing mounds. A venom used for a drug called rec... For a second time today, realization made something within her cephalothorax twitch.

Brown recluse.

The hairs on her legs suddenly tingled and she froze. From an apartment at the end of the hallway a long-legged spider exited and skittered along the floor toward the front of the building. The dark brown hairs on its violin shaped body were thick and had the look of velvet. Up the wall it scurried, through the opening to the third floor.

Gen had enough information. Time to get out of here and formulate a plan with Ven and Lucas to...

The hairs on her legs twitched, sending new stimulus to her brain. Latro. She smelled latro among the rec. What kind of queen would leave without investigating, to see if one of her subjects was in trouble?

No doubt in her mind that the drug lab was on the third floor. Obviously, the spiders living here willingly donated the main ingredient for rec. But the black widow venom needed for latro? If it were on the premises, then it was being taken by force. She didn't smell anyone from her cluster, but the brown recluse odors were too thick to sort through.

With very little webbing on the ceiling, she skittered to the opening with ease. As before, she started with the tip of one of her front legs. The funk of so many brown recluses collected in one area, their webbing musky, but the acrid chemicals needed to make latro and rec turned Gen's stomach and burned her sense of smell. She pressed on and eased her way to the third floor. Though darker, she saw movement throughout.

Electricity ran through her leg hairs.

A brown recluse on the ceiling above her.

She ducked back through the hole just as globs of webbing sprayed at her. Sticky strands gummed her back two right legs together. Awkwardly she retreated from the opening, then eyed the hole in the floor to the first floor. Too late. The spider that had ambushed her dropped to the second floor and blocked her egress.

Shrill chirps sounded from the third floor, a warning emitted from spiders rubbing their legs together. Clicking came from the apartments in response. The situation was growing dire.

Gen turned and sprayed sticky strands at the brown recluse that blocked the closest exit. Gen's two legs were still stuck together, hindering her speed and agility, but she hurried down the hallway floor, aware of the webbing mounds. Another spider shot from an apartment, and Gen sprayed webbing as she scurried by it. No pursuit, and she assumed she got it in its eyes.

Senses elevated, the input from the hairs on her legs set her brain on fire. Some of the mounds vibrated, a few burst open. A mammoth recluse pounced, and she scuttled up the wall to dodge it. Another spider sprung from an open doorway but missed as she moved to the ceiling. A mound close to the stairway opening at the back of the building twitched and split open. Dropping from the ceiling just as the recluse broke through its webbing shell, she landed on top of it and jammed her fangs past the hair, piercing its exoskeleton. It bucked and twisted, its long legs twitching, but she wrapped her six unfettered legs around its body. As she pumped venom into it, the spider crashed against the wall, smashing her against it. Whether it was blind panic or a calculated last gasp, the recluse sprung toward the stairway hole with Gen on piggyback, and twisted as they fell through.

Pain ripped through her body, stars dominating her vision as she slammed against the concrete of the first floor, the dying spider on top of her. A few heartbeats were all it took for the recluse's legs to curl inward, and that was all the time she could afford herself to gather her wits. Chirps and clicking noises from the second floor were approaching.

Aches rippled through her legs as she shoved the carcass off her and righted herself. Flinging the back door open, she turned back into her human form, sticky webs coating her right leg, and grabbed her clothes on the way out. Bare feet slapping against the parking lot, she ran toward safety. One naked blonde running from the building, pausing by the abandoned car just long enough to slip into her skirt and jacket, might go unseen. But the building was too close to houses. Any more naked people, let alone any giant spiders, flowing from the building would raise questions. Dark forms swirled inside the building's doorway, just long enough to pull the dead spider deeper into their lair.

Gen had found the species invading her territory and where they were making the drugs she wanted to get rid of. Now what?

CHAPTER 17

July 8th, Philadelphia

A few times when he was younger, Orion tried to pull fast-ones on his parents. Acting like he was going to a PG movie with designs to sneak into an R rating instead. Telling them he was going to a sleepover when he and Brennan had planned on going to a concert. Trying to sneak out of the house Halloween night with a carton of eggs and a can of shaving cream. His parents had always caught him. *What did I do wrong?*

The Philadelphia International Airport was the last place Orion expected to analyze failed transgressions of the past in order to commit a new one, but he needed to pull this off. He hated to lie in general but lying to his friends made the sick swirl in his gut a million times worse. A bubble that tasted like barf worked its way up his throat and ended in a stinging burp. *Okay, I think I need to control stuff like that.*

Sweaty palms, brows, hairline. He remembered his whole body getting sweaty and his eyes going wide whenever his parents started asking questions. Oh, yes, he remembered his voice trembling something fierce when he fabricated answers to their pointed questions.

"Are you sure you don't wanna come with us, kid?" Victor asked. Too caught up in his thoughts, her question made him jump, and his wide-eyed answer had the upswing of a question, "Yes, I'm sure?"

Calm the hell down, he reminded himself as Victor put a hand on his shoulder. She chuckled and said, "It's okay to be nervous. I mean, it's been a *whole day* since you've been miraculously cured of your flying-sickness."

Standing next to her, Celina elbowed Victor. "Be nice. This is the first time staying by himself in a strange city. I'd be nervous, too."

"You get nervous over, literally, everything."

"I'm sorry we all can't be as callous to the world as you," Celina said. She then dropped her voice and flexed her arms, "I'm Victor fucking Vegas. Nothing scares me. I eat razor blades and make men cry. Grrrr."

Victor stepped back and squinted, analyzing Celina as if she were a statue in a museum. "I can't tell if your impressions of me are getting better or worse."

Orion smiled and winked at Celina. "Better. Definitely better."

"You both still eat cereal with marshmallows, so clearly neither of you have discriminating taste. Now come here," Victor said as she hugged Orion. "Don't forget, you're not getting paid for time off."

Orion squeezed back and mumbled into her shoulder, "You're not my boss."

Celina's turn, her hug strong, comforting. "But I am, so I'm giving you vacation time. And I order you to please be safe. Don't take any chances. And text when you get settled into a hotel."

"'K."

Victor led the way to security, Celina behind her waving to Orion. He waved back even after they made it through and disappeared from view. Heart beating faster than nightclub music, Orion started to pace, but realized how suspicious he looked.

Not sure what else to do, Orion tightened his grip on his backpack and laptop bag, and followed the signs for taxis and shuttles, glancing over his shoulder one last time.

Once outside, he pulled up Uber and requested a pickup. A sigh of relief. He wasn't sure why he was so nervous, since he technically didn't lie to them. He just hadn't told them the whole reason why he wanted to stay in Philly.

The Uber ride dropped him off at the Holiday Inn. Check-in went smoother than expected; he just had to be polite and show his driver's license and credit card, though he still hated pretending to be John O. Miller.

The room was nice, the bed plenty big enough to do a few snow angels – a silly hotel room routine he performed ever since childhood, though it felt bitter-sweet since this was the first time he ever paid for and stayed in one by himself. *Okay, enough goofin'.*

Slouched cross-legged on the bed, he pulled up the internet on his laptop, sent an email, and then typed, "lucid dreaming" into the search bar. The theories. The history. The facts and the fiction. The studies. Orion read it all, absorbing every word. At first he took notes, but abandoned the effort, too excited to move onto the next article and the next, retaining the information far better than any other topic in school. The hours slipped away, pausing only to order pizza. Page after page, website upon website devoted to techniques on how to achieve lucid dreaming. And Orion read it all.

His phone pinged, a text from Victor: `We're in Chicago tell your hookers I said hi`

Another ping, this one from Celina: `Hi! We made it to Chicago safely. You be safe too. Goodnight!`

Good night. Yes, it was time to get some sleep. After replying to his texts, Orion ran through his nighttime routine, and checked his email once more. Nothing new in his inbox. Laptop shut. Lights out. Eyes closed. Grateful that he'd had the foresight to not drink any Red Bulls today, Orion closed his eyes and welcomed the blackness.

He must've fallen asleep quickly because he now strolled through a familiar setting, the blackness of his dreamscape. It didn't take long to come upon the shards of broken glass lying on the floor. This was good. When someone became aware that they were dreaming, one should create a comfortable environment. This was far from comfortable, but Orion had been here multiple times, so it was a good enough starting point.

Now, what next?

Dragons!

Within the blackness, Orion imagined a fantastical setting with pink skies, green clouds, and purple rivers flowing through a blue and yellow forest populated by dragons of all shapes and sizes. No matter how hard he wished, past the point of throbbing temples, he saw nothing but blackness. Catching his breath, he laughed at himself and mumbled, "How about you learn to crawl before you try sprinting, ass-hat."

Orion held out his hand, concentrating on his empty palm, and thought, *Baby dragon.*

Nothing.

Frowning, squinting, flexing his neck and jaw until his head shook.

Nothing.

Huffing, Orion paced in tight circles. This was his dreamscape. His world. He was an artist inside the blankest canvas possible and he couldn't create anything! His pacing took him closer to the broken shards. Tingles raced up and down his spine while he remembered why they were broken.

Bigby.

Was that what was holding him back? Fear? He certainly had a lot of it recently. The fear of a monster like Bigby living somewhere inside of his head. Not to mention the newly learned possibility of being hunted again. And withholding the truth from his friends. But... He *could* control something in his dreamscape.

The last time he was here, he saw memories of his childhood, of Aika. A sting at the back of his nose, a twist behind his ribs. He missed her. The prelude to tears taunted him as he shuffled around the graveyard of glass. He picked up a piece about a foot wide. "Aika, help me be brave."

A rainbow skipped across the surface of the glass, quickly followed by another and another. More colors slid across the glass, faster, until the colors combined and then separated into shapes, images. People. Aika. And himself, but much younger. He was sad, scared, gripping the straps of his Star Wars backpack with a death grip. First day of first grade!

The image flickered as Aika crouched down in front of his child-self. Confused about the flickering, Orion tilted the glass and realized the scene wasn't playing on the glass, rather the glass was projecting it. Turning the surface of the glass away from him, the scene continued to play out as if the blackness had a wall, like an old reel-to-reel home movie from the sixties. Orion smiled.

"I'm scared," the young Orion whimpered.

"Have I ever told you of Momotaro?" Aika asked, her smile soft, comforting.

With a pouting bottom lip, Orion shook his head.

"Well," Aika continued. "One day, an old married couple found a peach, but when they cut it open, they found a baby inside. They decided to keep him since they had no children of their own and named him Momotaro, the Peach Boy."

Young Orion's expression changed, his eyes now wider with wonder. "Peach Boy?"

"Yes. Every day, he grew stronger. By the time he was five years old, he was able to cut down a large tree by himself."

"By himself?"

Aika nodded. "Yes. Then one day his parents heard stories of a group of Oni ravaging the lands. The brave Peach Boy was old enough and strong enough, so he took it upon himself to leave his parents, seek out the Oni and drive them off his lands."

"Did he?"

Another nod. "He did. The brave Momotaro did what he felt he had to do, and along the way, he befriended a dog, a monkey, and a pheasant who helped him."

Like a street magician, Aika produced a peach in a plastic baggie from behind her back and put it into his lunch box. Now excited to leave home, the young Orion ran onto the school bus when it pulled to the curb and opened its doors. The scene faded to black, and Orion awoke in the hotel bed.

Crying and smiling with sweat pouring over his face, he sat up. Every first day of a new school year, she packed a peach in his lunch. He hadn't thought about that first day of school since… well, since it happened. But he was so happy to have seen that memory. He felt better, braver.

He used the bed sheet to wipe his face, and then leaned over to grab his phone off the nightstand. One in the morning – plenty of time to try lucid dreaming again. However, he couldn't resist checking his email.

A new email in his inbox.

`RE: your parents`

`Meet me tomorrow at the old Monticello Theater. 5:00 PM.`

He suddenly became too excited to go back to sleep.

CHAPTER 18

July 8th, Chicago

Silence cloaked the ambient sounds in the small back office of Club B-Sides, growing heavier upon Blaze's shoulders with every thudding heartbeat. Gen had just finished her story about the infiltration within the cluster of brown recluse spiders, including the discovery of a drug lab making both rec and latro. And that Scarlett was a brown recluse.

Betrayal nagged at the base of his skull.

Gen had followed him, going behind his back to investigate where Scarlett lived. But she did the right thing and she owed him nothing. They had become closer these past few days, but not as close as he had hoped. Winning her over wasn't the goal; helping her was. What more proof did he need that he was helping her than being included in this conversation. Much to Venom's chagrin.

Ven crossed his arms over his chest and leaned against the wall next to Gen's desk, glaring at Blaze, his abysmal eyes holding a multitude of threats. Blaze wondered if they had always been that black, or if the large man called forth the ebony eyes of his spider-self, ready to pounce and devour upon command. "Why is he here?"

"Seriously?" Lucas asked, sitting on a cheap, armless gray padded office chair. Blaze sat on its ugly twin, opposite Lucas. The blue haired man frowned and continued. "After what Gen just told us, the first thing out of your mouth is that you don't trust the guy who helped us find the other cluster and their drug lab? Don't be an asshole."

"He's not one of us, so why is he here?"

"Dude, he helped!"

"But why? What's his motivation? He's not like us, so why did he help look for an invasive cluster in our territory? He hasn't lived here long enough to be part of the local community. Why has he been so interested in finding the drug lab?"

116

"Oh, I think we all know the answer to that." Lucas's wicked gaze at Gen was overshadowed by his lascivious tone.

Gen sat straight in the chair behind her desk, grabbed a handful of papers from one of the stacks, and threw them at Lucas. Most pages peeled away midflight, but a good enough portion smacked against his head. "Grow the fuck up!"

"Damn it," Lucas moaned as he massaged the impact spot on his forehead. "You almost hit me in the eye! You could have poked my eye out."

"Don't be an asshole," Ven said.

A middle finger as a response.

Gen glared at Ven and said, "Not that I need to explain myself, but Blaze adds a different point of view. *That* is why he's here."

"Fine," Ven said with a growl. "What next?"

"Welfare check on the cluster," Gen said. "I smelled the black widow venom used for latro. They're getting it somewhere, meaning from someone in our cluster. I need to check out each member to see if anyone is missing."

"How many are in your cluster?" Blaze asked.

"Almost two dozen."

"Twenty-six," Ven corrected.

Gen winced and looked away, obviously trying to hide the disappointment with herself. Blaze could almost hear the admonishment in her head and took the opportunity to shoot a look of concern to Lucas. Ven put the cluster above all; Lucas put Gen above that. Luckily, Lucas picked up what Blaze was putting down and cleared his throat. "Ven and I can do the welfare check, Gen."

"That's not a bad idea," Blaze said. "Gen has a ton on her plate."

Gen's expression softened. "Thanks, Lucas, but I'll do it."

"You sure?" Lucas asked.

"Yes. I am the queen."

"Plus, you'll need to let them prepare for war," Ven added.

"We're not going to war," Gen said.

Ven uncrossed his arms and pushed away from the wall. "What? Why not?"

Even though a scowl chiseled its way across her forehead, Gen kept her tone even. "How would we even go about it? Attack their lair? It's in an area where there are plenty of people to watch dozens of human sized spiders attempt to kill each other. Which means we'd have to attack in broad day light, because we can't see for shit at night. Even if we try guerilla tactics, meaning we kill a couple of them then they kill a couple of us, it goes back and forth until there's no one left. We certainly can't add to our numbers in mass quantities, because the disappearance of men in one area wouldn't go unnoticed. Even if I chose that route, what good would it do since we already established that neither a head-to-head confrontation nor sneaky tactics are preferable?"

Jutting his jaw and grinding his teeth, Ven crossed his arms again. "What if we just burn the fucking building down?"

"That would be a big, fiery declaration of war with a big dose of retaliation. Scarlett knows who I am."

Ven and Lucas turned their attention to Blaze, hot looks of anger across their faces.

Gen waved at both of them. "Stop. Not his fault. I'm sure she knew who I was long before Blaze. Hell, she was probably using him to learn more."

Well, that stung. Blaze thought he was helping a young prostitute. Now he felt stupid for letting himself get used like that.

"Even though we know who and where this new cluster is, we're still kind of back at square one, aren't we?" Lucas asked.

"Fuck!" Gen yelled as she threw herself back into her chair and punched the air with both fists.

An awkward silence grew until *The Imperial March* played from Gen's phone. Confusion turned to annoyance when Gen looked at the screen. A single tap killed the noise, and she slammed it face down on her desk. Mere seconds later, Blaze's text tone chimed. From Victor: `Tell her to answer its important.`

The Imperial March played again. This time Blaze said, "Victor says it's important."

"Fuck sake," Gen grumbled as she snatched her phone from her desk. A tap and Victor's face appeared on her screen. "What do *you* want? And how the hell did you get ahold of my phone long enough to put your number in and give it a ringtone?"

"Hey, gorgeous," Victor replied. "I'll ignore the easy pickup line about having deft fingers so I can tell you Celina and I will be in town tomorrow. We need to meet up with you and Slimy Snakeskin Sammy."

Lucas laughed at Blaze.

"Now's not a good time, Victor," Gen said.

"I know, I know. But something's going on that involved the people on the list and we need your input and help."

"I told you back in Los Angeles that I don't care about—"

"Calista's back."

Gen and Blaze both went rigid, zapped by the same bolt of lightning. After exchanging a worrying look, Gen said, "Impossible. I killed her. And even if somehow I didn't, a whole burning building fell on her."

"Hey, trust me, I'm following your logic. I personally don't think it's her, but one name on her hitlist is dead and another was attacked. Evidence points in Calista's direction."

Gen stared at her phone, jaw muscles flexing as she chewed her options. "Meet here at the club tomorrow morning, ten o'clock."

Phone off. Gen looked at Lucas and Ven, tiredness evident in her voice. "I'm gonna do a wellness check. I'm not gonna mention why. Understood?"

"Yes," Venom and Lucas said in unison as they headed out of the office.

After a minute of silence, Blaze stood as well. "Anything I can do to help?"

Staring off into space, Gen tapped a pen on her desk. "No, I don't think so. Thanks."

"See you tomorrow." Blaze slowly shut the door behind him.

CHAPTER 19

July 9th, Philadelphia

The Monticello Theater. At least that was what the person on the other end of Orion's mystery emails had called it. Not much about it on the internet, just that it was a theater for plays and musicals, not movies, and there had been a fire. At first glance, it didn't seem all that bad. If not for the graffiti on the walls, it'd have a fancy appearance. The marquee was empty; no performances since 2002 according to the internet. Nothing about the front of the building suggested it was a victim of fire. A victim of time and neglect? Yes. Not fire. Unless that happened at the back of the building.

Orion's cell phone read 5:10p.m. The last email had asked him to be there by 5:00p.m. Orion didn't like that he hadn't arrived promptly, but he had awoken at the crack of noon and spent the rest of his day researching lucid dreaming. It was easy for him to lose track of time, a quality that Conner and Madison had harped on over the years.

Heavy chains and padlocks through the handles of the front doors kept him out and this neighborhood made him nervous. A bunch of three, four, five story buildings were crammed together. Boards covered windows and doors on the brick building across the street. The sidewalks had minimal foot traffic, as evidenced by the guy in thick blue pants and matching work shirt who huffed by while paying Orion no attention. Ditto with the four young people, laughing at lame conversation, probably heading for a bar.

5:15 and he paced in tight circles, eyeing the theater while keeping his head on a swivel. No more waiting. On his phone, he pulled up a siren app, and then readied the small canister of pepper spray in his pocket. After a deep inhale and four quick exhales, he walked into the alley leading to the back of the building.

Behind the theater was a small lot overgrown with weeds and speckled with broken glass. One dumpster looked like it had been forgotten about years ago. The stonework of the building's rear still had char streaks darkening it. The top of the building faded into the charcoal remains toward the back corner. While gawking at the burned section, he jumped when a door opened. A voice called out, "There you are! Christ, I've been looking all over for you."

Standing in the open doorway was an old man with thinning white hair slicked back. Even though he had a rounded belly, his gray suit fit loose everywhere else. The man's raspy voice completed the 1940s gangster vibe. "Don't worry about the roof. If it hasn't fallen yet, it ain't gonna today. Come on."

Orion approached with his pepper spray leading the way.

The old man rolled his eyes. "Put that away. You ain't gonna need it and you're more likely to spray your own eyes than mine. Plus, your age starts with a one while mine starts with a seven." He then held up a simple black cane as visual proof of his infirmity.

A curt nod and Orion put away his phone and pepper spray.

"Name's Harold Varvaro," he said, introducing himself as Orion followed him into the building and down a long hallway. "A fire of mysterious circumstance happened back in 2002. While looking for financial backers to rebuild the theater, it came to the public's attention that there'd been embezzlement, and the books were as fake as a porn star's tits. Around 2005, I bought the place for a song. I was making a killing in the art world, so I figured why not grab an investment property. Well, gentrification don't move as fast as some people think. Anyways, in 2006, I needed to disappear. If you learn one thing, Orion, it's that you gotta be smart and think ahead. I bought this place with a name and an account no one but me knows." As he concluded his spiel, they made their way into the main theater, the stage on their left. Limping to a stop, Harold patted his bad leg. "Fucked my leg up back in 2006. For the same reason I had to disappear."

Orion was getting better at recognizing social cues, and figured that Harold wanted him to ask, "Why did you have to disappear?"

Harold gestured to the stage as an answer.

Orion walked up the stairs as if they were boobytrapped. He had never been this close to a stage, let alone walked onto one. His parents had traveled to New York City for plays and musicals, but he never joined them. Theater wasn't his thing, but he had enough friends involved with his high school's plays, and he'd seen all the performances from ninth grade on up. They all had a similar form of set – hand crafted and painted bushes, trees, fences, buildings. But this theater had amazing seats, ornate decorations, beautiful murals. It even had a balcony! That grandeur made having no set on the stage more noticeable. But the stage wasn't empty.

In the center was a hospital bed, with an I.V. and heart monitor next to it. The monitor didn't make any noise, but numbers were displayed in digital red – blood pressure 110/70. Pulse 60. Not a single creak from the floorboards as Orion inched closer, though all he heard was the slosh of his heartbeat between his ears. Why wasn't this talkative Harold guy saying anything?

Orion crept onward, hoping nothing would spring from backstage or drop from the ceiling. Tunnel vision encroached and his ability to think became muddled. He needed to know who was lying on the bed.

A woman.

She had long black hair with a couple streaks of gray, and a skin tone that matched his, though her face was a bit sunken. He was a terrible judge of age, but Aika had celebrated her 40th birthday before the end of last year, and this woman looked about the same age as Aika. This woman looked old enough to be…

"My mother?"

"You're correct," Harold said.

Orion's mind seized. This woman was his mother; he knew it before Harold confirmed. *What do I do?* He had always dreamed about finding her and then giving her a big, squishing hug. *Can't hug someone in a bed, in a coma.* A secondary daydream had been to hold her hand. Orion slipped his hand into hers, gently intertwining their fingers together. Too many "love-conquers -all" stories left him disappointed when he got no reaction from her. No movement. Not even an extra blip on the heart monitor. He slid his hand away. "Why is she like this? What happened?"

Harold made his way across the stage toward the bed, the rhythmic thump of his cane sending arctic chills up Orion's spine. Harold stood next to

Orion. Both hands on his cane, he viewed the woman as if he and Orion were paying homage to a sick buddy. "Sorry, pal, I have no idea."

Orion's parents – his *adoptive* parents, Conner and Madison, who had lied to him his entire life – told him that she died at childbirth, meaning that it was *his* fault that she died. He had spent years believing that he had murdered his own mother. Yes, he knew that was too harsh a word to use, too weighty of an attitude to have, but the guilt always felt like a stone in his gut. A burst of crazy feelings swirled behind his chest like someone had shoved every emotion ever into a blender and hit "puree." Guilt took up a heavy spot in his belly. *Am I responsible for her condition?* "How…? How long has she been like this?"

"About four or five months before you were born. Been like this ever since."

"Just like this? In a coma for over eighteen years?"

"Actually, she was worse. For most of that time, her heart rate was real slow, blood pressure lower, breathing almost nonexistent. Not sure how she lasted as long as she did. It was like her body was in a weird form of stasis, or some kind of hibernation. Then all of a sudden, a few months ago, her vitals went crazy, spiking all over the place. After a minute or so, they calmed down and now her heart rate is stronger, blood pressure is good, her breathing is stable."

"A few months ago?"

"Yeah, March 29th to be exact."

Orion stiffened as if all his muscles flexed at once and his breath hitched.

"Whatsamatter, pal?" Harold asked, his tone way friendlier than warranted. "Did something happen to you on March 29th?"

"My nanny tried to kill me."

"Yeah? Why's that?"

"Because she said I…" *Have a dream monster living inside of me.* The thought made Orion more attentive, aware that Harold had been leading him down this conversational path. Needing to finish his statement, he went with, "…She said I was dangerous."

Harold grunted in approval as if Orion passed some sort of test.

123

Making a mental note to be more careful with his words, Orion looked back at his mother, the guilt slowly turning to dust and blowing away. *Did they know she was like this?* He wondered what Conner and Madison truly knew. They worked for a powerful man, one with enough resources to pay them to adopt Orion and observe him for unusual behavior. Maybe they had been lied to as well? After all, they had said they didn't even know his real mother's name. "What's her name?"

"Her name is Yume Dangan."

"Dangan? My nanny's name was Aika Dangan."

"Not related."

Wait...? It hurt to pull his eyes away, but he looked back to Harold. "How did you know my Nanny's last name?"

"Aika? Because she and I worked together. I rescued your mom from the hospital the day you were born. Aika and I have been taking care of her ever since. The day after your mom's condition changed, on March 30th, the news reports said that Aika had died in a car crash, taking you with her. I knew that was bullshit. A while back, Aika had found the go-bag your folks made for you, including your new ID. Next thing I know, John O. Miller graduated from an online high school and got an apartment in Las Vegas. Got a job at a café, too. Good for him."

"Why? Why were you two working together to keep my mom alive?"

Harold turned away from Yume and faced Orion, both hands resting on his cane. "Why'd Aika try to kill you?"

Orion stared at Harold, unblinking, silent.

Harold chuckled, sounding like he was gargling gravel. "Your generation, I tell ya. Master communicators, all of ya. It was because of your dad."

"You knew my dad?"

Whatever composure Harold had been displaying eroded away, like he had been pretending to be sane and could no longer maintain the act. "I met him a couple times."

"Is he alive? Like my mom?"

"No. Well, he's mostly dead."

"Mostly? What does that—?"

"You see, Orion, when you sleep and dream, you enter a dreamscape. Your own personal universe. Now, most people don't know shit about shit in the dreamscape. Hell, most people don't even know they're dreaming, let alone know they're in a dreamscape."

"Do you mean lucid dreaming?"

A darkness came over Harold as noticeable as a shadow. His brow furrowed as his eyes widened. "It goes beyond lucid fucking dreaming, Orion. It goes *way* beyond that. There are some people in this world who can go into other people's dreams. *I* had the ability to go into other people's dreamscapes. Eighteen years ago, I had a connection with someone who could *take me* from one dreamscape to another, someone who could control any dreamscape she entered. Someone who had the power of God when the world was asleep. Your dad had that power, too, the power of God, and *he* took my connection from me. He *stripped me* of my connection *to God*! Then Aika found me, asked me questions about the man I was working for. I asked her questions, too, and she told me your mother could go into people's dreams. That's why I've been caring for your mom, hoping she'd wake up one day, thank me for nursing her back to health, and become my new connection to the dreamscape. Be my new God!"

Harold took one step closer, the thump of his cane a judge's gavel sentencing Orion for a crime he didn't commit. With dark eyes under a heavy scowl, Harold continued, "Then Aika died and I pieced the puzzle together. She was watching over you, Orion, making sure you didn't have your parents' ability. Her dying in a car accident smelled like bullshit to me. She died because your ability to go into the dreamscape manifested itself. Either the man I used to work for killed her, or *you* killed her, and that'd only happen if you can do it, too! *You* can go into people's dreams!"

Heat radiated up Orion's neck and he had to tighten his stomach to keep from peeing himself when Harold grabbed his arm and yelled, "Take me into the dreamscape, boy! Let's go be God!"

Orion kicked the cane hard enough to send it clacking across the stage.

Harold toppled forward, releasing Orion's arm when his knee slammed onto the stage. "Fuck!"

Free from Harold's grip, Orion took a step back and grabbed his pepper spray from his pocket. Hands trembling, he fought with the safety snap, freeing it. But Harold lunged forward and smacked the canister from Orion's hand.

"Why don't you wanna be God, Orion? Who doesn't fucking wanna be God?"

One knee on the ground, Harold placed both hands on his other leg and pushed himself to a stand. Even without his cane he had good enough balance to charge toward Orion. The look of pure insanity in Harold's bloodshot eyes told Orion that he had no chance of winning a fight.

So he ran.

Off the stage.

Down the hallway.

Out the backdoor.

Down the closest street.

Confident he was heading in the right direction, Orion waited until after the third block to pull out his phone for directions back to the hotel. Two miles to the Holiday Inn and he ran the entire way, no matter how hot the fire in his legs raged. Panting to the point of gulping on the inhale and wheezing every exhale, Orion burst into his hotel room and headed for the bathroom sink. He cupped water into his mouth and then splashed more onto his burning face. The more he splashed, the more he cried, until his sorrow flowed to his knees, dissolving his will to stand. Sliding to the floor, Orion's crying worsened. Repeatedly smacking his head against the wall, he wailed, "Fuck! Fuck! Fuccccccck!"

Minutes, hours, days, he didn't know how long it took for him to run out of steam. The tears went away, but the pain – dear God, the pain – stayed, the hot pressure behind his chest so intense that his heart would turn into a diamond before the night was over. *What do I do?*

The cops? That seemed like the obvious choice, but was it the right one? He didn't know. He'd never in his life needed to call 911, which made him hesitant to call now. What would he even say? That his mother who had been in a coma for eighteen years was being held in an abandoned theater by some old dude who wanted Orion to escort him into other people's dreams? The cops would think he was crazy, maybe even arrest him. And the last thing he wanted to do was bring any attention to John O. Miller.

Then his phone buzzed.

Jacob McGovern was calling.

Too caught up in his own drama, he didn't wonder why, he just answered it. "Yeah?"

"Orion? Orion, you're not going to believe this," the excitement in Jacob's voice was obvious by how fast he spoke. "But after I met with the police at Preston's – everything's taken care of, by the way – I started thinking about my dad, so I went to the storage locker where his belongings are. And I found something! Do you have time to talk – sorry, I forgot to ask."

"Ummm...?" Orion whispered, his throat raw from crying, moaning, yelling. He then shook his head and ran his hand over his face. Sitting a little straighter, he cleared his throat. "Yeah."

"Would you be able to meet?"

Orion didn't know what to say. He hadn't been a legal adult for very long, so the instinct to run to Conner and Madison remained close to the surface. Not far behind were Victor and Celina, his new crutch. But he'd hid the reason why he stayed in Philly from them – the reason that bit him in the ass, leaving him a confused and crying mess on a hotel bathroom floor. Exhausted, his brain cells like used confetti, he damned away consequences and said, "Yeah. Yeah, let's meet up."

CHAPTER 20

July 9th, Chicago

Victor strolled into Club B-Sides with Celina. Gen had told them the doors would be unlocked and to come inside. The place looked vastly different from the last time they were here – dimmed lighting and half-filled with loud people, drinks in hands, standing around the small high-top tables or sitting at four-seat tables. A machete was needed to cut through the smoke. The air was electric and filled with the same possibility as shaking dice at a craps table.

Now, with the lights on… What a disappointment.

The room was just a room, made more boring by the gray cement floor, a worn orange-brown bar on the right, and a small stage up front. Despite the letdown, Victor smiled at the memory of when she'd been here three months ago. She and Celina were supposed to be on a "mission" – as Celina kept calling it – but there was magic that night. A bond formed between them, becoming sisters. As sudden as a knife through the heart, Victor remembered what happened at the end of the night. Not all magic was good.

Victor had lost her best friend, Murphy, discovering her dead body a few blocks away. Murdered and displayed on a giant spiderweb. She and Celina had fled the city via bus, their bond galvanizing. She never found out what happened to Murphy, but she had always suspected…

"Genocide," Victor said. "Great to see you as always."

Seated at one of the tables on the dull, boring gray cement floor, Gen snarled. "Victor." Blaze was sitting to her left and lounging back in his chair, hands linked behind his head with that damn smile. Lucas and Ven were sitting at the table as well – Lucas grinning like a child ready to pilfer cookies as soon as everyone turned around; Ven glaring and ready to murder upon command. The bouncer was at the table, too. What was his name? Vinnie, if Victor remembered correctly. She barely caught his name last time, when he had escorted her to the back room.

128

"I see the gang's all here," Victor said.

"Just going over preshow stuff," Lucas said as he stood. "Figuring out the set list for tonight." He pulled his chair out for Victor. As he walked past her, she felt the warmth of his breath across her cheek when he asked, "You gonna stay for the show?"

He was handsome enough, and the blue hair added to a look she liked, but the idea of him turning into a spider at any given moment? That made her feel too much like a fly. Not that she'd ever let him know that. Confidence was the perfect mask for everything. "Oh, sweety, I don't think you want me to stay."

"I know I don't," Ven growled as he stood.

"Yes, you do. You just don't want to admit it." Victor punctuated her statement with a wink.

One more sneer, and Ven joined Lucas as they walked toward the back of the club. Victor opted to keep her big mouth shut as she sat in Lucas's vacated seat; further instigation would do no good.

Vinnie stood as well, and Victor wondered if he was born wearing a black tee shirt with the word "Security" on it, because it clung to every single striation of his copious muscles. His hairless head was shaped like a bullet and his body was the gun ready to shoot. He offered his seat to Celina. "Hi. Umm... Here you go. I'm, umm, Vinnie. I don't know if we exchanged names the last time we met."

With the sour look of chewing on a lemon peel, Celina said, "You were too busy threatening to kick me out of the club the last time we met."

"Heh, yeah. Umm, sorry about that. I was just doing my job, trying to keep dangerous people away from Genocide."

"I was trying to tell you about dangerous people, but you didn't listen. I mean, do I look like a dangerous person?"

To most of the world, possibly. Her height was imposing, and she was nowhere as skinny as models or actresses. Standing next to each other, she had less than an inch on Vinnie, but his bulk made him a walking eclipse. The correct response would have been, "No," but Vinnie went with, "You were dressed differently then."

"I was dressed like a whore!"

Those words stung; Victor was the one who picked out Celina's outfit that night.

Vinnie scratched the back of his head and looked downward like a chastised toddler. "Well, uhh, that's definitely not what I thought, not how I'd describe it. I mean, I thought you looked nice, not that you don't look nice now, because you do, you do look nice and—"

"What the fuck is wrong with you?" Gen asked, eyebrows crunched together as she slowly shook her head.

Vinnie's blush ran from the base of his neck to the tip of his head. Still averting his eyes, he gestured to the chair for Celina. She tucked the back of her thin, knee-length sundress – sky blue to match her flats – and sat. As gently as petting a butterfly, he slid the chair under her. With a slight frown and pursed lips, she said, "Thank you."

"Yep," Vinnie said, and quickly retreated down the hallway to the back room.

After another stifled laugh, Victor glanced across the table to Blaze. She hated his impish smile as he turned his attention from Celina to her. "I know what you're thinking," Blaze said. "He's human."

"What's that have to do with anything?" Celina asked.

"I'll tell you later," Victor replied.

"So," Gen said, her permafrown in place as she leaned forward and put her elbows on the table. "Other than making my bouncer sound like an idiot, piss off my band members, and confuse the fuck out of me, is there an actual reason why you two are here?"

Celina folded her hands together on her lap and slouched, relinquishing all control of the conversation to Victor. They both had slept on the plane from Philly, but they used the hours before and after to devise a plan. It wasn't much of one. After discussing various scenarios and different twists and turns stemming from Gen's possible reactions, they decided that it'd be best to be direct and let Victor do the talking.

Victor reached into her jacket pocket and pulled out Corette's business card. Sliding it across the table, she said, "Two reasons. The first being this woman."

Gen read the card. "Corette Remington. Munition Investing. Why does this concern me at all?"

"She's special. Like you and your band, me, Celina, Goldy Snakenstein."

Blaze pulled out his phone to verify, and Victor said, "You won't find her on the list, but believe me, she's one of us."

"If she's not on the list, what makes you so sure?" Gen asked.

"The feeling."

"The feeling?"

"The blood red streaks in your platinum hair? That's a good look on you. Playing coy? Not so much. You know what feeling I'm talking about. The feeling we all got when we first met each other. Being on edge. Jittery. Wary."

"You both got that feeling around her?"

Celina nodded.

"Not only the *feeling*," Victor continued. "But a little something extra, like the way she speaks."

Gen chuckled. "The way she speaks? What does *that* mean?"

"She manipulates people with it. Like the way the Golden Creeper over here uses his smile."

"Hey!" Blaze snapped, sitting upright, smile falling. "What are you talking about?"

"I like his smile," Celina mumbled. "And his jacket."

"You shouldn't on either account," Victor said to Celina. She turned to Blaze and said, "Never go into acting, because no one's buying your interpretation of 'indignant.'"

A bit of a squint to his seedy eyes, Blaze gave a lopsided, wicked smirk. "I don't know about that, Victor. I've been told I'm a very good actor."

Blaze's smile took Victor right back to the one time she had sex in a cemetery – a junior in high school during her goth phase, excited by the risk of getting caught, turned on by the taboo, empowered by breaking social norms, but terrified about disturbing angry ghosts.

Through the fog of her own pheromones, she gestured to Blaze with both hands and said to Gen, "There. Right there. You see what he's doing, right?"

Gen and Blaze held an entire conversation with one prolonged look to each other. Blaze's smirk downgraded from evil to puckish. Gen sighed and slouched into her chair. "That still doesn't answer my original question – what does this have to do with me?"

As Victor told her story about Corette snaking the building she had earmarked for the Ashtons and her subsequent meeting with the woman in question, Gen didn't react, her cold eyes focused.

Blaze listened; no speaking, no smiling, no shenanigans as he showed genuine concern.

When finished, Gen worked the inside of her cheek with her teeth, a judge pondering evidence. "So, you believe Corette is dangerous because she screwed you out of a property purchase and then made you feel bad at a meeting?"

"There's a good chance she's trying to kill us."

"I doubt it."

"If it's not her, then it's Calista Lindquist."

That did it. That statement garnered something other than apathy or antagonism from Gen, exactly how Victor set it up.

Eyebrows knitting, Gen pulled her chair closer to the table. "I killed her."

"Are you sure?" Victor pulled out her phone, the kill-list on her screen, and pointed to Jacob. "Because we stopped this guy from getting killed by a blonde and his description of her matched Calista, including a tattoo." She then pointed to a picture of Preston. "This guy did get killed by a blonde and we found Corette's business card where he died."

"Does the description of your blonde include giant-ass fang marks on her left shoulder? Her blood tasted weird – I'm guessing from the God-only-knows drugs she probably took before her assault on us at the warehouse – but I pumped a metric shit-gallon of venom in her."

"Then it's Corette trying to kill us."

Waving her hands, Gen closed her eyes. "Stop! Just stop. You're grasping at straws. Blonde hair and business cards? That's your evidence?"

Victor hated the desperation in her voice, but it was rare when someone didn't eventually see that she was right. She turned in her chair to give Gen her full attention. "That's more than we had when Calista was first hunting us. We need your help to remove suspicion from one of them. You're the only business owner I know that Corette wouldn't be able to connect back to me. Contact her and tell her that you're looking to use her services. Set up a meeting. That way you and Golden Smiles can get your take on her. Then we—"

"No!" Gen shouted. She squeezed her eyes shut and rubbed them with her thumb-knuckles. When she opened them, Victor expected more anger, but Gen's tired, blood shot eyes emphasized the bags under them. "There is no 'us,' Victor. There is no 'then.' No 'next,' no plan. I have too much going on here, too many things that need my immediate attention."

"We just discovered the lab where a drug is being made that we're trying to get rid of," Blaze said.

Gen might have been tired, but she mustered enough energy to sneer at Blaze. He in turn gave a slight shrug and a nod toward Victor, clearly telling Gen that they needed to offer a legitimate reason for declining to help. Gen rolled her eyes and continued, "Like he said. The people making the drugs are dangerous. Right now, they are a *real* danger, not some venture capitalist or ghost."

"Do you want any help?" Celina asked. "Victor and I could—"

Gen strummed her fingers on the table. As testimony to how nice Celina was, Gen didn't yell when she said, "No. Thank you, Celina, but my kind will have it under control. With Blaze helping, we can't lose."

Celina looked at Victor for what to do next. This was a wasted trip. Though, Blaze's eyebrows were arched in pity. Maybe he understood the danger and would be willing to help if he weren't wrapped around Gen's pinkie? Victor would try him later. For now, she stood, and Celina followed.

"I'll keep you posted," she said to Blaze. With only a cursory glance to Gen as she turned to leave, Victor said, "Thanks for the hospitality."

CHAPTER 21

July 9th, Philadelphia

Orion thanked the Uber driver and entered the diner. Half of him felt like a badass grifter from a heist movie taking a meeting in a greasy-spoon, the other half was in no mood for such nonsense, still upset about the whole, "Orion is a coward and abandoned his mother," thing. *I couldn't have done anything*, he reminded himself. *Could I have?*

There had to be something he could do. Like what? Kick down the door and beat the crap out of Harold? He'd call that idea "the Victor solution," even though he thought the likelihood of winning a fight against that man was slim-to-none. Maybe he needed to tell Robert? But he wasn't available. Maybe he had to come clean with Victor and Celina? He'd call that idea, "the Orion is not only a coward, but a whiny coward solution."

As soon as Orion stepped foot into the brightly lit shrine to chrome and shimmering red upholstery, Jacob waved to him from a small booth in the back corner. Like he had seen in movies, he passed by a few slump-shouldered souls on worn stools lining the counter to the right, empty old booths on the left.

"Hi," Orion said as he sat opposite Jacob. A glass of water sat before him. "Sorry that I'm only eighteen."

The diner wasn't the first choice, Jacob having suggested a local bar. Cocking his head, Jacob regarded Orion with a quizzical look. A spark of realization flashed behind his eyes and he waved off Orion's apology. "No worries. I just needed to talk to you."

So upset by his earlier interaction with Harold, Orion accepted the opportunity to meet with Jacob but forgot to ask a few questions, one being, "Why did you call me?"

Jacob smiled and Orion felt like someone put a slug down the back of his shirt. When they had first met, Jacob had seemed so serious. Though, having four strangers barge in right when he got cut during a knife attack might have led to his sour attitude. Finding an old acquaintance murdered and then dealing with the police afterwards probably didn't help. But now, he seemed lighter, joy in his eyes. "Because I feel like I can trust you."

"Oh. Ummm… Thanks?"

Jacob opened his mouth like he was ready to give a speech and then closed it, eyes shifting, clearly thinking about what to say next. Leaning forward, he placed his hands on the table, ready to exchange secrets. "What do you know about your father?"

Orion tried to remember how much he and the others shared about their adventure together and what they had discovered. "Ummm…?"

"I think you know more than that. I mean, I don't blame you for holding back when we first met. It made sense. But you guys told me that Victor didn't know anything about her birth parents, which I believe, and Robert said that his parents were completely normal, which I don't believe. Celina shared some details about her birth father, which were terrifying. But you… Everyone was vague, only saying that you had recently discovered that your birth father was a monster."

Throat going dry, Orion grabbed the water and started gulping.

Chuckling, Jacob sat back. "No worries. Like I said, I get it. We had just met. You knew nothing about me other than my name was on some list along with yours and others. What I'm trying to say is… all the talk about fathers got me thinking about mine. See, he died when I was seven and I really didn't know much about him other than which storage unit had his possessions. After dealing with the police at Preston's, I went right to the unit and learned a little more about him. You asked me why I called you? Because you know more about your father than the other three know about theirs."

Orion hadn't really thought about it that way, but Jacob was right. "Yeah, I guess?"

"Tell me about him."

"Ummm…?"

"Come on, Orion." Jacob leaned forward again. Orion had never been involved in a business deal, but he felt like he was in one now, the way Jacob folded his hands together, the serious tone in his voice. Though he was over a decade older, he treated Orion like a peer, not a kid. Orion liked that. "We're involved in something together. I don't know what. Do you?"

"No."

"The only way we can unravel this mystery is by being honest with each other and sharing information, right?"

"Yeah. Yeah, that makes sense."

"Okay, then. Tell me about your father."

Orion started slowly, repeating how he had met the others under circumstances similar to how they had met Jacob, mentioning again that they had saved Orion from his nanny. Then Orion took the story further, sharing that his adoptive parents told him his father could go into other people's dreams. He told Jacob about Bigby and how the monster killed his friend Brennan and high school bully, Lance. Orion confessed that recently he had begun experimenting with his own dreamscape.

When he finally finished talking, he was surprised to find that he ate through breakfast and then lunch, despite being dinner time. He thought about dragging a few of the leftover fries through stray blobs of syrup, but remembered he tried that a few years ago and didn't like it. Jacob held a similar look as Orion's favorite art teacher – proud and encouraging. "That's quite a journey, Orion. How does that make you feel?"

"Ummm, scared, I think."

"Well, having that level of power can be frightening."

"Power?"

"Yes, power, Orion. That's what your father had. That's what *you* have. That's the *legacy* your father bequeathed to you."

Legacy. Power. Bequeathed. None of those words had ever been used by Orion when it came to himself. None of those words had come to mind when he thought about Bigby tearing into Brennan or the fear in his parents' eyes when they talked about his birth father. "I... I never thought about it that way."

"You should, Orion. You should. If you don't think about what you can do, then you'll never realize what you're capable of."

Orion sat back in his seat and looked out the window, the people on the city sidewalk walking under the streetlights, nothing more than faceless figures. *Capable of.* What was he capable of? Sure, he had been experimenting with lucid dreaming, with exploring his dreamscape. What was his end goal? Just to see if he could? To recreate a few memories? Or was he secretly trying to reconnect with Bigby? Trying to control his fears?

"Have *you* gone into other people's dreams?" Jacob asked, pulling Orion from his own thoughts.

Orion looked back to Jacob and absently tossed a French fry into his mouth. "No. I haven't tried."

"Are you sure? You talked about watching Bigby kill Lance and your friend Brennan. I don't think that happened in *your* dreamscape, right?"

Orion frowned. "Yeah. You're right. I must have been in their dreamscapes."

"That's what I thought." Jacob loomed closer, his eyes fiery with hunger. "I want you to go into my dreams."

Cold blizzard winds whipped through Orion. "What...? What did you ask?"

Never taking his eyes off Orion, Jacob reached into the courier bag next to him. Orion felt a little stupid for not noticing it until now. Jacob put a journal with a leather cover on the table. "This is what I found in storage. A diary written by my father before he died. This... this is now my only connection to him. I want to learn more about him, Orion, beyond what's written here. I want you to go into my dreams and show me who he is."

Orion jolted upright as if the booth seat shocked him. "I don't think I can do that. I mean, I didn't even know I could go into other people's dreams until a second ago. And I don't know anything about your father, so I wouldn't know how to show him to you."

"You don't need to know anything about him. I just need you to show me what *I* know about him. I mean, sometimes dreams pull memories from our subconscious, right? So, you go into my dreams and help me pull up memories of my father. Can you pull up memories?"

"No. I…" Why did he deny the question so quickly, especially since he didn't actually know the answer? "I don't know. Maybe? While experimenting with lucid dreaming I found some memories. I watched them as if I were watching a movie, but with raw emotion behind it. So… Maybe? Maybe I could pull up your memories."

Jacob clapped and pointed at Orion. "That's what I'm talking about. That's great. How about tonight? Do you want to try tonight?"

Orion slouched, deflated. Going into other people's dreams was what Harold rambled about, what he wanted Orion to do for him. This was different, though, right? Harold wanted Orion to act as a doorway, while Jacob asked him to be a guide. *God, this sucks!* "I just… I'm… I'm a little distracted, too much on my mind. It probably wouldn't work."

Orion thought Jacob was going to be mad. After all, the man across the table had to be disappointed to discover a helpful resource, only to have it suddenly fail him. Instead, Jacob's eyes rounded, his eyebrows arched. "Did something happen? Was it finding Preston the way we did?"

"No. Actually that isn't it. But something did happen." As Orion recounted the events of today, Jacob listened, really listened. He tensed when Orion mentioned Harold, gasped when Orion met his mother, cringed when Harold attacked him.

Jacob reached across the table and squeezed Orion's forearm. "Hey, man, you did the right thing. That Harold guy was obviously playing you. He lured you there to cause you harm. If you stayed and tried to fight… Well, there's a chance you wouldn't be here right now."

Orion shrugged. "I guess. You're right, but it's my mom, and I ran. I… should I have called the cops? I don't know. I freaked out and ran and now I don't know what to do."

"I understand." Jacob released Orion's arm and started to swirl his index finger in the air. "I have an idea. Let's meet up tomorrow morning and we'll go into the theater. We'll sneak around and scope it out. Your mom is probably still there. If Harold is gone, we'll rescue your mom. You said she's in a hospital bed, right? We can wheel her out and take her to an actual hospital. If that Harold guy is still there, *then* we call the cops. Either way, I'll be with you, your backup."

Warmth erupted behind Orion's chest. "Yeah?"

"Yes. Absolutely. After we get your mom settled and safe in a hospital, when *you* are comfortable, then we'll revisit the idea of you going into my dreams."

Yes. His guilt had been acting like a wall, blocking him from thinking of anything else. Coming up with a plan to save his mom destroyed the wall and allowed him to think about his power, his legacy, his bequeathment. "Yeah! I like this plan."

Jacob pumped his fist. "Yes! Excellent! Okay, go back to your hotel and get a good night sleep. I'll take care of the bill and research about dream telepathy tonight to see if I can help you out with that."

Orion stood and fist-bumped Jacob. "Awesome! Yeah! Thanks!"

As Orion left the diner, he tapped away at his phone for an Uber pickup, excited by a whole new world of possibility now laid out in front of him.

CHAPTER 22

July 9th, Chicago

Genocide closed the door to her apartment and leaned against it. After a deep sigh, she tapped the back of her head against the wood – not hard enough to see sparks, just hopeful that it would knock things into place and give her the answers to what she should do. A buzz from her pocket and she gave herself a few more cranial taps before picking up her phone; it had been exploding these past few hours.

After Victor and Celina left, Ven had jumped on her about their visit and how she was too accepting, then he jumped all over her about not confronting the brown recluse head-on. Lucas, God bless him, did his best to deflect. Ven then jumped on her about finding a permanent drummer – tonight's guest drummer was from another band just passing through town and had accepted a case of Wild Turkey as payment – and he or she needed to be a black widow. Lucas did his best to deflect that as well. Blaze, blessedly, kept his mouth shut and let everything play out without adding his opinion. Or his smile.

Before she had taken the stage, she sent a "check in" text to every member of the cluster. She should have let Ven and Lucas do it, but it wasn't their burden to bear. "I'm the fucking queen," she had said before Lucas could protest. Responses had poured in while she was on stage.

The performance was euphoric. It was supposed to have been a ninety minute set, but the stage acted as sanctuary and it felt too good to shut out the world, so she extended it to two hours. There were no problems while on stage. No brown recluse. No drug labs. No cluster. No business. No hitlist or threat of being potentially hunted again.

After the set, she gave the drummer the booze and bid him farewell. "I'll figure shit out tomorrow," were her last words to Lucas and Ven as she put on her coat and locked up the backroom office. On her way through the club toward the exit, she had waved goodbye to Blaze, parked on a barstool.

She had been answering text messages while walking from the club to her apartment. And now, with her head against the door, her phone buzzed again.

With a grunt, she pushed herself away and wandered to her bedroom. Her apartment was clean, the furniture new, the walls a blemish-free cream, and her hardwood floors scuff-free. No knickknacks, no plants, no artwork. But she had a respectable number of professionally framed posters of musicians, each signed with an authentic autograph. A black and white of Rotten and Vicious, Misfits with Danzig, Henry screaming with Black Flag, Billy's spiky blond hair in front of Generation X. NOFX, Wendy O and the Plasmatics, Dead Kennedys, and the queen – Joan Jett. Over two dozen smaller ones of bands that had played at her club took space on her bedroom walls. Everyone in those photos stared at her, judging her and finding her wanting. She squirmed out of her pants and mumbled, "Doubt you'd be doing any better."

Her phone buzzed again.

Time to get comfortable. She pulled on her favorite sweatpants – impossibly soft, black with "devil" written in a white, fluffy font up her right leg, and the word "angel" written in flame down her left leg. Bra pulled off strap by strap from under her tee. And then a pit sniff. Nothing offensive enough to warrant a shower or changing out of her tee shirt.

Her phone buzzed again.

During the show and on her way home, she had heard back from twenty -one of her cluster who weren't Ven and Lucas. The last three just checked in, each asking if there was anything to worry about. Back in her living room, she read the last text from Ven: `I can get a flame thrower I know a guy and we can burn the recluse out as soon as tomorrow`

"Fuck sake, Venom!" she yelled as she threw her phone at her couch. It bounced to the floor and she left it there, too pissed off to answer any of the texts. She flopped on her loveseat and grabbed the remote, the only item on her black glass coffee table. Her sixty-five-inch 4K Samsung sat atop her entertainment center, another black glass table with nothing else on it. The couch was in front of the television, but she preferred the loveseat set to the side because she could lay her head on the armrest and sprawl out, an ersatz chaise lounge.

Remote in hand, she brought the television to life and pulled up one of her favorite movies: *10 Things I Hate About You*.

No sooner had she hit "play" than a knock came from the door.

"The fuck?" she asked Julia Stiles and Heath Ledger when their faces appeared on the pause image.

Fists clenched, she stomped to the door and looked out the peephole. She didn't unclench them when she opened the door to greet Blaze. Smiling softly, he held a six-pack of green bottles as a form of offering.

"This is a helluva assumption," she said, crossing her arms.

"Not an assumption. An invitation."

"An invitation into my apartment?"

"An invitation to vent. You had a pretty heavy day. I'm offering a sympathetic ear and a tonic that has helped lighten heavy days for hundreds of years."

"Not in the mood for the company that comes with the sympathetic ear."

"I get it. But, please, take the beer."

"Thanks," she said as she accepted it. "Later."

She closed the door and counted to ten. Were she a betting woman, she would have wagered the club that Blaze would still be standing there when she opened the door. Smartass comment about male entitlement queued up, she opened the door and… would have lost the bet.

Poking out her head, she caught a glimpse of him turning the corner of her hallway. "Hey!"

After a heartbeat or two, he peeked around the corner, his upswept blond hair leading the way. "Me?"

"Yeah. You left?"

"You asked me to."

Gen had asked rowdy men in her club to take it down a notch and they'd respond by cranking it up two or three or ten notches. She'd ask Lucas not to be an asshole when interviewing drummers, and that encouraged him to be an even bigger one. She asked Ven to leave her alone for the night and he texted her nonsense about flamethrowers. Blaze had done everything she'd asked of him, the only man in her life to do so. "Yeah, well, it's kinda creepy to show up at my front door."

"Only way I knew how to contact you."

"You couldn't have texted?"

"I couldn't remember your number."

"If my phone wasn't in timeout right now, I'd call bullshit."

"Phone in timeout? I don't know what that means."

"It means men suck, but..." She tilted her head toward the open door, an invitation. She thought about asking how he'd found where she lived, but knew he'd have some douchey response like, "I have my sources."

"Thanks," he said, entering her place.

"No smiling," she replied.

He raised his hands as a form of surrender. "I can't promise that."

"Yeah, yeah, yeah. Have a seat on the couch," she said as she dropped the six-pack on the coffee table. Right as Blaze sat down, she realized he had the perfect view of what she was watching.

"Huh," he grunted. "Interesting."

Flopping down on her loveseat, she snapped, "What? You gonna go on and on why rom-coms are stupid."

"Not at all. I'm no movie expert, but the rom-coms I've seen are the only movies where good things happen to women on a consistent basis, after a contrived misunderstanding or two. Sci-Fi and fantasy, women are tokenized or damsels in need of rescuing. Thrillers and mysteries, they're supporting cast, at best. And horror? Hell, nothing worse for a woman than being in a horror movie. I get why most women like anything with the word 'rom' in it. After spending time with you, I can say without a doubt that you are not like most women, so *that* is why I'm surprised you like rom-coms."

That was definitely a compliment. Sure, when they first met, he had tried to get in her pants. But lately? Genuine. Altruistic. Supportive. And she'd been nothing but... less than kind. Still, he was a grifter who peddled favors and information, one who just showed up at her door with a six-pack and a sympathetic ear. He was another issue she didn't know how to deal with. However, he was offering to help with all her other issues, so she decided to share. "Rom-com movies are kinda like aquariums."

He sat forward, grabbing two beers from the six pack, and handing one to her. "Yeah?"

"Yeah. The environment is merely a portrayal of where these fish are from, a well-maintained setting, and the fish are prettier than what they'd be like in the wild, their natural habitats. They're fed the best foods, treated by experts and doctors, don't have to worry about predators or shelter. Even though aquariums are manicured fantasies, we still go to see the fish."

"Not that you needed to justify what you like, but it makes sense. I've never seen this one, so don't let me stop you."

Gen squinted and eyed him while she took a long pull from the bottle. She then asked, "Why are you here, Blaze?"

He took a swig and set the bottle on the coffee table. "Like I said, you had a heavy day. Wasn't sure if you wanted company or not, if you wanted to talk or not. If you did, I just wanted to give you that option."

"To talk?"

"If you want."

"About tonight?"

"About anything."

"You believe them, don't you?"

Blaze took his time leaning forward, and sipped his beer, clearly organizing his thoughts under the weight of Gen's scrutiny. "Victor and Celina flew to Chicago *from Vegas* just to talk to us. It makes me think they truly believe what they're saying."

"Victor's just trying to pull me into her drama. She lost money and now wants revenge."

"I don't know if I'd disagree with that, but I believe them about Jacob and Preston getting attacked. Even if Victor's motivations are multi-layered, I think Celina's are more pure."

It was Gen's turn to smirk; she knew the answer to her next question… "Are you sweet on Celina?"

Blaze shrugged and shook his head like he'd never thought about that question until now. "I can't answer that."

"Are you sweet on me?"

He returned her smirk, and looked away. "I can't answer that."

Gen let the tension linger while she enjoyed another swig, the bitterness tasting sweet. "But you believe the threat is real?"

Blaze looked back. "I do."

"Okay, then. Toss me my phone. It's on the floor over there."

Blaze did as asked. Gen tapped away at the phone when it was back in her hands. She set it next to her on the loveseat cushion and finished her beer. Patiently watching her, Blaze finished his. It was her turn to grab two beers from the six pack, and she handed one to him. "Just sent an email to Corette, offering an embarrassing amount of money to meet her tomorrow. Anything else we need to talk about?"

"Nope. We didn't even need to talk about that."

Gen grunted and twisted the cap off her beer. A few moments of silence and her phone buzzed. Surprised that Corette answered so quickly, Gen said, "Well, she's jumping on a plane first thing tomorrow morning, and meeting us late afternoon."

"Us?"

"Unless you don't want to join."

That fucking smile. "Wouldn't miss it for the world."

"I said no smiling."

He didn't stop, he just turned it toward the television. After another pull from the bottle, he said, "Are you gonna hit 'play?'"

"Are you gonna talk and say snarky shit throughout the movie?"

"I promise, not another word."

Wary, Gen started the movie and sipped her beer. After twenty minutes, Blaze was chuckling along with the story, and Gen started to relax. Against her better judgment, she got off the loveseat, grabbed the last two beers from the six pack, and sat next to Blaze on the couch. Tucking her feet under herself, she handed a bottle to Blaze. He didn't say a word, his smile comforting. They clinked bottles and enjoyed the rest of the movie.

CHAPTER 23

July 10th, Las Vegas

Celina's phone played a soft tinny ditty, growing louder every second. Normally she'd hit snooze a few times, but she grabbed her phone. 7:30a.m. Turned off her alarm, and sat up. She and Victor got home after midnight. Bone-tired from traipsing across the country and back within two days, Celina had aimed right for her bed. Her comfy, comfy bed that gave her bliss and sound sleep.

Sighing with rejuvenation, she slipped on her robe and headed for the kitchen, ready to start her day with a cup of coffee. She already smelled its warm aroma.

She screeched to a halt when she saw a man sitting at the table in the dining room.

Handsome.

Shirtless.

Drinking coffee.

Why did he look familiar?

After setting his mug down, he slid a second mug across the table, an invitation for Celina to join him. "Good morning."

Celina gripped her robe tightly, like an antebellum widow clutching her pearls. Clearly, Victor had chosen activities other than sleep after they had returned home last night.

Feeling like a guest in her own apartment, she sat at the table across from him and took the mug. "Thank you."

His gaze was heavy, his smile more playful than anyone should have this early in the morning. "This is really good coffee."

Celina took a sip. "Oh, this is one from the café. Hazelnut and chocolate blend."

"Café?"

"Yes. Victor and I own a tabletop game-themed café a few blocks away. It's—"

Victor stomped into the living room. "Why are you still here?"

The man jumped from the chair and hurried to put on his shirt. He then took another gulp of coffee and shrugged his shoulders. "You said I could grab a coffee before I go."

"Yeah. A coffee, not my roommate."

The man shrugged again on his way to the door.

Celina called out to him, "If you like the coffee, it's called 'Chocopoly' and the café is called Roll and—"

The door shut behind him.

"—Role… Wait! He was the Uber driver who picked us up at the airport last night. That's why he looked so familiar."

Victor shuffled into the kitchen and poured herself a cup of Chocopoly, then joined Celina in the living room. "You are correct. After we got back to the apartment, I couldn't sleep, so I ordered another ride. Feel free to laugh your ass off at the clever double entendre."

"Oh my God, if that weren't so gross, I'd call it a dad joke."

"You thought he was gross?"

"No. He was gorgeous. Whatever the hell you did with him and to him last night was undoubtedly gross."

Victor scowled. After clearing her throat, she said, "Speaking of gross, have we heard from Orion lately?"

Celina went rigid and grabbed her cellphone. "No, as a matter of fact, we haven't," she said, typing a text to Orion.

Victor grunted. She leaned to look over Celina's shoulder, watching her phone as if it would start to sing and dance at any moment.

"He's not answering me," Celina said. "I don't like this. I'm going to call him."

Victor grabbed the coffee pot from the kitchen and refilled both mugs. "Don't call him. He's hungover with a bed full of hookers."

"I highly doubt that."

Orion's sleepy face popped up on Celina's phone. Head on a pillow, one eye shut, the other half opened, he mumbled, "Yeah?"

Celina looked for a woman's face or arm or leg, any sign that a hooker might be sharing his bed. She couldn't see past Orion's mussed hair, but he was wearing a tee shirt. "Hey! It's... well, it's me. And Victor's here, too."

Rubbing his eyes, he mumbled, "Why are you calling so early?"

"It's almost 11:00 there!" Victor laughed as she shifted next to Celina. "Too much fun with Robert?"

"No. Jacob."

"Jacob?" Victor asked. "Jacob McGovern?"

"Umm, yeah? I'm helping him with stuff about his dad."

Celina gasped. Even Victor looked concerned. After a few seconds of wide-eyed silence, Celina asked, "Do you think that's a good idea?"

Even in bed, Orion managed a shrug. "Yeah, why not? We said we'd help each other, right? You said you wanted to help people on the list."

"Help, yes, but not blindly so. My father was dangerous and so was yours, and we all know about Gen's... family."

"Jacob doesn't know anything about his father," Orion said.

"It's reasonable to believe that his father might be dangerous. You said it yourself – there's a reason we're on the list and evidence seems to indicate that it's because of our parents, right?"

Crunching his eyebrows together, Orion huffed, "Yeah."

"So, you need to be careful when digging around a stranger's past. Especially since it seems like we're being hunted again. I mean, Jacob was attacked. If you need us, Victor and I can be on a plane in a few hours, and we can—"

"No!" Orion snapped. "See, this is what I'm talking about. This is why I didn't tell you I talked to Jacob. You can be really smothering. God, it's like I have four moms now."

Celina reeled back, his words slapping her face.

Victor, however, straightened in alert. "*Four* moms? Orion, did you find something out about your birth mom?"

His frown melted as he looked away. "Yeah."

"That's great news," Celina said, chirping. "Is she alive?"

"Yeah, but it's complicated. Look, I gotta go."

"What does that mean? How is—?"

Victor cut off Celina by squeezing her hand. "Hey, kid, sorry I jumped up your ass about Jacob. We just... Have you ever had someone con something from you? Something valuable?"

Orion's eyes moved back and forth as if reading notes in his head about his childhood. "My bike was stolen once."

"Yeah? Did someone trick you or lie to you to steal it?"

"Not really. I kept leaving it on the front lawn at night. My parents would always tell me to lock it up in the garage. The lock was such a pain in the ass, so I'd leave it in the lawn. After a couple weeks it was gone, so I guess it was stolen."

"What happened then?"

"My parents got me a new one. But I started putting it in the garage. I think I get what you're saying."

Do you? Celina yelled inside the privacy of her mind. *Do you really?*

Victor must have read her mind, because she squeezed Celina's hand again and said, "Celina and I are here for you, got it?"

Orion chewed his bottom lip and nodded.

"And no hookers and booze!" Celina added.

A quick snort and an unexpected chuckle. "I'll be fine. Bye."

Celina's phone went black. She mumbled, "I still want to jump on a plane to Philly."

"I know," Victor said as she rubbed Celina's back. "That's what makes you the sweetest person on the planet."

"Orion said he got what we were saying, but I don't think he did, and he shined a spotlight on the fact that he has no idea what consequences are."

"Hey, I was doing crazier and stupider shit than that at eighteen. He's a smart kid and he'll call us if shit gets too real. I'm just happy to be included as one of his four moms. Obviously, I'm the cool, hot mom."

Absently spinning her phone on the table and still in a mumbley mood, Celina said, "Well, I'm the momma bear, and God help Jacob if Orion gets hurt."

"I know you are. But these past few days bring up a good question – do we want to keep trying to find the rest of the people on the list?"

Over the past few months, the café had taken away attention and time. Celina and Victor had made cursory internet searches on the names, but nothing more, not even a scribbled note. Now that the café was open and there was the possibility of renewed danger – maybe even from Calista Lindquist, the same danger as before – it made sense. If for no other reason than to preemptively discover who might try to take advantage of Orion next. "Yes. Yes I do."

Victor headed for her bedroom. "Good. We'll come up with a plan for that and what to do about Corette tonight. Believe it or not, I'm actually going into the office today."

"'K," Celina said, unmoving from her seat, staring into space as her mind drifted. Why would Orion be so snippy toward her when all she wanted to do was help? Victor was right about his age, though. He was still a kid. Celina remembered eighteen, being confused and lost all the time. She also realized that she had no young people in her life besides Orion. No kids, no younger siblings, no job involving children. She spent all her time with people her age, but that didn't mean she should expect Orion to act and react like someone in his thirties. She should apologize to him for assigning such unrealistic standards to his thoughts and actions. She should call him right now. No! *That's the whole reason why he's mad at me!*

Now she missed her parents and wished she could apologize to them for acting like Orion when she was his age. But... had it been adolescent hormones? Or had her actions come from who she was, the daughter of Zebadiah Seeley, a kidnapper, rapist, and murderer? What was inside of her because of him?

"You haven't moved?" Victor asked as she strolled back into the kitchen.

Snapping from her trance, Celina checked her phone. Almost twenty minutes of being stuck in her muddy thoughts. "Yeah, sorry, I guess not. Just hoping Orion is okay and worried that Calista might be back." She then dropped her phone as it buzzed.

Victor chuckled. "Drama queen."

"It's Vinnie? Why is Vinnie calling? Is Gen having him check in on us?"

"Well, genius, there's only one way to find out."

The call was coming through on facetime, so Celina ran her hands through her hair and double checked to make sure her robe was cinched. "Hello?"

Vinnie's bald head took up her entire screen, hiding every bit of whatever was behind him. "Umm, hey. Hi. How are you?"

Celina wasn't sure why Gen had her goon call, but his interrogation skills were lacking. "Good. Soooo… Why are you calling?"

"Oh. Umm… yeah. I just wanted to call to see if you lost an earring when you were here."

"I don't wear earrings."

"Heh. Yeah, that's cool. It's just that I found one and it was pretty cool looking, so I wasn't sure if it was yours and if you had lost it, then you might be upset. That you lost it."

Where was this going? Celina didn't know what kind of game Gen was playing, but she didn't like it, especially since she thought they had a nice interaction last meeting. Okay, it wasn't nice, but it wasn't contentious either. Neither Victor nor Celina shared with Gen what they were going to do next, so maybe this was Gen's way of trying to find out? "I don't and I didn't. Thank you." Then a thought struck her, one that would pass through Victor's mind. "How did you get my number?"

"Umm… Blaze gave it to me. He said he didn't think you'd mind if I called."

Seriously? Blaze got her number from means unknown and now he was handing it out to Gen's flunkies? "Oh… Okay, I guess? Ummm…? Anything else?"

"Uhhh… no. That was all."

"You can tell Gen that we'll let her know what our plan is when we have one. Bye."

Celina tapped her phone off and crossed her arms. "What the hell was that about?"

Victor's face moved in slow motion from slack-jaw silence to large smile, culminating in laughter. "Oh, sweety! There was no earring!"

Celina frowned. "He said there was."

"Did he show you an earring?"

"No..."

"Oh my God. You're like a Redwood – freakishly tall and really dense. He likes you!"

All feeling evaporated from her cheeks, fingers, and toes. Unable to support the weight of this knowledge, Celina slouched in her chair. Even her lips were confused, unable to form any words beyond, "Wha...? Wha...?"

"You are my favorite television show! But as much as I'd love to stay and see the plot twists, I have to get going."

Celina replied, "Wha...? Why...? What?"

Victor shut the door behind her, and Celina heard her laugh again.

CHAPTER 24

July 10th, Philadelphia

Am I making the same damn mistake I just made yesterday? Orion wondered as he paced in front of The Monticello Theater. Well before noon, the mild anxiety of being on Philly streets after dark was no longer hindering the strong anxiety of meeting a stranger at a burned-out theater. *But Jacob isn't a stranger like Harold.*

Orion had done due diligence regarding Jacob McGovern. Well, he did a few internet searches and clicked through a bunch of social media posts. But he knew that Jacob grew up and lived in Philadelphia, started with a single investment in a restaurant and began partnering with all kinds of local businesses, most of which were still growing. He hit a level of success where his main activity turned to philanthropy. And, Orion had met and talked to Jacob. Twice! Okay, the first time wasn't under the best circumstances, but the second time was much better. They talked. They shared stories. Jacob wasn't anything like Harold! However, they both wanted the same thing from Orion.

But did they? Jacob asked for his help while Harold demanded it, threatened him to gain access to his abilities, even though he didn't know exactly what they were. Jacob was willing to face a crazy old man who held Orion's birth mother hostage in an abandoned theater. Wait, was it a hostage situation? Harold had been working with Aika for *eighteen years* to keep Orion's mother alive. That didn't sound like a hostage situation. But the look in Harold's eyes when Orion saw him… Terrifying. Madness. A crazed expression, how Orion envisioned most characters looked at the end of H.P. Lovecraft stories. Orion shivered even though it was a warm day. No, Jacob was nothing like Harold.

It was now after noon and Jacob was late. Maybe he was at the back of the building? Did they agree to meet in front or back? Heart revving, Orion stared down the alley to the back of the building… And almost jumped out of his skin when Jacob said from behind him, "Hey, sorry I'm late."

"Hey, no problem." Orion cleared his throat, hating how shaky his voice sounded, and tried again. "No problem."

Big smile on Jacob's face as he jostled the large nylon duffle bag in his hands. It rattled. "Took me a while to find this bag. It's one of those things that I knew was perfect for what I needed, but God, it took me forever."

The rattling sounded like loose tools. "What's in it?"

Charging into the alley, Jacob said, "You said the way in is through the back? Come on, I'll show you."

Orion followed Jacob while explaining what to expect and how the door opened to a hallway that led to the back of the stage, though Orion never took his eyes off the pointed shapes in the bag.

"Okay, got it," Jacob said.

At the door, Jacob dropped the bag and unzipped it. He handed a Louisville Slugger to Orion and kept a long crowbar for himself. Holding the bag open, he showed Orion what else was in it: first aid kit, a roll of ace bandage, a bottle of rubbing alcohol, a bottle of hydrogen peroxide, a flashlight, a pair of pliers, a large Philips head screwdriver, and a claw peen hammer. Orion's eyes went wide, wondering what would necessitate the things in that bag.

Jacob shrugged and said, "You can't be too prepared, right?"

"I guess," Orion whispered, ashamed he hadn't thought to bring *anything* other than himself. He cleared his throat and asked, "That bag is clanging, and it's kinda loud, isn't it? If we're trying to be sneaky?"

Jacob pulled out the flashlight, turned it on, and grabbed the bag's handles with the same hand. Nodding, he gripped the crowbar with his other hand. "You said there are rooms along the hallway before it takes us to the stage. We'll drop the bag off in one of them before we get too far."

"Sounds good." It didn't, but Orion had no idea what else to say. Holding a weapon and carrying around first aid made him afraid of why they'd need to use either. He opened the door and, thankfully, Jacob took the lead.

The flashlight helped but wasn't necessary. Plenty of afternoon sunlight made its way through the holes of the charred roof and burned rafters, past the layers of blue tarp. The half rotten carpet reeked of mildew from years of soaking up rainwater. Orion almost gagged and wondered how he didn't notice the smell last time.

Jacob stopped at the first room they came to and whispered, "No door. Easy access."

It was a dressing room, the flashlight beam highlighting the thick layer of dust on the vanity and costumes still on the rack. The mirror struggled to offer a reflection. Orion felt like he belonged here, where actors got ready to pretend to be someone else, to put on a performance. He needed that – make up, a costume, time to prepare to be someone other than a scared kid.

Neither of them ventured into the room, just stood close enough for Jacob to set the bag against the wall by the door. Should they need it – *God, I hope not* – Orion knew where it was. He did his best to walk beside Jacob, but the hallway wasn't quite wide enough, and he kept a pace behind, his sweaty hands strangling the bat's grip.

The next room on the other side of the hallway didn't have a door either. Having more of a ceiling, it was darker than the dressing room. Jacob's flashlight illuminated the interior, slow sweeps examining every nook. A storage room for props. Plenty of dust-caked set pieces for someone to hide behind, though Orion didn't see evidence of Harold or any other boogieman waiting patiently to pounce. A mouse scurried by, and Orion almost jumped, suppressing the urge to swing the bat wildly and fighting the jolt of electricity skittering dangerously close to his bladder. Luckily, he didn't react. The last thing he wanted was to look foolish in front of Jacob.

The next room had a door. Raising the crowbar over his head, ready to strike, Jacob shined the flashlight on the knob and gave a curt nod. Orion assumed Jacob wanted him to open it, so he wiped a wet palm over his pant leg and doubled his tight grip on the baseball bat. Deep breath. Orion reached for the doorknob.

Locked.

Jacob relaxed and gestured toward the end of the hallway. "The stage?"

Orion whispered, "The first set of steps takes you backstage, the next set takes you to the stage itself."

"Okay. Let's just go with an element of surprise. We'll run up the backstage stairs and jump him. I'll go first. Ready?"

No! But Orion nodded anyway.

Orion half expected Jacob to wave the crowbar around while screaming battle cries. This wasn't some video game or musclehead action movie. Jacob was smarter than that.

Crowbar ready, Jacob hurried along the hallway and climbed the first set of stairs, taking them to the backstage area.

Breath shaky, Orion followed despite his twisting guts telling him to turn back and make an anonymous phone call to the police. Up the stairs. Never one to play sports, he held the bat with both hands over his head, ready to swing downward like an ax. Curtains separated backstage from frontstage, but they weren't completely closed, leaving a small gap. This was it. Orion was going to save his mom.

Jacob rushed through the curtain opening and stepped left. Orion followed and stepped right as soon as he hit the stage.

Empty.

"What the fuck?" Orion muttered, scanning the stage floor as if he had simply lost a contact. His heart crashed into his ribcage as he spun, again and again, looking up into the rafters, out into the audience, between the curtains to the backstage. "What the fuck!" He was standing in the same spot as last time. He gestured wildly. "Here! She was right here. I stood here. Harold was here. And the bed was right fucking here! I swear!"

Putting a supportive hand on Orion's shoulder, Jacob said, "I believe you. There are scuff marks and wear spots and black streaks all over this area. It's obvious that he was afraid of you coming back with friends, and so he took her."

A vacuum of despair emptied Orion's insides, sucking out his hope, his spirit, his ability to think straight. He clutched a fistful of his own shirt to keep his chest from collapsing on itself, to stop it from pulling into the blackhole forming behind his bones. "Where? Where did he take her?"

"I don't know. I'm not going to lie, I don't know what you're feeling, but if I were this close to finding one of my parents, I'd be beyond pissed. Let's scour the place and see if we can find a clue where he might have gone."

"A clue?" Orion ran a shaky hand through his hair. "What kind of clue? What the hell would we even look for?"

Much calmer than Orion, Jacob squeezed his shoulder and said, "He was probably living here. Even if he wasn't, he spent a lot of time here. Maybe we find receipts to places he shopped for food, clothing, supplies. He needed I.V. fluids and medicines for your mom, so maybe we'll find where he got them from. He might have needed help moving her, so there might be a business card or a scrap of paper with a name and phone number. And to move her as quickly as he did means this was a contingency plan, so he might not have cleaned up, and left brochures, or notebooks, or maps lying around."

Whatever thoughts Orion had about Jacob using him had eroded after three hours of investigating the theater, from top to bottom, and into each and every room they found. No one would have done this for Orion. After the first hour, Orion chuckled thinking about the snarky comments Brennan would have made out of discomfort, fatigue, and boredom. Not Jacob, though. Never once did he waver, laser focused on exposing every shadow, every potential hiding place. Upbeat, even enthusiastic, he explored with the same vigor as if looking for answers to his own mysteries.

Finally, they ran out of places to search. Harold must've lived here, judging from the well-worn mattress backstage and the rudimentary shower system that had been installed in one of the restrooms. There was an empty rack in one of the storage rooms, and Jacob guessed it had been reserved for his clothes. No evidence of where he had gone, though, nor any hints as to where he got the medical supplies. The only paperwork found was empty fast -food wrappers.

"I'm sorry we haven't found anything," Jacob said as he zipped his duffle bag closed, all the equipment back inside. "If you want, we can do another sweep."

Mouth parched, stomach rumbling, muscles aching, Orion shook his head. "No, that's okay. We checked literally everywhere and didn't find any evidence of where he might have taken her. I can't imagine something jumping out at us a second time around."

"I understand."

When he and Jacob stepped outside, sunlight sliced through Orion's eyes and stabbed his brain. A few tearful blinks yielded funky colored afterimages, but a few more cleared them away. "So dark in there."

Jacob chuckled. "Yeah, it was. All right, I'll let you go, and we can connect tomorrow."

"Wait. What about me trying to go into your dreams tonight?"

"You need some time to process. A lot happened to you these past two days."

Orion agreed. The high from learning about his mother was indescribable. As was the devastating low from coming back to an empty theater. But other things happened as well – he stood up for himself to Victor and Celina, he navigated a strange city, and he made informed, adult decisions. He learned to trust his gut. He accepted help from a new friend, and he wasn't about to go back to being the spoiled, sheltered kid he was only a few months ago. "No. We're going to give it a try tonight. I insist."

"Are you sure?"

"Yes."

Jacob smiled and Orion's gut gurgled, a bubble of acid popping in the back of his throat. He blamed it on hunger.

CHAPTER 25

July 10th, Las Vegas

Victor entered the offices of Bouch & Becker, surprised to see a young, smiling woman behind the receptionist's desk. Halfway through wondering what happened to the young man who had been there, she remembered that she had promoted him. Bailey. *I remembered his name, so I'm getting a gold star today.*

The young woman opened her mouth, but Victor was in no mood, so she breezed past and said, "I'm one of the partners."

In her office, Bailey was sitting at a round table that fit four black leather chairs, accommodating enough to make any guest feel special. Since she never had guests, she thought the table and chairs were superfluous in her office. Six hundred square feet of three gray walls – the fourth being floor to ceiling windows. A big chunk of cherry wood desk with hand carved swirls and highbacked leather chair at one end of the room; a wall with two monitors mounted on it at the other end. Sixty inches each, the biggest and the best in the company.

Bailey's sky-blue shirt pulled across his chest, betraying that he worked out. His short brown hair had a conservative, yet modern style and his light green eyes were a conversation starter. Victor had at least four years on him, but his clean-shaven face made him look even younger, as did his wide-eyed surprise when she strolled in. "So... You don't have your own desk yet?"

Looking up from his laptop, he said, "You promoted me three days ago."

"That should be plenty of time for you to get your own workspace."

"I was told the paperwork is being held up."

"God damn it. Which asshole is holding up the paperwork?"

Bailey's gaze fell to the floor, weighed down by discomfort. "Ummm...?"

Victor snickered and sat at her desk. A shake of the mouse, a quick clatter of keystrokes, and she checked her work email. Sure enough, there was a form in her inbox regarding her new assistant's workspace. As she filled it out, she said, "It's me. I'm the asshole."

"Ummm...?" Bailey repeated. "I was told there'd be paperwork regarding my compensation package, too."

Scroll, scroll, scroll. Click, click, click. Paperwork sent to HR. Victor liked Bailey but she wasn't thrilled with the way he slouched – spooked and ready to run. She never had an assistant before. Well, a professional assistant at least. Murphy had been her personal assistant – her ability to get anything Victor needed was second to none. Could she train Bailey to fill that role? Only one way to find out. "Okay, someone will contact you in the next few days about an office or desk or something. Also, your fat raise for working with the best boss ever will be in effect as of three days ago."

Sitting straighter, no longer looking like he'd jump through the second story window at the faintest whisper of, "Boo," Bailey smiled. "Thank you."

Confidence. She needed to instill confidence. "I want you to know I mean that, being the best boss ever. Yeah, I can be a bastard, and yeah I have outbursts, but that's all directed at people who act like shit heels. If you never stab me in the back, then I'll always have yours."

Bailey nodded. "Understood."

Victor thought about asking if he knew how to hack into security systems, how many bar fights he'd been in, or if he knew how to hotwire a car. *Naaah, those are week-two questions.*

Back to her laptop, Victor tapped away requirements for Sugar Fix, Inc. production plant and emailed them to Bailey. Time to test his hunting skills. "This is what they need for production space. See what buildings you can find. I know there aren't many, so if you can't find one then we might have to make one, so look for available options."

"Is this to replace what Munitions Investments took from us?"

"Yes."

"Munitions Investments, one of the aforementioned shit-heels?"

Victor's heart warmed and she smiled. "Yes."

"Munitions Investments?" someone said from her doorway.

Marshall Becker's bulk filled the space as he took an exaggerated, long sip from his "TeqqCon 2010" coffee mug. Victor hated that mug. He only drank from it for show, as a power move. TeqqCon was a conference for upstart tech companies to gather and show off what they'd been working on. Fifteen years ago, in 2010, after a decade of limping along with minor success stories, Bouch & Becker were still struggling. Bouch wanted to fold, but Becker – imbued with a rare sense of fire and urgency – attended TeqqCon 2010, where he added seven companies to the portfolio. That accomplishment launched a period of unmitigated success.

Victor didn't hate the mug because he kept it as a trophy to remember the bold move; she hated *why* he broke it out when he did. It was his passive-aggressive way of rubbing salt into a wound. Corette had screwed over Victor, and Becker was gloating. Prick. He was irking her, so it was time to irk him back.

"Yeah, partner. They used a dirty, underhanded bullshit move to fuck with us, partner. Minor setback, partner."

Becker locked eyes with Victor and brought the mug to his lips again, slowly draining it. He broke eye contact to peer inside the mug like he was surprised that the coffee had disappeared. After a lip smack he said, "It's interesting that you keep calling me partner, because I'm not sure how long that will last."

Victor rolled her eyes. "Oh, please. Sugar Fix is still producing and profitable. Three months behind taking them to the next level. Six tops."

Eyebrows raised in mock surprise, Becker said, "Oh, when I mentioned Munition Investments, it wasn't in reference to them buying the building out from under Sugar Fix."

Victor's heart stopped in her chest. She made partner three months ago by landing two big investments, Sugar Fix and... Toes and fingers going numb, she asked, "If not them then... the Plimptons?"

Becker shrugged with an expression on his face that implied, "Whoops." Without another word, he left.

"No. No! No! Fucking no! Corette you bitch," Victor growled as she stabbed her keyboard with her fingers.

Bailey jumped from his chair and closed her office door. Hands folded in front of himself, he stood as a silent sentry against the door.

Glaring at the two monitors at the other end of the room, Victor came out from behind her desk and leaned against it, waiting for Dante Plimpton to answer. It took less than five seconds. He was obviously awaiting her call.

"Victor! What a surprise!" Dante's bold, booming voice matched his look – jet black hair and thick beard, as perfectly coiffed as a Greek statue. Straight teeth gleamed unnaturally white in his bright smile. He was head of the family business made up of himself and six others, and to get to the top in this family, he needed to be the loudest.

Half sitting on her desk, Victor crossed her arms. Plimpton Enterprises was made up of seven corporations, each family member owning one. Thanks to poorly crafted bylaws, the percentage of ownership was determined by the value of each family member's individual corporation, which they inflated via acquisitions of other companies, quality be damned. Three months ago, Victor closed a deal with them to consolidate the good companies under one umbrella, dump the bad ones, and do away with their antiquated bylaws. Now? "What the fuck, Dante?"

With a slow-motion shrug, the corners of his mouth drooped. "What the fuck what, Victor?"

"Oh, stop it. You're as coy as a brick through a window."

Dropping the wounded party act, he leaned forward, his face doubling in size on both screens. "Then you should have thought of that before you decided to fuck over me and my family."

Victor opted not to let him know that his comment made no sense. "How exactly did I fuck you or any of your family over."

"By stripping us of control! You took the best companies in the portfolio, put them into one pie, and took fifty-one percent of that pie. You now have the right to do whatever you want with those companies that my family and I worked so diligently to cultivate."

Victor's words shot from her mouth like machine gun bullets. "Cultivate? Jesus, Dante, how does cultivating equal buying random companies to bolster your egos? It's like saying you cultivated your art collection by hitting neighborhood yard sales!"

"There!" Dante backed away from the camera so he could better point at it, his meaty index finger taking up a quarter of Victor's office wall. "Right there! That flippant attitude of yours. Not only do you fuck us over, but you rub our faces in your insults. Family is *everything* to us, and these insults will not stand."

Victor scrubbed her fingers through her hair, then dragged her palms down her face. Once her fingertips reached her chin, she pressed her hands together and thrust them toward Dante. "You're right. I'm adopted and an only child, so I don't have the same family views that your family does. But that also means I don't have the same emotional connection. We all know that emotion and decision making don't always mix. Just like family and business don't always mix, which often leads to problems. You have to admit, Dante, that when you take a step back and look at your situation before you met me, you had problems."

"There are no problems caused by a family that can't be fixed by a family. And you are not part of my family."

"Neither is Corette."

Dante leaned forward again, the product in his black beard glistening. "But she's letting us keep it that way."

"Letting you keep—? What the holy and unholy hell are you talking about?"

"My family and I built a portfolio of forty-seven companies. The deal you strongarmed us into signing means that a new corporation will be formed and it will keep the companies you deem worthy."

"Right. The new corporation will end up with thirty companies and we'll sell the other seventeen. It's a slow process. We only have twenty moved over to the new corporation."

"And that's all you'll get! Corette is setting up a similar corporation, but my family and I will have sixty percent ownership! It may take weeks or months to get it all finalized, but my family and I will be back in control of our companies."

"Dante, you signed the papers. It's laid out in great detail that you need to—"

"I need to? I need to? No! I do not need to do what you say. I need to do what's right for my family."

"Right for your family? Our deal allows you and every one of your family members to cherry pick the roles they want in the umbrella corporation. If you try to break this deal, you know there will be lawyers."

Dante frowned so hard that Victor was surprised the screen didn't crack. "Lawyers? Bring your lawyers! It will be worth it, because... Well, I'm sure you know your Milton, Victor."

The screens went black.

Gripping the edge of her desk, Victor's wrists and fingers burned. The muscles between her shoulders turned to steel and a quiver played at her arms. "Bailey? Is Becker in his office?"

Bailey opened her door and peeked around the corner. "His door is open, but it doesn't look like he's in it."

"Can you get his mug for me, please?"

Bailey left and for the next few quiet seconds Victor grit her teeth so hard they hurt.

"Here you go," Bailey said when he returned.

Unclenching her body enough to accept the mug, she said, "Close the door. And stand behind me."

TeqqCon 2010. The famous glory moment when Becker brought to the company by bringing on seven companies. Fifteen years later, only one company was still in the portfolio; two were sold, one split away, and three failed. Becker held this firm to the mythological standards he had created fifteen years ago. However, that level of perfection within the story, not the results, was communicated to everyone via this mug. This stupid mother fucking mug in her hands. This mug that she'd love to crack over his head and into his nose. This mug that her anger painted blood red.

"FUCK!"

Like a rocket, she launched the mug across her office imagining she was aiming at Becker's face. The mug shattered against the wall, a web of cracked paint radiating from the dented impact point.

Victor panted, not realizing she had been holding her breath, her ragged inhales followed by growling exhales. The red dissipated from her vision, the thumping throughout her body subsided. A chill prickled her skin from the regret setting in. Understanding that she had a temper and controlling it were two different things. Losing it at work in front of an assistant made it worse, an assistant she only had for three days. Hopefully she hadn't scared him.

Bailey didn't look afraid, but the way he worked his fingers together said that he didn't know what he was supposed to do next. Victor assumed that he was wondering if it was his job to pick up the shattered porcelain. Call someone to fix the wall? Or quit because his boss was psycho?

She unlocked a small drawer in her desk and pulled out a wad of cash, her emergency stash. Uncertain as to how much it was – close to a thousand dollars, she believed – she slid it across her desk toward him. "I shouldn't have done that. Please don't report me to HR."

Staring at the cash, Bailey frowned, his back rigid. He slid the money back to Victor. "You don't need to pay for something you already have."

It wasn't a test, but he passed with flying colors anyway. "Thanks."

"Just remember that for my performance review. What's our next move?"

Our. He was starting to talk like Murphy. Good for him. "We call in a favor."

After locking away the cash, she grabbed her phone and tapped the name, "Golden Ass Hat." Arms crossed, she half-sat on her desk again and stared at the wall monitors, adjusting her expression to read somewhere between bored and miserable. When Blaze's face appeared, he winced, but then smiled. "Hey, Victor. What do I owe the pleasure?"

"Owe is right. I need dirt on Corette Remington of Munition Investments. Dirty as possible."

Blaze's smile wavered. After a quick look over his shoulder, he said, "I don't think that's a good idea."

"You owe me for the car, Blaze. Do this and I won't mention it again."

Jaw muscles worked as if chewing on her words. "Fine. The insults have to stop, too."

"Until you do something to piss me off again."

The smile returned. "Deal."

Victor hung up before his smile pissed her off. She turned to Bailey and said, "Now we wait. In the meantime, contact maintenance and let them know a dent of enigmatic origin has mysteriously appeared on my wall. If they push for a reason, tell them you witnessed me single handedly fight off a biker gang from the streets looking to exact their own form of vigilante justice. It was inspiring and it changed your life."

"You got it," Bailey said as he returned to his laptop. "One question, though – what did Dante mean about you 'know your Milton?'"

Victor chuckled. "He was referring to 'Paradise Lost' by John Milton. After the devil got cast from heaven, he said, 'Better to reign in hell then serve in heaven.'"

"Interesting analogy."

"Not a very accurate one, though, because he failed to take into consideration one piece of information."

"Which is?"

"That I am the fucking devil."

CHAPTER 26

July 10th, Chicago

Genocide stretched her legs across the booth's seat, her back against the graffiti covered wall, every once in a while flicking her eyes at Blaze who sat lazily across from her. She absent-mindedly played with the loose edge of duct tape covering a hole in the booth's seat-back while her left elbow rested on the table, a resin encasement of movie posters from the 60s and 70s Mexican cinema. Sitting here for over two hours, she doubted that any of the *Los Muertos que Bailan* staff would mind, considering they cultivated a punk rock vibe with the street art on the walls, red and purple lighting over the bar, and the mismatched and refurbished furniture. Every employee had more tattoos and facial piercings than any band that had played at Club B-Sides. It was all part of the aesthetic.

"Why not at my place?" she had asked when Blaze first suggested this restaurant for the meeting.

"Even though you didn't invite Lucas or Ven to participate, they'd still be hovering around. Plus, Club B-Sides barely serves bar snacks and I'm peckish for tacos."

Despite the dive bar feel, *Los Muertos que Bailan* served upscale dishes, never receiving a less than perfect critique in the papers and boasting a 4.9 on every website that allowed the general public to rate it. Whatever Blaze had been to her lately – she still couldn't refer to him as a friend, especially since she didn't refer to anyone else in her life that way – he had to have an ulterior motive for picking this place.

Though, it was kind of funny to see Corette taking a seat beside him.

Wearing a cream-colored suit, jacket unbuttoned over a plain white blouse, shin length skirt pleated, she looked painfully out of place, but never once showed the slightest sign of discomfort. Blaze, however…

When Gen and Blaze first arrived, he had been all smiles, no matter how many times she forbade him. Then Corette walked into the restaurant. Gen felt every bit of oxygen leave Blaze's body. At first, she thought it was infatuation. Corette was every bit as mousy as Celina, more so since she was tinier, and Blaze had an affinity for Celina. But Blaze looked at Corette as if she were a puzzle to be solved, a song with a title he couldn't quite remember.

The pleasantries were minimal, Corette giving a curt answer to how her flight had been before she jumped into business. True to what Victor and Celina had said – "the feeling" hit Gen, but she pushed past it and explained why she had contacted Munitions Investments. They ordered food, ate while Corette asked follow-up questions, and then she pulled out her laptop and went to work.

Two hours later, after research, emails, video calls – the location of where she worked be damned – and two money transfers from Gen, Corette shut her laptop and said, "Done. You'll have it in your hands in two days."

"Impossible," Gen said.

For the first time since arriving, Corette smiled. A tiny curl of her lips, but it conveyed enough confidence to back her words. "You just paid me quite a sum of money for impossible."

Blaze grinned. "So, now that you've moved mountains and parted seas, care to stay for a drink?"

Corette stood and brushed away any potential wrinkles from her suit. "Thank you, but not at this time."

"Thank you," Gen said, dubious about Corette's promise.

Corette packed her computer into her bag and produced two business cards. Placing them on the table, she said, "If you need anything else, don't hesitate to contact me. I'll be in town for a few days to force the paperwork through the city's process."

Gen watched Blaze watch Corette. Once the small woman in the business suit exited the restaurant, Blaze shook his head as if waking from a dream. Gen took a swig of beer and asked, "What'd you think?"

Blaze opened his mouth but paused. A sly smile played across his face as he grabbed his beer. Striking a more relaxed pose, he pulled slowly from the bottle. "You'll have to be more specific."

"Is she one of us? Like Celina and Victor seem to think?"

Blaze bit his bottom lip and nodded. "Yeah. Yeah, I think she is. That weird feeling when she first came in. Didn't you feel it?"

She offered a halfhearted shrug as a weak form of confirmation. "How about her voice? Victor said it was weird, like she could use it to manipulate people." *Like how you use your smile...* Gen kept that thought to herself, not wanting to traipse down some bullshit conversational tangent.

"I don't know. Her voice wasn't as soft as I was expecting, but not... I don't know... nothing weird or mystical or hypnotic or whatever Victor was talking about. However, we weren't adversarial to her as Victor undoubtedly was. I mean, when she was on the calls and meetings with the lawyers and bankers, they were all agreeable with what she was saying. Does she have some special influence, like what Victor was talking about?"

"Or maybe Corette is just exceptional at her job."

"Maybe a little of both?"

"So, you believe Victor?"

"Just because she and I didn't witness the same things, doesn't mean I don't believe her. She might be right."

"That's very trusting of you."

"I've seen 'interesting' things over these last few months. I mean, you're... umm..."

"A mutant, giant spider freak?"

"... a unique creature."

Gen smirked as she brought the bottle to her lips. "A unique creature."

Blaze drained his beer and signaled to their server for two more. Silence until the bottles arrived. "In L.A., Melissandra called you 'sister' and said you had a gift."

Thoughts of running away and sticking Blaze with the bill danced through Gen's head. After guzzling the remains of the beer she was holding, she clutched the one from the table with both hands. This would be the first time she talked about her situation since... "My mother. She was the queen of the black widows. Only the queen can reproduce, and the queen can only have daughters."

"The gift."

"If you wanna call it that."

Blaze was smart, something Gen was learning. And at least nice enough to look away as she thumbed the tear rolling down her cheek. Instead of badgering her about her last comment, he asked, "So your cluster is all male?"

"One other woman, my half-sister. We don't talk much. I actually don't talk with the rest of my cluster much either, other than Ven and Lucas. I'm a shitty queen."

"Seems like you respect everyone in your cluster enough to let them do their own thing."

Gen grimaced and wished that were true. Another gulp of beer. "I should hire you as my PR guy."

Blaze laughed. "Oh, I'm sure Ven and Lucas would love that. Since the queen can only give birth to females, how are those two and the other men in your cluster the way they are?"

"The queen can turn human men into spiders. Well, I *thought* it was only the queen, but Melissandra kinda demonstrated otherwise."

"The spiders that she controlled seemed… inhuman," Blaze said. "Different than your bandmates. More like animals."

"Drones. Kinda like ants or bees, the queen… or whoever, I guess… can assign a role to their underlings while creating them."

Blaze looked at Gen like she had said he was going to be her next meal.

"Don't worry." She chuckled and then held her index finger and thumb an inch apart. "I mean the little bugs. To the best of my knowledge, there are no half human, half insect creatures. Just us spiders."

Shifting in his seat, Blaze said, "Good to know. How many of your cluster did you make?"

"Just Lucas. I haven't been queen for long. About three years or so."

"Do you have to turn men into spiders in order to reproduce?"

Gen rolled her eyes and shook her head. "There it is."

"There what is?"

"Your ulterior motive."

170

"My motive is to understand the workings of a group of near-mythical creatures."

Swinging her feet off the booth's seat, she stomped her boots on the ground and rested her elbows on the table. Chin in her hands, she batted her eyelashes. "Yes, they must be spiders for me to reproduce, but not for me to have sex with. And men don't turn into spiders simply by having sex with me, before you ask."

Mimicking her gestures and finishing with his chin in his hands, Blaze said, "I wasn't gonna ask."

No smile. If he'd been smiling, then she'd know he was lying. Still, she sat back and flicked her fingers dismissively. "Sure you weren't."

Blaze sat back as well, taking his beer with him. "You're very suspicious of me."

"That's because you put your dick first."

"I get why people would think that. I get why people think a lot of things about me. Fast talker. Grifter. In it for myself. Sure, I do a lot of shady shit, work a few cons here and there, but the motivations behind them are to help those who could use my help. I don't put my dick first; I put my heart first."

"Men who 'put their hearts first' wear golf shirts and khakis, not snakeskin and python skin boots."

"On the contrary," Blaze said as Gen brought the bottle to her lips. "I'm sure you'd agree that the biggest troublemakers in bars like yours are douchebags in golf shirts and khakis 'walking on the wild side' by spending a few hours getting drunk and talking down to the regulars. A push, a shove, a few punches, possibly a broken beer bottle, and a police visit later, the douchebags get escorted out."

Gen sighed. Men who put their hearts first were a fucking myth. "So, you're hanging around because you think I need your help."

"Nope. I'm hanging around and helping when I can because... you're different."

"Yeah, I'm different. I'm not even fucking human."

Blaze set his beer down, body tightening and brows pinching with concern. "You're very fucking human. You have dreams and responsibilities. You work hard and make decisions that best serve these dreams and responsibilities. Three years ago, you became queen of a group of... unique creatures... which is when I'm assuming you learned that you were one. I'm also assuming that's when you became owner of a portfolio of businesses that I'm pretty sure you're not interested in. Three years ago, you became Atlas. It takes a hell of a lot longer than that to balance the weight of the world on your shoulders. You're angry. Frustrated. Confused. Pulled in different directions. Sounds pretty fucking human to me."

Gen grabbed her beer and looked away, not sure how to respond. A burn in her gut told her she needed to argue, but against what? His observations were accurate, even though she truly didn't feel human.

In the midst of her existential crisis, half the people in the restaurant started to cheer and clap.

Leaning out from the booth, Gen got a view deeper inside the restaurant. Pissed at herself for not noticing they had a small stage, she snarled as six musicians stood on it with two guitars, two trumpets, an accordion, and a small drum kit. As punk as the decor, the mariachi band played fast and hard, yet melodic enough to encourage dancing. People hopped from their seats and moved to the beat in the open area in front of the stage.

Gen turned back and Blaze greeted her with his biggest cat-chewing-on-a-canary grin. God, she hated that smile – it gave her the same tingle of excitement as stepping on the stage ready to sing a concert's first song. "You caught me. I do have an ulterior motive."

Squashing the fun tingles Blaze's smile caused, Gen leaned back into the booth and said, "Fuck no. Fuck off. Fuck you."

Blaze laughed and held up if hands as a form of surrender. "My ulterior motive was to give you an opportunity to unwind and have fun. I know you have a ton of responsibility waiting for you back at B-Sides. If I hadn't suggested a place like this, then you would have felt like you had to go back and deal with all that responsibility. Now, you have a choice. I'm not going to try to stop you from leaving or talk you into staying. All I'm gonna do is ask – wanna dance?"

"In case you didn't hear me the first time – Fuck no. Fuck off. Fuck you."

Still laughing, Blaze stood and took off his jacket to reveal the insanity of his Hawaiian shirt – sky blue background with clouds shaped like hands at his shoulders, dozens of individual cartoon snowflakes falling with outstretched arms as if they had been pushed toward the many broken and bloodied snowflake corpses along the bottom of the shirt. He tossed his jacket on the booth's seat. "I hear ya loud and clear, Gen. I'll take care of the check."

Using his smile like a jousting lance, he charged forth. Mouth moving nonstop, he ingratiated himself in the small crowd, dancing with everyone. Pelvis to pelvis, his hips moved in rhythm with one of the women for a minute or two until he spun away to engage with another woman in a modified tango. A half song later he was jumping and hopping with one of the men around a point in a circle only to have another woman back into him. They wriggled to the beat of the drums.

"Fuck no. Fuck off. Fuck you," Gen said to herself as she stood to leave…

…but walked toward the dance floor.

"Nice of you to join us," Blaze said over the music as Gen approached.

"Christ, are you going to talk the whole time?"

"I promise, not another word."

Just like the last time he said that to her, he followed through. Gen moved to the music, her hips, feet, arms, head. Free to move, nothing constricting her, nothing pinning her down. Her vision blurred as she allowed the music to enter her mind and evict all thoughts. No cluster. No band. No businesses. No invoices. No responsibilities. Weightless, she smiled song after song, minutes turning into an hour. Just the music.

Dancing.

Freedom.

Blaze.

Gen stopped dancing and simply watched Blaze, she felt… she didn't know what she felt. She spent her life stomping down certain emotions, pushing away other emotions, and ignoring the ones that remained. Then

Blaze came into her life. She didn't know she could still feel. Now she felt...
she still had no idea what.

Noticing her staring at him, Blaze stopped dancing. They locked eyes
and Gen felt...

Weak.

Blaze reached out, his elbow close to his hip. Then he extended his other
arm. That pose made him look like an awkward junior at a 1950s prom, but
the invitation was obvious and Gen obliged. Her hand in his, she hugged
him. His firm hand on her back made her feel even weaker.

Gen closed her eyes and rested her head on his shoulder. They simply
swayed back and forth as the rest of the world swirled around them.

CHAPTER 27

July 10th, Philadelphia

Black. That was all Orion saw – inky darkness. *Well, of course, all I should be able to see is darkness. My eyes are shut.*

Orion shifted in bed and hoped the noise didn't disturb Jacob. Although, it was doubtful he'd be able to hear anything over the white noise machine on the nightstand between them.

Jacob had shown up at Orion's hotel room around 9:00p.m., a travel mug of valerian root tea for each of them. At first Orion thought it was weird to have someone else sleep in his room, but Jacob had an easygoing way about him and explained that it was no different than traveling for business or going to an out-of-town convention. And after they had started talking, Orion's reservations melted away.

Through research, they both learned about the science behind dream telepathy – which was technically what Orion was attempting by trying to enter Jacob's dreams – and decided that proximity was important, especially for neophytes. The plan was for Jacob to think only about his childhood home, hoping that within his dream he could conjure memories, while Orion focused on entering Jacob's dream and guide him through his dreamscape. So, Orion eschewed energy drinks all day.

He lay on his back, his arms crossed over his chest. *Wait, this isn't some kind of military procedure. I don't sleep like this.* Orion rolled onto his left side, his back to Jacob. He could hear rhythmic breathing coming from the other bed – or was it the white noise machine? – and wondered if Jacob was asleep already.

Focusing on the black nothingness, Orion tried to force himself to go to sleep. *What if I don't sleep at all tonight? I can't believe that douchebag took my mother. C'mon, stop thinking about that. Let the tea do its thing. What the hell is valerian root anyway? Ugh, this sucks.* Orion shoved his hands in his pockets.

Jacob's gonna think I'm such a child. Frustrated, he kicked a small rock down the street. *What if I can't do this? What if...? Wait...*

Orion stopped walking, his feet on a road. He looked around. *Holy shit, I'm in the dreamscape – I'm asleep.*

The dream setting wasn't one he'd been to or seen before – a suburban neighborhood with small houses. Well, smaller than the one he had grown up in. Half of them were single story, the rest either bilevel or two story. They all had driveways, but only a few had garages. Shrubs and trees accented the neighborhood. No other signs of life, though.

Not knowing where he was or what he was looking for, Orion kept walking down the middle of the street. As he passed house after house, his excitement waned, replaced by a cold sense of unease. No movement behind any of the windows. No one outside. No kids playing, no adults working on the houses, yards, cars. The sky was blue. No, the sun was blue, casting an unwashed film on everything, like a coat of grime from lack of cleaning.

The front door of a split level flung open, and Jacob ran out, laughing and waving. "Orion! It worked! It worked!"

Orion smiled and jogged the rest of the way, dismayed that even in a dream his muscles were starting to get sore, leaving him slightly winded. Yeah, he thought it was cool that he was able to see in three dimensions and color, to hear Jacob's joy clearly, and feel sweat forming along his hairline, but he hated knowing that dying in the dreamscape would lead to real world death. "Hey! Yeah, it worked, right?"

Extending his arms, Jacob spun slowly as if showcasing gameshow prizes. "Fuck yeah it did! This is the neighborhood I grew up in." He stopped and pointed, giving a remote tour. "That's sweet Mrs. Montgomery's house. She made the best pies. Marcy my babysitter lives in that house there. I fell out of that tree when I was six. Luckily, I landed in that bush or I would have had broken bones. And this... this is my house. Come on in."

Jacob hurried back into the house. Following, Orion continued to look around the neighborhood. Didn't Jacob notice the unusual coloring? Was he blind to how dirty everything looked? The shrubs were so unkempt that they were creating exaggerated shadows. At least Orion *thought* the shrubs created the shadows. Were they moving? Orion blinked and rubbed his eyes. No, the shadows remained still. But Orion hurried into the house just in case.

On a small landing – on his right a set of stairs led upward, on his left a set of stairs led down – Orion called out, "Jacob?"

"Up here."

Orion jogged up the steps. Living room on the right, kitchen and dining room in front of him with a set of patio doors leading to the backyard. A hallway to the left led to four doors – a bathroom and small room on one side, a bedroom on the other, the master bedroom at the end of the hall. The same strange blue tint cast its hue upon everything in the house. Plain wallpaper peeled along the edges and seams. Cobwebs accented every corner of the ceiling and draped along the threadbare furniture. Dust on the carpet showed footprints. Jacob couldn't have possibly lived like this. But this was Jacob's dreamscape, his subconscious. A representation of how Jacob either viewed his house or remembered it. It had been twenty-three years. Would Orion view the house he grew up in like this after twenty-three years?

"Hey, how's it—?" Orion started to ask, but choked on his words, startled by what he saw as he got to the master bedroom. A man stood in the center of the room. Applying clown makeup.

Three small containers in his left hand, he dipped his fingers into the one and added more white grease paint to the first layer on his face. He then dug his index finger into a different jar, this time painting blue circles around his eyes. The third jar contained red paint, the color he used for his mouth. When finished, his eyes and smile grew wider and wider, his head like a balloon ready to pop. Squiggly lines of colorful static covered him, like an old television set failing. Once the static cleared away, the scene reset, and the clown repeated the painting process.

"What the fuck?" Orion whispered, not daring to cross the threshold, transfixed by the unnerving clown. He hadn't noticed the opened closet door until Jacob poked his head out. "Oh, hey. Him? Yeah, that's my father. His name's Collin."

"Whoa!" Orion's emotions squished together, leaving a gelatinous mess oozing around behind his chest. On one hand, it was awesome that Jacob got to see his father again, but on the other hand... He was a creepy clown! Did Jacob know this before asking Orion for help? Or did he just learn about it and come to terms with it super quickly? Either way, it seemed like no big deal to Jacob as he darted back inside the closet.

Keeping a wary eye on Jacob's clown dad, Orion walked into the bedroom. "Is...? Is this what you were expecting to find?"

Kneeling while rifling through papers in a cardboard box, Jacob answered, "Yes. Well, sort of. He mentioned in his journal that he fought against the subconscious societal tyranny of the mundane by donning clown makeup – white base, blue around his eyes, red mouth."

"Oh. Ok. That's... I guess that's kinda cool. So... What are you looking for? Can I help?"

Jacob pushed the box aside and grabbed one of the other eight. "I really don't know. I feel like there's so much more to my father that I want to learn. If I see something here, then it should exist in the real world, right?"

Orion shrugged. "Yeah, I guess so."

"Good, then I can find it there, too. My father kept this closet locked, but I was a sneaky kid. I mean, aren't we all? I wanted to come here to look through the memories of my seven-year-old self to see if I can find... I don't know. Something, you know? How about you check out the basement to see if there's anything interesting down there?"

"The basement?" Orion didn't like that he sounded like a frightened prepubescent.

Jacob chuckled while turning his attention to another box of junk in front of him. "Don't worry, it's a finished basement. A combination rec room and office space. Plenty of lighting. Not a scary basement."

Jacob's assurance did nothing to alleviate Orion's fear, but he tried to cover it up with, "I didn't mean it like that. I meant, would I be able to see details without you being there?"

"You should. Even though the dreamscape is mine, it's the whole dreamscape. You saw the neighborhood details when you first got here, right? And the details of the house when you first walked in, even though I wasn't with you?"

"Yeah, I guess."

"I mean, if you want to hang out here, that's cool, too, but all I'm going to be doing is rummaging through the closet. When I'm done, we can hit the basement together."

Orion couldn't stop his gaze from drifting to the clown in the middle of the room. Another static blur over his head and his face reset to paint-free. "No, that's okay. I'll head downstairs."

The basement's wall-to-wall carpeting was a thin piece of abstract art thrown over the concrete floor. Orion flipped the light switch at the bottom of the stairs which turned on one torch lamp against the far wall, illuminating most of the wood-paneled room to the right of the stairs. The left of the stairs offered darkness, so Orion went right.

A floor-to-ceiling entertainment center with television against the one wall, worn couch with stuffing poking from random area in the middle of the room, a metal desk with a bent leg tucked in the corner. Farther into the room, where the light struggled to reach, was a bar. At least Orion assumed it was a bar since shadows obscured the shape, but he was pretty confident he saw three barstools in front of it.

A rusty metal file cabinet, as tall as Orion, sat beside the desk. He pulled the top drawer open, warmth prickling his cheeks, feeling like he was peeking into someone's bathroom window. *No, he told me to look around. But look for what?* Hanging folders stored old and wrinkled forms filled with words he couldn't make out and numbers he didn't understand. Orion had no idea if any of it was important or not. Should he bring any of these folders to Jacob? Wasn't like he could bring all of them. There were too many! Not to mention three more drawers of—

TAP. TAP. TAP.

Orion froze in place. The noise came from the bar area.

TAP. TAP.

Holding his breath, he looked to the stairs. Jacob had told him there was nothing scary in the basement. Wrong!

TAP. TAP.

Orion backed away from the file cabinet, leaving the drawer open, trying to focus on the darkened bar. Something was there. Then he saw movement, the source of the…

TAP. TAP. TAP.

Fingernails. Extending from behind the bar, one set of long, thick nails dug into the top of the bar's counter. Branchlike fingers from the other chalky -white hand gripped the side. Making sure his balance was sound, Orion took another big step toward the stairs.

A face rose above the bar, emerging from the shadows. A ghastly white face, stretched and demonic, with strips of clumpy brown hair hanging from its head like Spanish moss. Ragged blue circles covered his eyes, a fist-sized red nose anchored his face, and a smear of glistening blood created a fake smile.

The clown inched farther out of the darkness. When he smiled, the corners of his gash-like mouth crept up his face, moving past his cheeks, higher than his pointed ears and cutting into his temples. Rippling lips split open to expose his teeth, pointed tusks shimmering under the saliva flowing from his mouth.

Orion sprinted to the escape, slamming into the stairwell wall, and took the stairs two at a time. He crashed into the front door when he got to the landing, but didn't stop, continuing up the other set of stairs and screaming, "Jacob! Jacob! We gotta get—"

The patio doors shattered, pebbles of glass raining to the floor like crystal confetti. A figure stepped into the dining room from outside and Orion jerked to a stop.

Calista Lindquist.

Wearing a form-fitting black tactical outfit, she drew two guns from the holsters strapped to her thighs and aimed them at Orion.

"Wake up," Orion said to himself as she stalked closer. "Wake up! Wake up!"

Jolting upright in the hotel bed, Orion yelled, "Wake up!"

"Whoa, whoa! Orion, it's me, Jacob. You're all right. You're okay," Jacob said, standing next to him.

Shaking, Orion wiped the sweat from his face, but more flowed despite his every swipe. Jacob handed him a glass of water and he drained it with big, loud gulps.

"Deep breaths. Deep breaths. You're okay," Jacob said, and sat.

Orion took long, deep breaths in and out. No clowns. No assassin psycho woman. After a few more exaggerated inhales and exhales, Orion checked his body for wounds or injuries.

"How you doing? Any better?" Jacob asked.

Orion ran his hands through his hair, droplets of sweat hitting the sheets. "Yeah. Yeah, I think so. Fuck, that was intense."

"I'll say," Jacob said. "What happened?"

Still panting, Orion wiped his face with the bed sheet. "The clown."

"My dad? Yeah, that was a little odd."

"No, the one in the basement."

"Whoa. You saw a clown in the basement?"

"Yeah, a weird, freaky one with long fingers and pointy teeth."

Jacob backed away from Orion's bed. "Seriously?"

Orion glared at Jacob. "Yeah, seriously. You said there was nothing scary down there."

"There never was. Are you afraid of clowns?"

"What? Why are you asking me that?"

"I'm guessing you were weirded out by my dad. Your fear must have been amplified when you went into a strange basement. There, you manifested a nightmare clown."

"I manifested? But it was your dreamscape."

"You must have some level of control, ability to manipulate other people's dreamscapes. I mean, you jumped into my dreamscape and guided me to a memory I had. If you think about it, it was you who architected the dreamscape, right? Plus, you said your father could control other people's dreamscapes, so it stands to reason that you can, too, even if you don't realize it, even if you don't have conscious control over it."

"Yeah, maybe."

As Jacob slid his jeans on over his boxers, he asked, "Is that clown what woke you up?"

"No. It was Calista Lindquist."

"Wait. You mean the assassin woman who had been hunting you?"

"Yeah."

"Okay, that's even weirder. Maybe it was a snowball effect. My dad weirded you out, which led to you seeing a scary clown, which led to you conjuring the most terrifying moment of your life."

Orion stretched, muscles tight as if he had actually walked along a street and bounced off walls while running up stairs. Jacob's explanations sounded logical, but were they accurate? Was he afraid of clowns? Did Orion manifest the nightmare elements within Jacob's memory dream?

"Damn, that was intense," Jacob said as he removed his sweat drenched tee shirt and grabbed a new one from his suitcase. "You didn't tell me that having you along in my dreamscape would be so sweaty. I feel like I ran a marathon." He then put on his shoes.

"Sorry. Thought it was just me who sweated like crazy. Are you leaving?"

Like a kid looking at his favorite dessert, Jacob nodded. "I am. It's four in the morning, but I'm way too wound up to go back to sleep, so I'm going to the storage unit and rummage around some more. I need to thank you, Orion. What you did was amazing and very helpful. In the boxes in my dream, I found awards and projects from school. I mean, they were stupid drawings and participation awards from when I was five, six, seven, but the fact that my dad kept them... Well, it really hit my sensitive spots."

"Umm."

Packed and dressed, Jacob headed toward the door. "More importantly, I saw that he had another journal. I couldn't get much from it, because I don't think I read it as a kid, but if it was in the closet, that means it exists in the real world, right?"

"Umm, yeah?"

Door open, Jacob said, "Let's meet for lunch. 12:00 at the diner where we met before. It should give me plenty of time with the storage unit and you can get more sleep."

"Uh huh."

The door latched shut and Orion flopped back on the bed. Eyes wide open, he wasn't sure if he'd ever sleep again.

CHAPTER 28

July 11th, Chicago

Women! Blaze thought as he shoved a crispy piece of bacon into his mouth. *Messin' with my head.*

Sitting in his usual spot in the Sun Up-N-Down Diner – the corner booth in the back – Blaze paused from his breakfast to rub his eyes, hoping to grind away his frustration. Sighing, he dug into his pancakes and stared at his phone. Victor had asked Blaze for a favor, and he owed her. But right now he wanted to renege, to text Jerry and tell him to call off his search for dirt on Corette Remington.

Victor had made her request before he met Corette. But things had changed when Blaze met the little blonde woman in the business suit. She had made quite an impact on him. Thank God he had been sitting down when she entered *Los Muertos que Bailan*. Whatever the "feeling" was that he got from the others like him, the one he got from Corette would have knocked him over had he not already been seated. His breath abandoned him like he'd been gut punched, the hair on the back of his neck turned to nails, and his goosebumps could have etched glass. It was stronger than the feeling he got when he first met any of them. Celina. Victor. Orion. Gen.

Scarlett.

The cold sweat of dread trickled down his spine. Gen was going to screw her over, and it was Blaze's fault. Well, Scarlett – a brown recluse – would undoubtedly see it that way after Gen drops the bombshell.

He was vulnerable. Not only did he stand no chance of surviving an attack from a human sized spider, but Scarlett might use him as a way to hurt Gen. So, instead of just injecting him with a lethal dose of venom, she might view his relationship with Gen as something of value, and web him into a cocoon to torture him. But… was his relationship with Gen anything of value to Gen? Would she protect him? Unknown. Hell, that was assuming he'd survive what Corette would do to him if she found out that he was involved with digging up damning information and giving it to Victor. *Christ, what if Victor's plans to fuck over Corette work too well? Could Corette trace it back to me?* A syrup covered acid bubble burst halfway up his throat.

All he wanted to do was help. He knew better, though. Sometimes to help one person, he needed to hurt another. But then he felt bad and wanted to help *that* person.

When he had first met Scarlett, he thought she was too young to resort to prostitution in order to make it through this world. Sure, she had a dangerous edge to her, so did most women in those situations. Desperation in her eyes. She could have killed Blaze when he started asking around about the rec. Instead, she warned him away from the topic. Gen assumed that Scarlett was the queen of the brown recluse spiders, but was she? Maybe Scarlett answered to someone else?

"Are you sweet on me?" Gen had asked him the other night. He didn't lie when he said he couldn't answer that question. She was like no other woman he had met before, and that intrigued him. Excited him. Drove him to want to help her. But he had no idea where he stood with her. Last night, they had danced.

Having her in his arms was exhilarating, yet comforting, as they slow danced nonstop for over an hour. Then she pulled away, keeping her hand in his. In that corner of the restaurant, lights flashed in different colors from the set the band provided, and he swore her cheeks glistened with tears. After an interminable gaze, she let go and walked away. Blaze didn't ask why she was crying, didn't suggest she stay, didn't say anything because he had promised.

No mention of when her next move would be against Scarlett, or what the hell that dance meant to her. Should he show up at her apartment again? No. That had been a risky move the first time around. Fuck it, he'd go to Club B-Sides tonight. As long as Vinnie didn't toss him, he'd chill at the bar until he got a chance to talk to Gen.

Blaze checked his phone again. No message yet from Jerry. Could he help Corette after he had turned on her by helping Victor? That depended on what Jerry found, so no use dwelling on what could be. Plus, Corette was rich and powerful, so he doubted she'd need anything that he might have to offer.

But there was something about her that made him feel the need to help her, something that pained him just thinking about her. *Guilt*, he surmised. *Guilt for fucking her over.*

As if his remorse was the necessary catalyst, his phone buzzed with Jerry's number displayed. Blaze answered, putting himself on video.

"Love the beautiful scenery you got there, Jerry. So warm and inviting, tropical even," Blaze said to the phone's black screen. Jerry was so damn paranoid about hiding his location.

"Ha ha, fuck you. For someone who abuses my good nature and generosity, you sure bust my balls a lot," Jerry said.

Jerry was right – Blaze owed him a few favors. "C'mon, what's a little nut-tap now and again between friends."

"Friends. You use that word, but I don't think it means what you think it means."

"True. A friend would tell a friend where in the world he was hiding."

"Not over a phone, smart guy. Anyway, if you're done being a douche, I got something on Corette."

This was it, the moment Blaze was dreading. He kept smiling, though, to hide the queasiness rumbling through his gut. "Is it bad?"

"Depends on your definition of good."

Blaze tapped away at his screen to get to his email. "Did you send me anything yet?"

"Not yet, because it needs a little explanation first."

"Explanation?"

"Remember the movie set massacre of '96?"

"Remember? No, I wasn't born yet."

"Have you heard about it at least?"

"Sounds familiar. I kinda remember reading something about it. Some guy killed a bunch of people on an Arizona farm where they were making a movie, right?"

"Close. It was a ranch in New Mexico. A serial killer got caught there using it as a playground."

Blaze shoveled a sloppy chunk of pancake into his mouth. "Okay, what does this have to do with anything?" His phone dinged with an email notification.

Jerry said, "I just sent you a clip from an underground VHS video magazine called *Eye Spy With My Knowing Eye* that dedicated itself to counter, alt, sub, anti-culture. Right after the movie set massacre happened, it hit the mainstream news for a minute and then was gone the next day. The producers of *Eye Spy* offered some cashola for an interview with anyone who was involved. Well, four hookers stepped forward. Go ahead and hit play."

Blaze retrieved the file from his email. As grainy as expected, the video focused on four young women. The intense height and volume of hair went with the times, as did the bright colors of their revealing outfits. Blinding shimmer on their Spandex pants, their tops every color of neon. One wore a pair of large-framed glasses, making her look more like a librarian than a prostitute, clearly satisfying a particular niche customer. The shot was pulled back, the quality of film low, and watching from his phone made it impossible to see details of their faces. Then the camera zoomed in on the girl on the left as a man's voice said, "We're here with four brave souls who survived a date with the devil himself, almost participants in a macabre tale of murder and mayhem. This is Babydoll." She was the shortest of the four and had chocolate brown hair and wore brown lipstick on her thin-lipped smile.

"And here we have Jinx," the narrator said as the camera panned to the right on a brunette. She gave a smoldering stare to the camera, then giggled after a few seconds.

The next girl was the one with the glasses. She had a lucid and focused look about her, and her smile seemed forced. "This is Beth."

The camera panned to the last of the four, a blonde with a big smile. "And finally, Starla."

Blaze gasped and dropped his phone to his lap.

It can't be! Fumbling, he picked it up with shaky hands and brought it closer for a better look. Sure enough, he knew the smiling blonde.

His mother.

Young, maybe not even twenty, with a hairstyle he had never seen on her before, but Blaze knew that face. He had seen it and loved it every day for the first twenty-two years of his life, from the day he was born until the day she died. He had two full shoe boxes under his bed filled with photos of that face. Megabytes worth of pictures were stored in one of his cloud folders. Starla, his mother.

Her real name was Estella Stanford, and she'd move to Los Angeles, probably shortly after this video. Blaze had no idea who these other girls were, because his mother had never talked much about her youth. He always assumed she came from a bad childhood, and he never wanted to bring up any subject that upset her.

The man off camera asked them questions, prodding them for their stories. They obliged, going on about being called out to a mansion-like house on a pig farm to party with a guy named Silas. Except for Beth, who admitted that she took a fancy to Silas' friend, Johnny. The house – the Boyle place, as they referred to it – was the property neighboring where the movie set massacre took place. Blaze barely caught much information, the world too muffled by the gauzy memories of his mother.

"Hey! Hey, Shaky McGee, can you even hear me?" Jerry's voice had made its way into Blaze's brain, snapping him back to reality.

Blaze swiped under his eyes, shooing away tears. "Yeah. Yeah, Jerry, I'm here."

"What the hell, man? You dropped the phone and it's been shaking the whole time, and… Are you crying? Why the fuck are you crying?"

"You sent me a video of my mom."

"Your…? Whoa! Which one is she?"

Blaze pointed at his screen, even though Jerry couldn't see the gesture. "Her. The blonde."

"Oh, thank God. I have a major thing for the hottie in the glasses."

"You're a piece of work, Jerry. A real piece of work. Why did you send me a video of my mother?"

"I didn't! Well, obviously, I did, but I didn't know she was in it. I sent you a video of Corette's mom."

Squinting, Blaze held his phone closer to his face. "Wait, what?" he asked, wondering to which girl Jerry referred.

"Babydoll's real name is Barbara Remington, and eight short months after filming this, she gave birth to a girl. I included a copy of the birth certificate in your email."

"That's... Well, that could be scandalous, depending on the person's viewpoint."

"Scandalous? Haven't you been paying attention? A psycho named Johnny Ghastson was arrested and took credit for each murder at the movie set and a handful of other ones before that. Dude, he willingly offered up incriminating evidence. The women just said that not only did Johnny have an accomplice, but they fucked him. Well, three of them fucked him, not my girl with the glasses. She fucked Johnny, but that's neither here nor there. So, your girl, Corette Remington – not only is her mom a hooker, but there's a good chance that her daddy is the accomplice to a literal massacre, or maybe even the killer himself."

Video paused on a closeup of Starla's face, Blaze muttered, "Yeah. Yeah, I guess that's pretty bad, isn't it?"

"I'd fucking say so. But... Does that mean you and Corette might have the same daddy?"

"Gotta go, Jerry. Thanks for the video. I owe you."

"You better believe you do! Wait, so you're not even thirty yet? Holy shit, I thought you were older, like forty—"

Blaze hung up on Jerry. Before he changed his mind and broke a promise for the first time in his life, he sent Victor an email and attached the video, birth certificate, and an explanation.

A weird sense of relief swept through him, washing away the heaviness in his heart. Not only had Jerry dug up something on Corette, but he uncovered something about Blaze as well. Maybe this explained the connection he had felt with Corette.

He flagged the waitress down. Queueing up the video for a long line of rewatches, he ordered lunch. He was going to be here for a while.

CHAPTER 29

July 11th, Philadelphia

All diners looked the same to Orion, not places he and his family ate at often, if ever, yet during his time in Philadelphia these were where he'd been eating the best. Blaze had mentioned that he loved diners, and Orion was beginning to make them a habit. He saw the appeal – any kind of food any time of day.

Pancakes, bacon, scrambled eggs. A breakfast similar to what he was used to. Though, when Aika cooked, she'd stretch the bacon into a smile on the pancakes, dollop on the eggs as eyes. Here, the food was prepped by a guy named Frank, or at least that's who the waitress yelled to when she went behind the counter.

Perched in a booth toward the back – in case Jacob got mad when Orion shared his news – he tapped his foot while shoveling eggs in his mouth. His stomach lurched when he looked up.

Jacob had entered and gleefully hurried his way over to Orion. Sliding into the seat across from him, Jacob set his dad's journal on the table.

"Hey," Jacob said.

Orion gulped down the eggs. "Hey."

"Last night, huh? Well, I guess technically this morning. That was pretty friggin' wild, though, right?"

"I'm heading back to Vegas." The words were hurried and possibly childish, but Orion needed to get them out quickly before Jacob got to talking.

Jacob's shine lost its luster, but he was taking the news better than Orion thought he would. "Oh yeah?"

Slouching, Orion spoke to his syrup-streaked plate. "Yeah. It's about time I get back home."

"I don't mean to sound crass or dismissive, but what's waiting for you there?"

Not sure why, but Orion felt offended, almost insulted. His tone strong, resolute in defending himself, he said, "My friends. My apartment. My job. I mean, don't you, like, have a job or something?"

Jacob sat back and held up his palms to block Orion's heated words. "Sorry, sorry. I didn't express myself well. First, you are correct, I do have a job, but I'm kind of the boss of different stuff, so I have a lot of latitude. Now, I have the time to learn about myself, my father. My legacy. Don't you want to learn more about your legacy? Your father? Find your mother? Why leave now? Why give up on yourself?"

"I'm not giving up on myself. And staying here won't help me find my mother. You and I went back to the theater, but she's gone. Harold took her and left no clue as to where. Calling the cops would do no good now. I'd feel better back home, where Victor and Celina could help me."

"You really think they'd be able to help you find your mother? Are they expert sleuths? Sure, they found you from Calista's hitlist, but come on, how many Orion Fogelbergs are there? It was easy for them to track you down, but your mother? Can they find a man named Harold Varvaro who's been living off the grid for literally as long as you've been alive?"

Orion shrugged. "They can be resourceful. They found other people from the list."

"They didn't find me. They didn't find Preston."

"We researched everyone on the list."

"Not well."

"There are seven Jacob McGoverns and three Preston Albrights."

"Orion, the picture of me on the list came straight from one of my social media pages."

"We were being hunted. We looked for the people on the list who would be the easiest and fastest to find."

Jacob made the same, sad face that Orion's high school guidance counselor once made when Orion said he wanted to be a graphic novel artist. Jacob settled his elbows on the table, his tone softening. "Then the searching stopped once it seemed like everyone was out of danger. Once Victor and Celina had the answers they were looking for."

"They helped me find an apartment and gave me a job."

"There's no denying that they helped you, but I can do everything they did for you. And I'm offering to continue to help you. My companies put social consciousness in the forefront. ReSole La Soul? For every pair of shoes we sell, we donate two to people in need. That means we're literally giving away two thirds of our potential profit. Would Victor do that?"

Orion shifted in his seat. He knew the answer but refused to give it voice. "Celina might."

Jacob sighed, making Orion feel even more pitiable. "I'm sure they'd at least attempt to help you find your mother. But how hard would they try? Someone attacked me, and possibly that same someone killed Preston. What are Victor and Celina doing about that now? Did they even say?"

The seat was becoming less and less comfortable, as if it had turned to sandpaper. Victor and Celina hadn't told him what they were doing about it, because he hadn't asked. In all the excitement about finding his mother and taking a journey into Jacob's dreamscape, he had forgotten about the possibility of being hunted... until he saw Calista in Jacob's dream. Stupid. "They went to Chicago to talk to Gen about it."

"How'd that go?"

Orion should have seen that question coming from a mile away, but he had no response other than a shoulder shrug.

"This is exactly what I'm talking about, Orion." Jacob spoke faster, but his demeanor remained sympathetic. "They're not including you in the big decisions. I don't want to use the term 'selfish,' but they haven't been focusing on your amazing ability. Or where you inherited it from. What are they doing to help you learn more about yourself?"

The answer was "nothing," but that was due to him not making much of an effort, until now. He received no help because he never requested it. Don't ask, don't get. When he first received Harold's email, he should have let Victor and Celina know, but he didn't. Sure, he trusted them, but they would have discouraged him. Dismissed the email as a scam. Or gone the complete opposite direction and forbade him from coming to Philly unless they came along and brought Gen and Blaze and Robert and the National Guard. "Ummm...?"

Jacob waved his hand in an unspoken apology. "That came off really harsh. It's obvious that Victor and Celina care about you and that you'd like to go back home to them. I got caught up in my own drama trying to learn about my dad and I thought you were interested in learning more about your dad by doing what he did – traversing the dreamscape."

Orion offered a weak smile. "No, it's okay. You're not wrong. I *do* want to learn more about my dad and the dreamscape and find my mom. I think getting that close to my birth mom has been making me think about my adoptive parents."

Lately, Orion had been missing Conner and Madison. They had lied to him about the circumstances of his life, adopting him because they'd been assigned to him by a mysterious man so powerful that they refused to speak the man's name. God, it made him angry to think they only adopted him because it was their job. But... They had given him a good life, a *great* life, and he missed them.

For his first eighteen years, the longest he had ever been away from them was four days. It had been three months since he last saw them, and the "farewell" came in the form of a go-bag with a fake identity while Madison lay bleeding on the floor. So angry. So sad. Maybe that was what it meant to be an adult – having more than one shitty emotion when thinking about the people he loved. Certainly applied to whenever he thought about Aika.

Not only was Orion an assignment for her too, but she tried to kill him. He should hate her. He should never want to think of her again. But a heavy chunk of rock formed behind his chest every time he thought of her. Sparks tingled behind his nose, cheeks, eyes as he thought about his recent visit to his own dreamscape when he saw her telling him the story of Momotaro. He wanted to go home to Las Vegas so he could go back to his dreamscape in comfort, and spend entire nights there looking at memories of Conner, Madison, and Aika.

But wasn't that what Jacob was asking for? Yes, it was freaky as hell that Jacob's memories contained creepy-ass clowns, but he was searching for something he had forgotten. Wait... "If it was a dream about memories, how were you able to snoop through your dad's closet?"

Jacob looked away and smirked. "I remembered his closet, and that he kept it locked, but he was terrible at hiding the key. I guess I was a precocious child, so one day – when I was seven, I found it and snooped around. After twenty-three years of life with its extreme ups and downs, my *conscious* memory of what was in the closet had dissolved away."

Orion nodded. "That makes sense."

With a sadness in his eyes, Jacob looked down. "Even as a little kid, I wanted to know my dad better, especially after I lost my mom. If it was going to be just me and him, then I wanted to know everything about him. That's why I snooped through his closets, his drawers, his desk, his file cabinets. I combed through every nook and cranny of that house trying to find his secrets, because I wanted to understand him better."

One spin of his fork, two, three, Orion sighed and said, "I'll stay."

"You don't have to. In fact, now I feel bad about making you change your mind."

"It's my mind to change." It sounded more snappish than he wished, but even though Jacob was the same age as Victor and Celina, he never acted like a parent or a role model, never acted like he knew better. He made Orion feel like a peer, and peers ask for help. "We're both on a journey of discovery, right? Learning about ourselves by learning about our parents. Well, it's a long journey and long journeys are better with company, right? Like a spiritual road trip, or something."

Good friends had a secret language. Whole conversations took place in an exchange of facial expressions and shifts in body language to convey complex emotions. Orion had that with Brennan and was now developing that with Jacob. He was appreciative of the offer, Orion could tell.

"Are you sure?" Jacob asked.

"Yep."

"Okay. Well, thank you." He then patted the journal. "This is what I was excited to tell you about. I found it this morning. A *second* journal."

Orion was legitimately excited for Jacob – another sign of friendship. "Yeah? Awesome! What'd you learn?"

"I haven't read it yet. I flipped through it and saw some names, though I don't know who they are. Yet."

"Do you want me to jump in your dreamscape again tonight?"

"Not tonight. Last night was pretty intense, and I won't know what to look for in my memories until I read this journal. Maybe then a name or two will become familiar. Let's take tonight off from the dreamscape. All I'm going to do today is read this journal and figure out what to look for when we hop back inside my head. And this will give you a chance to relax, recenter. Explore the city, or stay in your room, or catch up with Victor and Celina. Let's meet back here at noon tomorrow. What do *you* think?"

Orion nodded, satisfied that Jacob asked for his opinion. "I think this is a good plan."

"Perfect! All right. I'll see you tomorrow." A quick fist bump, and Jacob left.

Orion waved the waitress down to get the bill. A yawn accompanied his exit. A whole day with zero plans. He was going back to the hotel and take a nap.

CHAPTER 30

July 11th, Las Vegas

Victor smiled, her fingers itching to click "send" as she proofread her email. It made all the points she wanted to make, and punctuation was perfect. Satisfied, she released it to the internet superhighway, indulging in a bit of flourish and a loud, "Suck it, bitch!"

Propping her feet on her desk, she interlocked her fingers behind her head and leaned back in her chair. She made a bet with herself about how long it'd take to get a response. Under half an hour, guaranteed. Writing that email made coming into the office today worthwhile. Of course, now she had the rest of the day with nothing to do. She thought about looking for more investment opportunities, but the two biggest companies in her portfolio had been such a pain in her ass lately that she wanted to get them under control before she sought out more pains in the ass. She was frozen with Sugar Fix, Inc. until Bailey brought property options to her. That'd take about three or four days. Head over to Roll and Role and help Celina? *Nah. Not sure if my presence would make her more or less nervous about her date tonight. Wonder when Orion will be back?*

Victor grabbed her phone and sent: Hey kid how's it going?

Before she had a chance to toss it back onto her desk, he replied: Good thanks.

"Such a little shit," she mumbled.

Even though the first number on the clock wasn't double digits yet, she weighed the pros and cons of going to a casino, either at the roulette table or the bar. Or both. Before the "pros" list got too long – the only entry on the "cons" list was "hangover tomorrow" – Bailey entered her office.

Heading with determination to the table he used as an ersatz workspace, he gave her a quick nod. "Good morning, Sir."

Victor sneered. "Eww. Sir? There's a difference between identifying as a man and living life by following men's rules."

Setting his laptop case and attaché on the table, he said, "Sorry. Good morning, Ma'am."

Gagging, Victor dropped her feet to the floor and sat up. "Oh, God, that's worse. No need to be so formal. Victor is perfectly fine. No Victoria, though. And if I hear, 'Vicky,' I will literally throw you out the window and voluntarily turn myself in to the police."

"Somewhere between the heart-melting request of my mother to always be polite and the browbeating demands of my father's toxic masculinity to perpetually respect authority, I physically cannot call you, as my boss, by your first name."

"Wow. That's a lot to unpack. How about, 'Boss?' And only call me that within this building."

Bailey fished through his attaché and pulled out six manila folders. As he examined the contents, he said, "Sure thing, Boss, but I'll need to include standard working hours and work-related functions while outside the office."

Victor rolled her eyes. "Fine."

"Excellent. Good morning, Boss."

Victor grunted.

"So, why 'Victor,' and not 'Victoria?'"

"I learned early in my career as a businesswoman that when you sign emails 'Victoria' they tend to go unanswered. Signing them as 'Victor,' almost all of them get answered, and twice as fast. Victoria gets meetings canceled or postponed, if she even gets them. Victor's meetings are fully attended with the rare cancelation. Then, I took it a step further. Through observation, I noticed that young businesswomen rarely ask for what they deserve, often taking what's offered to them. Men? They barely ask, because they demand. I could give a dissertation, but you get the idea."

Bailey nodded as he organized the folders. He then crossed the office and handed them to Victor. "My boyfriend is constantly suggesting that I be more aggressive."

"I suggest you be you. Play to your strengths, but never inhibit yourself from exploring and learning. What are these?"

Bailey clasped his hands behind his back and said, "What you asked for. Three of them are existing buildings that could be converted into factories. The other three are parcels of land for sale that have potential regarding what we're looking for."

Pictures, descriptions, lists of costs, neighborhood demographics, histories. "Jesus, Bailey. Was your boyfriend okay with you completely ignoring him all night to obsess over this?"

"He's a bit of a dude-bro, but he's willing to do anything he can to help my career. Plus, he's away on a business trip."

"Still… This is friggin' amazing. Well, I know how I'm spending the rest of my—" Victor cut herself short when a funeral dirge played from her phone. Less than ten minutes. *I knew it!*

As Victor swiped to answer the call, Bailey closed her door and stepped to the side.

Dante Plimpton's frowning face inhabited both monitors on her back wall. Walking out from behind her desk, Victor savored the fact that this was the first time she hadn't been greeted by teeth so white they could blind a pilot coming in for a landing. "Oh, hey, Dante. What's up?"

"Cut the shit, Victor!" Dante snapped. Even his beard looked angry, more pointed than usual. "What the fuck did you just send me?"

"To what might you be referring? The video? Or the PDF?" Victor wondered if she could nominate herself for an Emmy with this performance of sugary sweet innocence. She then whisked her fingers through the air as if swiping away her previous questions. "Actually, never mind. Silly me, both files are related to each other. Did you happen to watch the video yet?"

"Of the hookers talking about some tragic event that happened twenty-nine years ago? Yeah. What does that have to do with Corette Remington's birth certificate?"

Victor tapped away at her phone and glanced at Bailey. He arched an eyebrow and cocked his head. After a quick wink, she tapped "send" on her phone and turned her attention back to Dante. "Almost forgot one more PDF.

The one now in your inbox is the waiver form, the one the video magazine made the hookers sign. They had to use their real names for legal purposes, and one of those legal names is Barbara Remington, AKA Babydoll. Babydoll is Corette's mother."

The crevices along Dante's forehead softened, forced away by his widening eyes. Victor crossed her arms. "You know, after your diatribe about family this and family that and family blah blah blah, it got me thinking about how moral and upstanding you must be viewed in the community since it's *very* obvious that you're all about family. I wonder how that community would react over you doing business with the daughter of a hooker?"

Through his thick beard, Dante twisted his lips and squinted. Victor knew that look. It was a, "It'll cause me grief, but I'll get over it" look. She considered it a challenge for her to add something tastier to the pot.

"Well, I'm sure *none* of the people who hold you in high regard would have any prejudice toward a daughter of a hooker, but...," Victor held the word for dramatic pause. "Well, did you happen to catch that the four young ladies were bragging about partying with the man responsible for the Movie-Set Massacre and his alleged accomplice? Now, if you notice Corette's birthdate on her official birth certificate, you'll see that it's verrrrrrry easy to assume that the man responsible for the Movie-Set Massacre and/or his alleged accomplice is her daddy. How about now, Dante? How will your 'family first' friends who hold you in high regard react to you doing business with the daughter of a mass-murderer?"

There it is! Victor saw exactly what she had been hoping for – the sheen of sweat across Dante's forehead with one, two, three beads of perspiration appearing along his hairline. She needed to get to know Bailey better, because she desperately wanted to bet with him which bead of sweat would fall first.

Dante chewed his lips and averted his eyes. "Well... I'm going to have to go back to my family and explain the situation, but it seems like there's a good chance we will not be working with Corette Remington and Munitions Investments after all."

"Fucking right you're not. And Dante?" Victor paused until Dante looked back into the camera. "The really important message to this call is this – I found that out about Corette in a day. One. Day. If I found all this about her so quickly, what do you think I'll find about *you* if I decide to start looking?"

Sweat droplet number one on the far right let go first, rolling quickly over his temple and disappearing into his beard. His cloud of indignant arrogance from the beginning of the call had rained away, leaving puddles of apprehension. That wasn't good enough for Victor as she put on her metaphorical rainboots and stomped. Grasping the six folders that Bailey had given her, she fanned them out in dramatic affect. "Or any of your family members? Are all six of them squeaky clean, Dante?"

If fear were food, Victor wouldn't need to eat for a week, savoring the deliciousness of Dante's shaking. "I… ummm… I am making an executive decision to terminate all communication to Munition Investments after informing them that we will no longer be doing business with Corette Remington."

"Perfect! Now, do me and Bouch & Becker a big favor, will you? Let me do what I do so you and your family can sit back while the money pours in. Got it?"

A few more newly formed sweat beads dropped from his hairline as he nodded vigorously. "Yes. Yes, I got it. I'm going to send some emails now."

Victor's screens went black. She then bowed deeply enough to rival any stage actor while Bailey offered a golf clap. "Nicely done, Boss. The use of props for improvisation was a great touch. I have a lot to learn from you."

Victor liked what Bailey had to offer, proving himself every time she asked something of him. He was smart, driven, and wanted to learn. Yes, he was going to be the new Murphy, but he had a lot to learn. Luckily for him, Victor was a great teacher. *Or a terrible influence. Nah. Great teacher!*

Tossing the folders onto her desk, she headed for her door and gestured for him to follow.

"I thought you said we were going to spend the rest of the day reviewing the properties?" Bailey asked.

"Change of plans. You said you wanted to learn, so the first lesson is to celebrate victories. What kind of strip club do you like?"

"I don't. Although, I find burlesque to be artistically interesting."

"Perfect. I know a place."

"At 10:00a.m.?"

Hand on the door handle, Victor shrugged. "Okay, casinos first, then burlesque. Happiness and fun starting now."

When she opened the door she almost crashed into Marshall Becker, his knuckles primed to knock on her door. "Oh! Victor! You leaving?"

"I am."

"You haven't seen my TeqqCon 2010 mug, have you? I can't seem to find it anywhere."

Victor opened her mouth to say something snarky, but to her surprise, Bailey beat her to the punch and said, "I believe I saw Mr. Bouch with it in the kitchen, Sir."

Becker scowled. Jowls wiggled as he snapped his head toward the direction of the kitchen. "Bouch? That fuckwad has been jealous of my mug for fifteen years now."

After Becker stormed away, Victor said, "Bailey?"

"Yes, Boss."

"Monday, you're getting a raise."

CHAPTER 31

July 11ᵗʰ, Las Vegas

Celina paced her living room. In her heart she had yet to accept it as hers, still having Victor's decoration fingerprints all over it. Though, there was very little decoration to it. The walls were white. *All* the walls in every room of the four-bedroom, two-bathroom apartment were white. Gray flooring – carpet in the living room / dining room area, faux wooden planks in the bedrooms, bathrooms, and kitchen – added no form of life. The closest thing to color was the couch, loveseat, and armchair. They were "cream" at best. Sure, the dining table was a gorgeous black with a bold woodgrain, but the side tables and lamps shimmered silver and glass.

Three pieces of artwork hung on the living room walls. On either side of the wall-mounted television were massive, poster-sized black and white photos – in shiny black frames, of course – of a snarling wolf. Each image was different, but the beast bared its teeth, ready to attack, tear, rend. The opposite wall held the third piece of artwork – a six-by-four-foot photo of a woman's mouth. Symmetrical and stunning, it split into a wicked smile, teeth with a perfection akin to God, lips rimmed in blood. Gums bloody, the crimson dripped over her chin from either corner of her mouth. It was obvious that the blood didn't belong to the subject, rather the victim she had torn into. The mouth was perfect and wicked and bloody because it was Victor's.

A brief stint in modeling after high school had led her to a gig for an anti-cruelness animal campaign. After two hours of dickering with tinted corn syrup and various levels of failure, Victor left the studio, marched across the street to a grocery store, grabbed the juiciest pack of T-Bone she could find, and upon returning to the studio, tore into the raw steak. The photographer and assistants completed the photoshoot in utter silence, and wrote her paycheck with shaking hands. According to her, "No, I didn't eat raw fucking meat. I spat it out. On their floor. I didn't give a shit about my career, or the client. I just needed quick cash for an investment or two. I like this piece because not only is it sexy as hell, but it's a reminder that there is a solution to every problem and sometimes you have to be a little vicious. Now, quit pacing your apartment – yes, *your* apartment – bitching about how colorless it is and get ahold of yourself."

Celina stopped walking in circles and shook her head. Victor had said the last sentence only in Celina's overactive imagination, knowing those would be her words if she were here now. The words she actually used before she left this morning were, "You're amazing. It's obvious he likes you, so just relax and have a good time tonight."

"Yeah, but I've never dated a guy so… so…" Celina had made fists and awkwardly flexed her biceps, striking a poor rendition of a bodybuilder's pose. "… Muscley."

Grabbing ahold of Celina's hands, Victor had said, "Settle down, Ms. Universe. First of all, never do that again and absolutely do not do that on your date tonight. Second of all, why are you so nervous? I know it's been a while since you had a date, but you're more wound up than usual."

Deep inhale, shaky exhale. "There's a lot going on. We had our grand opening. We flew to Philly and then Chicago and back. All of that within a week, which is crazy. Someone may or may not be hunting us and that someone may or may not be someone who may or may not be dead. And I'm *really* nervous about Orion being in Philadelphia."

Victor had put her hands on Celina's cheeks. They were warm, calming. "Yes, it's been a crazy week, and yes, there are a lot of question marks about us being hunted again. After bouncing from city to city, we've determined that Corette is involved with this, whatever the hell 'this' is. I got irons in the fire regarding her, so I'm hoping to take that on soon enough. In the meantime, if it makes you feel better, stay home from work today. That's one of the perks of being the girl-boss bitch owner."

A never-ending source of strength had poured from Victor. Celina drank her fill any chance she got. Feeling better about her choices, Celina took Victor's hands into hers. "I'm going into the café today. We've been open for a month and I feel bad for missing so many days."

That conversation was nine hours ago and Celina desperately needed a few gulps from Victor's unending well of strength. *Get a hold of yourself. It's just one date with a guy you're not entirely sure you like.*

Time check – ten minutes left until date time.

Celina moved her manicotti dinner from the delivery container to a plate and set it on the dining table, then uncorked an Apothic Red, her go-to wine, and poured a reasonable amount in a traditional long-stem. One last soul-cleansing breath, she sat at the table five minutes early and clicked away at her laptop to start the Zoom meeting. She was immediately greeted by Vinnie's ass.

A startled blush warmed her cheeks and she held her breath while assessing the situation. It seemed that his computer was on a table, and it had an unobstructed view into his kitchen, where Vinnie was standing with his back to her. Wearing a blue suit jacket and slacks – *thank God he's wearing pants!* – he opened the oven and pulled out a glass pan. Did he cook his own manicotti? Feelings of inadequacy suggested that Celina close her laptop, toss her dinner in the trash, and curl up under her bed covers

But then he turned around, and squinted at the camera. "Oh, damn! Celina? Sorry, I didn't realize I started the call."

She waved and immediately felt dumb. *What filters can I pull up to hide my sweating?* "Hi! No worries. So… You *cooked* for dinner?"

While plating his manicotti, he said, "Yeah. Did you?"

"Ummm…" She thought about lying, but nixed it. Why bother? "No. I ordered from a place down the street."

A ladle of sauce from a pan on the stove and a sprinkle of shredded cheese from a small bowl on the counter finished his plate. He hurried from the kitchen to the table and sat down. "Oh, cool. Yeah, so… Is it a good place? To eat? Well, I'm guessing it is."

"Yes. It is." Any additional words would send her tumbling along the road of awkwardness, so to stop herself, she took a sip from her glass.

"Good. That's good." Vinnie grabbed a bottle from off camera and filled his glass halfway. When he set the bottle down, Celina almost did a spit take. 2018 Penfolds Quantum bin 98. Nowhere near being an expert in the world of wine, she knew enough to recognize a bottle of wine that teetered on the edge between three and four digits.

"So…" Celina started as she set her glass down, but realized she had no follow-up to that lone word. Obvious questions about where he worked and what he did shriveled up like salted slugs. What did he know about Gen and her band members? He had to know they were giant spiders, right? Was he a giant spider as well, a member of Gen's cluster? No. Blaze had mentioned that he wasn't.

"So…?" Vinnie said after a few seconds of awkward silence, now becoming more so as he held a forkful of steaming manicotti.

"Sorry, it's been a while since I've done a video date. Not since the pandemic."

Vinnie chuckled and rolled his eyes. "God damn, what a fuckin' shit show that fuckin' mess was." He then froze, face stern and eyes wide, the manicotti no closer to his mouth. After clearing his throat and as meekly as his gruff voice would allow, he muttered, "Sorry for the unnecessary sentence enhancements."

Celina chuckled as it finally dawned on her – he was just as nervous as she was. Everything made sense now, from their first awkward conversation to their second awkward interaction to the awkward call about non-existent earrings. Not sure what he could possibly be nervous about, it gave her a strange sense of ease. "Did you forget who my best friend and roommate is? I've fucking heard worse."

Vinnie smiled. It did nothing to soften his face, instead an image of handsomeness was carved into a chunk of marble. *Damn, I'd love to tickle those dimples,* Victor's voice said inside Celina's head. *No, wait… that was my voice!* Celina cut a piece of manicotti with her fork and shoved it into her mouth before it could say anything Victor would say.

After the bite of his dinner finally made it to his mouth, he nodded. "Oh yeah, your best friend slash roommate is something else. My boss certainly does not like her."

"You know a lot about Gen's business dealings?"

A nod followed by a sip of wine. "I do. Not everything, but she shares stuff with me beyond the happenings of Club B-Sides and the band."

Too curious to stop herself, Celina asked, "Do you know about… *what…* she is?"

"You mean the queen of a bunch of giant spider creatures?"

"Umm, yeah, that."

"I do. Like I said, she shares quite a bit with me. She told me about what happened in L.A. a few months ago, and what you did. That's pretty bad-ass by the way, what you did."

Celina slouched, wanting to fold in on herself. Embarrassment burned its way up her neck to her whole face while her insides quivered, reliving the moment when she used a handsaw to cut into the body of a human-sized spider trying to eat her, and the blue slime of its blood had cascaded over her. She set her fork down and used a napkin to dap the corners of her mouth. "Umm, thanks? Are… Are you one as well?"'

"Nope. All human."

"Okay. Good. Not that there's anything wrong with, you know, not being human."

Vinnie called forth his dimples again and shook his head. "It's okay. I know what you mean. From what Gen told me, you're human, too?"

"To the best of my knowledge."

"Good. Again, not that there's anything wrong with not being human."

A blushing smile and Celina went in for a couple more bites. After another drink, she was surprised to find her glass empty. *Nothing calms the nerves like booze*, was her justification as she poured herself another. "So, do you know any other non-human people?"

Vinnie waited to finish chewing before he answered. "No. Well, sort of. Gen found out who's making the drugs. Another cluster of spiders – brown recluse – and the queen is a prostitute named Scarlett."

A million tiny legs scurried down Celina's spine from all the spider-talk. Another bite, another gulp of wine. "Well, that's good news. Now that she knows, what is she going to do?"

"Fuck her over." A pause to clear his throat. "Ah-hem. I mean that she contacted that Corette woman you and Victor told her about. Apparently, she's a kind of miracle worker, because she found something for Gen to use against Scarlett."

"Oh! That sounds... I don't know... Mean?"

Vinnie looked into the camera and said, "Maybe, but it's better than any other alternative. She can't involve the police, without the risk of exposing the cluster. This might shock you, but Venom wants to go to war with them. Gen would if she had to, but what she planned is the least violent option for now."

Police. War. Violent option. The weight of those words pressed down on her shoulders, causing her to slouch. She must have slumped dramatically, because Vinnie put his fork down and folded his hands together, elbows on the table. "Yeah, so, how about no more talk about spiders and drugs and that stuff. How's the new café going for ya?"

Sure, it was a question to change an awkward topic, but he seemed sincere. Celina shared, her enthusiasm growing the longer she talked.

A little gruff, but surprisingly sweet, Vinnie chatted warmly about his parents and his life in rural Minnesota. Gen was a great boss and paid well, giving him all the time he wanted to travel the world, a taste he had grown fond of from his time in the Army. Celina talked about her parents and recounted a few silly stories about her friends, a life far less exciting than his, yet his eyes sparkled with interest when she spoke. And, God, did she like his shirt – a simple white, collared shirt with no tie, the top two buttons undone. However, about halfway through dinner, a third button freed itself from the hole to expose the soft roll of hard muscles, his upper chest flexing anytime he moved. *Oh, I think the wine is doing wine things inside my head. I should call Victor when this date is over.*

Ninety minutes and two bottles of wine between them later, the date ended nicely with plans for a second.

Still using her computer, her screen came alive with Victor's open-mouth laughter accompanied by speakers thumping dance music. Celina wondered if she had slipped from "tipsy" to "super-drunk" when Victor's face changed from blue to green to yellow to red, but realized it was the spinning light in the background from wherever she was.

Victor yelled, "Hey, gorgeous! How was the date?"

"Good," Celina yelled back and giggled at how weird she sounded by herself.

"Can barely hear you, let me move to the back of the bus."

"You're on a bus?"

Victor turned her phone to show Celina a party bus with at least eighteen people. Most of the women wore sparkling gowns and Celina wondered if Victor kidnapped a beauty pageant, though when she brought her face closer to the screen, she swore a few of them might be men. The music was replaced by multiple voices, but when Victor flopped into the empty seat at the back of the bus, Celina could hear her much more clearly. "You said the date was good?"

"It was," Celina replied, no longer yelling. "I thought you texted me that you were doing a team building project with your employee, Bailey?"

"I am!" Victor turned the phone again to show Celina a well-dressed young man sitting between two blondes. "This is Bailey. You having fun, Bailey?"

The man raised the half-full martini glass in his hand. "Very much so, Boss."

Victor's face filled Celina's screen once again. "See? All good."

"That's a hell of a team building party bus."

"Bailey and I started out at a casino and were crushing roulette and then all of a sudden a bachelorette party crossed our path. Well, you know me."

"You tried to have sex with the bride-to-be?"

"Correct! But, to my surprise, she actually likes her fiancé. Anyway, we talked them into attending a drag burlesque show with us. One thing led to another which led to me calling a party bus."

"Of course, it did."

"I'm glad you called! And I'm happy you had a good date with Vinnie. I want details tomorrow."

"Tomorrow?"

"I may have struck out with the bachelorette, but the maid of honor gave me the green light. So did one of the drag queens. Her name is Bi Felicia."

Celina giggled again. All intentions to tell her about Gen contacting Corette dissipated like smoke from a crushed cigarette. It could wait. "Have fun! I'll see you tomorrow."

"Always! Love you!"

"Love you, too."

The screen went black. So did her mood since she couldn't discuss her date. The need to talk to someone made her itchy on the inside. Victor was out for the night. Orion was answering his texts with less than three words. Blaze was not the person to call with two bottles of wine in her. That left only one other person.

Click, click, click of the mouse. Celina tilted her wine glass and looked inside. Still empty. Probably for the better, especially when Robert's face popped up on her screen. "Hi, Celina. What's new?"

"Quite a bit, actually…"

CHAPTER 32

July 12th, Philadelphia

The diner again, for the fourth time. Orion strolled toward the eatery and could hear Madison's voice as if she were walking along next to him. "Son, you have every restaurant imaginable available to you in Philadelphia, yet you come to the same place over and over again. Why?"

He ate breakfast here this morning and was now back for lunch. Dinner last night and breakfast meeting with Jacob yesterday.

Feeling stupid for not having an answer, he pondered the question that his subconscious conjured. Loyalty? If he were truly a loyal person, he'd have shared more with Victor and Celina. Safety? If he wanted to stay safe, he'd have jumped on a plane yesterday. Comfort? Again, if he wanted comfort, he'd be back in his Las Vegas apartment. Laziness? God, he hoped laziness wasn't the answer or else that would call forth Conner's voice spouting off pithy quips about working hard. Stability? Orion pulled up on that one, hand resting on the diner's door handle.

Stability. That was something that had been woefully missing these past few months. Sure, there were plenty of eighteen-year-old kids uprooting themselves and moving halfway across the country, but they usually had a home to go back to. Visit their families. Contact their parents. Use the name they were born with, instead of learning to introduce themselves as "John O. Miller." Every time he started missing his old life and thinking of his adoptive parents as Mom and Dad instead of by their first names, the anger toward using his fake name arose.

"Hi, John," Matilda, the waitress older than his grandmother croaked at him as he walked through the doors.

"Hey," Orion muttered, heading for the back of the diner, the booth he always occupied every visit. Dang – his booth was taken by a man and a woman. Wait... The man was Jacob. Who was the woman?

The urge to turn and flee from a potential trap tingled at the base of his skull. The woman seemed to be somewhere between his age and Jacob's, and he shivered at a curious thought: *Is this a fix-up?* God, he hoped not. She wasn't his type, not that he had a "type." She was heavyset, but that didn't bother him. It was the fact that she looked like an amalgam of every kid who got busted for smoking by the dumpsters behind Orion's school: long greasy hair that was brown at the roots but grew out blonde even though he was confident she didn't dye it that way, an open-mouthed stare and a missing canine, a dullness behind her eyes. And she seemed blurry due to a jaundiced nicotine haze. *This couldn't be a fix-up, could it? Why does she look familiar?*

Keeping his eyes on her, Orion approached the table. "Hey, Jacob."

Smiling, Jacob gestured to the empty booth across the table. "Hey, Orion. So, a lot has happened since we last spoke."

Sliding across the upholstery, Orion said, "I can see that."

"This is Danielle Munch."

"Hi!" she said. When she nodded, she looked like a bird bobbing its head. "I'm like you guys. I'm on the list."

Orion brought his phone to life and pulled up the list. Sure enough, her face and name were there. "How'd you find her?"

With a heavy thump, Jacob repeatedly stabbed the small leather book on the table with his finger. "This. My father's second journal. It's much more detailed than the first and includes names. One of the names was an associate of his, Salvatore Munch."

"My dad," Danielle said, leaning forward as she spoke. "Salvatore was my dad, but he went by Sally. He was a delivery truck driver. Died when I was four, so I don't remember much about him."

"Sorry to hear that," Orion said.

"He was murdered."

Orion was surprised and unnerved by her complete candor. "Oh, wow. Really sorry to hear that."

"We think it was Calista Lindquist who killed him," Jacob said, the glee in his voice unbefitting the words. "And my father."

"Wait, what?"

211

Finger still thump, thump, thumping on the book, Jacob smiled like any cheesy used car salesmen in cheap commercials – impossibly bright, inviting, and ready to promise great deals. "Yep. I read it in here."

"Jacob, if Calista killed your dad, how could he have written it in the journal?"

A gentle elbow to Danielle's arm, then professor Jacob pointed to Orion, his star pupil. "See? I told you he was smart."

"Yep," Danielle confirmed, pigeon-like nodding hard enough to ripple her hair.

A warmth played across Orion's cheeks, never knowing how to accept compliments graciously. Conner and Madison had showered him with so many compliments he never deserved that he had no measuring stick to judge what was real and what was fiction when kind words came his way from someone else. Well, other than his art. He was better than the average artist, this much he knew. Thanking Jacob felt too weird, so he went with the slightly less awkward tactic of saying nothing while looking sheepish, awaiting an answer to his question.

Jacob relaxed into the booth, a more comfortable posture for a longer story. "My father had formed something like a committee dedicated to changing the narrow scope of how his society viewed its members."

Orion recalled Jacob's father putting on makeup. Clown makeup. "By..." Orion wasn't sure if his statement would be correct, but he finished it anyway. "...dressing as a clown?"

"It sounds outlandish, but yes. It was a farcical way to lean into the perceived slight. The thought that since society as a whole viewed others like him as a bunch of clowns, why not be the clown? But then twist it to make it your own. Unironically apply a visage more befitting the perceived expectations. Usurp the power from those who horde it and distribute it accordingly."

Jacob's rapid-fire words missed the target. "Hunh?"

"Your real face," Danielle said, chiming in with a voice heavy from tar and nicotine. "Paint on your own face, make it real."

"Real face? How would that help?"

"By taking something that's meant to be an insult and turning it to a point of pride."

That made sense. Not even a year ago, Lance the high school bully tripped Orion in the hallway between classes at peak population. The fall hurt, but not as bad as the laughter. Before anyone could pull out a phone and hit record, he popped back up and took a deep bow with great flourish. He then proclaimed that he had been practicing that move for months and loudly thanked his lovely assistant, Lance, for his small, but important, role in the routine. Red-faced, Lance moved on while the masses laughed with Orion instead of at him. "Like turning a prank against the person who played the prank on you."

"Exactly!" Jacob said, clapping. "Turning the prank on the prankster. Perfect analogy, Orion."

Orion jolted at the exuberance, but allowed himself a smirk, satisfied that he was understanding Jacob. "So, your dad wanted to prank the prankster. And society was the prankster?"

"Yes. Once upon a time, the term 'nerd' was derogatory, meant to make individuals feel bad about what they enjoyed and who they were. Over time, the term changed because 'nerd culture' swept through society. That's what my dad, Danielle's dad, and others were trying to do."

But... "What happened?"

"Calista Lindquist," Jacob said.

Orion leaned forward, elbows on the table, and whispered. "How was she involved?"

The three of them huddled close together like "the planning scene" from a heist movie. With Danielle staring at him, Jacob lowered his voice and explained. "Back in 2002, I lost my mother. She and my dad were on a camping trip, and she was... Well, let's just say Mother Nature can be cruel. Later that year my dad realized what a shitshow society is, and how he wanted to change it."

"Society treated him like a clown, so he became one," Orion said, making sure he was following along.

"Exactly. My dad's ideas were making so much sense that others joined him in their desire to show their true faces, to change society's perception of them by changing the definition. So, in their mind, a clown is not a person for comic relief. And they wanted others to see them for who they really were. They wore clown makeup, but there's nothing funny about them. They wanted their painted face to display emotion and to represent how they identified themselves. Not as funny clowns, but as real people wearing real faces outside of society's norms."

"Including your dad, right?" Orion asked Danielle.

Gape-mouth smile extending past her missing tooth, she nodded. "Yeah, right. Sally."

"Sally," Jacob repeated. "And others. Then one day, Calista shows up in Philadelphia and starts killing clowns, killing friends of my father."

"Whoa." *Wait. Philadelphia, 2002, clowns.* The puzzle only had three pieces, but it was enough to paint a clear picture in Orion's mind. Something he learned, seen on the internet. Muscles tensing, he pushed himself against the back of the booth. "Wasn't there like a big massacre at the King of Prussia Mall involving clowns back in 2002?"

"My father wasn't there for that. Neither was Danielle's. Yes, it involved clowns, but it was a different group of maniacs. They only wanted to kill people. And Calista was involved with that, too."

Calista. A weird, magic word that simultaneously worked as an answer to every question *and* as a demand for more questions. Orion released his death grip on the edge of the booth's seat but remained wary. He needed more information and assumed that sentiment was etched all over his face, because Jacob changed his tone from informative to accusatory. "She is a hunter. Sometimes she hunts monsters like the maniacs from the mall, but sometimes she is a monster and hunts people simply because they're different. Like my father. Like Danielle's father. Like me and you."

Jaw muscles working, Orion breathed through his nose, loud, hard.

Jacob continued. "A hunter who is cunning and extremely dangerous, willing to do anything, and to cross any line. See, she found my dad and started to date him. Then she set up an ambush for my father and a few of his friends. During that ambush, she killed Danielle's father... At the Monticello Theater."

"Whoa."

"Yeah. That ambush caused the fire. My father and a couple others escaped. He had just enough time to write an entry in his journal about it. Orion, you had asked how he could write in his journal after being killed by Calista. Well, he didn't. That was his last entry, and she was hot on his tail. There's only one logical conclusion."

Sympathy and fear weighed heavily upon Orion's shoulders. He slouched as he mumbled, "She got to him."

"Exactly."

Numb. Stunned. Upset. Empty. If Orion had the capacity to look inside his body, he'd see hollow blackness. He had no feelings whatsoever because he had no idea how he should feel. Even when Jacob finished his thought and said, "Which is why I'd like you to go into my dreams again tonight."

Orion mustered a shaky, "What'd you say?"

Jacob repeated, "I need you to go into my dreams tonight."

"But why? You said you wanted to better understand your dad, and you did that. You found his journals. You found out why he dressed like a clown. You found friends of his. What else are you looking for?"

The tapping started again, Jacob's finger on the leather cover of the journal. Jacob leaned farther toward Orion. "You're right, Orion. You are. But this journal unlocked a memory within me. Right after my father was found dead, my babysitter drove me to a house to meet up with a couple people, to 'keep me safe.' That was the day I went to live with my aunt. The memory that hit me like a freight train? It was Calista's house. I was inside Calista Lindquist's house. I was seven at the time, but I'm confident that someone mentioned an address."

"You want me to help you find the address to a killer's house?"

Orion must have said that louder than he thought, because both Jacob and Danielle looked around the restaurant to see if inquiring eyes had turned their way. Jacob answered, "Yes."

"What the fuck, dude? Why?"

"She's a hunter, right?"

"Yeah."

"What do all hunters have in common?"

Orion was in no mood for this back and forth, this meandering path Jacob had taken. However, the answer came easily. "They keep trophies."

"Exactly!" Jacob's stabbing index finger punctuated his statement. "She might have something of my father's, something of Danielle's father. Something of *your* father's."

A skin-prickling chill passed over Orion, as if a ghost passed through him. "*My* father?"

"I can't say for sure, but it's a possibility, right? Think about it – she hunted and killed my father four or five years before you were born. You know next to nothing about your father. If he is the monster you've been told, doesn't it make sense that Calista would have hunted him?"

Orion had found his mom, literally touched her with his own hands, only to have her taken from him. Other than her name, he had no leads or clues as to where she might be now. Instead of trying to find her, since he lost that opportunity back at the theater, he now had an opportunity to learn about his father. It was a longshot possibility that might lead to nothing, but his heart pushed him forward. It wanted hope. Optimism. Potential. Before his brain could veto, his heart spoke for him. "Okay. Let's do it."

CHAPTER 33

July 13th, Chicago

Gen stood in front of the building that Scarlett and her cluster of brown recluse used as a drug lab. Soon, that activity would come to an end.

"Sure you don't want us to come in with you?" the cop, Officer Delaney, asked. Arms crossed over his chest, he leaned against the driver side door of his cruiser, lights off. His partner, Officer McKeller, waited in a similar pose, half sitting on the trunk.

"We're sure," Gen replied. "We just asked you here in case there's any trouble."

Mouth drawn tight, he gave a slow up-down-up with his eyes. Tone dubious, he asked, "Sure *you* three ain't gonna be the trouble?"

Not upset by his assumption, Gen chuckled. She was wearing only three articles of clothing – midriff baring black leather jacket with fringe along the arms, a thigh-low black leather skirt with silver spikes running down the sides, and black ankle-high wedge boots, fringed and studded – yet achieved a look of maximum aggression. She chose this outfit because it took less than ten seconds to get out of, but Officer Delaney didn't need to know that. Lucas shared a similar logic, wearing nothing under his zipped leather jacket, black jeans, and unlaced army boots. Ven took a different approach with his style. Black jeans and boots, but he wore a black duster, covering a lump on his back. The officers probably assumed it was a growth of some sort and kept their mouths shut about it. "No trouble, Officer. Just want to get rid of the tenants. They're months behind on their rent and I decided to clear out the building. I don't want any trouble from them, so I want to try a soft touch."

Delany grunted but nodded to accept her reasoning. "What are you gonna do with the place?"

Three stories, solid structure, good bones. But Gen actually hadn't thought about what to do with it after today. "Don't know. Maybe fix up the apartments? Convert it to office space?"

"The possibilities are endless," Lucas chimed in, his wickedness in full effect. "Could be a night club. Could be a strip club. Could be a bakery or a cakery. Maybe a chop shop or—"

"If you say, 'donut shop,' we're fuckin' leaving," Delany said.

Lucas cocked his head and looked at the building. "I was gonna say, 'hospital,' but never mind."

His comment was met with an eye roll. "I don't give a shit what you do with it. I'm sure the neighborhood would be happy for the improvement."

Doors shut, curtains still, not a single resident curious about a police car outside the abandoned apartment building. Gen assumed this neighborhood had seen police often enough to become numb to the concept.

"Quit fucking around," Ven grumbled to Lucas. "Let's go."

Clapping his hands and rubbing them together, Lucas all but skipped beside Ven, and they approached the building. "Hell, yeah. Gotta figure out where the nurses' station will go."

Gen nodded to Delaney and followed her bandmates, thinking about firing them for the tenth time this week. It didn't take a psychologist to deduce that they had been acting out lately because she had been allowing Blaze more access to her life. Ven didn't like anyone who wasn't a part of the cluster. Lucas appreciated that she wanted a life beyond the band, the cluster, the businesses, but he got a little squirrely now and then. Maybe because she'd been seeking advice from Blaze? Lucas often filled the role of advisor, sometimes going as far as to handle certain matters of her businesses, like making sure paperwork was in order. Did he feel threatened that she might be fulfilling those needs with Blaze? After all, she turned to Blaze to accompany her for the meeting with Corette, and thanks to that meeting, they were able to do what they were doing right now.

The combination of the smoky glass due to layers of time-added grime, and sheets of yellowing newspapers taped all over the place made it impossible to see through the windows. Good thing, because as soon as she shut the door behind her, Scarlett and two large men stepped out from one of the apartments at the back of the building. Naked.

Gen drifted farther down the hall into the building, Ven a few steps behind her. Lucas stayed by the closed door and removed his clothes. After slipping into his black widow form, he scurried up the wall and sprayed webbing over the stairway hole to the second floor. It wouldn't stop any brown recluse waiting to scuttle through for an ambush, but it'd be a nuisance for the first few. For the others... Well, that was what Ven was for.

Stopping between the empty doorways of the first pair of apartments, he removed his duster and let it fall to the dirt-encrusted floor. With no fanfare, he unclipped a metallic nozzle with a large trigger. He could wield the flamethrower with one hand, but used both hands for more control. A hose ran from the back of the nozzle to a three gallon, cylindrical canister strapped to his back. Should an ambush come from the apartments on either side of the hallway, he'd fry them.

It wasn't a military grade liquid spewing dragon as Gen had assumed, more like a creative DIY alternative that used an aerosol propellant. In short, controlled bursts, Venom could use it without burning down the building. But Scarlett didn't need to know that.

Gen stopped halfway between the first pair of apartments and the second pair. She reached into a pocket inside her jacket and pulled out trifolded papers, and tossed then to Scarlett. Landing at her feet with a smack, an eddy of dust swirled around the papers.

Scarlett's furrowed glare didn't diminish as she picked them up and glanced through them. Gen thought the papers would burst into flame from the fire in Scarlett's eyes. Instead, she tore them up and tossed the confetti over her shoulder.

Unfortunately, she knew where this was going, so Gen unzipped her boots and stepped out of them. A quick shimmy and her skirt was on the ground followed by her jacket. "Doesn't matter. That was just a copy, the originals filed with the city. We all know that real-estate transactions normally take weeks, but I found a miracle worker. Honestly, I'm a little afraid of her considering how easily she did this. But, the deed is real. As of today, this building is mine. You and your cluster have five minutes to get out of here. Before you try anything too crazy, there are a couple of cops out front, so I suggest you all leave out the back."

Nope. Scarlett curdled into a brown recluse and scurried forward. Gen transformed into a black widow and held her ground. Rearing up on her back four legs, she used her middle two for balance and stabbed with her front two. The brown violin shaped spider was smaller, her legs covered with a fine fur. She was faster and more attuned to changes in the air. Harder for Gen to land an attack. However, she had six-eyes instead of eight, and smaller fangs. Though venomous, should she have been the size of a regular brown recluse, she'd struggle to pierce a human's skin with her bite. Even at this size, she'd have a difficult time injecting her poison into Gen, unless she got hold of a leg.

Arching her back where her thorax met her abdomen, Gen jabbed her front legs at Scarlett's head. The brown recluse struck a similar pose, attacking in a similar way. Gen kept her at bay, but Scarlett was angry, the frustration radiating from her. Scarlett leapt forward, focusing on Gen's right side, undoubtedly trying to trap one of her legs. Springing to her left, Gen scuttled up the wall to the ceiling and then dropped onto Scarlett's back, pinning her. She could have pierced Scarlett's exoskeleton with her fangs and pumped her full of venom, but... *God damn it, have I been hanging out with Blaze too much and his weird fucking zen attitude?* Benevolence took over. As a warning, Gen used three of her legs to bend back Scarlett's frontmost right leg and ran her fangs over it, demonstrating that she chose not to kill her. Gen scurried off Scarlett just enough to kick the brown recluse with her back legs, sending the defeated spider sliding down the hallway.

Back in her human form, Gen said, "It's over, Scarlett. You don't want a war with us. We don't want to kill any spiders, but we absolutely will, especially if we see any form of rec or latro on the streets. This is your only warning. And you have four minutes left."

Now human as well, Scarlett held her right arm close to her body, massaging her shoulder with her left hand. Still glaring at Gen, she said to one of the men behind her, "Go tell the others we're leaving."

"You can't be—"

"Go!" she yelled before her subordinate could argue any further.

He slipped into spider form and scurried up the wall and through the opening of the back stairwell to the second floor. Agitated clicks and whistles made their rounds along the second floor. But within a minute, clothing, shoes, large cloth bags, and small suitcases poured through the hole in the ceiling. Scarlett grabbed a few articles from the pile and put them on. One by one, more brown recluse crawled from the hole, changing into human form when they reached the ground.

Under the intense stares from each member of Scarlett's cluster, Gen crossed her arms over her chest and leaned against the wall, watching Scarlett get dressed, hoping to find the answer to the identity of the black widow traitor. One of the men, rivaling Venom in size and stature, focused his laser-beam glare on Gen, and asked Scarlett, "Where are we going?"

Not passing up an opportunity to display dominance, Gen said, "Far away from my fucking city, that's where."

Both the man and Scarlett shot Gen the, "I wasn't talking to you" look of annoyance. Scarlett said to him, "We'll hit the railroad tracks and figure it out from there. And then we'll figure out how to get back at this bitch."

The man grunted, slung one of the cloth sacks over his shoulder, and walked out of the building, never taking his heavy eyes off Gen until the door shut behind him. Others followed, each getting dressed and grabbing a bag of some sort. A few of the men had slack skin and looked like dullards, barely capable of putting on clothes and walking out the door. Simple drones. Gen assumed that one of them had poisoned Chet.

As much as Gen hated to admit it, she appreciated Venom's flamethrower. Only ten in Scarlett's cluster, but they stood more than a small chance of taking out Gen and her bandmates. Did Scarlett have members somewhere else? Doubtful. The look of raw anguish on that babydoll face told Gen that this was her only home. Why so small? Being queen was difficult, but Gen's cluster respected her, and willingly followed her commands. Maybe Scarlett had a hard time keeping everyone in line? Obviously, they had different management styles. Or maybe she shared Gen's similar feelings about being a mother for an entire species? It didn't matter now. Scarlett was the last of her cluster to leave the building.

Lucas skittered from the front of the building to the back along the ceiling and disappeared into the opening. Gen transformed back into her spider form and followed.

Dark, but enough ambient light allowed them to see without aid.

"Holy shit," Lucas said. "This is intense."

"Check the third floor. And be careful of traps," Gen ordered as she scrabbled farther into the second-floor living area.

Lucas did as he was told, leaving Gen to explore the second floor more thoroughly than the last time she was here. Mounds of webbing along the walls and rotting furniture. No personal items of any kind. Nothing of interest. Moving on.

The third floor was worse than the second. More than half the walls were missing, turning six apartments into one large room with unusual angles and alcoves. Thick patches of webbing covered every corner. Tables covered in glass tubes and cups, colorful liquids in them. At the end of the processing line were dozens of plastic bulbs with a pair of tiny needles protruding – the injectable delivery system for the drugs. None of this surprised her.

She wanted to see the raw material.

In the far corner of the room, she found two plastic tubs big enough to hold a couple gallons each. They were a quarter full; one with brown recluse venom, one with black widow venom. *Shit!*

Gen scuttled from one end of the room to the other, along the floor, the walls, the ceiling. There was no evidence that one of her cluster had been a hostage and forced to supply the venom. Neither was there evidence that Scarlett had it shipped in. That meant one of the spiders in Gen's cluster was willingly supplying it. *Shit!*

"Floor's cleared," Lucas said. "Want me and Ven to start taking out the trash?"

"Yes, but let me get rid of the cops first."

Mind racing on how to find her betrayer, Gen went back to the first floor and dressed.

Lucas stopped at the second floor and yelled down to Ven, "Toss the flamethrower up to me."

"No!" Ven yelled. "I don't like you touching my things!"

"Well, then I'm going to shoot *you* with *my* webbing and pull you up."

Ven made a retching noise while he started to unstrap the canister from his back.

Once outside, Gen sauntered toward the cops and smiled, doing her best impression of a soulless soccer mom at a fund-raising bake sale. "Thank you, officers. They offered no resistance and left out the back on their own accord."

"Big guy probably threatened them," Officer Delany said as he and McKeller shoved themselves off their car. As McKeller shut the passenger door, Delany paused, one foot in the car, and glared at the building. "The hell is that?"

Flashes of muted orange flickered behind the papered-up second floor windows. *God damn it, Ven! Can't wait two fucking minutes.* Keeping her expression soft, Gen said, "The other two are taking pictures of the mess."

Delany squinted one last time before grunting apathetically and getting into his cruiser. Gen thought about waving as they drove away but didn't want to give them any excuse to look back. Cracking her knuckles, she turned back to the building ready to bust a couple of skulls, but her phone buzzed with a text from Blaze: Can I come over to your apartment?

CHAPTER 34

July 12th, Philadelphia

Grimacing, Orion accepted the thermos of valerian root tea from Jacob. Just like two nights ago, Jacob met Orion in his hotel room and brought the nasty tasting concoction to help with sleep. Not a fan of water run through dried up yard waste, Orion chugged the entirety of the container to get the displeasure over with. "Ugh. Yuck." He then set the container on the nightstand next to his bed.

"Maybe I'll add milk to it next time," Jacob said with a chuckle, then plopped on the neighboring bed.

Orion snarled at the thought. "Adding milk to a pile of dead leaves? Worse cereal idea ever. No thanks. But... Thank you for telling Danielle not to join us."

"Trust me, it would have been uncomfortable for everyone if she was here right now. I just met her yesterday."

"So, you found her because your dad mentioned her dad's full name in his journal?"

"Yeah, they had the same last names. More than that, from his description, she gets her looks from her dad."

"Your dad went into that much detail?"

"Down to the face paint color schemes – their true faces as he called it."

"Whoa."

Jacob finished his tea and turned off the light over his bed, the sole source now leaving the room shockingly black. "Yeah. Some of them had really wild looks. Danielle's father, Sally, was bald and painted his entire head yellow, and had a straight black line over his mouth. Red circles over his eyes, the color dripping from the bottom."

"Wow. Like blood?"

"I guess? The craziest one was a dude named Delvin. White face paint and red around his mouth. The guy had blue hair and blue 'x's over his eyes.

224

What made it wild was he used cigarettes to burn the 'x's over his eyes and used fishhooks to hold his smile in place."

Orion wanted to jump out of bed, flip on the lights, and throw back an energy drink so that Jacob's words weren't the last thing he heard before falling asleep.

But he was already asleep – he was now walking down a suburban street with small houses on each side, cars in driveways. Jacob's neighborhood.

Jacob's boyhood home was at the end of a long block. Orion picked up his pace. The sky's creepy blue hue gave everything an ominous tint. The pavement. The sidewalks. The streetlights. The bushes. The bushes that rustled. Wait…

Across the street, a set of overgrown, ragged bushes shook as if something were moving through them. Something bigger than a person. The shaking stopped. Then they parted in the middle like curtains to reveal pointed teeth, framed by crimson red lips held into a permanent smile by fishhooks.

Orion started to jog, silently cursing Jacob for talking about creepy clowns right before falling asleep. *Why would he do that? Wait. If the clown with the fishhook smile is here, does that mean…?*

The door of an upcoming house creaked open. Five yellow snakes slithered out of the house, the tips curled around the door frame. No, not snakes – there were no heads. Worms? No. Bigger. Five more, each thicker than Orion's arms, each with a nail and knuckles. They wriggled from the darkness along the outside wall. Fingers. They were fingers attached to massive hands reaching out from the doorway. As Orion sprinted past the house, a face emerged from the threshold – bloated and the same shade of sickly yellow as the hands and fingers. Blood red circles over his eyes, a streak of pitch black across thick lips. Danielle's father, Sally.

Orion's legs never churned so fast in his life to Jacob's house, focusing on his footfalls so he didn't trip. So fast, he smacked his nose as he slammed into the door. A high-pitched cackle split the air as his sweaty hands slipped from the doorknob. *Please, God, just open!*

As if God was listening, the knob turned.

Feet still in run-mode, he threw the door open, fumbled inside, and slammed his body against the door to shut it. Panting, he tensed, expecting the monstrous clowns to crash against it. The cackling had stopped, but no way was he going back outside.

Got to find Jacob.

He gulped down air while on the landing, assessing his two options: downstairs into the creepy basement where a clown had attacked him during his last venture, or upstairs to where he had found Jacob the last time. Simple choice.

As he hurried up the stairs, he heard voices. Muffled. Electronic as if from a television. A light flickered along the walls of the living room. At the top of the stairs, Orion turned right and crept into the room. Sure enough, Jacob was sitting on a couch watching television, but Orion couldn't see what from this angle. Too pissed to care what was on, Orion rushed closer to the couch. Fuming, he wiped sweat from his face and dried his shaking hands on his pants. "Dude! What the hell? I'm being chased by Danielle's father and that other clown you talked about – Delvin. The fishhook weirdo named Delvin – and you're in here watching TV?"

Jacob didn't react, the light from the television playing over his face as he sat, relaxed and grinning.

"What's so important on the...?" Orion jolted back a few steps when he looked at the television. Calista Lindquist was storming across the screen, guns in hands. "Jacob? What's happening?"

Waving the remote like a stage magician's wand, Jacob turned off the television. "I haven't been simply watching TV for entertainment, I've been researching my memories. See, I knew what I was looking for wouldn't be found in my father's closet or in one of his filing cabinets. What I'm looking for isn't subliminal information that I happened to see but never consciously registered. It's something I overheard during an event I lived through."

Rising from the couch like a corpse reborn as a vampire – stronger, rejuvenated, powerful, singular of purpose – Jacob turned to Orion, shadows covering his eyes. Orion took a couple of steps backward, backing into the banister that separated the living room from the stairwell. This was still Jacob, still the man who helped Orion search an abandoned theater for his mother, the man who believed in Orion, the man who asked for Orion's help. Wasn't it?

Orion didn't like the way Jacob clasped his hands together behind his back, a clichéd move from someone ready to launch into a monologue. "I was struggling to think of a way to access my memory of being in Calista's house. I was there only once. But during one of the many discussions you and I had, you said that in your dreamscape you watched childhood memories play out like movies. That gave me the idea to use the television here to play back my memories. Well, it worked, so thank you for that. Calista's mom, of all people, mentioned the address to my aunt, so I got what I came for."

"Umm… You're welcome?" The air chilled, carrying ambient noises of movement. The hallway darkness quivered. Shapes approached the patio doors from outside. A feeling, a primal one that came from a hundred thousand years of evolution, told Orion to identify escape routes. The only one available, and easily accessible, was the front door via the small landing. "Can we leave now?"

"No. Well… I can leave, but…"

The implication punched Orion in the gut. When he was four-years old, shortly after starting preschool, one of his classmates promised him a Pokémon Poké Ball for the low price of five dollars. That night Orion stole a five-dollar bill from his father's wallet. The next day, he brought his newly purchased, oddly shaped Poké Ball home. Discovering that it was simply a raw egg painted to look like a Poké Ball created quite a mess in his bedroom, followed by a tear-filled admission to his parents that he had stolen money from them. He wasn't upset that he had been swindled, because kids can be cruel. They lie and these things happen. The fact that he was stupid enough to fall for it elicited nausea-inducing disgust with himself. Just like how he felt right now.

Sour impending vomit painted the back of his throat as, to no avail, he tried to leave the dreamscape. *Wake up. Wake up, wake up, wake up!*

"Are you trying to wake up?" Jacob chuckled. "I guess I need to spell it out for you since you didn't catch the hint. I added a little something extra to your tea that will keep you under for a while. Well, after my father and his two friends get you, I think you'll be under permanently."

Fingers like chalk-white spider legs curled around the corner of the hallway wall. Then a head peeked from the darkness with crimson rimmed teeth, like rows of dripping spikes, leading the way.

Breathing heavier, Orion stood frozen as Jacob's father, Collin – somehow now two or three times the size of a normal person – inched his way out from the cramped hallway. Then the squeal of unoiled metal pulled Orion's attention to the dining room. The patio doors slid open, and two more faces as big as the doorway poked through. Blood flowed from the eyes of the round yellow face with a black streak over his mouth, like a sociopath emoji. Greasy blue hair framed the other clown's milk white face. With burled skin and blue "X's for eyes, his scarlet smile was held into place by dozens of fishhooks. Giant barbs of curved metal substituted his teeth. Sally and Delvin were trying to squeeze their way into the house. "How... How did you make these clowns?"

"Me? Oh, not me, Orion. I don't have the power to conjure in the dreamscape. These are creations from *your* mind, *your* subconscious."

Now he knew why Jacob described the two clowns struggling to enter the house in detail right before sleep took hold. "Why are you trying to kill me?"

"You just don't seem that into being who you're meant to be. You speak of your father as if he were some kind of villain, as if he's not a part of you. You know nothing about him, not even his name, yet you're trying to deny the *legacy* he left for you. And then when you started to put together that my father might have been a part of the Mall Massacre of 2002, you were *disgusted*. When *Danielle* figured it out, she was *excited*."

"She figured it out just after meeting you?"

As soon as the words left his mouth, Orion realized that he wasn't done being stupid yet.

Jacob stuck out his bottom lip in mock pity. "Oh, Orion. You really should be smarter than this. Yeah, she and I have known each other for a while now."

Jacob's father, Collin, edged farther from the hallway, his fingers pulling him along. More than twice as tall as Orion, his legs were bent at uncomfortable angles. Everything between Orion's chest and hips turned to jelly. "You played me, didn't you?"

Jacob laughed, a rich full sound of amusement. "I get it now, why bad guys spill their plans. It's actually a rush, such a joy to gloat. Yes, I played you masterfully, especially making you and your idiot friends believe Calista was still alive. Now that I told you everything, I'm going to leave you with my father and his friends. I'm sure in the real world it will look like you had a heart attack or aneurism or stroke or something along those lines. You're going to die in my dreamscape, which, I guess, is in my brain, right? I don't have the ability to consciously bring myself back here, but I hope to come back and see if your corpse will still be here or not. Maybe I'll get an EEG in the real world to see if there's an Orion shaped blotch in my brain. Well, whatever."

Jacob wiggled his fingers as a goodbye to Orion, and faded away. Once he disappeared, the clowns sprung like tightly coiled springs. Sally and Delvin crashed into the house through the dining room, but Jacob's father was faster, pouncing from the hallway with streamers of cobwebs and swirls of dust behind him.

Left with no other choice, Orion planted his hands on the banister and swung his feet over. Action stars made similar leaps look easy, but when Orion tried it, his hands refused to let go. Toes cracked against the stairwell's wall; forehead banged against the banister. It hurt like Hell, but he fought back tears. Crying would do no good, only hinder his vision.

Having missed his target, Collin crept on his hands and knees toward the banister, toward Orion, and opened his mouth to expose his horrible teeth. Delvin scurried from the dining room, toppling the table and chairs as he raced toward the stairs, Sally close behind.

Orion's hand finally released the banister, and he dropped to the foyer. He hit the floor with an explosion in his left ankle and a blast from his right shoulder, but he pushed past the internal fire of pain and grabbed the doorknob. Door open, he flopped out, and whipped the door closed. A house rattling thump from at least one body slamming into the door as Orion limped away.

"Work, fucking work!" Orion screamed at his ankle as he pushed it to carry him away from the house. It didn't seem to be broken and the flexibility improved with every step. But where to run? Hiding wasn't a feasible option, especially since he didn't know this neighborhood, the houses, the landscapes, the cars. Wait… Car!

Parked right at the curb and unlocked, Orion jumped into the driver's seat. The keys were in the ignition and he thanked God that his subconscious exerted itself in a positive way for the first time in this damn dream. As he turned the key, he glanced in the rearview mirror just in time to see Jacob's house door blow off the hinges hard enough to splinter against the house across the street. Collin lumbered out first, quickly followed by Delvin, then Sally.

Throwing the car into drive, Orion hit the gas pedal. Tires spun on the pavement fast enough to draw smoke, and Collin's long fingers filled the rearview mirror. Just as the fingertips touched the car, the tires gained traction and propelled Orion away, pinning him against the seat. A sigh of relief was his only respite, a new thought conscripting his emotions: *Now where?*

CHAPTER 35

July 13th, Chicago

Slouching back in the booth of *Los Muertos que Bailan*, Blaze's leg jackhammered away. *Why am I so damn nervous?*

He wanted to call Jerry. *That would do no good*, he reminded himself. Nothing but snark and sarcasm, Jerry was not a sympathetic ear.

Gen was busy kicking a group of drug making half-human spider creatures out of her newly purchased building – a concept he never thought about before in his life.

Celina? Nah, she wouldn't understand and then Victor would jump down his throat to scratch whatever abusive itch she had.

Stop it. It's just a meeting, he scolded himself as he sat up and leaned his elbows on the table, hand on the recently delivered bottle of beer. *Just meeting with a woman who could be my half-sister.* Who wouldn't be nervous?

His leg started to jackhammer again.

He had few friends and fewer family. Being raised by a single mom who was a part-time this-and-that in between being a part-time prostitute so she could afford a shitty apartment in the low-rent area of Los Angeles didn't give him many opportunities to make connections, especially when most people were only looking out for themselves and/or actively looking to take advantage of others. He just knew that he needed to meet with Corette to discuss the video starring their moms as hookers. She was still in town and was familiar with this restaurant, so Blaze suggested it. Jaded by the lessons that life had taught him, he started to plan for what to do when she inevitably stood him up, and then his mind went to static white noise when she walked in.

He wanted to be a gentleman and stand, but thought that was too weird, so he sat in a strange limbo of body positioning, partially turned and tense. Of course, Corette was singularly focused, and paid no mind to the stupid way he sat.

She slid into the booth across the table from him. "Hello."

As slyly as possible, Blaze brought his legs back under the table and *smiled*. "Hey. Thanks for meeting with me."

"There's no need to do that," she said.

The world around him rippled as if he had stood up after downing six shots of hooch. Did this weird feeling come over him because of her voice? Was this what Victor had been talking about? A quick headshake to right everything, he asked, "Do what?"

"Try to use your smile to influence me. If you don't try to influence me, I won't influence you."

Blaze smiled again, this time small, socially pleasant. "Fair enough."

"Your email didn't state the nature of this meeting."

This was it. The moment of truth, where she throws Blaze's beer bottle at him and storms away. But how to phrase questions about what he saw? How the hell to explain to her what he had seen? "Ummm... Well, I have a... let's call him a friend. See, this friend has a unique ability to find anything, and I mean anything. He... ummm... He found something..."

Corette sighed. "He found an old clip from a defunct video magazine where a representative of that magazine interviewed four hookers about the Move Set Massacre of 1996, one of whom is my mother. And one of whom is your mother. You watched the video, probably more than once, and you have questions."

Blaze lost his smile. Jaw muscles tightening, he growled. "Yes, starting with, 'How the fuck did you know that?'"

"Why do you think the video was so easy to find?"

Never knowing how Jerry worked his magic, Blaze hadn't thought to ask how easy or difficult the information was to procure. "You knew about the video?"

"Obviously."

"Why did you make it so easy to find?"

"So, you'd get it and watch it, and learn that we are half-siblings."

Frowning as a headache punched him right between his eyes, Blaze ground his elbows against the table. "Why not come to me? Why the elaborate ruse?"

Face as expressionless as a porcelain doll's, mirth laced her words. "When you con someone, do you tell them the conclusion you want drawn? You lead the horse, you don't make it drink, right?"

The hairs along the back of his neck stood at attention. "That's when I'm manipulating someone. What are you trying to manipulate me into doing?"

"Find the truth."

"Okay, this ought to be good. After going through all that trouble to have me find the video, what truth do you want me to find?"

"About our father."

"So you believe that we have the same father?"

"Don't you?"

Stiff posture, blank expression. Her even tone infuriated Blaze. He wasn't sure if she was playing with him or if this was who she was – rigid, impassive. To be as successful as she was in business, she had to master those skills. Or she could just do that voice trick of hers.

"I know nothing about the man who the hookers were talking about," Blaze said.

"His name was Silas, and he was a part of the movie massacre that took place in New Mexico almost three decades ago. A man named Johnny Ghastson claimed responsibility for the murders, along with a dozen unrelated killings, and has been in prison ever since."

At least she was providing information. "And this makes you think we're half siblings?"

"That gives dimension to the situation," she said. "You and I were born a week apart. Sure, our mothers were prostitutes, and any one of their other clients could be your father or mine. But after we met, we felt something, like we were special to each other."

Blaze shrugged. "I also felt something when I first met Gen and Victor and Celina. I'm sure you did, too."

"I did, but I think ours was a deeper connection."

Blaze smirked. "Was it?"

His comment elicited a slight frown. Corette cocked her head and said, "Don't play coy."

The command hit Blaze, heavy and sticky inside his head. Well, if he hadn't believed Victor about Corette's mood-altering voice, he did now. *If she wants honesty, she'll get honesty. Time to show her what I can really do with a smile.* He leaned forward, eyes widened to intensify his power, bringing on the smile of someone who enjoyed playing with animal carcasses. Corette gasped and sat back, averting her eyes like a scolded child.

"Okay, now that we're done with our pissing contest," Blaze said, "I can believe you and I are siblings – the thing you do with your voice, how I make people feel with my smile. But I need to know what truth you want me to find about our father."

A quick adjustment to her suit jacket followed by aggressive swipes over wrinkles that didn't exist, Corette grabbed her cell phone and tapped away. "I have reason to believe that Calista Lindquist has something that belongs to our father."

"I think you know my next few questions are gonna start with words like what and how and why."

She placed her phone face down on the table, and then folded her hands next to it.

The restaurant door opened, and a man walked in, heading toward their booth. Moderate height and build, brown hair simply styled, golf shirt and jeans, he'd be completely forgettable if not for his smile. Blaze was somewhat of an expert on smiles and the one this guy had bordered between enthusiasm and psychosis.

Sliding into the booth beside Corette, he said, "Hi, Blaze. My name is Jacob McGovern."

Blaze frowned. Anytime he met someone new, he'd usher them down the path of diplomacy, discover their value and what they could offer. Not this guy, though. He didn't like the way Jacob looked at him. Uneasiness stirred within Blaze; it was like walking through a serial killer museum with the eyes in every portrait watching. "Name sounds familiar, but I'm not sure I like you looking at me like we're old classmates."

Jacob shifted in his seat and gestured with an implied apology. "Sorry. You're right. Please let me back up. I'm one of the faces on Calista's hitlist. I recently met friends of yours… or associates? Celina, Victor, Orion, and Robert."

Okay, that answered a couple questions. "Yeah. I remember your name now. You got attacked by Calista, right?"

Jacob and Corette exchanged glances. "Well… Not exactly."

"Not exactly?"

"I wanted to get everyone's attention, so I staged a scene."

"With Corette?"

"With an associate of ours."

"Did this associate kill Preston?"

Jacob shifted in his seat and rolled his shoulders.

For the first time since meeting her, Corette seemed tense, and studied her folded hands.

Jacob cleared his throat. "No. Preston's death had nothing to do with us. The cops said it was a break in gone wrong. I'm not proud to say this, but it helped the narrative Corette and I were trying to create, so we rolled with it."

Blaze chugged the rest of his beer and slammed the empty bottle on the table. He slid to the edge of the booth. "I don't know what kind of scam you're pulling, but I'm not gonna be a part of it. I'm outta here."

The look of confidence fell from Jacob's face as he reached for Blaze, but he then suddenly pulled his hand away.

Corette practically leapt across the table and squeezed Blaze's forearm. "Please wait."

The way she said, "please," touched him. Not in the weird way that made him uneasy. Not in the cold, almost robotic way she presented herself. Not in the nasty way that Victor had described her. But the way one person tried to connect to another person, like when a sibling needed help and no one else could understand. Grinding his teeth, Blaze could almost see complex formulas floating in front of him as he tried to calculate the potential angles these two might be playing. *Fuck it, I'm not good at math,* and he slid back in the booth. Wearing a "How can I get you into the car today?" used car salesman smile, Blaze said, "I'm listening, but the first sign of bullshit and I'm outta here."

"Fair enough," Jacob said.

But Blaze refused to look at him. He kept his attention on Corette. She released his arm and sat back, but there were enough cracks in her armor for him to glimpse the person hiding within.

She said, "I'm sure you realize our father was a monster. No doubt in my mind that he was involved with the movie massacre. I understand that Johnny Ghastson took credit for the murders, and there are crackpot theories swimming around the internet, easy enough to find. But… I feel it, Blaze." Hand over her heart, she tapped. Then made a fist, her blouse crumpling within angry fingers. Voice cracking, she repeated, "I *feel* it, Blaze. Do… do you know what I mean? *Really* feel it?"

Every word she spoke made Blaze's mouth dryer and dryer. Licking his lips, he nodded.

The tightness in Corette's face relaxed as she looked to Jacob and said, "It should be no surprise that Jacob's father… Well, he, too, did things that this society frowns upon."

So did Celina's father. And Orion's. Gen's species was one that gave many people nightmares. It made sense that Jacob was on Calista's hitlist. "Then what was the purpose of the over-the-top performance? You could have just approached us."

"You know that's not true," Jacob said, his words drowning in desperation. "Celina and Victor are focused on the café. Orion is too, along with his artwork. Robert has his gallery in Philly. Gen has her band and cluster, and you're focused on helping her. Corette and I needed to figure out who was interested in learning more about our parents. Learning who they were and their motivations."

"And getting everyone wound up was your best idea?"

With an expression of a kicked puppy, Jacob shrugged. "It worked, didn't it? I mean you're interested, right?"

Blaze turned to Corette. "What's this got to do with Calista having something of our father's?"

"Calista is a monster hunter. All hunters keep trophies."

"She hunted our father?"

"I think so. An actress named Brenda Haddon was supposed to be in the movie being filmed, but left when the killings first started. She's the mother of Dakota Haddon, Calista Lindquist's best friend when they were younger. There's a link there."

It was flimsy, but it was a link. "Okay, so even if Calista was the one who killed our father and kept something from him as a trophy, now what?"

"We get it back," Jacob said. "We get back everything that belongs to us."

"What belongs to us? Do you even know what 'trophies' Calista kept? What – in theory – she has that belonged to our fathers?"

"It could be anything from an invaluable piece of jewelry to something like a family photo. I'm looking for anything to bring me closer to my dad."

Blaze could guess the answer, but he asked Corette anyway, "And you?"

"I hardly believe our father had anything sentimental, but there could be a piece of evidence of his existence. Maybe something explaining why Johnny Ghastson took the blame for the massacre. There might not be anything, but this is the best lead we have to finding out who our father is."

"I'm assuming you know where to find these trophies?"

"I *just* recently found out that her house is in New York, which is why we haven't approached you until now. Even if there aren't trophies there, if she hunted our fathers, then she'll have files on them."

"You said, 'we.' You, Corette, and who else?"

"Another woman named Danielle. You, and anyone else you think would be willing to join us."

Blaze chuckled. "I haven't said I was joining you."

Corette placed her hand over Blaze's. "Please."

It was stupid. It was a bad idea. It was chasing a fairy tale. But if there was even the slightest chance of learning about his father, learning more about himself, he had to take it. "Fine. I'll come with you."

The maniacal smile returned to Jacob's face, and Blaze thought about changing his mind, but then he glanced at Corette. Her features fell from the tight pulls of worry to the soft landing of relief. She tapped away at her phone, and less than a second later Blaze's buzzed. An address.

"Meet us there in three hours," Corette said. "We'll take Jacob's private jet."

"Three hours," Blaze repeated as Jacob and Corette slid from the booth.

"Thank you," Corette said as they left.

Private Jet. *Well, at least I'm being stupid in style.* Before he left the restaurant, he sent Gen a text: Can I come over to your apartment?

CHAPTER 36

July 12th, the dreamscape

Using the entire length of his forearm, Orion wiped his nose. He then wicked away the tears blurring his vision and slapped his hand back onto the steering wheel, ready for any sudden change in the road. Right now, it was straight and obstruction-free, a paved cut through the skin of a barren desert. It didn't feel like a desert, though, since the temperature was perfect; the sweat pouring off him was from fear and panic.

The dull blue hue overlaying everything persisted, and the dried dirt landscape on either side of the road held no form of life. All that could change, at any instant. He needed to get out of here. But... how?

He didn't know how to make things work in his favor. If he was still in Jacob's dreamscape and Jacob was awake, then would this be the entirety of the world Orion found himself stranded in? Like a subconscious screensaver? If that were true, then he'd be driving along until Jacob fell asleep again. But maybe not? Jacob needed Orion's help to get to his childhood home in a neighborhood he was familiar with, something he couldn't have done on his own. Could Jacob appear here through his own power, in this desert? No, Jacob had said he couldn't. So, was Orion destined to drive through these desolate lands until he woke up? Or until the clowns ate him. Or could he change that?

Orion had little control in the dreamscape, and what he could control was only in *his* dreamscape, not someone else's. He had only been in two other people's dreamscapes before – Lance's and Brennan's – and he witnessed Bigby brutally slaughter each of them.

The only way to control anything in his dreamscape was to concentrate, and there was no way in Hell he was going to stop the car and meditate while three mutant clown monsters chased him, despite not seeing any sign of them in his mirrors. This was a dream, so they could be *anywhere*. No, he needed the comfort of his own dreamscape. How could he get there?

He was asleep and dreaming. Yes, he was in Jacob's dreamscape, and, no, he didn't understand the science or magic or whatever behind the how's and why's, but his father was able to jump from one dreamscape to another. Heck, he recently learned that his mother could do it, too. It was possible, and Orion was going to do it.

First step, how? *Think. How to get from one dreamscape to another? How do I* – Orion laughed at himself. Here he was, speeding down a highway in a car while wondering how to travel. He might as well be driving a Ford Metaphor.

Next step, concentrate on home.

Struggling to remember his apartment's address in Vegas, or even the wall color, he realized Vegas wasn't his home. Fredrick, Maryland was where he had lived for all but three months of his life. Yes, that was home. His house. But where to start, which road to take?

The image brought to mind was Downtown from the south. Approaching Carrol Creek, he passed by the homes and businesses tucked into two-story rows lining each side of the street. There was a beautiful wide walkway along the creek, paved with red brick, and a walking bridge that took pedestrians from one set of store fronts to the other. Clean. Well maintained. Orion took for granted how nice it was because he was too young to appreciate the efforts and aesthetics of civil engineering. Until he saw it on the horizon.

Finally, he recognized the buildings that lined the edges of the road, turning the desert into a town. The blank highway transformed into Market Street. Orion laughed as he neared the bridge that crossed Carrol Creek, taking him downtown. The buildings were gray. With no people or other cars, it looked like a desolate post-apocalyptic landscape, but a warmth bloomed within his chest. This was his dreamscape. He made it into his dreamscape and within one block, he'd cross the bridge into downtown and be away from those fucking clowns!

As soon as the tires touched the bridge into Downtown Fredrick, his plan went sideways.

Like the tentacles of a kraken, Sally's plump, squirming fingers blasted up from Carroll Creek on either side of the bridge and reached for Orion.

Orion tromped the accelerator and shot into town, fighting the steering wheel to keep from swerving out of control. Thankfully, no cars were parked along the abandoned streets.

Don't cry, don't cry! He couldn't afford to have tears blurring his vision.

Less than a block into Downtown, a sparkle of light from the roof of a square building on the corner of Market and Patrick caught his eye. The blue haired Delvin, the sunlight glinting off his fishhook smile, jumped from the roof. As tall as the surrounding two-story buildings, the clown didn't jump far, his feet shaking the road and cacking divots into the pavement.

Orion painted the road with a layer of tire as he made a squealing right onto Patrick Street. He only made it past a few store fronts before he smashed both feet against the brake pedal. A rubber burning fishtail, the stench pervasive and immediate, but he came to a complete stop before he ran into Jacob's father, Collin.

Like Delvin, Collin stood over twenty feet tall. Milk white skin draped over a skeletal frame like wet curtains. A distorted skull, long with a protruding jaw of spiked teeth, sported two flaps of blood red lips, blue circles around bulbous eyes. The clown's laughter, like warbling banshees echoing off the concrete canyon walls, penetrated Orion's bones. The creature lumbered forward, and bent down to view Orion through the passenger side window, its talon-like fingernails screeching across the car's roof.

Unable to take his eyes off the maniacal face, Orion fumbled blindly for the door handle. A click from the opening door, and he spilled out of the car, rolling onto the pavement.

Run!

An alleyway was up ahead. Less restrictive than any of the unfamiliar buildings around him, Orion forced his wobbly legs to carry him down the alley. It led to the back of Winchester Hall, the government building, and opened to a small parking area before curving left.

Wheezing, he followed the curve, but stopped in the middle of the parking area. The yellow clown, Sally. A twenty-foot-tall wall of undulation, the behemoth oozed its way toward Orion, tentacle fingers wriggling along the side of the buildings. Gleaming sheets of saliva cascaded over black-streaked swollen lips, spraying whenever he laughed with the sound of repeated cannon fire.

Orion backed away and turned toward the Winchester building, but Delvin crept around the side of it. Back the way he came was no longer an option either – Collin lurched closer, his fingernails gouging ruts into the sides of the buildings.

Don't cry! Don't cry! Impotent words with no meaning, tears gushed over his cheeks as he backed away from the encroaching clowns. The morbid sense of futility told him it was a blessing – his tears would blur the visual of his impending, eviscerating doom.

Orion pressed himself against a building. Rough and cold, the stone scraped his back as he dropped to the ground, his body wracking with sobs. There was nothing he could do other than wait for his imminent death. The clowns shuffled closer, their smiles growing bigger. They were in no hurry, Orion had nowhere to go, no one to help him. His abandonment was his own fault, he had failed to ask for help when he had the chance.

Should've told Celina and Victor what was going on.

Those women were brave. He needed brave friends but had none here where he needed them. No Victor. No Celina. No Aika and her stories of Momotaro.

Wait… Aika had told him that *he* was Momotaro. And *he* had friends! If Orion was Momotaro, then he had friends to help him!

I'm Momotaro. I'm Momotaro, Orion repeated, faster and faster, fists clenching tighter while he furrowed his brow past the point of headache.

The clowns didn't waiver while marching forward.

I'm Momotaro. I'm Momotaro.

Converging in the center of the parking lot, shoulder to shoulder, the clowns advanced.

I'm Momotaro. I'm Momotaro.

The stench of rotten cheese and burnt hair assaulted Orion as ligaments in his neck flared. He ground his teeth.

I'm Momotaro. I'm Momotaro.

Nightmare faces inched closer as six hands reached for him.

This is my dream! This is my world! And I'm Momo-fucking-taro!

The building behind Orion vibrated against his back, rumbling. The three clowns pulled up, then backed away. Orion scrambled to his feet, looking over his shoulder. Uneven chunks of broken stone fell from the top of the building as something inside pounded against the roof. The pounding intensified and more jagged debris crumbled to the ground. Orion, hyper aware of standing within reach of the monstrous jesters, heard and felt one more bone rattling slam, and then three heads poked free.

A dog.

A pheasant.

A monkey.

"Yes!" Orion shouted as he punched the air and jumped. "Fuck yeah! Fuck up those clowns!"

The building tumbled around the three newcomers, bricks falling from them like discarded clothing. All three humanoid creatures stepped forward, curling their anthropomorphized hands into fists. Muscles rippled along their arms, chests, back. The pheasant ruffled its feathers while the monkey curled its long tail into a tight coil. The upper lip of the dog's muzzle rippled as it growled, exposing glistening teeth. Orion's friends took another step forward.

Yes! Orion fought through fear and abandonment to tap into his strength, his power. Rescue came in the form of self-sufficiency, a rewarding crop seldom reaped over the past eighteen years. Now, he was going to savor every bite of this delicious ambrosia.

His friends – the ones *he* created in *his* dreamscape – attacked.

But…

Monkey charged at Sally, yet the clown didn't budge. The python fingers of his left hand wrapped around Monkey's torso, pinning his arms to his sides. Monkey screeched and kicked. Sally palmed the top of Monkey's head and twisted. A snap and Monkey's head now faced the wrong way, its simian features going slack. Glossy eyes bulged from its head and then popped out with a slorp as Sally crushed Monkey's skull. Block teeth from Monkey's upper jaw shot in different directions as the lower half of Monkey's jaw clattered to the ground followed by a wave of gray jelly.

Pheasant charged at Delvin, but the clown ducked under the attack and buried his face in the bird's chest. With grand, sweeping motions, Delvin raked his face across the bird's torso, back and forth, back and forth. Chunks of feather-covered meat twirled through the air while red gelatinous globs splashed to the ground. Squawking, the pheasant-beast tried to push the clown away with its hand-shaped talons, to no avail. The clown gripped the bird's wrists and yanked both arms from its body, arcs of blood dancing between arm and shoulder. Delvin slashed his face across the bird's body, through skin and muscle. Bones flung through the air like saplings caught in a crimson hurricane. Colorful tufts of feathers were caught in the dangling fishhooks of Delvin's face.

Dog charged Collin, but the clown reached out with its gnarled fingers and grabbed the animal's muzzle. A high-pitched whimper was the extent of Dog's attack. Wedging his clawed hands between Dog's upper and lower jaw, Jacob's father pulled. A snap. A coughed gurgle. The sloppy rip of skin as Collin continued to pull, tearing Dog in half vertically and laughing as blood and organs spilled over him as if he had just bashed open a gore-filled piñata. Collin's black tongue swept globs of furry meat from his lips.

Knees knocking with fear, Orion's legs gave out and he flopped onto the ground. All he had to do was some self-actualization and he was sure these clowns would disappear in a pop, like bursting a Freudian balloon. But these damn clowns were deep-rooted subconscious and unconscious manifestations of obstacles and fears. He had tried to defeat his fears, even reaching back into his childhood to pull forth a surefire way to turn bravery into a weapon. And failed.

The clowns returned their malevolent focus back on Orion. Faces gleefully smeared with washes of red muck, their smiles loomed closer.

All alone. Too frightened to cry anymore, Orion felt hopeless; terror had frozen his entire body.

No... wait! This was his dreamscape.

There was someone else he could call upon.

Someone who could help.

Bigby.

CHAPTER 37

July 13ᵗʰ, Chicago

Gen had spent the past two hours tearing apart the brown recluse lair that served as a drug lab, and needed a shower to get rid of the gut-twisting filth. She'd spent too much time there, the musky odors of the other cluster of spiders coating her. Though she had to scrub off a layer of ash, she was thankful Ven had brought his little flame thrower, even if it did leave a burning alcohol smell behind. The building still needed a Sisyphusian level of work, but at least it no longer resembled a brown recluse lair.

She finished drying off and then slipped on a tee shirt, so old that the smartass statement once printed on it had all but faded away. She didn't remember what it had once said, but the word "Fuck" took up most of the space, its outline was still visible. She got her sweatpants on just as a knock came from the door.

"Hey," she said when she opened the door, a certain level of excitement in her voice.

Leaning against the jamb, Blaze smiled and held out a six pack of beer. "Hey. Thanks for letting me come over."

Gen gave a single shoulder shrug. She appreciated his company, but the words remained locked inside her mouth. She accepted the six pack and nodded to the couch as an invite. "You don't need to bring me a tithing every time you come over. Especially since I own a bar with much better beer."

Mirthful, Blaze placed his hand over his heart, wounded by her words. "Ouch! I bare my soul to you by sharing my favorite beer."

Gen laughed. Setting the six pack on the coffee table, she pulled out two bottles and uncapped them. She flopped onto the couch and handed one to Blaze. "These are green bottles. No one's favorite beer comes in green bottles."

Laughing, Blaze sat next to her and clinked his bottle against hers. "True enough."

Gen took a long pull and studied Blaze, looking for a tell, a hint as to why he was here. A weird vibe came from him, washing over her as cold as ocean waves.

She tucked her feet under her hips and turned to give her full attention. "What's up?"

"How'd the meeting with Scarlett go?"

"No bloodshed, so I'm taking that as a win. I missed… umm… It would have been better if you could have been there."

"About that…" He stared forlorn at the bottle and picked at the label. His face was slack, either weary or sad. Or both. A quick head shake as if he suddenly realized he needed to leave whichever reality he had found himself in and return to this one. "I… I, uhh, met with Corette."

Trying not to laugh into her beer while she took another swig, Gen wondered why he seemed so upset by this confession. "And?"

Blaze explained everything. The favor for Victor. The video from thirty years ago. The better than even chance that he and Corette were siblings – now that Gen thought about it, she saw a resemblance – and Corette's weird boyfriend, Jacob, and his crazy request. Wait… Was Blaze considering joining those two to break into Calista Lindquist's house?

Still calm, Gen cracked into a second beer. "And?"

Blaze didn't smile, such a rarity that Gen glanced out her window to make sure there wasn't a line of tornadoes ripping through Chicago or a hurricane of flaming toads raining from the sky. A hand-swipe through his hair, and then Blaze grabbed a second beer. "I feel compelled to go with them."

"Are you sure it's not that weird voice-thing everyone says she can do?"

Eyes focused on the floor, he nodded. "I think that only lasts a few seconds or so."

"Is this Jacob the same one who prompted Victor and Celina to hop the first plane from Vegas to Chicago?"

"Yeah, I know how it sounds." He regarded Gen with his full attention. No smile. No manipulation. "That's why I'm here. To ask you to come with me."

Cold fireworks bloomed within Gen's chest. Her gut said, "Yes." But her mouth said, "Why do you even want to go?"

"I think they're right. Calista was a hunter, no doubt in my mind. She hunted us, and she maybe even hunted our parents. No matter how small the odds that I'll discover something about my father – trust me, I know they're next to zero – I have to take that chance. If nothing else, then I'll at least learn more about Corette, my sister."

"Why do you want me to go?"

A small smile, accompanied by a hint of pink on his cheeks. "I remember when we first met in that old car dealership used as a drug lab, when Calista found us. She had said something like, 'No matter how many spiders I kill, there's always more.' Remember?"

"I do."

"She killed spiders before. Not just little things found in houses. She meant *your kind*. I've learned a helluva lot about spiders these past few months, so I understand there are different species all over the place. But maybe Calista did her thing closer to home? Maybe she has something that belongs to you?"

Gen brought the bottle to her lips, surprised to find nothing in it. Placing the empty on the table, third bottle in her hand. "I... I really doubt it."

"Melissandra called you 'sister.' Was she really your sister?"

Memories twisted in her gut and she looked away. "Yeah. I think so, at least. My mother mentioned that I have a couple sisters, but they accepted me as the only queen."

After grabbing the last beer, Blaze made a gesture to imply, "Maybe that's not accurate."

Unable to look into Blaze's eyes, Gen turned to the early evening outside her window. Chicago was a big city. Earth was a big world. There would forever be more questions than answers. However, some answers were more pressing than others. "I can't. I... I..." Her breath hitched as her misty words turned to whispers. "I want to." A gulp from the bottle. A quick throat clear. Weariness melted her expression to nothingness as she looked back to Blaze. "But I really can't. Not after what I found in the building. Well, more like

248

what I didn't find – the source of the black widow venom used for the latro production."

Blaze sat forward and frowned, solving the different equations that statement laid out before him. "Oh. Oh, shit."

"Yeah. It's pretty obvious to me that someone in my cluster willingly supplied their venom. Now that Scarlett and her cluster are leaving town, I need to connect with members of my cluster and figure out who it is. The price I pay for being a shitty queen." Gen guzzled the rest of her beer.

"You let your cluster do their own thing, live their own lives. That doesn't make you a shitty queen. Do you want help?"

There it was again, that annoying burst of tingles behind her chest, as if she kept her good emotions in balloons and Blaze was the pin that popped them. Was he this selfless for everyone? Or just her?

She shook her head. "No. Fuck no, I'm not letting you miss this opportunity to get to know your newly discovered sister and possibly find out more about your father. You go to New York with them and don't come back until you found what you needed to find."

Blaze's jaw muscles rippled, chewing on his thoughts. Slowly, as if trying to carry the weight of the world on his shoulders, he stood and gently placed his empty bottle on the coffee table. "Yeah. Yeah, you're right. I will."

Gen stood; if she didn't, then she'd convince herself to convince him to stay a little longer. A little longer always turned into a lot longer. Plans would change, and she'd feel... Hell, she didn't know how'd she feel. She barely knew how she felt at this moment, let alone how she'd feel later after messing up Blaze's plans for her own selfish reasons. "Okay, then that's the plan."

Blaze nodded like he was trying to convince himself he should leave. "Yeah. Looks like that's the plan."

Gen opened the front door and Blaze stepped into the hallway. "Good luck. I hope you find what you're looking for. And... Be careful."

Blaze smiled. It was a fake one. Gen had seen a full range of what he offered, so she knew without a doubt that this was for show. "I will. I'll... ummm... I'll text along the way?"

His voice held the upswing of a question. Clearly, he was asking if he should bother, or if he should leave Chicago for good.

Gen smiled. Nothing as powerful as some of the whoppers Blaze was capable of, but she wanted to make sure she conveyed encouragement. "Yes. Please text me along the way. And I'll keep you posted about what I find here."

One last smile, a real one, and Blaze walked away. When he reached the end of the hall, Gen called out, "Hey!"

"Yeah?"

"Make sure you come back to Chicago when you're done."

Blaze gave a wink before he disappeared around the corner.

Gen shut the door.

A buzz from her phone directed her attention to a text from Lucas: You coming back to the club?

Tomorrow, she typed. Too busy right now.

Lucas replied with a dozen hands tossing the heavy-metal-devil-horns emojis. She dropped her phone on the coffee table and went to the fridge.

She hated being such a cliché. Big ball of molten steel spinning inside her stomach, level of hate. Write a song about it later, level of hate. But she couldn't help it. Fuck everything going on right now. Fuck the band. Fuck the club. Fuck her other businesses. Fuck the cluster. *Fuck my life.*

Gen curled up on the couch with a six pack of beer – good stuff, not the swill that Blaze brought – and hit play on the movie "10 Things I Hate About You."

And cried.

CHAPTER 38

"Bigby!" Orion called out to the sky. Whisps of blood-red clouds floated before a purple swirl of star-gorged cosmos. "Bigby! I need you!"

"No!" rang a woman's voice from somewhere, echoing among the buildings. "We cannot allow him to be free."

Allow Bigby to be free? That meant he was here, within Orion's dreamscape. That was the hope he needed to get to his feet. The trio of towering clowns continued toward him, pernicious smiles acting as the harbingers of death, six hands reaching for him. Orion ran. Forget heading for Winchester Hall – this was a nightmare, so the back door would undoubtedly be locked – Orion ran through the parking lot toward Church Street.

"If you don't free him," Orion yelled, "then I'll die!"

"Then Bigby will die. That is an acceptable trade."

"Not for me!" Orion replied, huffing as he ran to the small church across the street. Up the stairs. As expected, the doors were locked. "Damn it! Who are you?"

"Orion?" he heard from behind, this voice familiar. He turned.

Aika stood in the middle of the street. She looked exactly like the last time he saw her – including the large blood stain on the bottom half of her shirt – except for her missing right arm. It had been replaced by dozens of steel cables and thick chains which ran taut from her shoulder to the fluffy red clouds in the sky. "Orion, please understand. Bigby is too dangerous."

Cracks spiderwebbed along Winchester Hall across the street as it rumbled, chunks of stone falling away. The clowns obviously decided to plunder through it instead of around it.

"So you're just gonna let these clowns kill me? And who's that other woman saying that killing me in order to kill Bigby is okay?"

Orion's heart crumbled just like the building across the street when another woman appeared next to Aika – a woman who looked like an older version of his mother – and said, "I'm your grandmother and I've caged Bigby for the past eighteen years."

The dust from Winchester Hall's collapse was thick and sickly white. The cloud billowed in all directions, but thinned as it flowed across the street. There was enough dust to send Orion into a coughing fit, but it wasn't thick enough to hide the three clown silhouettes standing within the plume.

Orion ran his forearm across his face to wipe away snot and slobber, and then squinted to get a better look at the older woman. "My grandmother?"

He had seen his birth mother only once. Her eyes were closed and she was in a coma, but this woman was her spitting image, though the smoothness of youth was gone. Like Aika, her left arm was a tangle of steel cords and chains, stretching to an unseen point in the sky.

"Why do you want me to die?" Orion asked, practically whined, wiping dust from his face.

"I don't," she replied. Her non-flesh arm jerked, as did Aika's. "But Bigby is pure evil. If you die, then he dies."

"But I controlled him."

"It was one time and in a small burst."

"I can control him!" Orion shouted.

A sudden tug along the chains and cables made both women lurch forward. Orion looked up to see the cables and cords leading to an unseen point above thick rolls of deep red clouds. Was Bigby's cage up in those clouds? It had to be. Before he could ask, the dust from the collapsed building settled, and the clowns continued their pursuit, their repulsive smiles leading the way. The bell from the church tolled, and the clowns laughed.

"Orion, please!" Aika shouted as she set her feet and twisted her waist to tug at the cables and chains. "Stop!"

The clowns ambled onto the street, seemingly ignoring the two women standing in the middle of it.

"I can control him!" Orion yelled again, louder.

The church bell rang again, vibrating within Orion's chest.

The women stumbled after another tug from the mystery source within the clouds, a cry of pain from each of them.

Sally was twice as wide as either of the other clowns, and he led the procession, meaty fingers reaching for Orion who stood firm on the crooked church stairs. Crimson slobber dripped from the corners of frothing smiles. Delvin still had feathers stuck in his fishhook teeth.

The gong of the church bell shook the entire street.

"Orion, stop!"

The clowns cackled.

"I can control him!"

The closest buildings quaked, the church bell tolling louder.

The women screamed, falling to their knees. Their steel cables and chains fell slack to the ground as something plummeted from the sky and crashed through the church's roof.

The yellow clown's hand reached closer.

The church bell stopped.

His heart, his breath, the only noises as Orion slowly turned around to face the church doors.

A spine-chilling creek of unoiled metal and strained wood cut the air like a rusted knife. As the church doors opened, Orion stumbled down a few stairs, away from the gaping black maw of the holy house. A man in a tattered blue vested suit, mangled opera cape, and rumpled stove pipe top hat stood in the threshold.

Bigby. Plucking metal bands and cuffs from his body.

Frayed metal cord and broken links of chain sprouted from each shackle that he dropped to the ground like plucked flower petals. When the last cuff clattered down the church's steps, he smiled, razor blade teeth gleaming brightly in the dull world around him. Taking a moment to assess his body movements with a few arm stretches and a couple deep knee bends, he then took in the scene before him, and then the church behind him. His smile grew even wider as he turned back and winked at Orion.

"Thanks, little buddy, for getting me out of that cage. But, I'm gonna steal a move from my good buddy, HeyZeus, and ascend my ass outta here. Assume the position!" Bigby crossed his ankles and extended his arms out from his sides. "Keep your stigmata inside the ride at all times!" He began to float from the ground. "Later, losers!"

When Bigby ascended to the height of the cross on the church's tilted steeple, Orion reached his hand toward Bigby. And curled his fingers into a fist as if grabbing the dream monster's shirt.

"Hurrrk!" Bigby gagged as he stopped floating higher.

Orion pointed to Sally – the clown's gelatinous face slack from surprise, his fingers mere feet from Orion – and said, "Bigby! Kill!"

Bigby shot from the sky like a bullet from heaven, and pierced Sally's blobby gut. Rippling skin turned orange as globules of fat and blood oozed from the freshly formed gouge, and a gurgle emanated from within the twenty-foot-tall clown. Delvin and Collin backed away from their associate, frowns of curiosity accompanying their ghoulish smiles.

Aika and Orion's grandmother backed away as well, stepping closer toward Orion.

Sally shook, a jaundiced ocean of rolling waves crashing into each other. Tongue lolling from the corner of his mouth, he took a tiny, unstable step closer to Orion, arm still poised to grab him.

Orion uncurled his fingers.

Popping like a pimple, the yellow clown exploded. Orange and red gelatin globs rained down and spattered the ground while organs rolled and bounced like balls along the streets. Wearing Sally's intestines like a boa, a twenty-foot tall Bigby stood where the clown had once been, his blue top hat on the ground next to him.

Curtains of pink slime flowed over Bigby in sheets as he retrieved his hat. Gristle chunks slid from his stovepipe as he examined it, an exaggerated pull of his bottom lip to show intense scrutiny. He plucked a toe from the brim and tossed it aside. "Much better." All smiles, Bigby placed the dripping hat on his gore covered head.

Orion, his grandmother, and Aika didn't escape the scarlet goo. Glops dripped from the length of chain his grandmother held in her right hand as she walked up the stairs toward Orion. "I'm sorry, Grandson. I truly am. But there is no other way to stop Bigby."

"But I can control him. Watch!" Orion made a fist again and Bigby contorted in unnatural ways.

"Hey!" Bigby cried out. "Let me go!"

Wearing the insides of their exploded comrade, Delvin and Collin closed in from either side of Bigby.

Grandmother pulled the chain tight, the other end attached to her left shoulder, showing her intent to wrap it around Orion's neck. "No one can control him."

Orion slowly uncurled his fingers to show his grandmother that Bigby's freedom was determined by Orion's fist. Now with more freedom than a moment ago, Bigby twisted, lightly stretching and bending his body parts back into place. The clowns were drawing nearer, but he put his hands on his hips and scolded Orion. "Listen here, young man. I don't appreciate you hindering me like this. I am a dream eater, and I can't run around and eat people's dreams like I'm destined to if you—AAAGGH!"

Collin swiped his clawed hand across Bigby's back, drawing blood.

Bigby released a howl as shreds of blue cape and curls of his fetid skin flew through the air, followed by arcs of blood.

"*Senpai!*" Aika yelled, pointing upward at Bigby, her eyes wide as if witnessing a miracle. "*Senpai!* Bigby bleeds!"

Orion's grandmother watched as Delvin sank his barbed teeth into Bigby's left arm. The nightmare monster screamed again. Grabbing the clown's blue hair, Bigby spun and launched Delvin into Collin, knocking both into a nearby building. The clowns grimaced and growled as they crashed into the structure, sending broken bricks and glass shards everywhere.

While the clowns pushed and shoved each other, struggling to get to their feet, Bigby scrutinized his left arm, snarl pulled tight against razor blade teeth. Blood dripped from his wounded arm, splashing the pavement.

"*Senpai,*" Aika repeated, grabbing Grandmother's arm. "He is hurt, bleeding. This means he can die."

"How is this possible? We've tried to kill him in an uncountable number of ways."

"Maybe it's your grandson? Maybe he has the power to end Bigby?"

"Orion," his grandmother said, her voice softer. "You must allow the clowns to kill Bigby. This is the only way."

Orion slowly closed his fingers into a loose fist. Bigby growled as he hunched forward against his will. The clowns regained their footing and marched toward Bigby. Clutching his wounded arm, Bigby said, "If you kill me, then the clowns will kill you."

"Once Bigby is gone, we'll kill the clowns," Aika said.

On one knee and quaking with impotent struggle, Bigby turned away from Orion. Delvin was getting closer. "The liars are lying lies again. The ties that bind, bind the ties, so if I disappear, so do they, leaving you alone with the bad bozos."

"Is this true?" Orion asked his grandmother.

"No."

"Lies!" Bigby said with a roar.

"Will you and Aika disappear if Bigby dies?" Orion yelled.

"I don't know," his grandmother replied. "If we do, you need to remember that this is your dream, your subconscious. You manifested the clowns, so you can make them disappear."

"Says the bitch trained by a dream goddess!" Bigby shouted. "If it were that easy to make the clowns disappear, wouldn't you have already done so?"

Delvin loomed over Bigby, his smile ornamented with fishhooks growing in impossibly ways, his mouth open wide enough to threaten decapitation with one bite.

"Let it happen, Orion," Aika said.

"Orion!" Bigby said, his watery eyes pleading.

He was afraid. Was that a good thing? And what did that mean for Orion once they were finished with Bigby?

The curved metal dangling from Delvin's mouth danced across the top of Bigby's hat.

Orion uncurled his fingers.

Delvin lurched forward to swallow Bigby but halted when Bigby pressed his left hand against the clown's nose, thumb inside his upper jaw. He gripped the clown's lower jaw with his right hand. Bigby's smile gleamed with metal teeth as he stood. "Normally I'd say a funny comment here to highlight my sarcastic and delightfully macabre wit, but I find myself too distracted by my desire to do *this*!"

As if tearing a sheet of paper, Bigby ripped the clown in half. Organs piled by his feet in one bloody splash. Panting, Bigby dropped the two halves of the clown and ran his slimy pink tongue over his cracked lips. "Insert pithy statement here."

Orion wasn't sure what was happening let alone any rules that might apply. He did know that Bigby had the power to stop the clowns. He also knew that Bigby was the only one currently in his dreamscape who hadn't tried to kill him. Yet. From the way Aika and his grandmother talked, that sentiment could change at any second.

Now that Bigby had killed Delvin, Orion curled his fingers.

Snapping backward and freezing as if pinned against and invisible pole, Bigby yelped, and then growled, "Fuck, Orion! I get it! I get it! You're the big boss man in control, the Emperor Darth Voldemort Ruler of Barter Town King Cthulhu of the Fucking World! Now let me go!"

Collin stopped a few paces before Bigby and rolled his shoulders, blood dripping from his growing rictus. A quick shake of his right arm, and he pulled the cuff of his sleeve to show everyone watching that nothing was hidden inside. A snap of his left arm made an even grander gesture to avail any hidden tricks to the audience. As gently as plucking a butterfly from midflight, he used his index finger and thumb to pinch the tip of his squirming tongue, and then pulled.

Arm at full extension, the muculent appendage still attached to his mouth, Collin pulled it longer, like pink taffy. And there was still more. With every pull, his tongue drooped closer to the ground. When satisfied, Collin allowed a length to dangle, then twirled it. And then snapped it like a whip.

Bigby howled in pain as the lash drew blood from his ribs. A second slash pulled a spray from Bigby's arm.

Orion relaxed his thumb.

Bigby caught the third snap and severed it with a bite of his razor blade teeth. As he rolled his neck, he slurped, gulping down the length of tongue like a piece of wriggling spaghetti.

What was left of Collin's tongue flopped from his mouth. Eyes widened, lips pursed in an exaggerated look of shock, Collin held up his index finger. He gestured to the black daisy that suddenly appeared on his lapel, while holding a plastic squeeze bulb in his hand.

"Not falling for that, you no rent-a-Bozo," Bigby said. He grabbed a chunk of building and held it in front of him, shielding him from the flower.

Collin squeezed the bulb, and a stream of liquid shot from his crotch and drenched Bigby's left leg. Acid. Smoke accompanied the sounds and smells of sizzling meat as Bigby dropped, muscles in his left leg burnt through and no longer strong enough to support him.

Orion relaxed his index finger.

Led by a spew of profanities, Bigby launched himself at Collin. Each figure over twenty feet tall, their swings and kicks at each other inadvertently reduced a nearby building to rubble. A chomp and a twist, Bigby tore a chunk of meat from Collin's shoulder. With oversized red shoes, the clown kicked Bigby off him to the squeak of a bicycle horn.

Bigby crashed into a building across the street. Slow to get up, blood flowing from the rips in his shredded clothing, he limped to the middle of the street. Again, Collin stood before him, only a few steps away.

Collin fussed with his right sleeve, reached into it and pulled out a five-foot-long chicken. A real chicken, pink skin plucked clean. Burled talons in Collin's one hand, he held its belly with his other hand, the bird's face like a muzzle, pointed at Bigby. Collin squeezed.

A slimy spray of blood and entrails shot from the chicken's mouth. As organs slapped against his face and sluiced over his body, Bigby struggled to move, too caught up in the twists of intestines wrapping around him.

Collin tossed the chicken aside and slowly approached his captive. Thumb in his mouth, the clown blew it like a balloon, inflating his other hand. As his hand swelled bigger, nails and spikes grew from his skin with every puff.

Bigby gnawed at the wrap of intestine closest to his face, but it wasn't enough to free him as the clown loomed.

Fist the size of his chest and cloaked with the sheer number of deadly protrusions, Collin reeled his arm back.

Orion opened his hand.

Catching the biological mace on the downswing, Bigby stood and tore it from Collin's arm. Streamers of blood arced through the air as the clown shrieked.

"You can take your stupid clown tricks and shove them up your sphincter! In fact..." Bigby grabbed the clown by his shoulders and spun him half a rotation. Pulling his arm back, Bigby delivered an upper cut – right into Collin's ass. And didn't stop until his fist popped out of Collin's mouth. With Collin's lips frozen open midscream, Bigby grabbed the clown's jaw and pulled. With one yank, he turned Collin inside out. Beating heart and billowing lungs laid against muscle encased ribs. Gurgling stomach and twitching intestines rested in pillows of yellow fat. Collin's eyes peered through an inverted skull, impotently watching as his brain slid over his reversed body. Once it hit the pavement, Bigby stomped on it. "Now *that* wedgie belongs in the hall of fame!"

It was over. The malevolent presence that Orion had brought into his subconscious from Jacob's dreamscape was gone. The weight of fear lifted, he looked at his feet to make sure they were still on the ground.

Bigby started to float away, implying his escape, but before the nightmare master had a chance to act upon the freedom awarded with victory, Orion clenched his fist.

"Fuck!" Bigby yelled as he crumbled to the ground in the fetal position.

"Kill him!" his grandmother yelled. "You have the power to end the greatest threat humanity has ever encountered! Kill him now!"

"She's right, Orion," Aika added, her tone softer, more familiar. "He is a monster of unfathomable power and needs to be slain."

"Orion," Bigby gasped. "They're hiding the truth from you." He wheezed, his breath more labored with every word. Mimicking Darth Vader's voice, he said, "Orion, I am your father."

"Silence, Monster!" Aika yelled as she snapped her shoulder, the chains and cables flicking toward him. They wrapped around his mouth. "Orion, that is not true!"

"How do I know that?" Orion screamed, desperate to use his voice to cut through the lies. "How do I know anything? You helped raise me for eighteen years, and then one day, you tried to *kill me*."

"That was because of how dangerous Bigby is." Aika strode closer to Bigby, the chains growing from her shoulder. "This monster has to be stopped at any cost. Even if it meant killing the only person I ever loved, the only person who I consider my child."

"If you love me so much, then why didn't you tell me the truth?"

"Because she didn't know, Orion," his grandmother said. "She had no idea that Bigby was inside of you until he manifested himself a few months ago, killing your classmate and your friend."

"But now that I know, we can work together to figure something out. I can control him. You saw me. You saw me control him."

"It's not good enough," Grandmother said, and she tightened her grip on the cord in her right hand, signifying she was still going to strangle him. "You did not control him. You limited him."

"*Senpai*," Aika said, "Shinko, please. Let's figure out how Orion can kill him."

"It's too dangerous."

Orion shook his head and cried. "I can't believe I wanted to learn about you, to know who you are. All I wanted to do was learn about my family, where I came from. I wanted to learn about my parents. I mean, God, I want to find my mother again."

"Again? My… My daughter is still alive?"

"Yes. Yes, I saw her. She's, I don't know, in a coma or something. But I saw her, touched her, held her hand."

"Is she okay now?"

"I don't know. Some guy named Harold Varvaro has her. He disappeared with her. I was trying to find her again, and went to Jacob for help – he said he'd help me if I helped him. But he used me. Jacob lied to me to learn more about his father, and then... then... then *this!*" Orion waved his hands around at the devastated city block.

Grandmother looked away, squinting, as if watching a movie only she could see. Without warning, she turned to Bigby. The metal cables and chains dangling from her shoulder sprung toward Bigby, wrapping around him, throttling him. More and more until they covered every inch of him. Aika added to the coils until a sphere of chain and cable encased him. The women floated into the air, the sphere taut between them.

"Find your mother, Orion," Grandmother said. "But do *not* contact us again. And never call for Bigby for *any* reason!"

In a blink they disappeared.

"No!" Orion shouted to the heavens. "I have questions for you! I have so many questions! Come back! Come—"

The taste of blood surprised him. It wasn't residual clown blood. This was warm, fresh, salty. Carefully, he ran his tongue across his upper teeth, one tooth at a time, and cut his tongue.

One of his teeth was a razorblade.

Orion awoke with a start, sitting straight up in bed. He immediately jumped out from his tangle of sheets and ran to the bathroom. Light on. Mirror. Sweat cascaded over his face as he used his fingers to pull his lips away from his teeth. Not a single one of them was a razor.

But he still tasted blood.

CHAPTER 39

July 13th, Las Vegas

It had been a great day in the café and Celina couldn't wait to tell Victor about it. Steady customer flow. Zero complaints. Well, one complaint, but that was from a college-aged douchebag asking for a refund because he found a fingernail in his panini, and that was after he had finished the sandwich and coffee. However, he confessed the scam once Celina used her half-foot height advantage to loom over him. Even so, she missed Orion and decided that she'd text him in a bit.

"Honey, I'm home," she said as she entered the apartment.

Still wearing her suit, Victor languished on the couch with a glass of amber liquid. She laughed. "You're so fucking weird. You know that, right?"

"Yes, that's been proven by having you as my best friend, roommate, and business partner. And since you willingly hang out with me, that means you're pretty fucking weird, too."

Downing her drink in one gulp, Victor stood from the couch and smiled. "It actually pains me that I can't argue with your logic. Now, go get changed. I wanna go out tonight."

"Bad day in the office? Where are we going and how should I dress?"

"Just a long day, researching available places for Sugar Fix, Inc. Now, time to find someone else's bed to wake up in. Where we're going and how to dress depends on how bad you wanna hookup."

Celina thought she had steeled herself against Victor's forthrightness, the words out of her mouth more random than lottery numbers, but the heat of a blush bloomed through her cheeks. "I… ummm… I'm not sure I want to… hookup with anyone at the moment."

Victor approached and raised her hand, primed for a high-five. "All right! Setting up tongue time with the bouncer, I assume?"

Flat-browed, Celina crossed her arms over her chest and cocked her hip, giving a look that could only be interpreted as, "Seriously?"

Laughing, Victor pinched Celina's cheek. "God, you're so adorable when you get all serious and mature. Are you really so into him that you're willing to pass up the opportunity to let me help you get some action?"

Celina softened her expression and relaxed her stance. "I don't know if I'm into him or not. I already told you about our virtual date. I don't want to add an unnecessary layer of complication or drama by – as you put it – waking up in someone else's bed."

Victor shrugged. "I mean, I am the author of *The Victor Vegas Book of Sloppy Love*, so I think I know —"

Thankfully, the doorbell stopped Victor from whatever perverted path she was about to traipse down. But seconds later, a desperate knock on the door followed. Victor got to the door first and looked through the peep hole, just as another knock hit the door, startling her. "It's Orion?"

Celina stood behind Victor as she opened the door, Orion's knuckles primed to rap again. The hallway blurred, Orion the sole focus of Celina's attention.

After a few seconds of blinking, like he needed to register where he was, he lowered his hand. Slouching more than usual, as if weighed down by the bags under his eyes, he seemed lost, almost confused. Voice so cracked that his words crumbled as they left his mouth, his body shook harder and harder. "Victor? I... I came straight from the airport. Straight from... Straight from Philly, because... because..." In a burst of life, he dropped his bags, lurched forward, and wrapped his arms around Victor, desperation in his hug. Celina's heart broke as his body wracked with blubbering sobs. "You were right! I shouldn't have stayed there! I should have come home with you two!"

The prickle of concern skittered along Celina's spine. She assumed Victor would push him away and make a sarcastic comment about him getting snot and tears on her expensive suit. Mercifully, Victor hugged him back, one hand on the back of his head as she pressed her cheek against his scalp. "Hey, Kid, it's okay. You're home, you're safe. Whatever happened, we'll fix it, okay?"

Celina went to the kitchen to get a glass of water, but remembered this was Orion, so she opted for a Red Bull from the fridge. When she returned,

Victor was rubbing circles on Orion's back while he dragged his forearm across his nose.

"Sorry for the mess," Orion said.

"No worries, Kid," Victor said.

"We're always here for you, Orion," Celina added as she handed him the energy drink.

"Thank you. Can I come in?"

"Yeah, get in here! Even though I refuse to let you live here, this is your home." Victor guided him to sit at the dining table where he cracked open the can and downed a few glugs.

Sitting next to him, Celina placed her hand on his forearm. "What happened in Philadelphia? Are you okay?"

Guzzling through two more Red Bulls and eventually a glass of water – Celina forced him to drink it, concerned about his hydration – Orion shared everything that happened.

Celina gasped when he mentioned finding his mother and Victor rankled when he explained that a man named Harold Varvaro had kidnapped her. They both pulled their phones to access the list to look up Danielle Munch. The air crackled with emotional electricity from Victor when Orion explained how Jacob had used him. And both women listened in stunned silence as he shared what happened in his dreamscape. Clowns. Bigby. Aika. His grandmother.

Victor closed her eyes and waved her hands. "So, wait. You're saying that your nanny and your grandmother are alive inside your head?"

Orion nodded.

"And tried to kill you in your dream?"

"Yeah, to keep a monster that my father created from being unleashed on the world. Apparently, they can't hurt him, but he can be hurt in *my* dreamscape? Or *I* can hurt him? I don't know, but now they're trying to figure out a way to kill Bigby for good without killing me."

With an exhale strong enough to puff her cheeks, Victor slouched in her chair and ran her hand through her hair. "God damn, that's some fucked up hillbilly drama right there."

Celina squeezed Orion's forearm. "What she's trying to say is we'll do everything we can to help you find your mother again."

Victor sat up and tapped away on her phone. "Fuck yeah we will. I'm sending a message to Bailey telling him to find out everything he can on this Harold Varvaro."

Either from sharing his woes or from accepting the offered help, Orion seemed airier, lighter, a weight lifted from his shoulders. "Thanks. I appreciate that. But... Shouldn't we tell the others about Jacob?"

Poking at her phone, Celina said, "I'll call Blaze."

"Wait, don't!"

Celina and Orion jerked at Victor's explosive blurt.

Canceling her call before it went through, Celina slapped her phone down on the table. "Okay! Why not?"

"He might be involved with Jacob's nefarious mustache-twirling."

"Jacob never mentioned Blaze," Orion said.

"Maybe not, but he never mentioned Corette to you either, and she *has* to be involved. Let's not forget, he was her 'client' and the reason this whole mess got started. We can't discount the fact that we went to Chicago to talk to Gen about her. After initially stating she didn't want to be involved, Gen turned around and started working with Corette. Where Gen goes, Blaze is sure to follow."

"Whoa," Orion whispered. "Fuck."

"Okay. How about Robert?" Celina asked. "He brought Jacob to our attention, but he extricated himself from everything."

Victor looked away, pondering the situation. She then pulled out her phone and less than a minute later, Robert's face was on the screen.

"Victor?" Robert said. "What a pleasant surprise."

"I'd normally make a smartass comment, but this call's serious in nature. I have Celina and the Kid with me."

Celina and Orion huddled closer to Victor's phone. Robert's face brought a tickle to Celina's insides and then guilt brought Vinnie to the forefront of her mind. A bloom of warmth ran up her neck, now embarrassed that she was thinking about such things at a time like this.

"Hi, everyone," Robert said. "Give me a second to head back to the office."

Behind him, paintings streaked along the background while he moved through the gallery. After a few seconds, Robert set the phone down, the backdrop now the wood paneling of the gallery's back office. "Sorry about that," he said. "What's going on? I was going to ask Orion if he wanted to come to the gallery today, but… You're back in Vegas?"

Victor relayed what Orion had gone through, abbreviating it down to Jacob tricking Orion. She then added her experiences with Corette and confessed that she had Blaze dig up a video involving Corette's young mother.

"Orion, did Jacob mention why he was looking for where Calista lived?" Robert asked, his tone soothing, inviting.

Orion shrugged. "Just that she might have something of his father's. He said since she's a hunter, she probably kept trophies."

"Did he say why he decided to attempt to murder you in his dreamscape rather than bring you along?"

"Yeah. I wasn't into my 'legacy,' or whatever. Danielle was super excited about her dad being a clown, but since I viewed my dad as a monster, he said I didn't have what it takes."

Robert nodded, a slight furrow in his brow. "Okay, so it seems like Jacob only wants to work with those on the list who want to know more about their parents. Heck, it seems like he's recruiting. I have his contact information, so I'll reach out to him and say I want to find out more about my father. It might take some finesse, but I think I can pull it off. I'll keep everyone posted."

Celina didn't like the idea, didn't like Robert putting himself in the line of fire like that, especially by himself. But there was no better way to find out what Jacob was truly up to, or how dangerous he might be.

After their goodbyes, Victor pulled off her tie and stood from the table. "All right, Kid. You're staying here tonight. Give me a minute to get into more appropriate clothes, then it's pizza and movies for the rest of the evening."

Orion smiled, a look of cherubic glee. Yes, he was an adult, but Victor's nickname for him was spot on. A kid, that's what he was. A kid who lived through a tragedy this week. Two, if Celina counted losing his mother immediately after finding her.

"Awesome! I know who to order from," he said, thumbs dancing across his phone's screen.

Victor headed for her bedroom, but when she got to her door, she shot a look to Celina. In the short period of time that they'd known each other, they had developed their own special, non-verbal language, and Victor had more concerns than what she had voiced, obviously keeping them to herself for Orion's benefit. Her look to Celina said as much. *Tomorrow. We'll cover those concerns tomorrow.* As for now Victor said, "Orion, don't friggin' order extra pepperoni five times on one pizza."

CHAPTER 40

July 14th, Las Vegas

Victor woke up alone and without a hangover. At first, she was mad at Orion for dumping ice water on her libido. However, her more enlightened parts reminded her that Jacob and Corette were to blame for killing her boner last night. "Assholes," she mumbled as she got out of bed. She slipped on the closest pair of cotton shorts and tee shirt before stomping out of the bedroom.

Orion slouched at the dining table eating a bowl of cereal. With a vacant face, he looked like any other teenager when not scrolling through their phone. Though, once he noticed he wasn't alone, he sat up, eyes bright and beaming. "Good morning."

"Back at ya, Kid. Did you start any coffee?"

"No. I don't drink it. It's gross."

Victor started the process, and sneered. "Gross? What's wrong with you? It's the lifeblood of society."

"It's dirt water. And it smells like Satan's vomit."

"You're a fuckin' weird one, Kid." Victor pressed the start button on the coffee machine and headed back to her bedroom. Shower. Get dressed. Pack a bag with three days' worth of clothes. Ready to devour the world.

When she exited her bedroom again, Orion was still at the table eating cereal. She double-checked her watch – twenty minutes since she last saw him, and he was still chowing.

Celina flitted about the kitchen in her sky-blue pajamas and astoundingly large bear slippers. The smells of sizzling bacon overlapped with the aroma of freshly cooked pancakes. "Good morning!"

Full coffee mug already on the table, Victor sauntered over and indulged, slurping obnoxiously, eyeing Orion over the rim. He rolled his eyes, then countered by slurping the last of his milk from the bowl. Victor laughed.

"You sure you don't want pancakes or bacon?" Celina asked Orion as she delivered two full plates to the table.

"Naah. I'm good, thanks." He deposited his bowl and spoon into the sink. "I'm gonna head back to my apartment."

"Might not be a good idea to go to work today," Celina said, she and Victor accompanying him to the door. "I know the owner and I'm pretty sure she'd be sympathetic to your situation."

"Yeah, I'm good. I'd feel better staying busy and being around people."

"Okay. Let me know if you change your mind."

Celina hugged Orion, but when he turned to Victor with open arms, she pressed her palm against his forehead. "Nope. You get one a year. Any more than that and people will think I'm a pedophile."

Crunching his face as if exposed to raw sewage, Orion said, "I'm eighteen. You know that."

"I know that, but they don't know that."

"They? They who?"

"The They that's Them. The They and Them involved with everything. You know, the They and Them who are the They and Them whenever anyone says, 'They,' or 'Them.'"

"I'm sure They and Them both know I'm eighteen."

"I doubt it and I'm not entirely sure you are."

"But—"

"Still no hug, you little perv."

Hard enough to almost knock Victor off her feet, Orion rolled his eyes. "Whatever." As he trudged out the door, he said to Celina, "See you at the café."

Shaking her head, Celina shut the door and scolded, "Why are you so mean to him?"

Victor headed back to the table and took a seat in front of her breakfast. "Pfft. That was hardly mean. That was just playing. You know, kinda like when someone uses a laser pointer with a cat."

"You're a piece of work, Victor Vegas," Celina said as she plopped in the chair across from Victor.

"I agree. Something like the ceiling of the Sistine Chapel, I'd say."

Celina laughed.

Victor loved her melodic laughter, so it stung when she cut it short by saying, "I'm heading out of town today. I'll be gone for a few days."

Bottom lip sticking out, Celina pouted. "Well, boo!"

Victor smirked and changed the topic so she wouldn't have to lie. "Hey, you'll have the apartment to yourself if you want to do naughty things in front of the camera for Vinnie."

Celina stuck out her tongue. As she turned her attention back to her plate, she said, "I might research other people from the hitlist."

A chill ran through Victor cold enough to drop the temperature of her eggs. "Be careful, Celina. If you find anyone, don't contact them until I get back. We could still be in someone's crosshairs."

"Orion said that Calista thing was a ruse by Jacob."

"Yep. But I think we were so relieved by that news we forgot about Preston."

"Preston?" Celina's eyes darted back and forth as she processed Victor's words. "Oh... Oh shit."

"Yes, exactly. Jacob said he knew him, and he was very dead. If it wasn't Calista, then who killed him?"

"Oh, God! You don't think it was Jacob, do you?"

"I don't know what to think."

"Okay. I'll contact Robert to warn him."

"Well, regarding Robert..."

"You're just a big ray of sunshine this morning, aren't you?"

No longer hungry, Victor put her silverware on her plate and slid it aside. Elbows on the table, she leaned in. "Think about the conversation we had with him last night."

Breaking Celina's heart was worse than willingly breaking her own, but Victor had to. "Last night, he listened patiently and said he was going to join Jacob and the others and go to Calista's. I think that's very selfless and brave of Robert to contact Jacob and say that he's curious about his... father? Why does that sound so weird?"

Victor swallowed down the lump in the back of her throat and watched confusion play across her friend's face. Then Celina's expression slid into sad realization. Victor reached across the table and grabbed Celina's hand. "Because ever since we met him, he's always said that both of his parents are normal. Both parents."

Frowning, Celina looked away and squinted, as if watching her memories play out in front of her like a movie. "And he had said that in front of Jacob, that both his parents were normal and perfectly boring."

After letting Celina stew in her own thoughts for a few seconds, Victor squeezed her hand to get her attention. "Hey. That's just me playing devil's advocate for one possible scenario. The father thing might have been an unintentional slip because Orion was talking about his father and Jacob's father, and Danielle's father. And Robert's charming. We both know that he can talk his way into Jacob's weird little caper."

Celina nodded, but still looked maudlin.

Victor continued, her tone lighter this time. "We just need to be careful. That's all I'm saying. Let's learn from Orion's prepubescent mistakes."

A chuckle followed by a headshake. Celina squeezed Victor's hand and stood. "You're right. We don't have enough information. Let's wait to see what Robert reports. In the meantime, I'm going to get ready to go to the café. Don't leave without me."

Victor winked and shot Celina with two finger guns. "You got it."

Once Celina's bedroom door closed, Victor pulled out her phone and called Bailey. His face appeared on her screen, stoic as ever. "Good morning, Boss."

"Did you leave your apartment yet?"

"Not yet. What do you need?"

"For you to pack about three days' worth of clothes. We're going on a field trip."

"Excellent. May I ask to where and for what purpose."

"Chicago and for me to see how resourceful you are."

"Could you elaborate?"

"We're looking for a woman named Scarlett. Honestly, that's about all we have to go on, so we'll test your street smarts."

"As my boyfriend likes to tease me – all of my smarts are in books."

"Can you hand someone a twenty dollar bill every time they answer a question?"

"Yes, I believe I can do that."

"You're on your way to becoming a street professor. Meet me in the office in an hour."

"Confirmed."

Victor hung up and placed her phone face down on the table as if she could hide from her own shame – she hadn't technically lied to Celina, yet. But if the question as to where she was going came up, then she'd have to. Plausible deniability. She wasn't sure if whatever Celina and Vinnie were doing would go anywhere – she kind of hoped it would, because they'd make a cute couple; a *large*, cute couple – but she didn't want to screw it up by attempting to find the enemy of Vinnie's boss. Of course, if it weren't for Celina going on a virtual date with Vinnie, then Victor wouldn't have known about Genocide working with Corette. She didn't like that.

Pocketing her phone, she went to her room to get her bags. "Time to fuck some shit up."

CHAPTER 41

July 14th, upstate New York

Blaze's phone buzzed inside his jacket. Making sure to keep the screen low so the car window didn't reflect his messages, he read the text from Gen: `Hows it going?`

He shared the back row of the Ford Expedition with Robert, but angled himself with his right thigh on the seat and half his back wedged against the door. Even though his sister sat in the passenger seat next to Jacob, he wasn't sure if he trusted her yet. He didn't trust anyone else in the car, especially Danielle, seated alone in the middle row. Meeting her only a handful of hours ago, there was no way he'd trust her. He hated the way she licked her lips whenever she looked at him. And trusting Robert? Not for a second.

Sure, Blaze started the cycle of distrust by stealing the keys to Victor's rental car from Robert while in Los Angeles, but he didn't deserve the glare he got from Robert when everyone met up a few hours ago. The silent side-eye was unwarranted, in Blaze's mind. Hell, what was Robert doing here? The bullshit song and dance about wanting to learn about his father didn't fly, either. During their time together in Los Angeles, Robert bragged about his parents being normal as normal gets. So, why the change in tune?

`Weird` Blaze typed back.

`Yeah?`

`On our way to calistas house Roberts with us`

`Really? Y?`

`No idea and corette and jacob are in a relationship`

`Weird. Anyone else joining?`

`Some girl named danielle weird vibe`

`Weird.`

Blaze smirked at Gen's response; she was clearly being a smartass.

`Hows the cleanup of the new building find anything useful`

`No. Ven wants to level it. Lucas wants to turn it into a strip club.`

`Sounds about right shit I think we are here`

`Good luck.`

Blaze pocketed his phone and squinted through the darkness to get a clearer view out the window as Jacob guided the Expedition off the main road. Trees. Nothing but trees and brush lined the thin, but paved, driveway.

"Whoa," Danielle whispered when they pulled up to the house.

Getting out of the car, Blaze nodded in agreement.

A few more minutes before twilight called it quits for the day, just enough color in the world made out the house. Sleek, modern design of asymmetry and roof pitched just enough not to be considered flat. More glass than most office buildings, the house was impressive. Blaze guessed it to be well over 5,000 square feet. Maybe 6,000.

"Whoa," Danielle said again, this time standing next to Blaze.

"Yeah," Blaze replied. "Now what?"

"Now this," Jacob said, pressing a button on the key fob. Blaze didn't like his monomaniacal enthusiasm.

The back hatch lifted to reveal locked carry cases and zipped duffle bags. While Danielle joined Jacob in unlatching and unzipping the contents, passing hushed questions and answers between them, Blaze and Robert drifted closer to Corette.

Robert stood quietly, arms crossed over his chest, jaw muscles flexing, eyes focusing only on the two sifting through tools and equipment.

Hands in his pockets, Blaze leaned close to Corette. Even though they were the only five people in the forest, he still felt obliged to whisper, "What's that they're going through?"

"Over the past year, Jacob and Danielle have become rather good at breaking into places. Of course, Jacob spares no expense to get what he wants, including the latest in burglary equipment," Corette whispered back.

Blaze nodded and then cuffed Robert's arm with a friendly familiarity unbefitting their limited and contentious relationship. "Hear that, Bobby? Nothing but the best to help us find out more about our fathers, right?"

Robert turned and Blaze shrank away, like a monkey after pulling on a lion's tail. Within the darkness, Blaze finally saw the spark flickering behind Robert's eyes, the fire that burned within them all, the sign that meant he belonged. Blaze didn't get "the feeling" when he had first met Robert – or Jacob or Danielle for that matter – the itch in his skull that came from meeting special individuals. But with Jacob and Danielle, Blaze could tell why they were on Calista's list, could see the monsters that lurked within. Robert boasted about having normal parents, and up until this second, Blaze could have believed that lie. Now? Now Blaze saw that there might be a labyrinth of shadows inside Robert, but make no mistake, a monster lived in the center of it all.

"I already know everything I need to know about my parents. I'm only here to find out why I'm on Calista's list. And *never* call me anything other than Robert again."

A salute and a wink, then Blaze sauntered to the Expedition. "Need any help?"

"Here," Jacob said and handed a big, unzipped duffle bag to Blaze, a jumble of thin, metallic poles clanking inside. "Let's do this."

Jacob and Danielle led the way, pointing to potential access points, but they quickly settled on the lower corner of the window that acted as an entire wall. Jacob took the bag from Blaze and emptied it. He assembled a tripod while Danielle fiddled with a box about the size of her head. The box attached perfectly to the tripod. When they turned it on, it projected red beams through the glass and onto the wall behind it. She and Jacob turned a few of the box's knobs and the beams formed an outline of a four-foot by four-foot square. Danielle continued to work the box while Jacob grabbed another duffle bag and set up rigging against the window. A rigid frame of thin black poles matched the proportions of the glowing perimeter of the square. A fist-sized object dangled in the center, four black cables attached to each pole of the contraption. "Ready."

More lines appeared on the window, all angled toward the bright red dot in the center. The object within the frame came to life with a whirr, then shifted to a buzz as it slowly followed along one of the red lines. While the equipment did its job, Danielle connected wires from the rigging to the window's frame.

Jacob smiled – Blaze still hated that stupid grin – and pointed to the laser emitting box on the tripod. "This measures the thickness of the glass and estimates its composition, then it calculates the best places to cut, and how deep, within the confines of the parameters. The glass cutter follows the direction. Should be about ten minutes."

"Why not just toss a rock through the glass?" Blaze asked.

"You'd need a rock the size of a car," Jacob said. "And even though Calista is dead, there's still electricity to the house, which means the security system is probably active. Right now, Danielle's setting up an electrical bypass."

"The house still has electricity?"

"Yeah. You know how rich people are. Her accountants and money managers are probably paying all the bills with no questions asked and no idea that she's dead."

Fascinated and impressed with its speed, Blaze couldn't help but get lost in the machine's efficiency. Burglary wasn't his thing. He'd robbed more than a few times for a variety of reasons; he just didn't like it. Too much planning for too many variables that were impossible to plan for. And not all high risk led to high reward. Sometimes the safe was empty. That thought made him slink closer to Corette again and whisper, "Do they know what they're looking for?"

"They do."

"Do you and I know what we're looking for?"

Corette wasn't an expressive individual, but her face went slack. "Not exactly."

That'd have to be good enough for Blaze. Any follow-up questions would push her away, not bring her closer.

Hot coals flared in his gut when he glanced at Robert. He wanted to mess with him, maybe even call him Bobby again, but his brain doused water on the thoughts. *That won't help right now. Don't be the one to ruin this mission.*

A few more minutes later, both machines stopped. Pulling a short handled sledgehammer from one of the duffels, Jacob stood before the window. "Does anyone mind if I do the honors?"

Robert remained silent and Blaze offered a nod of encouragement while the women expressed consent. A well-placed hit in the center brought large chunks of glass to the ground. Jacob laughed as he hurried away from the falling debris.

Danielle whooped, pumping her fist in the air.

Jacob slipped in through the hole. Once inside, he waved for everyone to join him, and they gathered at the entry of a long hall. Phones became ersatz flashlights for everyone.

Corette took Jacob by the arm and congratulated him as they walked down the hallway, paintings adorning the wall. Together, just a loving couple touring through an art gallery. Danielle strolled behind them.

Robert flashed a look at Blaze. A desperation in his eyes, a fear-driven solidarity. Blaze didn't know what to make of it, simply shining his light on the paintings as he brought up the rear.

The art was impressive. Though no expert, if any of these paintings found a way into his possession, he could get five digits for them, six for a couple others. Maybe he should be nicer to Robert, the gallery owner, and work up a scheme with him?

The hallway opened to a living room hued in whites and grays, accented by black. An orange beanbag chair in the center of the room was the only color. Attached and on the other side of the hallway wall was the kitchen, same monochrome scheme. The decoration was sparse: a painting that was nothing but slashes of black paint on a white canvas, a white vase on a glass end table, and stylish black and gray brick around the fireplace. Blaze ran his fingers along the back of the couch, centered in the room and facing the fireplace, and thought, *There's good money to be made peddling in death.* But there was something not right about the room... What specifically, he couldn't say.

It took less than a minute to find the opened door to the basement.

"And we're not suspicious?" Blaze asked as Jacob started down the stairs, Corette close behind.

"No. We're lucky that the door's open. Do you see how thick it is? And the security lock on it? If it were closed, we'd have to spend a lot of time on it, and we don't even know if what we're looking for is down there. If the basement is too scary for you, then you can check out the rest of the house. There's gotta be a bunch of less scary rooms."

"Yeah, yeah, yeah," Blaze mumbled as he gestured for Danielle and Robert to walk ahead of him.

Once Jacob made it down the stairs, light dispersed the dark with the flip of a switch. "Holy shit!"

"Oh my God," Corette said as she stepped off the stairs and disappeared from Blaze's view.

It was Danielle's turn to register surprise, "Fuuuuuuuuuuck..."

Robert didn't voice his shock, but it was displayed all over his face with wide eyes and gaping mouth.

Once Blaze stepped onto the gray cement floor and turned the corner, he thought the reactions were understated.

They found Calista's trophy room.

Dozens of trophies.

A simple rectangular room well over a hundred feet long. Four cylindrical support columns spaced evenly apart, ran down the center. Both walls running the length of the room had built-in shelves with overhead spotlights highlighting the objects on display. Pedestals, each about four feet tall, were placed unevenly across the room. On every pedestal sat a display case, a two-foot glass cube with a haunting item inside each one.

A bear head.

A giant reptilian clawed hand.

A skinned face draped over a plastic head.

Black feathers, the air rippling around them.

Tools and small machine parts.

Bones, teeth, body parts.

Fighting the urge to run into the room and explore, Blaze stayed back and watched where everyone else meandered. The tiny smile on Corette's stern face looked out of place as she wandered deeper into the room, gawking at the trophies as if browsing for the perfect dress in a boutique.

Danielle and Jacob knew what they were looking for. Ignoring everything else, they hurried through the room, giving cursory glances, until they found it.

They laughed and hugged.

A seed.

The size and shape of a football, there was no mistaking what it was. A gold plate inscription on the gray column read: "Master Poppy."

"We found him!" Jacob all but squealed.

"Congratulations!" Corette said as she made her way next to Jacob and kissed him.

Jacob wasted no time in taking the lid off the display case and reaching inside. Hands shaking, he removed the seed and held it with reverence, tears in his eyes. "I found him, Dad."

Danielle pumped her fist each time she said, "Yes! Yes! Yes!"

Robert ignored the trio, drifting to a pedestal on the opposite wall, a large section displaying more than a few alien and barbaric surgical tools. In the display case on a nearby pedestal was a book, bound in worn brown leather. Standing before it, Robert only stared.

Blaze stepped farther into the room, and his heartbeat sped up. Another step and his breath hitched. Another and his fingertips started to tingle. Something in here called to him, pulled him closer. Something on the shelves on the closest wall. Guiding him. The spell wavered when he passed a ten-foot stretch of wall displaying spider fangs, a few pair labeled "Black Widow." Gen had told him that she had met her mother, so Blaze pushed down the uneasy feelings of her possibly knowing the owners of these fangs. He continued past them, and the gnawing sense of familiarity returned, the nonverbal whisper. Heat radiated through his body, sweat rolling down his neck. He worried about his ribs shattering from how hard his heart smashed into them. The slosh of his flowing blood echoed between his ears, his vision blurring with every beat.

Then it all stopped.

Released from the constriction, he gasped, a big inhale of relief.

"I feel it, too," Corette said, standing beside him, staring at the lone item on the shelf in front of them.

A baseball sized, colorless resin sphere. A clump of thick black powder, an explosion forever frozen in time, was in the center. The gold name plate on the shelf held one word: "Silas."

Blaze reached for it, then hesitated, fearful of touching God. The sense that this sphere belonged to him, was him, took over and he plucked it from its stand. "Why do you think it called to us?"

"I don't know, but it has something to do with our father, don't you think? I can feel it."

"Yeah. Yeah, I feel it, too." Blaze slowly rotated the sphere, wondering what about it pertained to their father. And why. Slowly, his focus shifted to the sphere's surface. Then it hit him, what seemed wrong about everything upstairs. With his other hand, he wiped his fingers along the surface of the shelf.

No dust.

The shelves and the objects were dust-free. The glass cubes on the pedestals were also dust and streak-free. "Guys, I think we—"

A fraction of a second later, thunder cracked, and half of Danielle's head exploded. Chunks of wet meat and bone bits pelted Blaze's face hard enough to sting.

Despite the shock, everyone ducked just as Danielle's lifeless body collapsed in a heap, her blood flowing across the floor like spilled paint.

"Okay, you little fuckers. You interrupted Mama's special seaweed wrap healing time."

That voice. Blaze knew that voice. That voice belonged to a dead woman.

Peeking around the pedestal he hid behind, he saw the voice's owner, and she was very much alive and well.

Calista Lindquist.

Blonde hair wet and slicked back, she stood at the bottom of the stairs with a 9mm in each of her hands, wearing nothing but dangling strips of slimy seaweed and looking like a vengeful goddess excited to smite. Barefoot and silent as she crept farther into the trophy room, she disappeared from Blaze's view. "I spy with my little eye a bunch of dead pricks."

The room's acoustics sent her voice everywhere and nowhere. "Come on, you shit-heels, don't make this any harder than it has to be. I had a rough three months recovering and I'm feeling a little lazy. Could you do me a favor by sticking your stupid faces out for me to shoot?"

Blaze, stuck between a pedestal and the wall, couldn't see anyone else, not even Corette who had been standing next to him a moment ago. Blood whirled like a tornado inside his head, and all he heard was his pounding heart. Did everyone else get out? Was he alone in a graveyard with the grim reaper? No noises other than... clicking? A dry, hard sound from above, like someone gnashing their teeth together.

Trembling and holding the resin sphere with both hands, he looked up fully expecting to see a gun barrel pointed down at him. He wasn't sure if what he saw was better or worse. The pedestal he hid behind held a bear's head. With blinking, human eyes. And gnashing teeth.

"I'm gonna cut your heads off and replace your eyeballs with googly eyes," Calista said as she stepped out from behind a pedestal ten feet away, gun aimed at Blaze.

Blaze kicked with both feet, toppling the pedestal before she could shoot. The display case slammed against the floor hard enough to knock off the lid and send the bear-head tumbling out.

"No!" Calista shrieked. "Zebadiah!"

Blaze didn't know the significance of what he had done, only that it served as a distraction. He popped to his feet and sprinted toward the stairs. Everyone was way ahead of him, running up the stairs in the order they had come down, sprinting through the house, and dashing out of the hole cut through the glass wall. Blaze barely got both feet in the Expedition as Jacob put it in gear and tramped the gas pedal.

"Everyone okay?" Robert asked, clutching the leather-bound book on his lap.

"Not Danielle!" Jacob snapped. "You two said Calista was dead. You said you killed her!"

"We did!" Blaze snapped back.

"Clearly fucking not!"

Once he guided the SUV from the driveway, Jacob sped along the main road.

"We need to slow down," Corette said, voice as calm and stoic as ever. On her lap was the seed that Jacob was after. "No need to attract police."

Jacob did as suggested, but yelled, "That doesn't matter now that we have the most dangerous person on Earth after us!"

"Now what are we going to do?" Blaze asked.

No one answered as they sped toward the highway.

CHAPTER 42

July 1st, Philadelphia

Robert paced the hotel room. "Show yourself!"

He hated renting a hotel room in the same city where he lived, but no way was he going to invite four strangers into his house. And he had plenty of charms and spells protecting his place from the witch, a few designed to keep her from entering. "They'll be here soon, so you need to appear. Show yourself and tell me your plan!"

A chill rippled through the room, her harbinger. A serpent's hiss slithered through the air, intensifying in pitch and volume until the piercing whistle of a boiling tea kettle drilled through Robert's brain. He refused to cover his ears and give the witch any satisfaction, so he endured the suffering. Once the shrill stopped, sudden silence rang in his ears. Lights flickered and darkness gathered in the corner closest to Robert. Blackened veins, like dead vines, pulsated as they crept from the darkness, worming along the wall. A thumping emanated, growing louder and fuller, giving a heartbeat to the entire room. Clawed fingers shot from the abyss, followed by a rictus of yellowed teeth surrounded by a halo of cracked and wrinkled skin. Gray clumps of hair draped from her scalp like Spanish moss attached to a long dead tree. The witch had revealed herself.

With a breath like burning mildew, she said, "You need to mind your manners, whelp! When a puppy barks like a big dog, some find it cute. I find it sickening."

"Then stop treating me like a cur! Don't forget, you need me far more than I need you."

Like claws raking over a tombstone, she laughed. "Oh, do I now? Who will kill your father for you now that the hunter is dead?"

Robert tried to temper his emotions, especially in front of the witch, but he couldn't stop frowning. She moved close enough for Robert to see the odor vapors rippling just above her putrid skin. She ran a cragged finger over his cheek, her long fingernail dry and brittle. "Oh, my dear boy, you didn't think the deal you made with the hunter was a secret from me, did you?"

Not sure if he would escape from his next maneuver alive, or if he'd have to spend the rest of his life as a newt, Robert grabbed her hand and squeezed. "I knew my deal with Calista was no secret. I also know you made a promise to kill my father *years* ago. And I also know very well that you know who my employer is."

His last comment was a thinly vailed threat, Robert unsure of its severity. There must have been enough weight behind it, because the witch yanked her hand free and retreated, replying in a sharp tone. "I will fulfill my promise when I get what I want!"

"And what is that? You have yet to share your plans any sooner than the day before you need them enacted. Right now, four strangers are on their way to this hotel room and I don't even know why."

The witch smiled, and Robert felt like he had eaten a bowl of live maggots. The black rags she called robes flowed to the floor, casting an illusion that she was floating closer to him.

Levity in her words, she said, "Silly child. My lack of trust in you should be met with pride, not anger. It means I think you're clever."

"Bull shit. But I'm clever enough to know how to turn a doorknob and leave this room."

"So pigheaded! Just like your father." She tapped her index finger to his nose, and then turned back toward the black hole that had spawned her. "Introduce these new friends to your other friends."

"Why?"

"These new friends took the hunter's death as a sign to find her trophies. You'll help them, of course, but they need to meet your old friends, specifically the boy."

"Orion? What does he have to do with this?"

"He's the roadmap that will guide you and your new friends to the hunter's lair."

"What's in it for you?"

"A book. You'll know it when you see it. I need you to get it for me."

Robert squinted and crossed his arms over his chest. "You need this book? You never once mentioned this to me before."

The witch stepped into the darkness as if it were another room, then paused to turn and point a finger at Robert. "You are not someone with whom I need to share my desires!"

Robert rolled his eyes. A knock came from the door. "Be gone, witch."

The witch offered one last hiss before entering the shrinking hole. The shadows retreated once Robert got to the door. But before he opened it, he gave one last rueful glance over his shoulder. Satisfied that she was gone, he pulled a small plastic bag from his pocket. Clasped in his right fist was a piece of the witch's broken fingernail. There had to be a spell out there where this could come in handy, so he dropped her nail in the baggie. *Maybe I'll find such a spell once I find the book.* Robert pulled up on that thought. Was the book she wanted a spell book? He had always assumed that she knew every spell possible – she was The Coven of One after all. But what other book could she possibly want?

Another knock on the door interrupted his self-conjecture, and he opened it with enough force that the four people on the other side reeled back. Following a few gape-mouthed stares, the man in front stuck out his hand. "Hey, I'm Jacob McGovern."

Shaking hands, he said, "Robert Harrington."

"Oh, we know who you are." Jacob then pointed to the others one at a time. "This is my girlfriend, Corette. This is my best friend, Preston. And she's Danielle. May we come in?"

Robert stepped aside and gestured for them to enter. "Absolutely."

His hotel room had plenty of seating; Jacob, Corette, and Preston on the couch, Danielle in the desk chair. Robert opted to stand, leaning against the wall. He didn't like the way Danielle and Preston looked at him, stars in their eyes like he was a celebrity.

"Sorry for being a creeper," Danielle said, "but you're... God damn, man. You're fucking royalty."

"Yeah," Preston added. "Yeah, your father is up there. Top tier, like Jacob's father."

Leeches squirmed under Robert's skin. Jacob's father had been connected with the King of Prussia Mall Massacre. Robert was only six at the time, but he remembered the communal terror. The same kind of terror that his own father manufactured and reveled in. The same kind of terror that needed to be stopped. And to have four people this close to him wishing to continue where their parents left off while praising the bastard he intended to kill? Disgusting. He'd rather deal with the witch. But, he smiled, an actor playing a part. "Thank you. So... You want to find Calista Lindquist's trophy room?"

"We do," Jacob said. "And we have a plan..."

CHAPTER 43

July 8th, Abington, PA

Jacob brought his Mustang to a stop, parking in front of Preston's house. An advantage of owning a couple of private jets was beating the others to the destination by hours. He hurried to Preston's front door and knocked.

Preston answered with a lip quivering smile. "Hey. How's the plan going?"

Jacob let himself in and quickly shut the door behind him. "Just about perfectly."

Preston shook a fist in the air. "Yes! This is so fucking awesome."

It was awesome, though Jacob was surprisingly hesitant about what he had to do next. *No thinking like that! This is to continue Dad's legacy. This is to reclaim what was stolen from me.* "You bet it is. So, do you have the costume?"

Preston clapped his hands and scurried to the side of the couch where he procured a black trash bag. Handing it to Jacob, he said, "Just like you told me. All of it's in here."

Preston had a habit of getting lost while traveling the path of goal completion, so Jacob opened the bag to confirm its contents. Black body suit. Black gloves. Black army boots. Blonde wig. "Excellent. Great job, Preston."

"Did they buy it? Did I look like her?"

Jacob put his hand on Preston's shoulder. "They are confused, debating whether or not Calista is actually dead. Thanks to your perfect timing, a couple of them think she's alive."

Preston clapped again as he stepped out from Jacob's grip and spun a few times. "Yes! Yes, awesome!"

"It is. But it's time for the next part of the plan."

Preston stopped spinning, and his smile faded. He indulged in his familiar nervous tick, fingers rhythmically plucking on the skin of his neck. "So... Umm... Why do we want them to think Calista is alive?"

"Doubt. Doubt creates weakness. Doubt is how we make them weaker. We only need a few of them to doubt that Calista is dead, and that will weaken their group. I need to separate the dream boy from them, and I can't do that if their group's bond is too strong."

Preston was all smiles again. "Okay. Yep. That makes sense. Now what?"

"This." While Jacob had explained the situation, he had held his hands behind his back, putting a glove on his right hand. He then grabbed the knife he had tucked inside his belt and jammed the blade into Preston's ribs.

Eyes wide with shock, Preston clasped Jacob's shoulders.

Placing a hand on Preston's cheek, the other still gripping the imbedded knife, Jacob guided his friend to sit on the couch. Seated next to him, Jacob never broke eye contact.

Struggling to breathe, Preston's blinking became more pronounced. "I love you."

"Love you, too," Jacob choked out, forcing himself not to cry. Now wasn't the time. Now was the time to pick up where his father had left off, but he needed the seed that Calista undoubtedly had as a trophy.

Tears rolled from Preston's eyes as his body twitched. "I've been wearing the makeup. The same pattern as my dad."

"Me, too." And it felt great. If time had afforded it, Jacob would have slathered on white face paint, topped by blue circles over his eyes, and a big red mouth. His true face. The face of his father. The face Jacob had worn whenever he went out to learn the ways of his father, to learn how to kill. He'd disposed of a half-dozen homeless people so far, but Preston's death was personal, and he couldn't stop the tears. Giving a quick glance to the coffee table, he said, "Chinese and pizza for your last meal?"

Through chest rattling convulsions, Preston gurgled one last time. "I like Chinese food and pizza."

A cough. A full body spasm. A twisted gurgle. A full body relax.

In through his nose, out through his mouth, Jacob took deep breaths and released the knife. He stood and stared at the newly made corpse, marveled at his friend's acceptance and conviction toward the cause. Preston knew what needed to be done, knew that this was the only way to get to Orion.

Jacob opened the trash bag and pulled out the wig. Wrapping a few strands around his finger, he pulled them free. One strand on the coffee table. One on the floor by the door. One in the doorway between the living room and kitchen. The morons on their way would have to find one of these, right? If not, Jacob was confident that he could manipulate their attention.

Satisfied that the scene was set, he pulled the knife from Preston's ribs. A gush of blood splashed over Preston's hip and flowed to the couch.

Both the knife and glove went into the trash bag. *Time to go,* Jacob told himself. *Don't look. Don't look.* But he couldn't help it, and looked back to Preston.

A burn in the back of his throat was the precursor to more tears. In an act of catharsis, possibly self-forgiveness, he set the trash bag down and pointed both thumbs to himself. "Just stick with me and everything will be great."

Jacob wiped away his tears and then laughed. Harder. Harder. Louder. From the belly. Chest heaving laughter with a shrill cackle amplifying it. Just like Dad.

The Progeny of Devils series, book 1

THE TRUTH
IN THEIR BLOOD

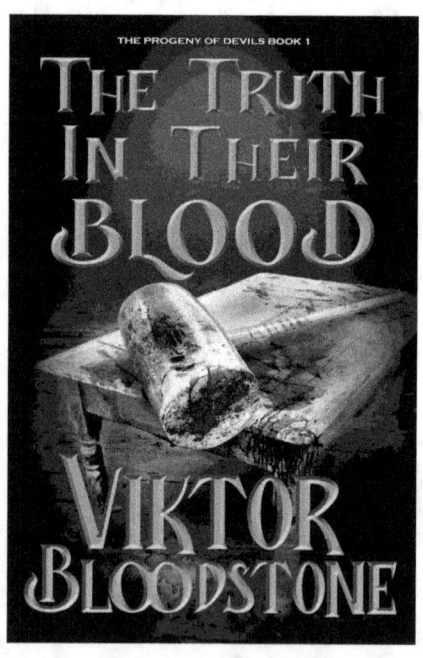

www.fortresspublishinginc.com

The *Legacy of Devils* series:

Hammer and Blood

www.fortresspublishinginc.com

The *Legacy of Devils* series:

The Dream Eaters

www.fortresspublishinginc.com

The *Killer of Devils* series:

BOOK 1: CLOWNS

www.fortresspublishinginc.com

Discover the secret origins of Orion's father and Robert's father. Those stories can be found in

Hellbent

An anthology by Hellbender Books.

www.sunburypress.com

Viktor Bloodstone

is

Brian Koscienski

Chris Pisano

Jeff Young

www.novelguys.com